THE

DEATH

OF CARTHAGE

Robin E. Levin

Order this book online at www.trafford.com
or email orders@trafford.com

Most Trafford titles are also available at major online book retailers.

Printed in the United States of America.

ISBN: 978-1-4269-9607-8 (sc)
ISBN: 978-1-4269-9608-5 (hc)
ISBN: 978-1-4269-9609-2 (e)

Library of Congress Control Number: 2011917032

Trafford rev. 12/05/2011

 www.trafford.com

North America & international
toll-free: 1 888 232 4444 (USA & Canada)
phone: 250 383 6864 ♦ fax: 812 355 4082

TIME LINE FOR CARTHAGE MUST BE DESTROYED

236 B.C. :Publius Cornelius Scipio Africanus born

235 B.C. :Lucius Tullius Varro (fictional) and Marcus Porcius Cato born

218 B.C. : Start of Second Punic War. Siege of Saguntum,(Spain) Battle of Ticinus (Italy), Battle of Trebia (Italy) Battle of Cissa (Spain)

217 B.C.: Battle of Trasimene (Italy)

216 B.C.: Battle of Cannae (Italy)

215 B.C.:Battle of Dertosa (Spain)

211 B.C. :Battles of the Upper Baetis (Spain)

210 B.C. :Hannibal briefly besieges Rome. Publius Cornelius Scipio Africanus volunteers to be Proconsul in Spain

209 B.C.:Siege and Conquest of New Carthage by Scipio Africanus (Spain)

208 B.C. :Battle of Baecula (Spain)

207 B.C.:Battle of the Metaurus (Italy)

206 B.C.: Battle of Ilipa, (Spain) Sucro Mutiny, Embassy by Scipio Africanus to Cirta to negotiate a treaty with King Syphax

205 B.C.: Publius Cornelius Scipio Africanus elected Consul in Rome.

204 B.C. :Scipio goes to Sicily to prepare for invasion of Africa, raise and train an army and recruit veterans of Cannae.

203 B.C. Scipio invades Africa. Battle of Cirta, (North Africa) Battle of the Great Plains.(North Africa)

202 B.C.: Battle of Zama. (North Africa) Peace treaty with Carthage on Roman terms.

183 B.C. Publius Cornelius Scipio Africanus dies

149 B.C. Marcus Porcius Cato dies

Time Line for The Death of Carthage

235 B.C. Births of Marcus Porcius Cato and Lucius Tullius Varro Silvius

234 B.C. Birth of Enneus Tullius

218 B.C. Beginning of Second Punic War-Siege of Saguntum. Battle of Ticinus.

217 B.C. Battle of Lake Trasimene. Enneus Tullius captured and transported to Greece

207 B.C. Birth of Hector Tullius, AKA Ectorius Tullius

202 B.C. Battle of Zama, end of Second Punic War

200 B.C. Beginning of Second Macedonian War.

196 B.C. Enneus Tullius and his family freed from captivity in Greece, returned to Rome

195 B.C. Consulship of Marcus Porcius Cato

194 B.C. Triumph of Titus Quinctius Flamininus

190 B.C. Battle of Magnesia, Lucius Cornelius Scipio Asiaticus defeats Antiochus III of the Seleucid Dynasty.

187 B.C. First attempted prosecution of Lucius Cornelius Scipio Asiaticus for fiscal malfeasance. Failed

185 B.C. Attempted prosecution of Publius Cornelius Scipio Africanus for bribery. Not completed.

183 B.C. Second attempted prosecution of Lucius Cornelius Scipio Africanus for fiscal malfeasance.
Successful

168 B.C. Battle of Pydna, Lucius Aemelius Paullus defeats Perseus of Macedon, ending the Antigonid dynasty.

167 B.C. Polybius sent to Italy as a hostage along with 1000 other Achaean notables. Polybius takes a position as tutor to the sons of Lucius Aemelius Paullus.

161 B.C. Demetrius Sotor escapes from Rome assisted by Polybius and others. Becomes ruler of the Seleucid dynasty.

152 B.C. Death of Lucius Tullius Varro Silvius

151 B.C. Carthage fights battle with Numidian kingdom of Masinissa. Decisive Carthaginian defeat.

150 B.C. Polybius and other surviving Achaean hostages permitted to return to Achaea.

149 B.C. Rome declares war on Carthage. Death of Marcus Porcius Cato.

146 B.C. Consulship of Publius Cornelius Scipio Africanus Minor. Carthage defeated and destroyed. Surviving inhabitants sold into Slavery.

CARTHAGE MUST BE DESTROYED
The Memoirs of a Roman Soldier

Publius Cornelius Scipio Africanus

CHAPTER 1

"When I come to age, I shall pursue the Romans with fire and sword and enact again the doom of Troy. The Gods shall not stop my career, nor the treaty that bars the sword, neither the lofty Alps nor the Tarpeian Rock. I swear to this purpose by the divinity of our native god of war, and by the shade of Elissa."

Hannibal's childhood oath to his father Hamilcar Barca taken at the temple of Elissa at Carthage.
From Punica, Book I by Silius Italicus"

My first experience of battle came unexpectedly. It was in the month of quintilis, during the first year of the second Punic war. Consul Publius Cornelius Scipio, concerned that Hannibal might be leading his forces toward the Alps, sent his cavalry unit, three hundred strong, along with some Gallic auxiliary, to reconnoiter the area along the Rhone river, north of Massilia. We met Hannibal's Numidian cavalry by chance and fell to battle. The Numidians were renown for their horsemanship and their courage. They rode bareback and wore no armor. I, myself, was accoutered in the usual fashion of a Roman cavalryman with helmet, chain mail, greaves and a large round shield. I envied the Numidian his comfort, but not his relative vulnerability!

A Numidian charged toward me and threw his spear with great speed and force. Fortunately, I saw it on time and deflected it with my shield, then, with intense concentration, I aimed and launched my own pilum with as much force as I could, and it struck the Numidian in the chest. My years of training on the Campus Martius had paid off. He was knocked off his horse and blood spurted from the wound and also from his mouth. He looked to be just a youth of about my own age. He writhed for a few moments and then lay still. The memory of the scene has stayed with me until this day. I thought to myself "This will most likely be my own fate soon, maybe today!" But there was little time to reflect. I rode off to face my next assailant.

No one can possibly understand battle who hasn't experienced it. The shouts of the soldiers, the screams of the wounded, the smell of blood and entrails, the ground strewn with corpses, the heat, the thirst, the fear. To endure it I had to block out all concerns except two-the necessity to avoid being killed or wounded by the enemy and the necessity to kill the enemy. When I threw my weapon I aimed to kill, not to wound, and most of the time I accomplished my aim. The goddess Fortuna was with me that day and I survived five or six more encounters. The Numidians persisted until they had used up their projectile weapons, and declining close combat with swords they rode off to rejoin their leader, Hannibal Barca.

How was it that I, Lucius Tullius Varro, found myself in an occupation so contrary to my natural inclinations? I have always been the kindest and gentlest of souls. In the sixteen years that I served in the Roman cavalry I never had the slightest animosity toward the enemy on the battlefield. In fact, I sympathized with my victims-just not enough to permit them to slay me!

My fate was sealed from the time I was born. I was not of patrician birth but among plebeians my family was highly ranked. We were of equestrian status, the mercantile class just below the patricians. We were expected to fill the ranks of the Roman cavalry. My father had done military service as a cavalry soldier in the wars with the Ligurians and the Samnites and against the Carthaginians in the first Punic war. After ten campaigns he had been allowed to retire had had been awarded a small amount of land. His affairs had prospered, and he had married and fathered four children, including two sons. But then his wife had died and he married my mother and fathered myself and two sisters. The eldest son would inherit my father's estate. I had no prospects whatever, other than to take my chances as a soldier.

My father made this clear on the night that I took on the toga virilis. (The long toga worn by Roman men, as opposed to the toga praetexta, the short toga worn by boys.) We had had a small ceremony at our house, with a few friends and neighbors invited. After the guests had departed my father bade me come into his study and told me to sit down. He poured me a cup of wine. "You're a man now, under Roman custom, Lucius," he said "and old enough to drink wine." My relationship with my father had always been distant and limited as he was a very busy man, and this may have been the first time we had ever had a talk of any length.

"You've grown like a weed in the last year." he said "I'm glad to hear that you have been active in training on the Campus Martius and show some promise as a soldier. I suspect that you will soon be called to service. I myself saw service in ten campaigns. There has scarcely been a year, since the days of Romulus, that Rome has been at peace, so I'm sure you'll see your share of war. Now listen to what I have to say. A soldier may die bravely or he may die a coward. If he dies a coward he will not be remembered except in ignominy. If he dies bravely he will bring honor to himself, to his family and to his country. I fervently hope that you survive your service, but if you die, I do not want to hear that you died a coward. Promise me this."

"Yes father." I said. According to Roman thinking you died a coward if a spear entered your body from the back and a brave man if it entered from the front.

He continued "The Roman soldier is, I believe, superior to that of any other nation. The key to our superiority as soldiers is discipline. I have had you tutored in Roman history, so you must remember the story of the Consul Manlius Torquatus who had his own son executed for disobeying his orders. The soldiers had been ordered not to engage the Gauls under any provocation and young Manlius could not resist a challenge to personal combat with a champion of the Gauls. He won the fight and beheaded the Gaul. In turn he was beheaded at the command of his father the Consul for disobeying strict orders. Many of the younger soldiers felt the punishment too harsh, but I, for one, would have done the same. Discipline is everything. Without it an army can not function. Bear that in mind and never disobey an order."

"Yes, father." I replied. My father was very strict and I knew better than to talk back to him. We would never be close. The best that could be said about him was that he was not brutal.

I had begun training on the Campus Martius when I was about fourteen. I was not naturally athletic. I was tall and thin, and did not have the muscular body of the ideal soldier, but I was determined to become adept at handling both sword and spear. I went to the Campus Martius nearly every day and practiced throwing javelins and pila until I could hit my target nearly one hundred percent of the time. Then I practiced likewise with my left arm, in case my right arm should be disabled in a battle.

Among the young men training on the Campus Martius in those days, the acknowledged leader was a sixteen year old patrician named Publius Cornelius Scipio. His family was one of the oldest and most prominent in Rome. My diligence and rapid improvement in the arts of weaponry soon drew his attention and he took me under his wing. He had a younger brother named Lucius who was about a year younger than me, and he was always goading him to exert himself a bit more. I was both proud and embarrassed one day when he said to his brother "Now watch Lucius Tullius Varro, here, Lucius. He's better at throwing the pilum with his left hand than you are with your right!" At his bidding I demonstrated.

"Yes," said Lucius Scipio, "But he's left handed, isn't he?"

"No, I'm right handed," I said, "And I'm actually quite a bit better with my right hand."

"Now Lucius Tullius comes here every day and practices," said Publius Scipio. "and I want you to do the same!"

Publius Scipio was unusually affable for a patrician, and he was the type of boy that fathers would point out as an example to emulate. He always stayed within the boundaries of propriety and he was unusually religious for a Roman youth. He frequently went to the temple of Jupiter "I like to be in the presence of the god" he would say. "It helps me clear my head." He was studying to be a priest of the Salian rites. Not particularly religious myself, I silently thought "De gustabus non disputandum est" (roughly, "no accounting for taste.") Although I was certainly glad to be counted among his friends, I was definitely in the second tier. His closest friends were Gaius Laelius and Valerius Galba. But he encouraged me to tag along whenever a group of us got together for refreshment after a day of drilling and practice with arms.

Not long after I took on the toga virilis, my father once again summoned me to his study. "Lucius" he said "some time ago I arranged a marriage for you with Silvia Tertia, the daughter of that Silvius who owns the stable in Subura. He's prosperous and there will be a significant dowry. And of course, you will never want for a good horse." This was one of the very few times I ever saw my father smile. "She has come of age now and we have consulted a haruspex for an auspicious wedding date. You will married on the nones of April. I would advise you to get her with child before you are assigned to a legion. We will see that she and the baby are comfortable. This will be the traditional form of marriage which permits no divorce."

I have to admit I was shocked. The idea of marriage had never even crossed my mind! I was a randy as any other boy of fifteen and had even accepted some minor sexual favors from the lower sorts of girls, but marriage? But I knew there was no use arguing with my father and after a while I accepted the idea and even started to look forward to it.

Not long after this we visited Silvius and I met my future wife for the first time. She was fourteen years old, short, with curly black hair and rosy cheeks and a sweet disposition. She was already proficient in sewing, weaving, wool working, and needlework. She looked at me with a mixture of awe and apprehension, which turned to delight when I placed my ring upon her hand. We were allowed to hold hands and we chatted about how many children we would have and what they would achieve in their lives.

In April we were married. Silvia came to my father's house in a procession of her relatives, friends and neighbors. I took her from her mother's arms and carried her across my father's threshold. Avowing her fidelity she said the traditional phrase: "Quando tu Gaius ego Gaia." After several hours of feasting and merrymaking the two of us retired to my room.

She giggled. "Oh, Lucius, I'm scared! My sister says it hurts the first time."

"I don't want to hurt you, Silvia, but we don't want to disappoint the matrons of your family or mine." I said. "We don't have to do anything right away, let's hug and kiss for a while and drink some wine. My brother says the wine will make you forget the pain."

We took our time and got to know each other. It was a night of giggles, wine, kisses, caresses and chatter, and in the end we were successful in presenting the matrons with evidence of her virginity. I thought myself to be the luckiest man in the world to be so enamored of my wife. I knew it didn't always happen that way. Somehow I couldn't imagine either my mother or my father doing what we had done this night.

Is it possible for a man to love two women? I don't mean in the casual manner of a philanderer, but in a way that is pure, honest and honorable? I know my friends and acquaintances gossiped and smirked behind my back, and it is difficult to make others understand such an unusual situation, but I think of my first love as worldly and my second as other-worldly. If I worshiped my heroine, it in no way detracted from my love for Silvia. Silvia was the best of wives, the best of mothers and I always loved her whole-heartedly and without reservation, no matter what others might think or say.

If Silvia was everything a Roman would want in a wife, her father, Caius Silvius proved an unexpected bonus. The father of four daughters, he had always yearned for a son, and whereas his first two daughter had married men well into their twenties, I was young enough for him to take under his wing. I found in him the father I had always wanted. "Son" He said to me "If you're going to be a soldier, I would strongly recommend that you join the cavalry, and with your marriage to my daughter you've come to exactly the right place." He assigned one of his slaves to mentor me in the arts of horsemanship, and after several months I could control his most spirited stallions. I divided my time between the Campus Martius and my equestrian training. Silvius, like my father, had served in the Roman cavalry for ten years and he personally undertook to teach me techniques for launching weapons from horseback. He encouraged me to practice my skills every day. My efforts paid off one day when Publius Scipio took me aside and said "I've heard that you are becoming quite a good horseman, Lucius, I will recommend you to my father for his cavalry unit." Publius Scipio's father had just been elected consul, so this was a great honor. After thanking him profusely, I ran to Silvius to tell him the exciting news. "Well, my boy." he grinned, "You will make me a proud father-in-law!"

Not long after this, Publius Scipio invited me to his family's villa to meet his father, the consul. "My father likes to meet his new recruits in person" he said "especially those who will serve in the cavalry."

I was awed by the stateliness and grandeur of the villa. The fountains, the tile work, the statues and other works of art. There were fresco paintings on the walls and the work was of higher quality than anything I had ever seen. One of the frescoes depicted Hercules defeating Cacus. Another depicted the funeral games of Aeneus, and a third depicted Romulus slaying his brother Remus. Looking at this third painting Publius Scipio remarked: "That's the problem with twins. In every other close relationship it is clear who is superior and who is inferior and the inferior bends his will to the superior. But with identical twins, both of whom are equal in every way, neither will bend his will to the other, and if they come into conflict, one must destroy the other. That's also the way of nations, as we remember from the Trojan war, and that will happen with Rome and Carthage. Eventually one will be destroyed by the other."

"Will there be another war with Carthage?" I asked

"It's already started." replied Scipio. "The Roman client city of Saguntum in Hispania has been destroyed by the Carthaginians under Hannibal Barca in violation of the treaty that ended the previous war with Carthage, and my father has been assigned to Hispania to attend to Roman interests there. He will try to restrain Hannibal. If he accepts you into his cavalry unit you will be going with him."

"My father says that the Roman soldiery is the best in the world." I said. "Surely we will be victorious in any war with Carthage."

"I would think so," said Publius Scipio, "But the Carthaginians have powerful allies to draw upon, such as Syphax in Cirta and Gala, the king of the Numidians. The Numidians are renown as horsemen. We may be overcome by sheer numbers. In the first Punic war the Carthaginians even allied with Xanthippus, the King of Sparta, who dealt our forces a stunning blow." He paused briefly. "Did you know that in Sparta the mothers tell their sons as they go off to war 'Come back with your shield, or on it.'"

I laughed. "In Rome the fathers would say such a thing, not the mothers. But how do you know so much about the world outside of Italia? I have only studied Roman affairs."

"My father believes that if you are going to be a general you must learn everything you can about Rome's potential enemies, their strengths and their weaknesses," said Scipio, "so that when the time comes you can form strategies to defeat them. This knowledge can also be useful in forming strategic alliances. My tutors were well provided for. Some of them were Greeks and they acquainted me thoroughly with Greek history. I'm a great admirer of the Greeks."

The dinner that night was an informal affair and we sat upright at the table rather than reclining on couches as is customary in patrician households on more formal occasions. Even so, the food was several cuts above the plain fare served in my father's household. There were three courses. The first was a gustatio, an appetizer made with soft boiled eggs, pine nuts, pepper, honey, and garum, a fish sauce. The main course was a fried veal escalope with raisins, and there was a nut tart for dessert. The food was accompanied by mulsum, a mixture of boiled wine and honey. It seemed that the Scipioni regularly ate the type of meals that my father's household would reserve for the most festive occasions.

As we sat down to eat, Publius introduced me to the elder Scipio for the first time. He was the general whom I would serve for the next seven years. "My son has told me a bit about you, Lucius," he said. "He says that you are a fine horseman and are competent with the sword and the javelin. You certainly have the right body shape for a cavalryman-long and lean."

I was in awe of this man. He had all the gravitas and auctoritas one might demand of a Roman general and I could see where young Publius Scipio got his good looks and his keen intelligence. All I could answer was "Yes sir."

"I understand that your father-in-law is the owner of a large stable in Subura. Why don't you ask him to come and see me to discuss the procurement of some good horses." I suddenly felt a sense of importance, as though I was now a part of something much greater than myself.

"I will do that, first thing tomorrow. When would be a good time?"

"As soon as possible." replied the Consul. "I will send you home with a letter for him so he will be able to get past my guards. We have received word that the Carthaginians under Hannibal have utterly destroyed Saguntum and have slain nearly the entire population. It is too late to help our allies, we can only avenge them. We have sent an embassy to Carthage to determine if Hannibal acted on his own or with the support of the Carthaginian senate. If his actions were authorized by Carthage, then our treaty has been broken and war with Carthage is certain. We are trying to raise as many men and horses as possible in a short time. I hope you will come with us. From what my son says, you will make a fine cavalryman."

As we ate the Consul held forth on the nature of the Carthaginians and the political situation that had brought about this new conflict. "The Poeni" (Phoenicians) he said, "were a people who lived on the eastern shore of the Red Sea east of Egypt. They prospered for centuries by sea trade, but were eventually conquered by the Assyrians and later the Persians. But, like the Greeks, they established colonies in distant places where they traded, and the largest and most prosperous of these colonies is Carthage. Carthage has prospered for centuries by trade, and as long as Rome was small and not very powerful they offered us treaties of friendship and we had good relations. We were even in an alliance against Phyrrhus of Epirus. But some forty-five years ago the Mamertines, Campanians who had taken the city of Messana in Sicily, asked Rome to come to their aid when they were attacked by the Carthaginians. I don't know why Rome consented to do this because the Mamertines were a despicable lot, but perhaps it was because we were concerned that the Carthaginians would expand their influence over the whole of Sicily.

"The war lasted for 23 years and cost vast numbers of casualties. In the end, however, Rome was victorious and won control over Sicily and some of the other islands in the area. The terms of the truce impoverished Carthage temporarily and we hoped for a lasting peace. During the past twenty years, however, the Carthaginian lust for empire has re-awakened and they have built cities, including a very wealthy New Carthage (Cartagena) in Hispania and are in the process of extending their influence over the whole of Hispania."

"Politically, Carthage is divided into factions. One, under Hanno the Great, opposes expansion by force, while the other, formed originally by the late Hamilcar Barca is avid for conquest. Hamilcar's son-in-law Hasdrubal has recently died and his army has fallen to the command of Hamilcar's sons Hannibal, Hasdrubal and Mago. Hannibal, in particular is a hot-headed young man and he has taken it upon himself to destroy Saguntum. Saguntum was a loyal client state of Rome and these actions are in clear violation of our treaty. I think that both Rome and Carthage now see war as inevitable. I just hope it doesn't last twenty-three years like the last one did."

I wanted to hear more, but young Scipio was already aware of all this and changed the subject. "Father," he asked, "Do you think it is better for a commander to be feared by his men or loved by them?" I think he may have asked the question for my benefit.

The Consul looked thoughtful for a moment. "Well, it's absolutely necessary that your men fear you." he said, "Or discipline will be too lax. But I don't think that one precludes the other, and ideally, you want them to love you as well. There is only one way to achieve this balance. You must mete out discipline to wrongdoers, but your men must perceive that punishments are just and fair. It is not a good idea to punish the many for the crimes of a few. The object is to make an example of the ringleaders in any disruption, but only the ringleaders. Personally, I detest the practice of decimation, where each decury (unit of ten soldiers) must draw lots and slay one of their number. It's wasteful and you may lose some of your best men. Investigate each instance of misbehavior thoroughly and punish only the miscreants. Roman discipline is harsh, but that of the Carthaginians is even harsher. In the last war they crucified their own generals after they lost a battle. I may die in battle some day, but, unless I fall into the hands of the enemy, I don't ever expect to be crucified. Rome reserves that punishment for slaves and foreigners."

"I might mete out that punishment to Roman deserters." said the younger Scipio. And, as it happened, some day he would.

The consul provided me with the letter for my father-in-law and I was dismissed. Publius Scipio accompanied me to the gate and said "I would like to go with my father to Hispania, but I am staying here to assist in the levies. I wonder if you might do me a great favor."

"Certainly" I said

"You read and write, don't you?" he asked

"Yes," I replied

"I want you to send me written accounts of everything of importance that goes on in my father's camp. Find out who the good soldiers are and who can not be trusted. Let me know your observations of the habits of the Hispanian inhabitants. Any information that can possibly be useful to me when I eventually get there. You can post your letters through Marcus Aemilius, my Father's lieutenant. He's a friend of mine."

"I'm at your service, Publius." I replied. "Just don't slay the messenger if it's bad news!"

He laughed and we embraced. We already had what could be considered a patron-client relationship. In Rome most social and commercial affairs are handled in the context of such relationships. These relationships exist at all levels of society, but the most influential and powerful of such arrangements are between wealthy patricians and their followers. The wealthier you are, the more likely you are to field a large number of clients, and a large clientele gives it's patron power.

I returned home and announced the news to the household. My father was not surprised. "I have long believed that this day would come." he said "We have prepared for it as well as we could. The rest will be up to the goddess Fortuna." But my mother and Silvia would not forebear to weep. Mother composed herself without too much difficulty but when I joined Silvia in our bed chamber she was weeping bitterly. "Lucius, can't you at least wait until Summer?" She cried. I said "Silvia, you know I can't. War doesn't wait for a convenient time." She sniffed. "I didn't want to tell you this but I haven't had my courses in three months and your mother thinks I'm with child. We went to see Auntie Lavinia, the midwife, and she looked at my breasts and also said she thought I was."

I was stunned. I hardly knew what to say! "Unfortunately, Silvia, a baby doesn't wait for a convenient time either. I can not fail Rome when she's at war. I have a duty. The duty to our country takes precedence even over the duty to our family. If every Roman soldier shirked his duty we would soon all become slaves!"

"We're already slaves," cried Silvia "And Rome is a harsh master!"

This was the first time since we were married that we had quarreled or even disagreed. "You mustn't say things like that, Silvia." I said sternly. "Anyway, I'd rather be a slave to Rome than a slave to a Samnite or a Carthaginian, and, if you think about it, so would you!"

She continued to weep. "But what if you die, Lucius, what will I do?"

"Silvia, if I shirk my duty I may as well be dead." Then I recited the old saw that has been handed down from generation to generation of Romans: "Dulcet et decorum est pro patria mori."

I put my arms around her and said "Let's not quarrel about what we can do nothing about. It appears that we are going to have a child. It is my duty to serve Rome, and it is your duty to nurture this child. We must both do our duty. I may die in war or I may come back to you, but it does neither of us any good for you to fret and cry about it. Please be strong for me."

"I love you, Lucius, whatever happens," she said "But I wish to Jupiter it could be different. I only want to be a good wife to you, so I will do what you say." At last she calmed herself and fell asleep in my arms. "Women!" I thought to myself. But then I considered that I would much rather that Roman women be like my mother and Silvia than like the women of Sparta. Leave hardness and masculinity to the men.

I had a lot to do the following week to prepare for my coming voyage with Consul Scipio's fleet. My father-in-law, Gaius Silvius, gave me an excellent stallion and he assigned to me one of his grooms, a man named Brunius, whose knowledge of horses and skill at handling them far exceeded my own. Brunius was a Campanian by birth and those people begin riding when barely weaned. Brunius appeared to be in his thirties and was stolid and taciturn, but his knowledge of horses would prove very useful to me after I joined the cavalry. Brunius was also assigned a stallion which would be at my disposal if mine should be injured or killed in battle.

Silvius had been a cavalryman in the previous Punic war and was able to advise me on what gear, clothing, weapons, shield and other provisions I would need. He had kept a gladius hispanica (Spanish sword, probably adopted from Spanish mercenaries during the first Punic war), and he gave it to me, saying that it was an excellent weapon for defending oneself once one's spears were used up, as often happens in battle. But he said "When you get to Hispania, try to get yourself a falcata, it's a sword used by the natives and it's similar to the Greek kopis. It's the best sort of sword for a cavalryman." Upon Silvius' advice I acquired a helmet, greaves and a lorica of chain mail. My father supplied me with a number of pila and his large round shield.

I visited with a number of my friends from the Campus Martius. They gathered around me and expressed awe and envy that I had been chosen for the consul's cavalry legion. One of them, Gaius Laelius, a close friend of Publius Scipio, and a young man of equestrian rank like myself, said "You're so lucky, Lucius, that you have a father-in-law who owns a stable and you can practice with the best horses. I wish I were a better horseman."

Of the seven or eight youths I met with that day, Gaius Laelius was the only one I would ever see again.

A few days later a man brought a package to my father's door and bade the servant woman to give it to me. It contained several dozen sheets of parchment as well as two styli and two ceramic vials of high quality ink. There was also a supply of sealing wax and a seal with my name inscribed on it. Finally there were a dozen leather pouches to enclose the parchments. I knew that these items could only have come from Publius Scipio and that he was completely serious about wanting me to report to him. My father, unaware of the gifts from Scipio, also presented me with a dozen sheets of parchment, a stylus and a vial of ink.

CHAPTER 2

Two days later I said farewell to my family. Silvius and his family were also there to see me off. Brunius and I joined the procession to Pisa, from where the Consul Scipio's sixty ships would transport two legions, consisting, each of about 4500 infantry and 300 horse, as well as 14,000 allied infantry and sixteen hundred horse to Massilia (Marseilles) a large city of Greek origin in the south of Gaul. We traveled by way of the Etrurian and Ligurian coasts and then passed the mountains of the Salyes. Unfortunately, I could not well appreciate the spectacular scenery. I had never been at sea before and rapidly became sea sick. I was not alone in this, as almost all the other soldiers suffered likewise. We had to endure the jibes and laughter of the experienced sailors and it left us weak and lethargic when we arrived at Massilia.

We set up camp at the mouth of the Rhone river. Roman camps are always on the same plan and each group of eight tent-mates knows exactly where their tent will be in relation to the others. The infantry men set up the usual ramparts and other fortifications of a Roman military camp, while we cavalrymen set up facilities for the care of our horses. The military tribune of our legion was young Scipio's friend Marcus Aemilius and he introduced himself to me saying "Publius has told me about you and asked that I assign you to assist the quartermaster. He says your father-in-law owns a large stable and that you know a lot about horses."

"Whatever I don't know I can ask my groom, Brunius." I said. "He knows everything there is to know about horses."

"Good," replied Marcus Aemilius. "Is he a slave or a freeman?"

"As far as I'm concerned he's a freeman. If my father-in-law doesn't free him I'll buy his freedom myself when I get back to Rome."

We discussed Publius' request that I write reports for him. "Let me know when you have something to report to Publius and I'll see that you have time and facilities to do your writing. Give me anything you write and don't show anything to anyone else."

A few days later, the ambassadors who had been sent to Carthage and had traveled from thence through Hispania arrived at our camp on the Rhone. Somewhat to my surprise I was invited to sit in on their debriefing in the Consul's tent. It occurred to me later that the Consul had given tacit consent to his son's information gathering arrangements and wanted me to report whatever I heard to young Scipio.

The Ambassador's report was grim and they spared us nothing. The ambassadors were all elderly men highly esteemed in Rome: Quintus Fabius Maximus, Marcus Livius, Lucius Aemilius, Caius Licinius and Quintus Baebius. They had been sent by Rome to inquire whether Hannibal had been acting on his own volition in destroying Saguntum, or whether he had acted at the behest of the government of Carthage in violation of the treaty. If he acted contrary to the wishes of the Carthaginians, then war might still be averted if the Carthaginians were willing to surrender Hannibal to the Romans for punishment. The ambassadors described how old Hanno, the implacable enemy to Hannibal's faction spoke the to the Carthaginian assembly in vain, trying to convince them to disown Hannibal. He warned that no good would come of this war.

"It is against Carthage that Hannibal is now moving his vineae and towers." He said "It is Carthage that he is shaking with his battering ram. The ruins of Saguntum (Oh that I may prove a false prophet!) will fall on our heads and the war commenced against the Saguntines must be continued against the Romans. Shall we therefore deliver up Hannibal? In what relates to him I am aware that my authority is of little weight on account of my enmity with his father. But I rejoice that Hamilcar perished, for this reason, that had he lived we should have now been engaged in a war with the Romans; and this youth, as the fury and firebrand of this war, I hate and detest! I therefore give my opinion, that ambassadors be sent immediately to Rome to satisfy the senate; others to tell Hannibal to lead away his army from Saguntum, and to deliver Hannibal himself according to the treaty to the Romans; and I propose a third embassy to make restitution to the Saguntines."*1

Unfortunately, old Hanno's wise counsel fell on deaf ears as nearly all of the Carthaginian senators were in thrall to the Barcine faction and devoted to Hannibal. They accused Hanno of having spoken with more malignity than Flaccus Valerius, the Roman ambassador. They then claimed that the war had been started by the Saguntines themselves and that the Roman people acted unjustly if they preferred the Saguntines to their most ancient alliance with the Carthaginians. The embassy ended with a declaration of hostilities on both sides.

The ambassadors then traveled through Hispania in an attempt to enlist various local tribes to their side against the Carthaginians. In this they had little success. The leader of one of these tribes, the Volciani gave the following reason for not siding with the Romans. "What sense of shame have ye, Romans, to ask of us that we should prefer your friendship to that of the Carthaginians when you, their allies, betrayed the Saguntines with greater cruelty than that with which the Carthaginians, their enemies, destroyed them? Methinks you should look for allies where the massacre of Saguntum is unknown. The ruins of Saguntum will remain a warning as melancholy as memorable to the states of Hispania, that no one should confide in the faith or alliance of Rome."*2

When the ambassadors passed through the lands of the Gauls, their reception was even more unpleasant. Laughter and derision greeted their proposal that the Gauls refuse passage to the Carthaginian on their way to Italy. They were told "Why should we Gauls take the war on ourselves and expose our own lands to be laid waste instead of those of others. We don't consider the Romans friends nor the Carthaginians enemies, so why should we take up arms on behalf of the Romans against the Carthaginians?" Indeed the long enmity between the cis-alpine Gauls and the Romans was well known to the Gauls of northern Hispania and Southern Gaul, and, in general, they did not look favorably upon the Romans.

All of these tidings from the ambassadors were disturbing to me and I thought that young Scipio should be made aware of these events so I immediately wrote down all that I had learned, and I entrusted my report to Marcus Aemilius.

A few day later Consul Scipio received intelligence that Hannibal had crossed the Pyrenees and was preparing to cross the Rhone. Hannibal had succeeded in either neutralizing or making alliances with most of the Gallic tribes in the region. Only the Volcae offered resistance, but Hannibal's forces drove them off.

Consul Scipio sent out a band of three hundred Roman cavalry with Massilian guides and Gallic auxiliaries to reconnoiter the land and see if they could locate the Carthaginian forces. I was among those chosen for this mission. After a few days we encountered a band of 500 Numidian horsemen which had been sent out for a similar purpose by Hannibal. This would be my first experience in combat, and in that one day I ceased to be a boy and became a man. As onerous as my duty was, I performed it with skill and competence, as half a dozen shades in Hades might testify.

There were heavy casualties on both sides. We lost one hundred and sixty dead including Romans and Gallic auxiliaries, and we killed over two hundred of the enemy. We considered this a Roman victory since their casualties outnumbered ours and we had put the Numidians to rout. Unfortunately, this did not presage any Roman victories over the forces of Hannibal anytime in the near future.

We, the survivors, collected the dead on both sides and constructed a large pyre where we burned them. We then attempted to get the wounded to safety. I tried to carry a man who had been wounded in the thigh on my horse, but he was unable to tolerate the motion of the horse and he soon begged me to put him back on the ground and let him die. Seeing my distress, the centurion assured me that they would send a wagon for any wounded soldiers unable to make it back to camp. Back in Consul Scipio's camp the next day, Brunius tended first to my horse and then to my minor injuries. He insisted upon cleaning any breaches in the skin with alcohol which stung painfully, but which Brunius claimed would "prevent the rot."

Consul Scipio was eager to engage Hannibal's forces in battle, but when we reached the camp where Hannibal had been, it was empty and abandoned. Hannibal had already marched his forces east to the land of the Allobroges. Hannibal, for his part, had no desire to engage Scipio and dissipate his strength even before reaching Italy. Scipio then reasoned that it would serve no good purpose to pursue Hannibal on his way to the Alps. Hannibal was wont to make alliances with the Gallic tribes by buying their leaders off with gold and we would probably dissipate our own strength by trying to force our way through hostile territory. Besides, we were certainly not prepared or equipped to cross the Alps!

Thus Consul Scipio made a decision to return to Italy with only a few of his men and raise an army which would meet Hannibal once he crossed the Alps. He believed that the arduous passage would weaken Hannibal's men and diminish their numbers, and that the Romans would have the advantage of fighting on familiar Italian soil.

In order to maintain the defense of Rome's interests in Hispania, he sent his legions, including myself, with his brother Cneius Scipio back by ships to Emporion on the northeast coast of Hispania.

Hannibal had left his general, Hanno, son of Bromilcar, in charge of the Carthaginian forces in northern Hispania, and, south of the Iberus, a large force of Carthaginians and their allies was commanded by Hannibal's brother Hasdrubal.

CHAPTER 3

Cneius Scipio was the elder brother of Publius Cornelius and had been consul in his own right a few years earlier. I was now under his command. Cneius Scipio's first order of business was to bring the tribes north of the Iberus back into the Roman sphere of influence. He did this by renewing old alliances and forming new ones. After a few days in our camp at Emporion I was surprised by a summons to his tent.

"Marcus Aemilius has informed me that you are corresponding with my nephew, young Publius Scipio." He said. "He says that your writing is clear and succinct and easily legible. He also told me that you acquitted yourself well in the battle against Hannibal's Numidian horsemen. Were you afraid?"

"Yes sir," I replied. He looked nonplussed for a moment and I wondered if I should have lied. But then he laughed and said "I like an honest soldier!"

Cneius Scipio had, if anything, even more gravitas and auctoritas than his brother and all I could answer was "Yes sir."

"Your cognomen is Varro? There was a Titus Lucinius Varro in the cavalry unit I served in under Regulus in the previous war against Carthage."

"My father!" I said

"A good man." said the Proconsul. "Quite a bit older than me. Surprised that he would have a son as young as you."

I smiled ruefully. "I was his son by his second wife. He was nearly fifty when I was born."

"I see." he said. "The reason that I asked to see you is that I have a number of scouts engaged in gathering information about the native tribes hereabout. Unfortunately, they are all local men who don't read or write Latin. I want them to report to you and I want you to write down all the information they offer. We need to know who is influential among the tribes and how these men may be induced to cast their lots with Rome. I will see that you have your own tent and a good supply of oil for your lamps so that everything you do will be done in private. These reports will be seen only by Marcus Aemilius and myself. Do you speak any other languages besides Latin?"

"I know a little Greek." I replied.

"I would advise you to try to learn the Celtiberian tongue if you can. It may become very useful in our work. The Celtiberians need to be handled very carefully. They are very proud and quite savage. I will encourage my Celtiberian scouts to teach you."

"Yes sir." I replied

"And one more thing." he said. "Once engaged in this work you will know too much. Should you at some point fall into the hands of the Carthaginians your duty is clear. You will be given a flask of poison. It will spare you from a very unpleasant session of torture at their hands." It occurred to me that if the Carthaginians crucify their own defeated generals, what might they not do to a captured Roman soldier?

"Yes sir" I replied. "May I keep my groom Brunius with me in my hut? He's quite illiterate and he will have no idea what I'm doing."

"Yes, if you trust him. But be very careful about who sees your activities." replied the Proconsul. "And you may continue corresponding with my nephew. Always give these letters to Marcus Aemilius, as before."

I was at a loss to decide whether this new assignment was a blessing or a curse. Certainly it was a privilege to have my own tent, and I was relieved of many of the mundane activities of an ordinary soldier such as sentry duty, stable duty and road construction. Cneius Scipio wanted me to be available whenever one of his scouts made his appearance. After my first experience in battle I was quite certain that my fate would be to die of a battle wound, but now it seemed just as likely that I would die by my own hand of poison! And learn Celtiberian? I had no idea how I might go about that. The Greeks, at least, have a written language. The Celtiberians do not. And all the writing. I had no idea when I joined Consul Scipio's cavalry legion that my most likely ailment might be writer's cramp!

It was Marcus Aemilius who gave me the poison. He instructed me that after a few months the liquid might evaporate and become too thick to easily be poured, or it might lose its effectiveness, so he told me that I must bring the flask back to him every three months and I would be given a replacement. I followed this practice faithfully the entire time that I served in Cneius Scipio's intelligence organization, so that when the day came that I was forced by circumstances to reach for the flask, I had every confidence of its efficacy.

The Iberian peninsula is shaped roughly in a square, and I took a parchment and drew a square and divided it into 25 sub squares, hoping to develop some idea of the physical and political geography of the place. Emporion originated as a Greek colony and many of the coastal inhabitants trace their ancestry to the Greeks. Further inland are the Ilergites, the Sedetani and the Ausitani. To the northwest are the Vascones, and across the Iberus are many groups of Celtiberians. As in most places the coastal peoples are more settled and more civilized, supporting themselves by farming and trade. The inland peoples are semi-nomadic and more primitive and warlike. These people were quite independent and owed fealty neither to the Romans nor to the Carthaginians and many of their leaders did not scruple to play one side against the other. This made it very difficult for me to know whom to trust!

After I was set up in my own tent with only Brunius as a companion, I began to be visited by various tribesmen who would give me intelligence about their communities and their leaders and the attitudes of both the leaders and the people toward the Romans and the Carthaginians. I often had to struggle to understand the broken Latin of our informants, but I wrote down everything I could. I also started to accompany Cneius Scipio when he made journeys to meet with tribal leaders. Cneius was a natural politician like his brother and his nephew and, just by his personal influence, he won many of the wavering tribal leaders to Rome's side.

One of the Celtiberians who reported to me was Armon. He was a friendly, very gregarious sort and we quickly became friends. I asked him if he would start teaching me the language and when he came to see me he would spend an hour or so teaching me words and phrases. I devised ways to render most of the sounds of the language into Roman lettering, and where there was no corresponding sound in the Latin language I found ways to improvise. I wrote down everything and studied my lists of words and phrases every day and eventually began to build up a vocabulary. One day I invited him to dinner and we ate a mess that Brunius had prepared.

"How do you eat this?" he said, laughing. "I've never had anything quite this bad!"

Brunius' cooking was not very tasty, but I had been eating it for months and had never thought much about it. It was just another hardship of military life. "Well, he may not be much of a cook." I said. "but I don't know how to cook at all, so it's the best we can do."

"What you need here is a woman." he said "And I know just the one!"

"Armon." I said "a Roman military camp is no place for a woman!"

"Well, she's an orphan and she's been in bad company all of her life." He said "She's used to rough and crude men. With winter coming her kinfolk don't want the extra mouth to feed and we need to find her a situation. She can cook, clean, sew, fetch water and firewood, anything you want!"

He was not to be denied and a few days later he came to my tent with the girl, Ala, in tow. She was hardly more than a child. About fifteen years old, she had honey colored hair, green eyes and translucent skin. She was very thin and underdeveloped. I thought her exquisite looking but nothing about her provoked my lust. She was wary and brittle and I thought of her in much the way I would a feral cat-beautiful, but you didn't want to get too close. Brunius was happy to surrender the cooking duties to her and he avoided her like the plague. He was not happy when I told him he had to accompany her when she went out early in the morning to gather firewood and fetch water, but she was terrified of the soldiers and would not venture out of the tent alone.

It did not take long for the soldiers to become aware of her presence, and one day as I passed a group of infantrymen one of them said "Longus! I hear you got a woman in your tent! Is that your wife?" (since I was tall and lean I'd acquired the agnomen "Longus" in some quarters.)

"No", I replied "She's just a servant."

"But you are going to bed her, aren't you?" said my inquisitor.

"Only if she insists." I replied.

The group broke into raucous laughter. "Look at Longus here, such a gentleman! The woman has to insist!"

The story rapidly made the rounds of the camp and for a few days there were silly grins and suppressed laughter wherever I went.

In any case she never insisted and I had the intuitive feeling that she would like and respect me more if I kept my distance. I did encourage her to teach me Celtiberian and thus was able to justify her presence to Marcus Aemilius and Cneius Scipio when they inquired about her. And she was a better cook than Brunius. The selection of food stuffs at the camp market didn't satisfy her, so she would insist that Brunius or I take her into Emporion, where she would lay in a supply of spices and herbs. She would use these to flavor dishes of organ meats and poultry. It seemed that the Celtiberians were also fond of octopus, which they called polpo, and she would prepare it with coarse salt, rosemary and olive oil; and eels and sausages were also on the menu. When she was able to procure honey she would even make desserts, such as cuajada, a dish made from curdled ewe's milk, honey and walnuts, and sometimes she would make an almond tart. The next time I invited Armon to dine at our tent he was much more pleased with the food. "I think I'll be visiting you more often now that I know I can get a decent meal here!" He said

Ala seemed to emerge from her shell when she went to Emporion. She loved looking at the goods in the shops, especially the jewelry shops. She would ask the shopkeepers all sorts of questions about metals and precious stones. I paid both her and Brunius a small wage and she loved to buy items of clothing and trinkets.

With my own tent and two servants I lived a life of relative ease in those days. I was unable to keep my literary activities entirely secret so I started to develop a clientele of illiterate soldiers who paid me to write letters home for them. I made them provide their own parchment and charged them ten sesterces a page. I started to feel relatively affluent. Cavalry men get three times the pay of infantry men, although we need to expend some of that extra pay on the care of our horses, but it was nice to earn some extra income. I was able to increase the wages I paid Brunius and Ala.

I didn't want to lose my martial skills, or get too soft, so I would go out every morning before breakfast and exercise my horse and practice throwing pila and javelins.

Cneius Scipio's efforts to win over the population of northern Hispania were so successful that Hanno became alarmed and decided to offer battle. Scipio was not inclined to wait until such time as Hanno might be joined by Hannibal's brother Hasdrubal, so he gladly took up the challenge, and a battle took place near a town called Cissa. I took part in the battle but most of the fighting was done by the infantry. We defeated Hanno without much loss to ourselves. Six thousand of the Carthaginian forces were killed and two thousand made prisoner, including Hanno himself and several of his chief officers. The best thing was that Hanno's camp contained not only the possessions of his own soldiers but also the possessions of the forces who had accompanied Hannibal to Italy, which they had left behind so as not to be too heavily encumbered on their march. We all shared in the booty and I acquired a number of silver items and even some gold. This was the first time I'd experienced this particular benefit of a military career. I gave Brunius a silver bowl and a gold coin and I gave Ala some silver jewelry that I purchased in Emporion and a little silver box to keep it in. She was amazed and delighted. It was the first time I'd ever seen her smile. "Gratzia! Gratzia!" She cried in her newly acquired Latin. I also bought silver and gold jewelry to bring home to Silvia, and kept some nice bowls for my mother. Not wanting to be too encumbered with possessions, I sold the rest for coins.

The prisoners we captured were sold in Emporion as slaves, except for Hanno himself, and his most important officers who were sent to Rome in chains. I was able to get a good look at this enemy whose implements of torture in my imagination I had once greatly feared, and he seemed a quite ordinary and undistinguished person.

It was shortly after this battle that I received a letter in my father's hand telling me that Silvia had given birth to a little boy that they had named Lucius after me. I was, as the same time, thrilled by the news and deeply homesick. I determined that once I had completed two years of service I would ask Cneius Scipio for a furlough.

Our elation at defeating Hanno was soon dampened by the news from Italy. Hannibal had succeeded in crossing the Alps, with, after some losses, about 40,000 foot soldiers, 8000 cavalry including Numidians and Iberians, and 37 elephants. He recruited numerous allies from among the Ligurians and the Cis-alpine Gauls. With a hastily raised army of relatively inexperienced troops, Consul Publius Scipio engaged in a battle with Hannibal's forces at the River Ticinus. The consul was badly wounded and escaped with his life only because young Publius Scipio saw that his father was in danger and boldly charged through the enemy lines to rescue him. The Consul was able to flee with most of his forces to Placentia.

The other consul for the year, Tiberius Sempronius Longus was recalled from Sicily to deal with Hannibal. Consul Scipio tried to discourage Sempronius from open engagement with Hannibal. Perhaps he sensed that Hannibal possessed a military genius beyond his own abilities or those of Sempronius, and that confronting him on his own terms might prove disastrous to the Romans. Sempronius was eager for battle and harangued Scipio even at his sick bed. In December Sempronius gave battle at the Trebia River and was utterly defeated by Hannibal. Out of some 40,000 troops on the Roman side, nearly half were killed, wounded or captured. Worse was to come.

Sometime after our victory over Hanno, Vigodan, one of Cneius Scipio's scouts among the Ilergetes came to my tent. He was agitated and clearly frightened. He said that Hasdrubal, the brother of Hannibal had personally conducted an embassy to the Illergetes and had recruited their leaders to the Carthaginian cause, and that he was encouraging the youth of the Ilergetes to make raids on neighboring peoples who were Roman allies. I felt that this news was too important to brook any delay and took him directly to see Cneius Scipio.

The Proconsul listened carefully to the man and then ordered two cohorts of troops to investigate. Seeing the destruction, he ordered his army to invade the state of the Ilergetes and lay siege to their capital Athanagia. In a few days they surrendered and submitted to Rome. He fined them a sum of money and took hostages. He also took action against the Ausetani who were also aligned with Hasdrubal. After a long siege of their city their leader fled to Hasdrubal and they surrendered, agreeing to pay twenty talents of silver.

I thought that these measures would put an end to the problems with the locals, but not long after that time Armon came to my tent with disturbing news. He said that Vigodan was dead. Supporters of the Carthaginians had killed him and Armon believed that they planned to eliminate any local tribes people that they suspected were working for Scipio. "I think I had better go to ground in Celtiberia," he said "And I think you should come with me, both you and Ala."

"I don't think Cneius Scipio would let me go." I said. "He needs me here."

"He has no choice." said Armon. "Let me explain a few things to him. Come with me."

We went to Cneius Scipio's tent and asked to see the general in private. Scipio was perturbed to hear of the death of Vigodan. "Now I'm a target." said Armon, "And I'm going to hide out in Celtiberia in a village of my kinsmen. Longus, here, is also a target." He said, referring to me. "With what he knows about our intelligence operations, Hasdrubal will pay a gold talent to get him on his rack. And Longus is already tall enough!" Armon laughed heartily at his own jest, and Scipio could not suppress a chuckle. But I was starting to feel sick to my stomach!

"Lucius knows what to do if he's captured." said Cneius Scipio grimly.

"But I think the plan is to take him by surprise and strip him before he can get the poison into his mouth!" replied Armon. I was getting weak kneed by this time. "There's a plan?!" I thought to myself.

"Vigodan gave me the names of some of the Carthaginian agents among the Ilergetes before he died." Armon continued. "I think he knew that they were coming after him. I will give these names to Longus to write down for you. You can take action against them. But in the mean time we need to get Longus out of harm's way. Let him come with me to Celtiberia and we will return when it's safer. This way Longus will increase his knowledge of the Celtiberian language and be able to give you intelligence on the customs and attitudes of our people so that you can make alliances with them. Although the day you put your trust in the Celtiberians is the day you should give up your command!" Again Armon laughed heartily at his own jest. The Proconsul only smiled. There would come a time when I would wish that Cneius Scipio had paid more attention to Armon's jests!

The proconsul reluctantly agreed to the plan and we started to make preparations for our journey. "Is it really necessary for Ala to come?" I asked. "I thought her kinfolk didn't like her."

"I don't want to leave her here." he said. "We'll buy her a supply of grain to give them. They like her a lot more when she feeds them than when they have to feed her! We will also have to get her a pony. I will give you some Celtiberian clothes so you won't look so conspicuously Roman, although I doubt that I'll be able to find anything long enough in the legs." Unlike we Romans, who wear tunics or togae, the Celtiberians wear britches and it took some getting used to.

We paid a brief visit to Emporion to purchase the pony and lay in a supply of grain and other supplies for traveling. Ala used her paltry savings to buy nice items of clothing and jewelry for her kinswomen. I think she wanted to impress them that she had improved her station in the world.

We left at dawn the following day. "Was there really a plan to kidnap me?" I asked Armon. "Well," he said, "That's exactly what I would do if I were them. When dealing with the enemy you have to be able to figure out what he's thinking."

The journey took several days. At night we found sheltered places to build a fire. But one day we came to a cave and Armon said we would sleep there. "This is a very sacred place." he said "Only a few of the local people know about it. We don't like people coming here because it contains a great treasure."

"How do you keep people from stealing the treasure?" I asked

"The treasure can't be stolen," he said "But it can be destroyed, and that's what we seek to prevent. Therefore you must never tell a soul what you've seen here."

He bade me bring torches, and as many oil lamps as I could and follow him into the cave. We had to remove a number of large rocks from the entrance to gain access. I hardly thought it was worth the effort. But when we got into the large chamber and lit the lamps, what I saw absolutely amazed me. There were paintings of bulls! They were amazingly well executed, with shadings that made them almost seem alive. There were also stick figures of men with spears attacking the beasts. The art was obviously done by very primitive people but people with great artistic talent and mastery of perspective.

"Who made these paintings?" I asked

"We don't know." replied Armon "The first people in the world, we think. But we believe that this is a sacred place and that there is great power here. I think that if we stay here we may absorb some of this power into our spirits and it will protect us."

I just nodded. I had long since learned not to argue with another person about their religious beliefs. But perhaps he was right, for this was the first night in nearly a week that I slept soundly and had no nightmares or anxieties. I awoke very refreshed in the morning.

"You look good this morning." said Armon "not so troubled or anxious. I told you this was a good place. Woe betide anyone who destroys these paintings."

Not wishing to argue, I said "I will treat them as sacred, just as if this were the temple of Jupiter."

The next day we came to Carrach, the village where Armon's mother lived. I can not really render the name of the village into Latin because there is no Latin letter for the last sound in the name. The pronunciation is something you might achieve by clearing your throat!

Armon's kinfolk gathered around us and welcomed us. They even seemed happy to see Ala, especially when she gave them sacks of grain and the clothing and jewelry she had brought with her. It seemed that Ala was the natural child of one of Armon's mother's cousins. Ala's mother had died some years ago and her father was unknown, which conferred upon Ala a very low status. But they seemed to be treating her kindly enough and soon she was chattering happily with the women folk.

The people live in round thatched huts and survive by a combination of farming, herding cattle and sheep and fishing. Like Romans, they value military skill and valor, but unlike Romans they are not very disciplined and men are much more independent. Young Scipio had said that every human relationship other than twins was unequal. This doesn't seem to be so true among the Celtiberian men. Each man seemed to be his own boss!

I still recall my several months in Carrach as the happiest and most carefree of my life. There was no one to order me about or tell me what to do. I did try to help my hosts with chores and manual labor but it was all voluntary. Every day I would go with Armon's nephews, both adolescents, to chop wood, fetch water, or clear land for planting. One day, soon after I arrived, the men invited me to go hunting with them. They asked if I had ever hunted. "I've never killed animals, only people." I replied. My answer startled them. "Well, I'm a soldier." I explained. "I've killed people in battle, but I grew up in the big city of Rome and there are not a lot of animals to kill there." I went along on the hunt and enjoyed it, but I never got a chance to kill anything. My companions bagged some birds, rabbits and a fox. Armon's nephew Andor slew a deer and we had a good feast of venison that night.

At night they would eat and drink and sing and dance and play musical instruments. Everything was done in a primitive and uninhibited way and if they got too drunk fights were likely to break out, but their fellows would break them up before anyone got seriously hurt. I learned some of their songs and they taught me some of their men's dances. Men and women each had their own dances. I continued to study their language and got fluent enough to carry on a simple conversation. I wrote down all of my observations of their customs and habits with a mind to send the information to young Publius Scipio.

After several months Armon traveled back alone to Emporion to see if conditions were safe for us to return. Scipio had eliminated the men on Vigodan's list and made clear that he wanted me to resume my services for him. So Armon returned to Carrach to fetch Ala and me back to Emporion.

Scipio had to recruit some new scouts to replace a few that had actually been eliminated by the sympathizers of the Carthaginians, proving that Armon had been right, at least as far as the personal danger to himself. I still wondered if I had actually been in danger, and if, perhaps, I was still in danger, but I decided not to worry about it an threw myself into my work. I wrote a long treatise about the Celtiberians and sent it off to young Publius Scipio.

CHAPTER 4

We continued to get bad news from Italy. The consuls elected to replace Publius Cornelius Scipio and Tiberius Sempronius were Gnaeus Servillius Geminus and Gaius Flaminius. Flaminius was a man of quick temper who listened to no wise counsel. Several months after the disastrous battle of Trebia, Flaminius lead his consular army of 30,000 men into an even more disastrous battle at Lake Trasimene. Again Hannibal outflanked the Roman general and in the slaughter that followed, 15,000 Romans were killed including Flaminius. Some ten thousand managed to escape the carnage and made their way back to Rome. A group of 6,000 who escaped were captured the next day by Hannibal's cavalry chief Maharbal. Maharbal promised them safe passage if they would surrender their weapons, but when they did so they were put into chains and sold into slavery. From such actions we Romans derive our expression "Punic faith."

Rome was reeling from its losses. In desperate times the Roman assembly would elect a dictator and this was just such a time. The man they elected was Quintus Fabius Maximus, one of the ambassadors I had met when he came through Massilia on his way back to Rome after the ill-starred embassy to Carthage.

Quintus Fabius was the exact opposite of Sempronius and Flaminius in temperament. He was cautious and cunning. He consistently avoided any direct engagement with Hannibal, but constantly harassed Hannibal's forces and attempted to deprive them of provisions. Those tactics earned him the agnomen Cunctator-the dalayer. The agnomen was originally a pejorative applied by Fabius' detractors who thought that he was too cautious, but it came to be used admiringly by his supporters who felt that Fabius' tactics were the only rational course given Rome's present weakness in manpower and Hannibal's manifestly consummate skill as a general and a destroyer of Roman armies. Whether or not one agrees with Fabius' tactics, one will have to give the man credit for cunning. Among the generals who served Rome in the second Punic war, Gaius Flaminius, Lucius Aemilius Paullus, Gaius Servilius Geminus, Marcus Manucius Rufus, Tiberius Sempronius Graccus, Cneius Fulvius, Cneius Cornelius Scipio, Publius Cornelius Scipio the elder, Marcus Claudius Marcellus and Titus Quintus Crispinus all died in battle. Quintus Fabius died in his bed from conditions brought on by old age.

But the people of Rome grew impatient with Quintus Fabius and his delaying tactics and demanded that consuls be elected who would give Hannibal battle. They elected as consuls Lucius Aemilius Paullus and Caius Terentius Varro. The combined forces of the two consuls may have numbered 80,000 Roman and allied infantry, and six thousand Roman and allied horse, while Hannibal's forces consisted of only 32,000 heavy infantry, 8000 light infantry and 10,000 horse. But the new consuls were inexperienced generals and were easily outsmarted by Hannibal's brilliant military tactics. The battle of Cannae was far more of a disaster for Rome than even the battle of Trasimene. At least 50,000 were killed and 4000 taken prisoner. The dead included 20 officers of consular or praetorian rank, thirty senators and three hundred persons of noble descent. It was the worst military disaster in Rome's history. Perhaps the worst military disaster in any country's history! And yet, somehow, Rome survived.

Those of us stationed in Hispania wondered if there would be a Rome to go home to. We wondered when our legions would be summoned to go back to Italy and defend our city. But no such summons ever came. In fact, Publius Cornelius Scipio, now recovered from the wounds he had received at Ticinus, returned to Hispania to assume command of his legions. I was once again under his command.

When the winter following the news of the battle of Cannae arrived, I petitioned Publius Cornelius Scipio for a furlough to spend the winter in Rome. There was little military activity going on in Hispania at the time and I told him that I had fathered a son that I had never seen. I told him I would return in the Spring assuming that I wasn't needed to defend the walls of Rome. Publius Scipio granted permission for the furlough and asked me to bear a letter from him to his son. Other soldiers also asked me to carry their letters home to Rome and my baggage was filled with letters. They each paid me a small fee for the service. I took Brunius with me but bringing Ala would have been awkward, so Armon took her home to Carrach, again laden with grain and presents for her kinfolk.

The sea voyage to Pisa was particularly rough this time of year, but at least there was less likelihood of being captured by Carthaginian naval forces. We resigned ourselves to enduring seasickness. Our horses were vociferous in their complaints!

When we got to Rome I rode to my father's house and Brunius to his old lodgings at Silvius' stable. The whole family seemed transported with joy at my arrival. They crowded around me, the women showering me with hugs and kisses and everyone asking me an endless stream of questions. Silvia let my mother and sisters have the first crack at my attentions because she knew that she would have me to herself later on. I met my little boy for the first time. He had Silvia's black hair and rosy cheeks and looked like he would be handsome. He was just starting to talk. He was shy at first but after a few days he began to call me Papa. After the women went off to prepare a celebratory dinner, my father sat me down at the table with some bread and wine.

"You look so much older now and more mature than when you left!" he said. "I'm glad you're back! So many families hereabouts will never see their sons again." He looked as though he might cry, but he contained himself. "These are bad times for Rome, Lucius, very bad times. You know, two of your mother's nephews are dead. Remember little Enneus? Dead at Trasimene, and Gaius, dead at Cannae. I can scarcely credit my own luck. I must be the only father I know with three live grown sons!"

I hardly knew what to say. "Well, I've been very lucky myself. I've only been in two battles so far and I spend most of my time gathering and writing down information for Proconsul Scipio so my life isn't arduous at all. I even have two servants!" We talked for a while and then we all sat down to dinner. Our family had never lived lavishly so everything seemed the way it had always been in terms of the amount and availability of food. I distributed presents I had gotten in Emporium for each of my family members. I gave mother the silver bowls I had gotten as booty in Hanno's camp and everyone was interested in the story of how we had defeated him.

I thought about my cousins Enneas and Gaius, fine young men, both. Such a waste of good lives this war was. Enneas, in particular, had been a prodigy, the best student our Greek tutor Athenagoras ever had. He could recite nearly the whole of the Iliad and Odyssey by heart in Greek!

Normally, little Lucius slept with his mother, but my family wanted me to be alone with Silvia so my sister, Tullia, took the child to her house which was close by. When we retired to our bedchamber Silvia clung to me. "Lucius, I want to cry, but I won't. It would just upset you. Do you know that they passed a law forbidding even women to cry in public? I have had to learn to control myself. Somehow we have to keep up each others spirits, we Roman men and women, because there is just too much pain and death. It's overwhelming!"

"Silvia, if you want to cry, please do. I think I may soon want to weep myself, and no law is going to stop me!" I laughed

"Oh, Lucius, I love you. I love you!" she exclaimed. "I'm so glad you've come back! What do you think of your son?"

"A fine little boy, Silvia. You've done a great job." I began to caress and kiss her and we forgot all of our troubles in our lovemaking. "It's been so long, Silvia, I'd nearly forgotten what it was like to sleep in a bed and make love with my beautiful wife!"

The next day Silvia and I went over to her father's house for dinner. There was a noticeable decline in Silvius' opulence. His stable was struggling because it was now impossible to obtain horses from Campania. After Cannae the Campanians had made an alliance with Hannibal, and, in fact, Hannibal's army was wintering in Capua, a most opulent city, where it was said that they were eating, drinking, whoring and generally getting soft. When Brunius was told that Campania had allied itself with Hannibal he was a little shocked, but he said "Campania goes with Hannibal, but I go with Rome." and that was the end of that.

"I never thought that I would consider myself blessed to have four daughters!" said Silvius. "But then losing a son-in-law is almost as bad as losing a son." His youngest daughter, Aelia, had recently married but her young husband had been taken in the levies and had been killed at Cannae. Aelia was back at Silvius' home since Silvius was more affluent than her husband's family and Aelia was more comfortable in her father's house. "Now, with Campania gone I'm having to breed my own horses. I have several mares expecting foals in the Spring. It's so much better if you can buy your horses. It's a lot of expense and trouble to raise them yourself and it takes so long before your investment pays off. How was it in Hispania?" he asked.

"It's a beautiful country." I said. "The people are kind of wild, but interesting. Thank you for letting me have Brunius. He's been a big help to me. The horse you gave me is wonderful too, I just wish I could get it to tolerate sea voyages."

"Most people barely tolerate sea voyages, so why would a horse?" he laughed. I got up the courage to bring up Brunius' status. "You know, if it's possible I'd like to buy Brunius from you and manumit him."

"Well, I gave him to you, so he's yours, and you can do what you like with him." said Silvius

"I never asked him how he became a slave" I said. "The subject was just too awkward."

"Oh, his father got deeply into debt and sold him." he said "He's a good man and I have long since gotten my money's worth from him. I figured you could use a good groom in Hispania."

I decided that I would manumit Brunius the first chance I got.

The next day I sought out Publius Scipio and gave him the letter from his father. He seemed delighted to see me. "Lucius, come to dinner tomorrow at my father's villa, just the two of us. We have so much to talk about!"

I spent the rest of the day delivering the letters that I had been charged with. Every family invited me in for bread and wine. Everyone was so grateful to me for bringing them news from their sons. These days live sons were precious and their letters were treasured. If the family had no members who were literate, I read the letter to them as they gathered around the table. In some cases they asked me to come back when I had time so that they could dictate a letter to me for their son with the news from home. In a number of cases the son who wrote from Hispania had had brothers who had died in one of the battles in Italy. This work was emotionally wrenching to me as I could see that these family members were bravely doing all they could to refrain from breaking down and weeping in front of me.

The following day I went back to Publius Scipio's villa. I had not been there since that evening when I had met his father the Consul for the first time, a week or two before I had left for Hispania. It had changed little but something about it seemed forlorn.

Publius Scipio greeted me with a bear hug. "It's so nice to see you, Lucius. You look good! And thank you for all the news and information you've sent me from Hispania. I always look forward to your correspondence. I really enjoyed your report about the Celtiberians. Do you ever envy them? How free they are?"

"Sometimes I do." I replied. "I really enjoyed my time among them. They seem to have more choices than we do. I always felt that I never had any choice other than to become a soldier."

"Nor did I" said Scipio "And I'll probably die a soldier. But the problem with the Celtiberians is that they will not be able to maintain their independence. They will become a subject people. If you want to stay free you have to have good leaders and good followers in a disciplined military structure. Without that they will eventually be crushed either by Carthage or by Rome or by some other great power that emerges in the future."

Then his continence grew grave. "Our friends from the Campus Martius are nearly all dead now." I was getting weary by now of listening to litanies of grief, but I knew he needed to vent so I let him go on. "Martius Casca died at Cannae. Tiberius Licinius at Trebia, Gaius Terentius at Cannae, and Marcus Livius at Trasimene. Velarius Galba was on my head. He was with me at Ticinus when I led the charge to break through the Carthaginian line to save my father, and they cut him down."

"But if you hadn't done that you father would have been killed, or worse, taken by Hannibal!" I said.

"Yes, and Velarius would likely have died at Trasimene or Cannae anyway. Gaius Clodius and Marcus Junius both survived Cannae but they are in the fifth legion and the assembly passed a law that the soldiers who survived Cannae by retreating must serve in Sicily until the end of the war, no matter how long it takes. It's not right!" said Publius Scipio. "There's no disgrace in escaping the carnage once the battle is over and living to fight another day. I've done that myself more than once! They don't enforce that law with nobility like myself, only with the lower classes. Rome is badly in need of some social reforms, but that, I'm afraid, is not my province. My province is to insure that Rome survives. Reforms will have to await a generation of peace.

"After Cannae some of the surviving nobility wanted to give up the fight and emigrate. Lucius Caecilius Metellus and a number of his followers advocated this course. I went to their lodgings with Gaius Laelius and several of our friends and we publicly swore an oath that we would die before we abandoned Rome. Than I forced Metellus and his friends to take this same oath at sword point."

"Publius," I said "How did it happen? How did Hannibal defeat a Roman army twice the size of his own?"

"Well, Lucius" Publius Scipio replied "Hannibal's strategy and tactics are not new. The same gambit was used by the Athenians at Marathon nearly three hundred years ago to defeat a Persian army much larger than their own. It works like this: You put your weakest troops in the center of your line and the strong ones on the wings. In this case Hannibal's weakest troops were his Ligurian and Celtic foot, and his stronger ones were his heavy armed Hispanian foot and his Hispanian and Numidian Cavalry. Then when your enemy engages your weak troops, they slowly retreat and your enemy slowly advances. In time you send your wings forward to envelop the enemy on all sides. Your cavalry prevent any of their foot from escaping. Then you cut them all down. That's what happened at Trebia, Trasimene, and at Cannae. Hannibal may not have invented this maneuver, in fact his father Hamilcar Barca provided him with the best Greek tutors, but he has become a master at it."

"Edepol!" I said. "So he did the same thing three times and we Romans kept making the same mistakes! But what do you think of Quintus Fabius?"

"Well, if you're dealing with a military genius and you're not one yourself . . . . In that case Fabius' tactics make sense!" He laughed. "At least Fabius has kept himself alive and has not lost tens of thousands of men. But some day I plan to fight Hannibal Barca with my own legions, and I intend to beat him at his own game!"

Publius Scipio drew my attention to a gold ring that he wore. These rings are customarily worn by men of the patrician and equestrian classes. He stared directly into my eyes, his face livid and his eyes ablaze with fury: "After the battle of Cannae was over, Hannibal sent his men out to the field to search for any upper class Roman dead, and . . . . and they pried the gold rings off of the dead fingers and collected them all in an urn. Then he sent the urn by ship to Carthago and had them pour the rings out onto the floor of the Carthaginian senate. There were over two hundred of them. We will avenge them, Lucius Tullius Varro. We will avenge them!"

His voice sent shivers down my spine, and at that moment I believe utterly and completely in his words. He did not disappoint me.

CHAPTER 5

As depressing as the mood and situation in Rome was, I enjoyed being with my family and helping out at Silvius' stable. I resolved to spend every winter here if I could get permission. A cavalryman is expected to participate in ten military campaigns and I had participated in only two in three years so I didn't know how long it would take me to complete my service, especially since the war was likely to continue for a long time to come. Hannibal had offered terms of peace after Cannae, but the senate and assembly had refused them. Everyone was wondering when he was going to lay siege to Rome. He didn't seem to be in any hurry to do that. Perhaps he wanted to cement alliances with the rest of Italy to leave us isolated first, or perhaps he just enjoyed being the cat in a cat and mouse game and wanted it to continue. It is said that Hannibal's general Maharbal had urged Hannibal to march on Rome immediately after his huge victory at Cannae and that Hannibal had considered doing so, but had decided against it. Maharbal in exasperation told Hannibal "It seems that the gods don't grant all their gifts to one man. You know very well how to win a victory, Hannibal, but you don't know how to use one!"*3

When Spring came and there was still no evidence that a siege was immanent, Brunius and I made our way back to Pisa and thence to Emporion to rejoin Scipio's legions. Brunius wore his cap of liberty, as I had manumitted him. We traveled to Ibera where the armies of both Scipio brothers were laying siege to the town, which had been allied to the Carthaginians. It was believed that Hasdrubal, Hannibal's brother, had been given orders by the Carthaginian senate to bring his army to Italy to reinforce Hannibal.

The Scipios wanted to stop him. Hasdrubal came north to the Iberus and lay siege to the town of Dertosa, which was allied with Rome. Cneius and Publius Scipio then decided to abandon the siege of Ibera and give battle to Hasdrubal at Dertosa. This would be my third campaign. Hasdrubal's strategy in this battle was very similar to Hannibal's strategy at Trebia, Trasimene and Cannae, but this time it failed. Both sides suffered heavy casualties, but, in the end the Carthaginian forces were routed. I was wounded early in the battle by a spear to the left shoulder and taken back to camp, so I saw little action. When we took Hasdrubal's camp our soldiers were again allowed to divide up the spoils. My wound prevented me from going there and claiming any spoil in person, but Marcus Aemilius saw to it that I received my share of the booty. The battle put an end, at least temporarily, to Hasdrubal's plans to bring reinforcements to Hannibal in Italy. Not only that, but the Carthaginians decided to send Hannibal's brother Mago to Hispania to reinforce Hasdrubal, rather than to Italy as originally planned. Had Hannibal received these reinforcements the war in Italy might have turned out differently.

After the battle of Dertosa we returned to our base camp near Emporion, and after recovering from my wound I resumed my old work of receiving intelligence. As a result of our victory at Dertosa, more and more of the Hispanian tribes were aligning themselves with Rome and since the Scipios were able to recruit scouts from these tribes, taking their reports kept me very busy. Armon came to see me and brought Ala back.

During the next three years the situation in Hispania was stable and no major conflicts took place. With Hannibal laying waste to much of Italy, it was not possible to get reinforcements from Italy. Hasdrubal, on the other hand, was reinforced by his brother Mago and by another Carthaginian general, Hasdrubal, son of Gisco. He also had three thousand Numidian horsemen under Masinissa, and 7500 Hispanian foot under Indibilis, a chieftain of the Ilergetes. For a time Hasdrubal's attention was diverted by a rebellion encouraged by the Scipios of Syphax, king of Cirta. Cirta was a neighbor of Carthage and was inhabited by Numidian tribes. The Carthaginians considered it a client state.

During this time, I was permitted to go to Rome every winter to stay with my family. Twice Silvia had gotten pregnant during my visits and gave birth to daughters. In the Spring I would go back to Hispania and resume my work for Cneius Scipio.

After the rebellion of Syphax was put down Hasdrubal returned to Hispania and encamped north of New Carthage. The Scipios suspected that Hasdrubal was once again planning to go to Italy and reinforce Hannibal. They decided that they should try to eliminate him as a threat altogether. For this purpose Gneius Scipio recruited a force of 20,000 Celtiberian mercenaries. One of their leaders was a man named Gorgo. One day I heard Ala outside our tent arguing loudly with a man in Celtiberian. I knew enough of the language by now to get the gist of what they were saying.

"So this is where you've been all this time, Ala, with this Roman puppy!" the man said.

"Get your hands off me, Gorgo! Go away!" Screamed Ala.

"Surely you must know that I love you, Ala!" Said Gorgo.

"Surely you must know that I hate you, Gorgo!" replied Ala.

I walked out of the tent to see what was going on. Gorgo glared at me malignantly and stalked off. "Idiot!" I thought to myself. "If you're seeking to molest a feral cat, don't complain to me if she scratches your eyes out!"

"He could have at least granted me the dignitas of calling me a dog rather than a puppy." I joked when he left.

Ala was in no mood for jokes. "Gorgo grants no man dignitas." she replied. "He befilths everything he touches. Bad bad man. I hate him. I hate him!"

I asked Armon about Gorgo the next time I saw him. "I don't trust him," he said "He has a very bad reputation. It's a mistake for Cneius Scipio to rely on the likes of him. He'll sell himself and his men to the highest bidder, and Hasdrubal has a lot of money."

I made up my mind to go to Cneius Scipio with my concerns but he had gone south to reconnoiter the territory around the Upper Baetis. Hasdrubal Barca had separated his forces from Hasdrubal Gisco and Mago and the Scipios formed a plan that one of them, Publius, would take a force of 20,000 Roman and allied forces to attack Hasdrubal Gisco, Mago, and their Hispanian allies at Castulo, while Cneius Scipio would take ten thousand Roman troops plus 20,000 Celtiberian mercenaries to attack Hasdrubal Barca. Both operations proved disastrous. Publius Scipio first attacked the Hispanian troops under the Ilergete chieftain Indibilis and was inflicting heavy casualties, but when Masinissa arrived with his Numidian cavalry, the tide turned against Publius Scipio and his army. The subsequent arrival of Hasdrubal Gisco and Mago precipitated a slaughter of the Roman forces and by day's end Proconsul Publius Cornelius Scipio lay dead on the field of battle.

CHAPTER 6

I was with the forces of Cneius Scipio, one of about 300 cavalrymen. I had never gotten a chance to talk with the proconsul about my concerns regarding the Celtiberians, and Cneius Scipio believed that our forces were much stronger than they were. The Carthaginians had bribed the Celtiberians to leave the battle. Once aware that the Celtiberians had deserted, Cneius Scipio ordered us to retreat at night northward toward the Iberus. The next day the Numidians caught up with us and inflicted heavy casualties. The following day Hasdrubal Gisco and Mago arrived and carried on a wholesale slaughter of our forces. Cneius Scipio died in the battle only a few days after his brother Publius had.

Somehow I escaped with a small group of cavalrymen. There were four of us and we rode northward and crossed the Iberus into the territory of the Celtiberians. When our horses were exhausted we decided to set up camp in a clearing in the woods. I was preparing a fire when suddenly three armed men burst into the clearing. I recognized Gorgo. He gave orders to kill everyone, except for Cneius Scipio's puppy who was worth money to them. Taken by surprise my companions were easily dispatched. Since the Roman cavalrymen still wore their chain mail, the Celtiberians cut their jugular veins and there was blood everywhere. I tried to reach for my flask of poison but Gorgo jabbed his spear into my hand, wounding it to the bone. While the others restrained me he felt around for the flask, and, finding it, he said "I'll take this for now, Puppy. Maybe Hasdrubal will let you have it back after you've told him everything you know." He was leering at me. His expression could only be described as lust! "And we'll each enjoy some Greek love with the Puppy before we sell him to Hasdrubal!" he laughed. I felt every muscle in my body tense up.

Suddenly I heard a loud Celtiberian war cry. "Yaaaa!" It was Ala and she was armed with a falcata! She wielded it with a skill I have rarely seen in a man, let alone in a woman! This time it was she who had the element of surprise and with three strokes of the weapon she dispatched Gorgo and his two companions. There was blood everywhere. My tunic was soaked with it. This was no feral cat. This was a lioness!

She pulled me to my feet and said "We go, now!" Without further words we each mounted a horse and headed east. I followed her to the cave with the paintings. The wound on my hand prevented me from helping her remove the rocks from the entrance to the cave so she had to do it herself. We had no oil lamp and the cave was dark, but she said "We safe here."

"Armon is dead." she said. "They came for him, to sell him to Hasdrubal, and he took the poison."

"That must have been why Gorgo suspected that I was about to take poison," I thought to myself

I spoke for the first time. "Ala, how did you do that? That was amazing! I didn't know you could use a falcata!"

"When the man you most hate tries to kill the man you most love, it makes you twice as strong." she said.

"You knew Gorgo from before?"

"He was with my mother. He made her with baby and then he beat her and she died. He did bad things to me. Very bad man. I hate him, always." She said. "You are the first man besides Armon that ever treated me decent. When you're an orphan men take advantage.

"Gorgo couldn't understand how much I hated him and he thought he owned me. After Armon died, Gorgo ordered me to come with him. I heard them discussing their plans. They left me with one of his men when they went to attack your camp. I wrenched the falcata out of the man's hand and killed him with it. Then I followed their trail to your camp."

She had a pouch with some jerky in it and she shared it with me. There was a stream nearby and we drank some water. "Your clothes are caked with blood" she said. "Take them off and I'll wash them in the stream." Then, in the cave that night she insisted! Under the circumstances I didn't see how I could deny her.

"I love you, Lucius." she said.

"I'm your slave, Ala, now and forever." I replied. I still loved Silvia and felt bad about betraying her, but I was now too much in debt to this woman to deny her anything.

"I'm your slave, Ala, but what will I tell my wife?"

She laughed. "I don't take you from your wife, Lucius. This is what I want. You take me to Rome and get me a shop, like the ones in Emporion, and you bring me jewelry from Hispania and I sell it to the Roman ladies. Sometimes you come and visit me and we make love. You can keep your wife." Under the circumstances her demands seemed perfectly reasonable and I agreed to do whatever I could to bring her ambitions to fruition. On her trips to Emporion, Ala had been fascinated by the jewelry shops and had tried to learn everything she could about gold, silver and precious stones. When I thought about it I wasn't too surprised by her strange requests.

After a few days travel we arrived at our camp at Emporion. The wound in my had become purulent, but did not develop gangrene. The physician said I was very lucky. When Brunius saw me he wept with joy. And when I told him what Ala had done, the freedman symbolically removed his cap of liberty and knelt before her saying "Ala, I am your slave!" She laughed. "Oh, don't be silly, Brunius. Put that cap back on. I like you much more as free man than as slave."

"Sorry, Brunius," I said. "Only I can be her slave."

Over the next few weeks the survivors of the battles of the Upper Baetis came drifting into Emporion. There were some 8000 out of an original thirty three thousand Roman Soldiers. Proportionately, our losses may have been worse than at Cannae! Publius Cornelius Scipio had been right when he said the a good commander would be both feared and loved by his men. Every one of us had loved Publius Cornelius and Cneius Cornelius Scipio, and we were in mourning for them. We resolved that at all costs we would hold onto our corner of Northeastern Hispania. And, as it happened, Fortuna sent us a leader.

His name was Lucius Marcius. Like me, he was the son of a Roman knight, not a patrician, and, like me, he'd had a long and close association with Cneius Scipio. Unlike me, he was a man of exceptional military abilities and genius. He collected the troops which had been dispersed in the flight from the battles of the Upper Baetis and drafted some that had been left in the garrisons to form an army, which he united with the surviving troops under Titus Tonteius, the lieutenant-general of Publius Scipio. We fortified our camp and re-established traditional Roman discipline and military practices. In an assembly of all the surviving soldiers we unanimously elected Lucius Marcius as our supreme commander. Now this would not sit well with the conservative officials and senators in Rome. Soldiers were not allowed to elect their own leaders. Leadership was always to be conferred by the Roman Senate and Assembly, and, in the end, Lucius Marcius was denied the recognition and honors he should have received. But I bear witness to the fact that he was the man most responsible for the survival of what was left of the armies of Publius and Cneius Scipio.

We received word that Hasdrubal, son of Gisco, had crossed the Iberus to finish the work of the Upper Baetis. As the enemy approached, many of the soldiers, remembering our fallen generals, fell into fits of grief and lamentations, some beating their heads, some raising their hands to heaven and arraigning the gods, others prostrating themselves on the ground and each invoking the name of his own former commander. Marcius remonstrated with them:

"Why have you given yourselves up to womanish and unavailing lamentations rather than summon up all of your courage to protect yourselves and the commonwealth and not suffer our generals to be unavenged?"

But when we heard the shouts and the trumpets of the enemy and saw them approach the rampart, our grief turned to rage and fury and we ran to our arms and rushed to the gates to charge the enemy. The Carthaginians were not expecting such resistance. After eight years of war they still did not understand Romans! They wondered how so many enemies could have sprung up so suddenly as the army had been almost annihilated, and what could have inspired men who had been vanquished and routed with such boldness and confidence in themselves? We routed Hasdrubal Gisco's troops and began to pursue them to their camp, but Marcius called the retreat. I myself was caught up in the spirit of battle despite my injured right hand. I killed with my left.

The Carthaginians assumed that we had stopped the pursuit out of fear and had no suspicion that we would be bold enough to attack their camp, so they were careless about fortifying and guarding it. Again they showed no understanding of Romans! We learned that Mago had also now crossed the Iberus and had set up camp about six miles from Hasdrubal Gisco's camp. Concerned that Hasdrubal Gisco and Mago would soon unite, and perhaps be joined as well by the forces of Hasdrubal Barca, Marcius conceived of a bold plan. He called us all to an assembly and, to the best of my memory, this is what he said.

"I am much honored that you men have conferred upon me this command, but this is a heavy and anxious charge. For me this has been a time of great grief and mourning and the Scipios ever disturb me with anxious cares by day and dreams by night, frequently rousing me from my sleep and imploring me not to suffer themselves nor their soldiers, your companions in this war, who had been victorious in this country for eight years, nor the Roman Commonwealth, to remain unavenged. They enjoin me to follow their discipline and their plans. There was no one more obedient to their commands while they were alive than I, so that after their death, I would seek to perform what I believe they would have done if they still lived.

"You, my soldiers, should not show your respect for them by lamentations and tears, but whenever the memory of those men shall occur to you, you should go into battle as though you saw them encouraging you and giving you the signal.

"Yesterday you proved to the enemy that the Roman name had not become extinct with the Scipios and the energy and valor of that people which had not been overwhelmed by the disaster at Cannae, would emerge from the severest storms of fortune.

"Now, since you dared so much of your own accord, I have a mind to try how much you will dare when authorized by your general, for yesterday, when I gave the signal for retreat while you were pursuing the routed enemy, I did not wish to break your spirit but to reserve it for greater glory and more advantageous opportunities, so that you might afterward, when prepared and armed, seize the occasion of attacking your enemy while off their guard, unarmed, and even buried in sleep. That opportunity is now at hand. The enemy has left his camp unfortified and unguarded. There is nothing whatever which the enemy fear less at the present time than that we, who were a little while ago besieged and assaulted, should aggressively assault their camp ourselves!

"Let us dare, then, to do that which it is incredible that we should have the courage to attempt. It will be most easy from the very fact of its appearing most difficult. At the third watch of the night I will lead you hither in silence. I have ascertained by means of scouts that they have no regular succession of watches, and no proper outposts. Our shout at the gates, when heard, and the first assault, will carry their camp. Then let that carnage be made among them, torpid with sleep, terrified at the unexpected tumult and overpowered while lying in their beds.

"I know that this measure appears to you a daring one, but, in difficult times and almost desperate circumstances, the boldest counsels are always the safest. If we do not seize this opportunity there is danger that all of the generals and their forces will unite and how should we be able to withstand three generals and three armies whom Cneius Scipio with his army unimpaired could not withstand? As our generals perished by dividing their forces, so the enemy may be overpowered while separated and divided. Now depart, with the favor of the gods, and refresh yourselves, so that refreshed and vigorous you may burst into the enemy's camp with the same spirit which you have defended your own"*4

We were thrilled by this prospect of resistance and revenge that Lucius Marcius offered us, and his plan succeeded beyond our wildest dreams! The camps of Hasdrubal Gisco and Mago were six miles apart, and Lucius Marcius placed a cohort and some cavalry, myself among the latter, in between the two camps, so that when the soldiers from Hasdrubal Gisco's camp were routed and tried to flee to the camp of Mago, we intercepted them and killed them to a man. Once having destroyed the camp of Hasdrubal Gisco we attacked the camp of Mago and routed his soldiers as well. Unfortunately, both Hasdrubal Gisco and Mago Barca escaped unharmed, but this action put an end to their attempt to annihilate us, and our time in Hispania was tranquil until Publius Scipio arrived from Rome to lead us to the siege of New Carthage.

From the two camps we gathered a great deal of booty. One of the most noteworthy items was a silver shield of one hundred and thirty-eight pound weight with the image embossed upon it of Hasdrubal Barca. Hannibal, from depictions I've seen was a comely man, but, his brother Hasdrubal appeared rather porcine.

CHAPTER 7

Those soldiers who had been acquainted with me and Ala noticed that our previously aloof relationship had developed into intimacy. I made no secret of the relationship, nor of the reason for it, and there was not a man who sought to disparage it. Ala had acquired an agnomen, Falcata, and now she could move about the camp like a queen and not a soldier would leer at her or treat her with the slightest disrespect. In fact, when it became known that she was planning to establish a jewelry shop in Rome, hundreds of soldiers gave her presents of jewelry that they had stored with their booty.

I had to envy Lucius Marcius' nocturnal visits from the deceased Scipioni. My own dreams were tormented by far less exulted beings, such as the deceased Gorgo and shadowy figures of Carthaginian torturers intent upon extracting secrets from me by extreme measures. I was much in need of the comfort that Ala could, and did, provide. Whereas my Silvia was affectionate but passive, Ala, my lioness, was far more aggressive and experimental in our love making. I surmised that she had been sexually abused by Gorgo and others, but I believe that I was the first man that she voluntarily made love to. The first man that she actually loved. My initial reluctance soon developed into devotion and passion.

It is considered a cause of pudor (shame) to a Roman man to have his life saved by a woman, but personally, this didn't bother me in the least. Gratitudo (gratitude) was more important than pudor as far as I was concerned. Someday Marcus Porcius Cato would tell me "Varro, you have

51

no dignitas at all!" Dignitas is important to a man who follows the cursus honorus and who has serious political ambitions. My only ambition was to survive this war and live in peace and tranquility with my family. Marcus Porcius Cato can have all the dignitas he can muster, but I have not the slightest desire to trade my life for his.

I sent a report of the events of the battles of the Upper Baetis to Publius Cornelius Scipio along with heavy condolences on the loss of his father and uncle. I also sent word to my father that I had survived. I'm sure that they had feared that I was among the multitude of the dead.

I asked permission of Lucius Marcius to sail to Rome for the Winter, and it was granted. Again my baggage was laden with letters from my fellow soldiers to bring to their families in Rome. This time both Brunius and Ala would accompany me and I would find a place for Ala to set up shop. In addition to the jewelry that the soldiers had given her, we procured a goodly supply from the shops of Emporion. Since jewelry was tempting to steal, I thought it best to hire a trustworthy man to protect Ala and her goods. Of course, I knew that Ala Falcata needed no protection. It was the potential thief who would benefit from the arrangement by having his life preserved.

My family was ecstatic when I arrived. Word of the disaster at the Upper Baetis had reached Rome some months before and they believed that I had probably died. Even the letter to my father did not quite persuade them otherwise. My son, Lucius, was now seven years old and my daughters Tullia and Lidia were four and two. I tried to spend as much time with them as I could. One night at dinner it was Lucius who notice the spear wound on my hand.

"Papa, what happened to your hand?" he asked

"That's a wound from a spear." I said. "I was in a battle."

"Does it hurt?" he asked.

"It did," I said, "But it doesn't any more".

Lucius looked puzzled and a little worried. "Papa," he said "Will I be a soldier?"

Silvia gave me a meaningful glance. I knew that this was going to be a difficult conversation. "If Rome is at peace you won't have to be, Lucius" I said. "If Rome is at war, than every able bodied man must be a soldier."

"But Rome is never, ever at peace!" said Silvia

"Peace will come someday." I said. "Eventually people get tired of fighting."

My sister Tullia and her husband Marcus were at the table and he joked "Three more wounds like that, Lucius, and they'll think you were crucified!"

"Marcus!" cried Tullia, "That isn't even funny!"

I thought to myself, "They'd think it even less funny if they knew how I actually got this wound!"

I went to see Publius Scipio, and, as usual, he greeted me warmly, and thanked me for the letter I had written conveying news of Hispania and my condolences. "I'm going to Hispania to take the place of my father and uncle." he said. "Do you remember Gaius Laelius?"

"Of course!" I said "I knew him from our days at the Campus Martius! The son of a plebeian knight, like myself."

"And one of the few of us to have survived" said Publius Scipio. "He was at Ticinus with me when I rescued my father. I trust him more than anyone else in the world, and he is going to help me subdue Hispania and conquer Carthago. He will command a fleet. More than this I can't reveal to you. Our plans must be kept completely secret. Not that I don't trust you, but if Hasdrubal Barca put a price on your head . . . ."

"I doubt that Hasdrubal Barca is aware of my existence." I said. "I think that the attempted kidnapping was completely that scoundrel Gorgo's idea.

But, you're right. It's better not to tell me anything because I'm truly not certain how I would bear up under torture."

"Let's hope you never have to find out!" said Publius Scipio. "How are Silvia and the children?"

"Lucius is a fine boy, very intelligent, and the girls are delightful. Silvia is truly the best wife a man could have!"

"Then you must be a very happy man" Said Publius Scipio. I was tempted to confess my dilemma of having two women to him but Scipio was very proper and conventional when it came to these matters, as, ordinarily, I was myself, so I didn't think he would understand.

"I just wish I didn't have to spend so much time away from home." I said

"Unfortunately, that's a soldier's lot." he said. "It may be several years before I get back to Rome once I leave for Hispania. And as for you, I would like you to be one of my military tribunes."

My jaw, dropped open. "Military tribune? I've never been a decurion! The only person I've ever given orders to was a servant!"

"My uncle had a special use for you which precluded giving you command." he said "And you did a superb job for him in that capacity. But I have other uses for you. You've been in the Roman army for eight years and it is time you learned to command men."

I was almost speechless. "I'm truly honored, Publius." I said

"I'm sure you will earn the honor." he replied. "I will be requesting the command of Hispania in a few weeks. I believe I will get it because no one else wants it. Then Laelius and I will assemble an army and a fleet. We still have 8000 good men in Hispania thanks to the efforts of Lucius Marcius, but we need quite a few more to carry out my plans. I want you to stay in Rome with me until I leave and help Laelius and myself with our preparations."

"That would suit me perfectly, Publius. There's really not much going on right now in Hispania."

"And how shall I deal with Lucius Marcius when I get there?" asked Publius Scipio "The senate does not approve of him getting himself elected to command by the troops."

I don't think that Publius Scipio had ever seen me as angry as I was just at that moment. "The senate can go drown itself, Publius! Without Lucius Marcius there would not be 8000 Roman soldiers in Hispania now; there would be none!"

"I think you're right, Lucius" said Publius Scipio. "I will treat Lucius Marcius with the honor and respect he deserves. It's a pity that he won't get any of that from the senate and people of Rome."

We embraced and I conveyed my condolences once more. "Let me know when I can be of service, Publius"

"It will be a soon as I get my commission." Said Publius Scipio.

I went to see Ala regularly at her shop in Quirinal. She was absolutely thrilled about her situation and completely in her element. The change in her from a feral cat to an independent, poised and self-confident young woman was remarkable. It was not the best time to start a business in Rome, with a protracted war going on, and the Oppian laws in effect, which limited the finery that women could wear, but there were still people with money and women who liked jewelry, so the shop was profitable. Of course there were a few problems. Ala was illiterate and could barely count. I had to advise her in matters of taxes and fees. I found a sixteen year old plebeian school boy to help her keep her books. Manlius was short and had a club foot and so would never be in the army. Poor and desperate women would come to her and sell her their jewelry so that they would have money to eat, and Ala would resell the pieces at a small profit. She lived comfortably in a room at the back of the shop.

In most cases a Roman child born with a club foot would be exposed at birth, but it would have been awkward for me to ask Manlius how it was he had been permitted to live. I can only assume that both his father and grandfather had been away at some war when he was born and his mother could not bring herself to do what was expected. In any case, Manlius was a great help to Ala.

The matrons of Rome are not renown for minding their own business and refraining from gossip, so it shouldn't have been a surprise to me to come home one day and find Silvia pouting and tearful.

"Lucius, have I not been a good wife to you?" she asked

"Of course you have, Silvia," I said "You're the best wife a man could possibly have!"

"Then why do I keep hearing rumors that you are seeing another woman, a foreigner who sells jewelry in Quirinal?"

"I'm sorry Silvia." I replied "But it can't be helped. I'm her slave."

"You're her slave?" Her voice rose to a high pitch. "Lucius, I've always loved you and thought I understood you, but this is something I don't understand and can't continence!"

"Then let me explain, Silvia," I said. "I never wanted to hurt you. But I worship the ground this woman walks on, I kiss her feet, and so should you!"

"What?" Cried Silvia, a most shocked expression on her face.

"This woman is Ala Falcata, who single-handedly killed three Celtiberian ruffians to save the life of a Roman soldier. That Roman soldier was me! I'm in debt Silvia, and it's a debt that must be paid! Do you know what the Carthaginians would do to a Roman spy to get him to talk?"

"You're a spy?" she whispered, still looking shocked.

"I work in intelligence." I said "And I know many things that Hasdrubal Barca, the brother of Hannibal, would like to know. And these ruffians were about to sell me to him when Ala killed them" I showed her my hand with the scar "They did this to me to prevent me from taking my poison."

"Poison!" She repeated

"Yes," I said, "A soldier working in intelligence must take poison if captured. It's his duty. He can't allow information to be extracted from him by torture. Ala Falcata saved me from that. I owe her everything!"

She began to cry. "Oh, Lucius!"

"Silvia," I said "You're the woman I love. I'm with you because I want to be. I'm with her because I have to be. There's a difference between love and gratitude. You are the woman I love, she is the woman I owe."

Silvia calmed herself and I put my arms around her. "If I had had a choice, Silvia, I never would have been a soldier. You were right years ago when you said we are all slaves and that Rome is a harsh master. But there are things we can do nothing about. I can do nothing about Rome and I can do nothing about Ala Falcata!"

We made love and she seemed pretty much restored to her usual serene self. Of course I should have known that curiosity would get the better of her and she would arrange to visit Ala on her own.

Ala told me of the visit some weeks later. "A woman came to the shop last week and was looking at the jewelry. I asked her if she was interested in anything in particular and she looked at me very strangely. She stared at me for a long time. Then she said 'My name is Silvia, the wife of Lucius Tullius Varro. I just wanted to know if it were true.'"

"If what were true?" I asked

'If it were true that you killed three men to save my husband's life. I need to hear that from you.'

"Yes, it's true. The man who held the spear to Lucius' chest was the most evil man in the world. He caused my mother's death. I was happy to kill him."

"She took my hand. 'We both love the same man' she said 'and you are a much more beautiful woman than I.'

"Yes" I said "I love Lucius. He was the first man to treat me with respect. I know you can not live without him, and neither can I."

'Well, If I can love you, Ala, and I love you for what you did, than you can love Lucius'

"So your wife kissed me and we embraced and she left."

I had to admire my wife's largeness of spirit. Truly the best wife a man could ever have! I think it's a most remarkable thing to have two women who each love you so profoundly that neither will seek to deprive you of the love of the other!

I have to admit that, despite the onerous demands of my military duties, I have been a most fortunate man. I have been lucky in love and lucky in war. My affairs have prospered and my family has been a great satisfaction to me. Never has fortune deserted me. Thus I can not envy my commanding officer, Publius Cornelius Scipio Africanus, as accomplished as he was. Despite devoting so much of his life to the salvation of his country, he was eventually to taste the bitter fruit of his country's ingratitude.

CHAPTER 8

The Roman senate commissioned Claudius Nero to go over to Hispania and take the command from Lucius Marcius. He was given 6000 Roman foot and 300 horse and another 6000 allied foot and 800 horse from the Latin confederacy. He set up a base camp at Tarraco, a city to the south of Emporion. At this time, Hasdrubal Barca was encamped at the black stones in Ausetania, between the towns of Illiturgi and Mentissa. Nero seized the entrance to this defile and had Hasdrubal and his men trapped. Hasdrubal then sent an embassy to Nero and offered that if he and his troops were allowed to depart unharmed, he would quit Hispania altogether. But Hasdrubal dragged out the negotiations over the course of days, and, little by little all of his troops escaped the defile and on a morning with heavy mist Hasdrubal himself escaped from the camp with his cavalry and elephants. Nero, perceiving, at last, that he had been tricked, pursued the Carthaginians but Hasdrubal declined a battle. Punic fidelity!

It was clear that a strong leader must be found for Hispania. The senate resolved that there should be an assembly of the people for the purpose of electing a proconsul for Hispania. I accompanied Publius Scipio and Gaius Laelius to this assembly. As Publius Scipio had predicted, not a single one of the eminent men of Rome volunteered for the commission! Suddenly, Publius Cornelius Scipio, son of that Publius Cornelius Scipio who had fallen at the battle of the Upper Baetis, took a place on an eminence where he could be seen by all, and declared himself a candidate for the proconsulship. He was 25 years old. Despite his youth, such was the confidence that he inspired that he was elected unanimously by all the centuries!

I informed my family that I would be going once again to Hispania, with Publius Scipio. Silvia by now had learned not to weep at my parting. I told them that Publius intended to make me a military tribune, and that, of course, would bring a large increase in pay. I went to visit Ala and she accepted the news with aplomb. I also visited Silvius at his stables and hired Brunius once again to be my groom. Silvius gave me a fine young stallion. I was not in the habit of naming my horses, but I decided to call this one Indibilis, after the chieftain of the Ilergetes, just because I thought that Indibilis sounded like a fine name for a horse. There is precedence for naming your horse. Alexander the Great called his horse Boucephalis-cow head, because he perceived that his head resembled that of a cow!

Publius Scipio gathered up ten thousand infantry and one thousand horse and we set sail with a fleet of thirty quinquerimes from the mouth of the Tiber, landing once more in Emporion. In addition to Publius Scipio, and Gaius Laelius, we brought along the propraetor Marcus Junius Silanus to assist in the management of affairs. By this time I had been on a number of sea voyages and was able to enjoy the spectacular scenery of the Tuscan Alps, the Gallic Gulf and the Pyrenees.

After we arrived in Emporion a number of local tribes north of the Iberus sent embassies to Publius Scipio to make alliances. Publius kept me near him because I knew many of these tribesmen from my work with Cneius Scipio and I was able to tell him who was reliable and who might not be trusted.

It was around this time that I started to shave my beard on a regular basis. Publius Scipio believed that a soldier should be clean shaven because in close combat an enemy soldier could grab onto one's beard and use it to immobilize the head so that he could strike at the neck with his sword. Scipio shaved regularly and wanted his officers to do the same to set an example to their subordinates. He assigned a detail of barbers to each of his legions.

When we reached the winter quarters of the army, where the survivors of the battles of the Upper Baetis were quartered, Publius Scipio assembled the men and bestowed lavish praises and commendations on them, that although they had received two such disastrous blows in succession they had retained possession of the province and had not allowed the enemy to reap any advantage from their successes. They had excluded the enemy entirely from the lands north of the Iberus and had honorably protected their allies. He also honored and lavished praises on Lucius Marcius and retained him as his lieutenant general, inferior in command only to himself, Gaius Laelius and Marcus Junius Silanus. This gave me great satisfaction, because, in my estimation, Lucius Marcius was second in valor, greatness and worthiness only to Publius Cornelius Scipio.

He regaled the soldiers with a long harangue recapitulating the events of the war and informing them that now everything was going well in Italy. In Sicily, Syracuse and Agrigentum had been captured and the Carthaginians had been entirely expelled from the island. In Italy Arpi had been recovered and Capua taken. Hannibal had now been driven into the remotest corner of Bruttium. He told them that "My own mind, which has hitherto been to me the truest prophet, presages that Hispania will soon be ours; that the whole Carthaginian name will be in a short time banished from the land, and will fill both the sea and the land with ignominious flight . . . . Only do you, my soldiers, favor the name of Scipio, favor the offspring of your generals, a scion springing up from the trunks which have been cut down. Come then veterans, lead your new commander and your new army across the Iberus, lead us across into a country which you have often traversed, with many a deed of valor. I will soon bring it to pass that, as you now trace in me a likeness to my father and uncle in my features, countenance and figure, I will so restore a copy of their genius, honor and courage, to you, that every man of you shall say that his commander, Scipio, has either returned to life, or been born again."*6

At this point, none of the three Carthaginian generals in Hispania seemed minded to give battle. Hasdrubal, son of Gisco had gone to Gades on the Atlantic coast, Mago into the midland parts of the Hispania above the forest of Castulo, and Hasdrubal Barca was wintering in the neighborhood of Saguntum.

Publius Scipio left Marcus Silanus with three thousand infantry and three hundred horse to guard our province and then he led us across the Iberus and southward toward New Carthage. There were twenty-five thousand infantry and twenty-five hundred horse. He had told no one but Gaius Laelius of his plans. He had sent Laelius with his fleet to blockade the city. It was arranged that both army and fleet would arrive at New Carthage on the same day-the seventh day after crossing the Iberus.

We had been expecting to be led to battle against one of three Carthaginian generals, most likely Mago, and we were surprised at our destination. But Scipio called us to an assembly and explained his reasoning:

"Soldiers, what we are about to do is attack a city, but this city is not just any city. Our conquest of this city will have profound advantages to our cause. The conquest of this city holds the key to the conquest of Hispania and, ultimately, to Roman victory in this present war against Carthage!

"Here, in New Carthage are the hostages of all the most distinguished kings and states of Hispania, and as soon as you shall have gained possession of these they will immediately deliver into your hands everything which is now subject to the Carthaginians.

"Here is the whole of the enemy's treasure, without which they can not carry on the war, and which will be most serviceable to us in conciliating the affections of the barbarians. Here are their engines, their arms, their tackle and every requisite in war; which will at once supply you, and leave the enemy destitute.

"Besides, we shall gain possession of a city, not only of the greatest beauty and wealth, but also the most convenient in having an excellent harbor, by means of which we may be supplied with every requisite for carrying on the war both by sea and land.

"Great as are these advantages we shall thus gain, we shall deprive our enemies of much greater. This is their citadel, their granary, their treasury, their magazine, their receptacle for everything. Hence there is a direct passage into Africa. This is the only station for a fleet between the Pyrenees and Gades. This gives to Africa the command of all Hispania. But as I perceive you are arrayed and marshaled, let us pass on to the assault of New Carthage, with our whole strength and with undaunted courage."*7

I realized that this was the plan that Publius Scipio had conceived of in Rome that he had declined to reveal to me. I was staggered by his genius. He had found the Carthaginians' jugular and he would now bleed them dry!

The assault on the walls of the city was not immediately successful. Mago, the Carthaginian general, (not the same Mago who was Hannibal's brother), defended the city with 10,000 troops, and he stationed two thousand of the townsmen on the walls facing the Roman Camp. He then led his troops out of the city to battle with swords, as spears would have been of little use in the confined space. They fell upon our men who were working on the siege engines. After some struggle we drove them back within their walls. The enemy stationed upon the walls of the city threw down all kinds of missiles on the Romans who were trying to scale the walls with ladders. Scipio, protected by the shields of three stout young men, exhorted the men and cheered them on, but the walls were too high to be mounted by our scalades.

Scipio, however, noticed that there was a part of the city where the walls were low and which was washed by a lagoon. At low tide the water of this lagoon was only knee deep. So Scipio waited until low tide and lead a group of 500 men with ladders to that portion of the wall, which was undefended, and mounted it, thus gaining access to the city. They then proceeded to the gate and did battle with the defenders. They succeeded in breaking down the gate and the Romans poured into the city. Mago and his troops fled to the citadel and made an effort to defend it, but it was taken at the first assault.

Great carnage attended the entrance of our troops into the city. Every man over the age of puberty was put to the sword, but this came to an end once Mago surrendered. Some ten thousand males of free conditions were captured. Those who were citizens of New Carthage were freed and allowed to keep their property. There were also 2000 artisans taken who were pressed into the service of Rome, but promised emancipation if they addressed themselves strenuously to the service of the war. Young men and able bodied slaves were assigned to the fleet as rowers.

The Carthaginians had taken and kept quite a number of hostages from the various Iberian tribes in order to assure their continued loyalty. These included the wife of Mandonius, the brother of Indibilis, the chieftain of the Ilergetes, for whom I had named my horse. They also included the daughters of Indibilis. Mandonius' wife threw herself at the feet of Scipio, imploring him to give particularly strict injunctions to their guardians with respect to the care and treatment of females. Scipio assured her that the strictest propriety would be maintained. He declaimed:

"Out of regard for that discipline which I, myself and the Roman nation maintain, I should take care that nothing, which is anywhere held sacred, should be violated among us. In the present case your virtue and your rank cause me to observe it more strictly; for not even in the midst of misfortunes have you forgotten the delicacy becoming matrons."*8

These hostages were treated with the greatest consideration and all were restored to their homes. This went a long way toward assuring the loyalty of the Hispanian tribes to Rome.

There was a vast amount of plunder, including an immense quantity of military stores: One hundred and twenty large capatultae and two hundred and eighty-one smaller ones, twenty three large ballistae and fifty-two smaller ones, and great quantities of missile weapons. There was also an immense quantity of gold and silver, and there were 20,000 pecks of wheat and two hundred seventy thousand of barley. One hundred and thirteen ships were captured and boarded in the harbor, some laden with corn and arms. Now all of this would benefit Rome, and be brought to bear in our efforts to defeat the Carthaginians. The eventual impact of taking New Carthage could not be over-estimated.

Scipio dispatched Gaius Laelius to Rome in a quinquereme with an impressive amount of booty and with Mago and other important prisoners to give the word of his victory. A thanksgiving of three days was declared in the city.

For the 8000 veterans of the armies of Cneius and Publius Scipio, we who had been defeated at the battles of the Upper Baetis, we who had been so wretched and downtrodden, we who had so desperately resisted our own annihilation at the hands of Hasdrubal Gisco scarcely a year before, the conquest of New Carthage represented an unbelievable and overwhelming change of fortune. It was as though the poorest of the poor had become the richest of the rich! It was as though a slave had become consul! It was as though we had been taken from a dank prison cell and lodged in an opulent palace! We could now envision a future in which Carthage would be completely subdued, never to trouble our nation again, and where Rome would become the beacon of civilization to the world.

True to his word, Scipio promoted me to military tribune. Owing to my somewhat undeserved reputation of being a complete gentleman where women were concerned (and I don't know that he would have done this had he been aware that I was a bigamist), he put me in charge of the welfare of the female hostages. Since a number of the women were Celtiberian, my knowledge of the language was useful. I made friends with them and even joined them in their singing, remembering some of the songs I had learned in Carrach.

One of the hostages was a young Celtiberian woman of astounding beauty. In feature there was some resemblance to Ala, but whereas Ala had been a wretched little feral cat of the lowest status, this woman seemed more like the most pampered kitten in the most opulent of Roman households. I brought her to see Scipio and he inquired of her as to her country and parentage. She told him that she was betrothed to a young prince of the Celtiberians, one Allucius. Her parents and fiance had traveled from Celtiberia bearing gold and sliver with which to ransom her. Allucius was desperately enamored of her.

Scipio summoned the family to him and addressed the young prince: "A young man myself, I address myself to a young man, and therefore there need be the less reserve in this conversation. As soon as your intended bride, having been captured by my soldiers, was brought into my presence, and I was informed that she was endeared to you, which her beauty rendered probable, considering that I should myself wish that my affection for my intended bride, though excessive, should meet with indulgence, could I enjoy the pleasures suited to my age (particularly in an honorable and lawful love) and were my mind not engrossed by public affairs, I indulge as far as I can your passion. Your mistress, while under my protection, has received as much respect as under the roof of her own parents, you father-in-law and mother-in-law. She has been kept in perfect safety for you.

"The only reward I bargain for in return for the service I have rendered you, is that you would be a friend to the Roman people, and if you believe that I am a true man, as these nations knew my father and uncle to have been heretofore, that you would feel assured that in the Roman state there are many like us, and that there is no nation in the world at the present time with which you or those belonging to you would be better to be in friendship"*9

Allucius was overwhelmed with gratitude and he clung to Scipio's right hand, and invoked all the gods to recompense him in his behalf since he, himself, was far from possessing means proportioned either to his own wishes or to Scipio's deserts. Her parents then entreated Scipio to accept the very large weight of gold that they had brought to redeem their daughter, saying that if he would accept this gift they would feel as grateful for it as they did for the restoration of their daughter inviolate. They were so earnest in their entreaties that Scipio promised to accept the gold and ordered it to be laid at his feet. Then he called Allucius forth and said "To the dowry which you are about to receive from your father-in-law, let these marriage presents from me also be added." And he bid Allucius to take away the gold and keep it for himself.

Allucius returned to Celtiberia singing the praises of Scipio, observing that "A most godlike youth has come among us, who conquers everything, not only by arms but by kindness and generosity." He then made a levy among his dependents and returned to Scipio a few days later with 1400 chosen horsemen. I told Scipio that at least this would be a group of Celtiberian warriors he might rely on!

It was by such acts of kindness and generosity that Publius Scipio made warm alliances with many of the peoples of Hispania over the next few years. He was even able to win over the likes of Indibilis and Mandonius, who had been staunch allies of the Carthaginians, at least for a time.

During our time at New Carthage, Publius Scipio was constantly busy. He was determined to keep his army fit and battle ready. He instituted a program of rigorous exercise and discipline for his troops. On the first day he had the legions under arms perform evolutions through a space of four miles. The second day they were to repair and clean their arms before their tents. On the third day they engaged in an imitation of regular battle with wooden swords, throwing javelins with the points covered with balls. On the fourth day they rested and on the fifth they again performed evolutions under arms. Then this same cycle would begin again. His rowers and mariners, pushing out to sea when the weather was calm engaged in mock battles to test the manageability of their ships.

Owing to my duties involving the welfare of the Hispanian hostages, I was not required to take part in these activities, but I persisted in my habit of exercising my horse the first thing in the morning and practicing marksmanship with my weapons. I knew that once the hostages had been returned to their respective tribes, I would be called upon to lead a cavalry unit into battle.

The two thousand artisans that had been pressed into the service of Rome were collected together in a public workshop and Publius Scipio went around to inspect their works, which were carried on eagerly by the artificers in the workshops, armory and docks, who were eager to earn their emancipation. He saw to the repair of the walls which had been damaged, and made sure that the inadequate walls accessed by the lagoon, by which he, himself had entered the city, were built up substantially so that no other would-be conqueror could gain access to the city that way.

After all these works were completed, the booty appropriately dispensed, and the Hispanian hostages restored to their rightful tribes and families, he left a garrison at New Carthage and we set out for Tarraco. I assisted him in dealing with the many tribal embassies we met along the way and we formed alliances with nearly all the peoples dwelling north of the Iberus and many of the tribes dwelling in the South as well.

While at Tarraco, I received a letter from Titus, my eldest half brother. He said that my father had died and that he had taken over the family business, a workshop for making funerary statues. He also informed me that Silvia had given birth to a fine baby boy and that she had named him Titus, after my father.

I also got a letter from Ala, written by Manlius. She said that her business was doing well and that Manlius was teaching her to read and write in Latin and do sums. She hoped that she would be able to write the next letter herself.

CHAPTER 9

The following Spring, when Laelius had returned from Rome, we marched forth from Taracco to engage the forces of Hasdrubal Barca. On the way, we encountered Indibilis and his brother Mandonius of the Ilergetes who had been allied with the Carthaginians. Indibilis spoke for both, saying:

"I know well that the name of deserter is an object of execration to former allies and of suspicion to new ones. Never the less, it is not without great reason that we desert our former allies and offer ourselves to your service. We have, in the past, rendered the Carthaginian generals great services, and have been repaid with rapacity and insolence, together with every kind of injury committed against ourselves and our countrymen. My person has up until now been with the Carthaginians, but my heart has long been with the Romans, whom I believe have right and justice on their side. We only entreat you to judge us at this time, not as vile deserters, nor as respected allies, but reserve your judgment and estimate our services according to what sort of men you should find us to be from experience from this day on."

Publius Scipio replied "I will do so in every particular, and not consider you deserters who did not look on an alliance as binding where no law, divine or human, was unviolated."*10 Publius Scipio then restored to them their wives and children who had been hostages at New Carthage, and their forces joined ours on the way to Baecula, where lay the army of Hasdrubal Barca. We had thirty-five thousand soldiers to the enemy's twenty-five thousand, but Hasdrubal held the high ground. Nevertheless, Scipio engineered a pincer movement similar to the one Hannibal had engineered at Cannae and our victory was decisive. We killed six thousand of the enemy and captured twelve thousand. Scipio released all the Hispanian prisoners without ransom, and ordered the quaestor to sell the African prisoners as slaves. Most of the Carthaginians escaped with Hasdrubal. We set to work plundering Hasdrubal's camp for it's rich booty.

The grateful Hispanians crowded around Publius Scipio and one and all saluted him as a king. But Publius admonished them that, in his estimation, the most honorable title was that of general, which his soldiers had conferred on him. The title of king, revered in other countries, was something that was reviled in Rome, and that even if they, in their own minds, thought of him as kingly, they must abstain from the use of the term.

If the truth be known, Publius Scipio's strict injunction against allowing the Hispanians, or anyone else, to address him as king was not a question of humility or modesty but a matter of self-preservation. You have only to look at the case of Marcus Manlius Capitolinus, the Roman hero of the Gallic siege of the Capitoline citadel nearly 200 years before the time of which I write. Manlius later became consul and was very popular with the common people for a time, but he was execrated by the patricians for championing the cause of plebeian debtors who were being taken into slavery. These patricians made the unfounded claim that Manlius had the ambition to become king, and he was thrown to his death from the Tarpaeian rock! No prominent Roman will allow the word "king" to be associated with his name.

Among the African prisoners there was a full-grown youth, remarkably handsome, who claimed to be of royal blood. The quaestor sent him to Scipio who asked him who he was, where he was born, and why, at his age he was in the camp. He said that he was a Numidian named Massiva, and that being left an orphan by his father, he had been educated by his maternal grandfather Gala, the king of the Numidians. He had come to Hispania with his uncle Masinissa, who had come with a body of cavalry to assist the Carthaginians. On account of his youth and lack of experience in battle, Masinissa had forbidden him to take part in the battle, but on the day of the battle he had clandestinely taken a horse and arms, and without the knowledge of his uncle, had gone out into the field. He had been thrown from his horse and taken prisoner by the Romans. Scipio ordered that the youth be treated kindly and, after he had taken care of some other affairs, summoned him and ask him whether he wished to return to Masinissa. The boy wept with joy at the prospect and Scipio presented him with a gold ring, a vest with a broad purple border, a cloak with a gold clasp and a horse, and ordered a party of horse to escort him as far as he chose. This act of kindness would bear delicious fruit, for Masinissa would some day desert to the Romans and be a critical ally in the defeat of Carthage.

After the battle of Baecula Scipio spent his time cementing his alliances with the Hispanian tribes and we returned to Tarraco.

Meanwhile, Mago and Hasdrubal Gisco joined up with the defeated Hasdrubal Barca to confer and decide their next course of action. It was resolved that Hasdrubal Barca would raise an army from among those Hispanian states that were still aligned with Carthage and would bring it across the Alps to Italy to join with Hannibal. Mago would deliver his army to Hasdrubal Gisco and pass over to the Baleares with a large sum of money to hire auxiliaries. Hasdrubal Gisco would retire with his armies to the remotest part of Lusitania (Portugal) to avoid any encounter with the Romans. Masinissa and his horsemen would be encouraged to shift from place to place and ravage the territories of their enemies.

The next year Mago returned to Hispania with reinforcements from the Baleares and Carthage sent a new general, Hanno, with more troops. (This, or course, was not the same general Hanno whom we had captured at Cissa. There were several general Hannos in the second Punic war, as well as several general Magos.) The Carthaginians were also recruiting heavily among the tribes of Celtiberia, although, as we Roman found out to our grief, the Celtiberians are most unreliable as allies. As it happened, they were no more reliable to the Carthaginians than they had been to the Romans!

Scipio dispatched Marcus Junius Silanus with 10,000 foot and 500 horse to deal with this new threat. As I was now a military tribune, I led the 500 horse. We moved so rapidly that we caught up with their forces even before they were aware of our approach and we immediately attacked the Celtiberian camp where there was no proper watch or guard. We routed and dispersed them before the Carthaginians could come to their aid. Mago fled with almost all of his cavalry and 2000 foot, retreating back to Gades, but we captured Hanno and a number of his men.

As we were pursuing the fleeing enemy, some of Masinissa's Numidian cavalry charged our unit and I saw one of them unhorse one of my men with a javelin. I drew my sword and pursued the Numidian as he approached the Roman soldier to finish him off. When I caught up with him I thrust my sword into his back, penetrating the heart and he fell, dying, from his horse. I then dismounted and helped the soldier onto my horse and rode off to get him to safety. This was not the first time I had ever done something of this sort, but it was the first time that the person I had tried to save survived to report the incident to the general. The young man's name was Aurelius Servilius and he was from a patrician family. It is customary in such a circumstance for the beneficiary to acknowledge his rescuer as a parent and render them appropriate honors for the rest of their lives. Of course, I didn't expect any such treatment, especially from a patrician, but Servilius has continued to give me tokens of his gratitude periodically ever since. In any event, Publius Scipio awarded me with the grass crown, a symbol of great prestige to a Roman soldier.

CHAPTER 10

There would yet be one more major battle fought in Hispania, but first I must digress to talk of Hasdrubal's expedition to Italy. In many ways, this war between Rome and Carthage would hinge on whether Hasdrubal would succeed in bringing his reinforcements to Italy and joining forces with his brother Hannibal.

The two Roman heroes of this story were an unlikely pair. Gaius Claudius Nero was that same Nero who had been outsmarted in Hispania by Hasdrubal's Punic fidelity before Publius Scipio was sent to replace him. He had no great record of military achievement. Marcus Livius, the other consul was a bitter man. He had last fought for Rome, successfully, in a battle against the Illyrians shortly before the second Punic war began. He was, however, many say unjustly, impeached for some financial malfeasance, and he took his disgrace very hard, retiring to his estate, growing his beard, wearing rags and refusing to have anything to do with public life. His friends persisted in trying to get him back to Rome and back into the Senate, and eventually they got him to cut his beard and dress respectably and attend senatorial meetings, but he rarely spoke and participated only minimally. Rome was in disarray at the time when Hasdrubal crossed the Alps to reinforce his brother because both consuls, Marcus Marcellus, who had had considerable success against Hannibal, and his co-consul Titus Quintus Crispinus had died in battle and there was a serious void of military leadership. Otherwise you certainly wouldn't have expected either Gaius Claudius Nero nor Marcus Livius to have been elected consul.

Marcus Livius hated Gaius Claudius Nero because he had been one of his most vociferous accusers, but the senators thought that, as a careful and prudent man he would make a good counterpoint to the rash and impetuous Nero, and he did have a good military background. But Livius strongly resisted the honor. "Isn't it a profound inconsistency" he said "that having withheld their pity from me when arrayed in a mourning garment and a criminal, they now force upon me the white gown against my will? That honors and punishments are heaped upon the same person? If they esteem me a good person, why had they thus passed a sentence of condemnation upon me as a wicked and guilty one. If they had proved me a guilty man, why should they thus trust me with a second consulate after having improperly committed to me the first?"

The senators rebuked him saying "Marcus Furius Camillus, too, being recalled from exile, had reinstated his country when shaken from her very base. We must soothe the anger of our country just as we would of parents, by patience and resignation."*10 With many such arguments the senators at last persuaded Marcus Livius to accept the consulship with his enemy Gaius Claudius Nero. Quintus Fabius attempted to effect a reconciliation between the two consuls, but Livius was inexorable, saying "There's no need for a reconciliation, for we will both use greater diligence and activity in everything we do for fear that we give our colleague, who is an enemy, an opportunity of advancing himself at our own expense." However, once in office, the two consuls conducted affairs of state in apparent friendship and unanimity. It was decided that Gaius Claudius Nero would go south to Bruttium and Lucania to act against Hannibal, and that Marcus Livius would go to Gaul to face Hasdrubal Barca, who it was reported was now approaching the Alps. Hasdrubal had recruited a vast number of Ligurians and Gauls and his numbers now amounted to some 48,000 infantry, 8000 cavalry and 15 elephants.

With some four legions, Marcus Livius hesitated to give battle to Hasdrubal's hordes and allowed him to advance into Italy as far as the Metaurus River. Hasdrubal sent messengers to Hannibal with instructions that he should meet him in South Umbria. However, the messengers, two Gauls and two Numidians, got lost upon the roads and were intercepted by Roman soldiers. Under threat of torture they revealed their letters which were translated and the information was given to the consul Gaius Claudius Nero. Deciding that the letters were genuine and not some example of

Punic trickery, Nero decided that the situation was too urgent to ignore. If the letters were genuine than Hannibal would have no knowledge that his brother was in Italy. Nero chose 7000 battle hardened veterans and proceeded on a march to Marcus Livius' camp, with a mind to reinforce his co-consul and urge him to battle with Hasdrubal. He sent a letter of his intention to the Senate and sent messengers to Marcus Livius to inform him that he was coming. On the march, his veterans were provisioned by farmers and townspeople they met along the way. Well wishers lined the roads and Nero was even able to recruit some retired veterans and able bodied youths to add to his numbers.

After six days they arrived at the camp of Marcus Livius. In order that Hasdrubal would be unaware that these reinforcements had arrived, Nero sent his forces into the camp at night. In order that it not appear that the camp had expanded, each one of Nero's men were taken into a tent of one of Livius' soldiers. Each tribune received a tribune, each horseman a horseman and each foot soldier a foot soldier.

Gaius Claudius Nero argued vehemently that the engagement must begin the next day, despite the fatigue of his own troops who had been marching rapidly for six days. He was worried lest Hannibal realize that he had been tricked and then move to destroy Nero's own leaderless troops in Bruttium. That day, the Romans under Nero, Livius and the Praetor Porcius Licinus assembled their forces for battle and Hasdrubal drew up his own forces to meet the challenge.

But Hasdrubal began to get suspicious. He was an astute man with keen eyesight and he noticed things a lesser general might not. The Romans had more cavalry than he had expected. Some of the Roman soldiers were dirty, disheveled and sunburned as though they had been on a long journey. Some of the shields looked old and tarnished. In addition, he had heard trumpets herald the arrival of an important person the evening before, and that morning the trumpets had sounded twice in the camp of Marcus Livius and only once in the camp of Porcius Licinus. He realized that he was facing not one, but two consuls.

This meant that Nero had come from Bruttium. Could the Romans have intercepted his messengers? Had Hannibal been defeated, allowing the consul to leave his province? Hasdrubal sounded the retreat and his troops returned to their camp. The Romans did not attempt to take the fortified camp, and when nightfall came, Hasdrubal quietly led his forces out of the camp and marched northward toward the river Metaurus, intending, very likely, to return to Gaul. But the river was swollen with rain water and there was no place to cross. The armies of Nero, Livius and Porcius caught up with Hasdrubal and, in the ensuing battle, annihilated his forces. Hasdrubal fought on until the end, and then realizing that here was no point in trying to escape with his army gone, he charged a Roman cavalry cohort and was killed. Nero evidently carried a special grudge against Hasdrubal, who had made such a fool of him in Hispania and he had Hasdrubal's head cut off and later arranged for it to be thrown into the camp of Hannibal. Hannibal was said to have muttered when he saw it that "Thus we learn the destiny of Carthage."

Some Romans say that the battle of the Metaurus was the Carthaginians' Cannae, and I wish I could agree, but I can not. Hasdrubal's army was a mercenary army. Very few of the dead were Carthaginian. After Cannae a law was passed in Rome forbidding women to weep in public. No such law was ever needed in Carthage. The wails of mothers, wives and orphans might be heard in Liguria, in Cisalpine Gaul, in Gaul, in Celtiberia and other parts of Hispania, in Numidia and in Mauritania, but they were rarely heard in Carthage.

After my own army under Cneius Scipio was destroyed due to the defection of mercenaries, I came to detest the practice of using them. Publius Scipio used mercenaries when it suited his purposes, but he was never foolish enough to trust them. I believe that the day when Rome comes to rely too heavily on mercenaries will be the day that Rome starts to fail.

Publius Scipio receive quite a bit of criticism from his detractors in Rome, particularly from Quintus Fabius, for allowing Hasdrubal Barca to raise an army and leave Hispania. I believe that he failed to pursue Hasdrubal for much the same reasons his father declined to pursue Hannibal on his way to the alps eleven years earlier-that he did not want to exhaust his forces in climbing the Pyrenees or in contending with hostile Gallic tribes, and that our forces were not prepared to cross the Alps.

CHAPTER 11

After the battle of Baecula, with Hanno captured and Mago Barca having left Hispania, Hasdrubal Gisco split up his troops in various fortified towns. Scipio was not about to try to dislodge Hasdrubal's forces, but he did send his brother Lucius to capture the town of Orinx where the Carthaginians kept a goodly supply of money, grain and armament.

In the Spring, Mago returned from the Beleares with newly recruited forces to join those of Hasdrubal Gisco and Masinissa. With combined forces of some 60,000, they would make one more effort to recover Hispania for the Carthaginians. The battle took place at Ilipa. Before this battle, Scipio feared that our camp was vulnerable to an attack by Masinissa's cavalry. He sent me, with 400 horsemen behind a hill to wait for them, and when they came to attack the camp we attacked them and drove them off with heavy losses. I must have killed eight or ten myself.

In the days before the battle the Carthaginians brought their forces out each day arrayed for battle. Scipio would wait until late morning or early afternoon and then bring his forces out to stand in battle array. I was puzzled by the way he distributed his forces, with his strongest troops in the van and the weaker ones on the flanks, just the opposite of the way he himself had told me it should be done. He declined battle on the first day and then repeated the same procedure the following day. He rode by where I was stationed and he must have seen my look of consternation.

"Lucius," he asked "Is something troubling you?"

"Well," I replied "The troop positioning seems strange." He laughed and said "Just wait, Lucius, just wait."

When I went out to observe the enemy I noticed that they too had their strength in the van and their weak forces on the flanks in imitation of Scipio. I suddenly understood Scipio's game and laughed. "Those fools!" I said to myself.

After having done this for three or four days, on the morning of the battle Scipio called on us to rise before dawn and have breakfast and then go out to the field in battle array. Of course, this time he put his mercenary Celtiberian and other Hispanian troops in the van and his heavy infantry and cavalry in the wings. Mago and Hasdrubal quickly marshaled their troops to meet us and they came out to the field unfed. And they still had their strong troops in the van and their weak on the flanks!

Scipio allowed the battle to proceed slowly, so that when the heavy fighting started in the afternoon, the unfed enemy troops were weak and fatigued. Then he expertly performed the same type of double envelopment maneuvers that Hannibal had performed at Cannae, with much the same result. We would have completely annihilated them that day if a violent storm hadn't arisen. As it was, I led the cavalry in pursuit of them the next day and we destroyed all but about 6,000 of them, who managed to find refuge on a mountain, along with their general Hasdrubal Gisco. Both Hasdrubal Gisco and Mago escaped and the remnant taking refuge on the mountain, facing starvation and thirst, soon surrendered. Hispania was at last quit of the Carthaginians!

Masinissa and some of his men had survived and they came to Scipio under a flag of truce. "I would like to offer my services to Rome." he said, "But as King Gala has died, I must return to my country and establish my power there. When I have achieved my goal, then I am at your service. I have come to detest the Carthaginians, and I believe that Rome will prevail." Having fought against Masinissa a number of times and having seen what a superb warrior he was, Scipio was in no frame of mind to decline a gift.

CHAPTER 12

After the battle of Ilipa, when the Carthaginians had, more or less, been cleared from Hispania, Scipio turned his attention to pacifying the Hispanian tribes. There were two cities in proximity to the battlefield of Baecula, on the upper reaches of the Baetis river, which had switched allegiances from Rome to Carthage immediately after the defeats of Cneius and Publius Scipio. They were Illiturgis and Castulo. Illiturgis was the more egregious of the two because Roman survivors of the battle, thinking the city was still in friendly hands, sought refuge there and were cruelly put to death. That might have been my own fate had my companions and I gone in that direction rather than toward Celtiberia.

I was sent with Lucius Marcius to lay siege to Castulo, while Scipio took his forces to Illiturgis. The Illiturgi knew that Scipio's intent was not conquest but dire punishment and they put up fierce resistance, even the women and children taking up arms. Scipio's soldiers admired their desperate courage and when Scipio perceived a lessening of their fighting spirit he felt it necessary to remind them of their betrayed comrades. "The need for salutary vengeance should make you fight more fiercely against these villains than against the Carthaginians. Our quarrel with the Carthaginians is for empire and glory, and almost without exasperation, but the kind of perfidy and cruelty shown in this city must be punished." *11 He shamed the laggard troops and the city was taken. Contrary to Scipio's usual inclination to spare the innocent, every man, woman and child in Illiturgis was slain, and the city razed to the ground.

I am not a man who condones the killing of women and children under any circumstances. But I do have to admit that the news of the massacre brought a quick end to our siege at Castulo. The city surrendered and was treated with clemency.

After these actions we returned to New Carthage and Scipio held games in honor of the gods and in memory of his father and uncle. I easily won prizes for horsemanship and javelin throwing. No one challenged me to personal combat.

Soon after this event, Publius Scipio fell ill. I'm not certain what the ailment was, but he took to his bed and could not attend to the business of the army. I believe that if he had remained healthy, the sorry affair of the mutiny at Sucro would not have occurred. Sucro is midway between New Carthage and Tarraco. The soldiers there had fallen out of discipline, and probably as a result of Scipio's long illness, their pay had fallen into arrears. There had even been a rumor among them that Scipio had died. They drove their tribunes out of the camp and elected two common soldiers, Atrius and Albius, who had been the chief instigators, as tribunes. There was even some talk among them of joining forces with Indibilis and Mandonius, our inconstant allies, who were now in rebellion.

Upon hearing of these things, Scipio wanted to get to the bottom of this matter, so he sent seven tribunes, myself included, to meet with the discontented men. We were given instructions not to upbraid them but merely to listen to their concerns. We met with the men in small groups, because, under the circumstances, calling an assembly might have been hazardous. I listened to their complaints and took notes. We listed each man and the amount of pay he thought he was owed. The men were mostly rustics and uneducated, such as could easily be led into error. I rather felt sorry for them. I knew that they were at the mercy of Publius Scipio, and that, if he so wished, every one of them could be crucified.

Scipio issued a proclamation that the soldiers should come to New Carthage to receive their back pay. They decided to march to New Carthage as a body. When they arrived we tribunes welcomed them amicably and invited their leaders to sup with us. Scipio had given orders to bar all exits from the camp.

Once separated from their fellows, the ringleaders were arrested and put into chains. Scipio revealed that the plan was to publicly scourge and execute these men on the morrow after addressing, in no uncertain terms, the rest of the rabble.

Unfortunately, I was conscious of a weakness in myself. It may have been inborn or it may have been that those few moments of profound and abject terror I had experienced at the hands of Gorgo, before Ala rescued me, had deranged my mind. I was afraid that I would have a severe physical reaction if I were to watch the scourging and executions. Embarrassed to take my concerns to Scipio, I went to Gaius Laelius instead.

"Gaius," I said "I wonder if I might have stable duty or something tomorrow and absent myself from the punishments. I'm not good with these things."

"Absolutely not!" he replied. "We need every hand present to guard the rabble and if these men make any trouble at all we will put them to the sword. And there can be no perception of reluctance or dissent. I'm surprised, Lucius. How many men have you killed in battle?"

"I don't knew, a few hundred I'm sure." I replied. "But it's not a problem in battle. It's only a problem if I have to stand there and watch. In battle you have enemy soldiers who are trying to kill you. These are Romans who are bound and helpless."

"These men are traitors, Lucius." Said Gaius Laelius, "and Scipio is absolutely right to make an example of them. You remember how Rome's first Consul, Junius Brutus, condemned his own sons to this same punishment after they were found to have conspired with Tarquin. And he forced himself to watch the scourgings and executions. If he could watch his own sons thus punished, you should be able to watch the punishment of men who are nothing to you."

"Do you think that, perhaps, I am unfit to be a soldier?" I asked him.

"Certainly not, Lucius." he replied. "I have seen you in battle and you are one of the best. It's no accident that you have survived twelve years of this war. And did you not receive the grass crown last year? But I can not give you leave to shirk your duty tomorrow no matter how unpleasant it may be for you."

I slept poorly that night and rose early, breakfasted and dressed in full uniform including helmet, shield and chain mail. I brought along javelins and my sword.

Scipio began to speak to the assembled mutineers:

"I feel that I am at a loss to know how to address you. Can I call you countrymen, who have revolted from your country? Or soldiers, who have rejected the command and authority of your general and violated your solemn oath? Can I call you enemies? I recognize the persons, faces, dress and mien of fellow countrymen, but I perceive the actions, expressions and intentions of enemies! For what have you wished and hoped for but what the Illiturgi and Lacetani did?

"Are your grievances so profound that they justify these actions? Since I took command here you have always been paid in full, until such time as I became too sick to supervise the distributions. Mercenary troops may, indeed, sometimes be pardoned for revolting against their employers, but no pardon can be extended to those who are fighting for themselves and their wives and children. For that is just as if a man who said he'd been wronged by his father over money matters were to take up arms and kill him who was the author of his life.

"If the cause is not merely a grievance, is it because you hoped for more profit and plunder by taking service with the enemy? If so, who would be your possible allies? Men like Indibilis and Mandonius. A fine thing to put trust in such turncoats!

"You may recall the legion that revolted in Rhegium. They were beheaded to a man. But at least they put themselves under the command of a military tribune. You have put yourselves under the command of men with no rank or standing at all! And what hope of successful revolt could you have entertained? Even if the rumor that I was dead had been correct, did you imagine that such tried leaders as Marcus Silanus, Gaius Laelius and my brother Lucius Scipio would have failed to avenge this insult to Rome?

"Nevertheless, I will plead for you to Rome and with myself-using this plea universally acknowledged among men-that all multitudes are easily misled and easily impelled to excesses. A multitude ever appears to be and actually is of the same character as the leaders and counselors it happens to have. Just as I have been ill in body, I believe that you have been ill in mind, under the influence of ignoble men. Therefore, I too, on the present occasion, consent to be reconciled to you and grant you an amnesty. But with the guilty instigators of revolt we refuse to be reconciled, and have decided to punish them for their offenses."*12

Those of us circling the assembly clashed our swords on our shields to strike terror into the mutineers, and the herald called out the names of the condemned, who were brought out naked and in chains into the midst of the assembly.

The scourgings and executions were supervised by the centurion Appius Virginius, a brutish looking man with bulging arms like those you might observe on a blacksmith. It was reputed that his very appearance on a battlefield was enough to put the enemy to rout. I knew him well enough, however, to know that, if you were neither an enemy soldier nor a condemned prisoner, you had nothing to fear from Appius Virginius.

When the scourging began I heard the screams of the condemned and saw blood oozing from their lacerated backs. But it was only when I saw the first beheading that I dropped to my knees and, with several heaves, deposited my entire breakfast on the ground. What was worse, my action inspired some others with similar constitutions to do the same, including a number of the mutineers. There were murmurs and curses and suppressed laughter. I had made a mockery of an occasion which had been intended to be completely serious and solemn.

One of the other tribunes, Aulus Galba, who was senior to me, came up and said, sternly but without rancor "I will have to report this, Varro. Go to your quarters and stay there until you're summoned."

"Yes sir." I replied, and summoning what dignitas I could muster, I walked toward my hut. I lay down and turned my face to the wall. I had never been a person inclined to complain or sulk, but I felt more dispirited just than than I ever had in my life. I was quite sure that Scipio, whom I knew to be a just man, would not inflict a harsh punishment for something he must know I had no control over. And had this been a serious matter, I would have been placed in chains rather than confined to quarters. I had had a spotless military record. Per my father's injunction I had never disobeyed an order. So I tried to think what might be the consequences of a weak stomach. The mildest would be a reprimand. Demotion was also possible. The most serious possibility would be to be dismissed and sent back to Rome in disgrace. I would have loved to return to Rome, and I had options for making an adequate, if not lavish living to support Silvia and my four children. I could work for Silvius, I could work for my half brother in the family business, or I could help Ala in her jewelry business. But I didn't want to return to Rome in disgrace!

I considered that even in the absence of official punishment, I would likely acquire an appalling agnomen, Roman soldiers being the way they are. I would be Lucius Tullius Varro Vomitor!

I wondered if I could apply for an honorable discharge. Had I been in ten campaigns? There was the skirmish with the Numidians, where I saw my first blood, there was Cissa, there was Dertosa, there was Upper Baetis, there was Hasdrubal Gisco's attack upon our camp, and there was our counter attack against his camp and Mago's, there was New Carthage, Baecula, Ilipas, and Castulo. If all of those counted, I had my ten and I should be eligible.

Late in the day, Brunius returned from his chores at the stable. When he saw me in an uncharacteristic state of melancholy he exclaimed "Padrone! What ails you?" I smiled weakly and said "Bad stomach." I was not up to telling him what had happened. I waited all that day and the next for a summons, but it never came. With all that was going on, I was certainly not a high priority item. Brunius was sympathetic and tried to get me to take some wine and bread, but my appetite was further diminished by the smell of smoke from the pyre where they were burning the bodies of the executed men.

I was not summoned to see Scipio. Instead, he came to see me! He motioned Brunius to leave the room and sat at my table. I got up from my bed and took a chair across from him. "I heard you were ill." he said. "I just came by to see how you were."

I wouldn't look at him. "I'm sorry, sir." I muttered

"Look at me, Lucius" he said. Reluctantly I raised my eyes to meet his gaze.

"Lucius," he said. "A good commander knows the strengths and weaknesses of his men. Remember when I assigned you to the care of the women hostages we found at New Carthage? I did that because I knew you to be a kind and gentle man, and I needed just that sort of man for the job. And you did a superb job. You allayed the understandable fears of those poor women and made them feel safe. You even joined them in singing songs in their own language! No one but you could have done that! Because of this I was able to make alliances with a dozen tribes that had been in thrall to the Carthaginians. You did me a very valuable service. Now what would have happened if I had put Appius Virginius in charge of the female hostages and you in charge of executions?"

The notion was so absurd that I had to laugh!

"Exactly!" Said Scipio. "Just as you align your men on the battlefield according to their strengths and abilities, so do you use your men for the tasks they are suited for, and not for the tasks they are unsuited for. If Rome had an infantry full of Appius Virginiuses, we would have defeated Carthage long ago. But I could say the same thing if Rome had a cavalry full of Lucius Varros. Where Virginius is brute force, you are skill and finesse, and that's what makes you a superb cavalryman."

I looked at him in astonishment. "I'm flattered that you think so" I said "But Publius, by Hercules, I'm sick to death of this war!"

"And I'm not?" he asked. "Lucius, I want to end this war. I want to end it and I need your help. We have virtually eliminated Carthage from Hispania and now it's time to go to Africa and beard the lion in its den.

I am going first to meet with Syphax and I want you to come with me. I want him to meet some of Rome's better citizens. Then I am going to Rome to stand for election to consul. I want you to help me with that too. I will raise an army and invade Africa and Hannibal will quit Italy to defend his city. I need you to help me raise and train a cavalry force. I need your horsemanship and skill with weapons as an example for the men to follow. If you feel you must leave, Lucius, I won't stop you. You will get the most honorable discharge, but I really want you to stay with me, Lucius. Do this for me, but do this also for our friends from the Campus Martius who died at Ticinus and Trebia and Trasimene and Cannae. Do this for the memory of Cneius and Publius Scipio!"

I didn't know what to say, so for a long time I said nothing and we sat in silence. At last he said "Think about it, Lucius. And come to dinner with me. I want people to see what esteem I hold you in. And next time you have a problem, come to me with it. Gaius Laelius did exactly what he was required to do. But I would have given you a different answer."

I followed him to his quarters and supped with the most important people in the camp. He made it clear that I was a boyhood friend and there was the tacit message that no one was to give me grief over what had happened the day before. There would be no ugly agnomen. I knew that, as much as I yearned to be a civilian, I could not deny him my continued service.

CHAPTER 13

Publius Scipio considered an alliance with Syphax, the king of the western Numidians, the Maseasyli, critical to his designs in Africa. He had sent Gaius Laelius to treat with Syphax and Syphax had appeared willing to make a treaty with Rome, but he insisted on doing it with Scipio in person. In two Quinquerimes he and Laelius sailed from New Carthage to Syphax' city of Cirta. He asked me to come along in order to record the terms of a possible treaty and also to observe what I could of the country and its customs. The sea was calm that day with only an occasional light breeze so we had to rely mainly on our oarsmen.

We were all a little bored, so Scipio asked me "Why don't you sing one of the songs the Celtiberians taught you. I'd like to hear it." I was rather surprised, but I gave it my best effort. It was a sad song, about a woman who waits in vain for her husband to come home. I must have done a creditable job because I received approbation, even from the oarsmen.

"You like the Celtiberians, don't you?" asked Scipio.

"Yes and no," I said. "I know you detest them for the role they played in Cneius' death, and, indeed, they can be treacherous, but one of them, Armon, went out of his way to protect me when my life was in danger, and he ended his life by poison to avoid being forced to give information to Hasdrubal, and my Celtiberian servant girl killed three men to save my life. I enjoyed my time among them. We and the Carthaginians have brought them nothing but grief. We have brought war to people who want nothing more than to be left in peace. I don't blame them if they hate both of our nations."

"Then you think Rome is wrong to pursue empire?" He asked.

"Well, no," I replied "Because if we don't, someone else will, and likely they will be worse than we are."

Laelius spoke: "Your servant girl killed three men? That must have been something to behold!"

"It was, indeed!" I replied. "You never saw such fury, nor such skill, in a man or a woman!"

"I've seen you kill in battle, Lucius, and you're so businesslike about it. No exasperation or rancor at all" said Laelius. "It's as though 'sorry friend, nothing personal, but if one of us must die, I'd just as soon it were you!'"

I laughed. "I'm a different person on the battlefield than I am in ordinary life. Nay, a different creature altogether, a monster, perhaps. Appius Virginius is also businesslike when he kills, but I couldn't do what he does."

"A weak stomach!" laughed Gaius Laelius

Keeping a straight face with difficulty, Scipio said "You have my permission to vomit whenever you want, Lucius, as long as you don't do it on me!"

As we approached the harbor, we were thrown into consternation. There were seven Carthaginian triremes and they were heading toward us. Our oarsmen rowed as fast as they could, and luckily for us there arose a strong breeze. Once inside the harbor the Carthaginians dared not attack us, lest they give offense to our host, Syphax.

As it happened, the Carthaginian triremes bore the party of Hasdrubal Gisco, who was stopping by Cirta on his way from Gades to Carthage. King Syphax considered it a great honor that two such notable personages as Publius Scipio and Hasdrubal Gisco should have arrived at his city on the same day to solicit peace and friendship. He suggested that Scipio and Hasdrubal meet in a conference and negotiate and end to their differences, but Scipio declared that he was not empowered to treat with the Carthaginians. He could do nothing without the command of the Roman senate.

Syphax did prevail upon Scipio to allow us to attend the same entertainment as the Carthaginians. We all supped at the king's table and, at the behest of King Syphax, Scipio and Hasdrubal were seated on the same couch, and they carried on a lively conversation. Scipio, always charming, was at his best and genuinely charmed the Carthaginian general. The two conversed for a long time and I wondered if Scipio mentioned Ilipa and Hasdrubal Gisco's strategic mistakes at that battle, but thinking about it, I rather doubt it for two reasons: Scipio's natural politeness, and the notion that you don't want to tutor your enemies in the arts of war.

Hasdrubal Gisco was heard to say that Scipio "Appeared to him more to be admired for the qualities he displayed on a personal interview with him than for his exploits in war, and I have no doubt that Syphax and his kingdom are already at the disposal of the Romans, such are the abilities that Scipio possesses for gaining the esteem of others. Therefore it is incumbent upon us, the Carthagainians, not more to inquire by what means we lost Spain, than to consider how we might retain possession of Africa. It was not from a desire to visit foreign countries, or roam about delightful coasts that so great a Roman captain, leaving a recently subdued province, and his armies, had crossed into Africa with only two ships, entering an enemy's territory, and committing himself to the untried honor of the King, but in pursuance of a hope he had conceived of subduing Africa."*13

Hasdrubal Gisco was exactly correct in this analysis, and Scipio did succeed in obtaining a treaty with King Syphax, the terms of which I duly wrote down.

Hasdrubal Gisco did, however, have one hidden asset which would undo the entire accomplishment of our endeavor at Cirta: his beautiful daughter, Sophonisba.

When we returned to New Carthage, Scipio made preparations to return to Rome to run for Consul. But first, as the last order of business in Hispania, we marched to Ilergetes to but down the rebellion of Indibilis and Mandonius. With heavy use of cavalry we defeated them decisively, but we lost twelve hundred killed and over a thousand wounded. Among the Ilergetes and their allies the only survivors were those who did not take part in the battle, light armed troops who remained watching from a hill above the valley. Indibilis sent Mandonius to sue for peace, and, after upbraiding the chieftain scathingly, Scipio treated them magnanimously.

Scipio sailed to Rome with ten ships, and I was ecstatic to be going home at last. The day before we sailed, Scipio sought me out and told me more about his plans to run for consul. I asked him if there would be room on one of his ships to bring Indibilis.

"Indibilis?" he repeated, looking shocked

"My stallion." I said "I named him after the chieftain. Do you think the man would be honored or insulted if he knew?"

Scipio laughed. "Honored, I'm sure. But I hope your horse is a more faithful ally than his namesake! I've reserved a place for the horses on one of the ships."

Upon arriving at Rome, Scipio obtained an audience of the senate in the Temple of Bellona and related all of his accomplishment in Hispania. He had gone against four Carthaginian generals, four victorious armies, and now there was not one Carthaginian in that country. He brought to the treasury fourteen thousand three hundred and forty-two pounds of silver and a great quantity of silver coins.

Lucius Veturius Philo held the assembly for the election of consuls and Scipio was named consul unanimously by vote of all the centuries. His co-consul was Licinius Crassus, chief pontiff.

I had not been home in four years and my reunion with my family was awkward. The children were virtually strangers and I had never even seen little Titus. The paterfamilias of the household was now my eldest brother

Titus, with whom I had never been close. It was strange that my father should be absent. I was aware that he had died, but the fact never really struck home to me until now. My wife was more mature and there was a reserve about her that she hadn't had before.

"Will you be staying with us now, Lucius?" she asked "Are you not retiring from the army after all these years?"

"I wish I could, Silvia." I said "But our job is not done. Scipio wants to end this war, once and for all. He plans to go to Africa and take Carthage. He needs to raise and train a cavalry, and he's asked me to help him. I'll be able to stay in Rome until he obtains his commission."

"Promise me this, Lucius," She said "That you will not let our sons, Lucius and Titus ever join the army unless some foreign potentate invades Italy."

"Silvia, I will not encourage them to join the army" I said. "But they will have to train on the Campus Martius so that they will be ready if another Hannibal should ever come along. I hope that that will never happen."

I went to see Ala and was amazed at how much her Latin had improved. She had moved her little shop into a larger space and was selling a number of items other than Jewelry: ceramics, statuettes, kitchenware, lamps and the like. She was doing very well. I gave her a bag full of all the jewelry I had obtained as booty over the past four years. "There are men who want to marry me" she said "But I don't think I'm interested. I think I have the best life here in Rome that a woman can have. I love you for bringing me here and helping me start the business!"

"It was the least I could do, Ala." I said "You are lucky. You are the freest person I know. I never had any sort of freedom. My father chose my wife, although I was certainly lucky with the choice, and my father chose my occupation, in which death was more probable than not. I wouldn't marry if I were you, Ala. You don't want to lose your freedom."

I told her of how I had sung the Celtiberian ballad at the behest of Scipio and she exclaimed "I remember that song!" and began to sing it. I joined her and I'm sure it must have amazed her Roman neighbors to hear the two of us singing the poignant lay in Celtiberian! There were tears in her eyes and I asked "Do you miss Celtiberia?"

"There are things I miss, Lucius, but I would never go back there where, as a lowly person, I was so mistreated. I am much happier here. I love you Lucius, and if you weren't married, I would marry you. You are the only man I trust enough to marry." She closed her shop and we retired to her room for an evening of feasting, wine and love making.

CHAPTER 14

Scipio took his plan to invade Africa to the senate. While the centuries were strongly in support of him, there was a strong faction in the senate that opposed the plan, and this faction was led by none other than the Cunctator himself, Quintus Fabius Maximus.

Fabius pointed out that the senate had not declared Africa to be a province of Rome and that Scipio would have no jurisdiction there. He brought out the possible imputation that he, himself might be motivated by jealousy. "But if neither my past life and character, nor a dictatorship together with five consulships, and so much glory acquired, both in peace and war, that I am more likely to loathe it than to desire more, exempt me from such a suspicion, then let my age, at least, acquit me. For what rivalry can there exist between myself and a man who is not equal in years even to my son?"

He gave faint praise to Scipio's accomplishments in Hispania and averred that, rather than carry the war into Africa, Scipio should go after Hannibal in Italy. "Why then do you not apply yourself to this, and carry the war in a straightforward manner to the place where Hannibal is, rather than pursue that circuitous course, according to which you expect that when you shall have crossed over into Africa, Hannibal will follow you thither? Do you seek to obtain the distinguished honor of having finished the Punic war? After you have defended your own possession, for this is naturally the first object, then proceed to attack those of others. Let there be peace in Italy before there is war in Africa."

He went on to point out the difference between Hispania and Africa. Rome at least had had a province in Hispania and the remains of Scipio's armies. There had still been tribes there which were friendly to Rome and hostile to Carthage. "The rest of your achievements, nor do I wish to disparage them, are by no means to be compared with what you will have to do in the war in Africa, where there is not a single harbor open to receive our fleet, no part of the country at peace with us, no state in alliance, no king in friendship with us, nor room in any part to take up a position or to advance. Whichever way you turn, all is hostility and danger. Do you trust in the Numidians and Syphax? Your father and uncle were not cut off by the arms of their enemies until they were duped by the treachery of their Celtiberian allies, nor were you, yourself exposed to so much danger from Mago and Hasdrubal, the generals of your enemies as from Indibilis and Mandonius whom you had received into friendship. Can you place any confidence in the Numidians after having experienced a defection in your own soldiers?" (A reference to Sucro, which I thought was a low blow.) "The Carthaginians defended Hispania in a very different manner than that in which they will defend the walls of their capital, the temples of their gods, their alters and their hearths; when their terrified wives will attend them on the way to battle and their little children will run to them.

"Will Hannibal, who has now, for a long time, been unavailingly soliciting succors from home, be rendered more powerful in men and arms when occupying the remotest corner of the Bruttian territory or when near to Carthage and supported by all Africa? What sort of policy is yours, to prefer fighting where your own forces will be diminished by half and the enemy's greatly augmented, to encountering the enemy when you will have two armies against one, and that one wearied with so many battles, and so protracted and laborious a service?

"Consider how far this policy corresponds with that of your parent. He, setting out in his consulship in Hispania, returned from his province into Italy, that he might meet Hannibal on his descent from the Alps while you are going to leave Italy, when Hannibal is there, not because you consider such a course beneficial to the state, but because it will redound to your own honor and glory."

I found Fabius' speech, which I do not quote in its entirety, to be condescending, but I could see how it might be persuasive, especially to the older and more conservative of the senators.

Publius Scipio stood up to reply, addressing himself first to the question of Fabius' jealousy.

"Even Quintus Fabius himself has observed, conscript fathers, in the commencement of his speech, that in the opinion he gave, a feeling of jealousy might be suspected. And, though I dare not myself charge so great a man with harboring that feeling, yet, whether it is owing to a defect in his language, or to the fact, that suspicion has certainly not been removed. For he has so magnified his own honors and the fame of his exploits, in order to do away with the imputation of envy, that it would appear that I am rivaled by every obscure person, but not by himself, because as he enjoys a eminence above everybody else, an eminence to which I do not deny that I also aspire, he is unwilling that I should be placed upon a level with him. He has represented himself as an old man, as one who has gone through every gradation of honor, and me as below the age even of his son. As if he supposed that the desire for glory did not exceed the limits of human life. For my own part, I do not deny that I am desirous, not only to attain to the share of glory which you possess, Quintus Fabius, but (and in saying it I mean no offense) if I can, to exceed it!"

"Quintus Fabius also mentioned what a great degree of danger I should incur, should I cross over into Africa, so that he appeared solicitous on my account, and not only for the state and the army. But whence has this concern for me so suddenly sprung? When my father and uncle were slain, when their two armies were cut up almost to a man, when Hispania was lost, when four armies of the Carthaginians and four generals kept possession of everything by terror and by arms, when a general was sought to take command of that war, and no one came forward besides myself, not one had the courage to declare himself a candidate: when the Roman people had conferred command on me, although only 25 years of age, why was it that no one made mention of my age, of the strength of the enemy, of the difficulty of the war, or of the recent destruction of my father and uncle?

"Has some greater disaster been suffered in Africa now than had at that time befallen us in Hispania? Are there larger armies in Africa, more and better generals then there were in Hispania? Was my age then more mature for conducting a war than now? Can a war with a Carthaginian enemy be carried on with greater convenience in Hispania than in Africa? After having routed and put to flight four Carthaginian armies, after having captured by force or reduced to submission by fear, so many cities, after having entirely subdued everything as far as the ocean, so many petty princes, so many savage nations, after having regained the possession of the whole of Hispania, so that no trace of war remains, it is an easy matter to make light of my services, just as easy as it would be, should I return victorious from Africa, to make light of those very circumstances which are now magnified in order that they may appear formidable, for the purpose of detaining me here.

"What need is there of ancient and foreign examples to remind of what sort of thing it is to boldly carry terror against an enemy, and removing the danger from oneself, to bring another into peril? Can there be a stronger instance than Hannibal himself, or one more to the point? It makes a great difference whether you devastate the territories of another or see your own destroyed by fire and sword. He who brings danger upon another has more spirit than he who repels it. When you have entered the territory of an enemy, you may have a near view of his advantages and disadvantages. Hannibal did not expect that it would come to pass that so many of the states in Italy would come over to him as did so after the defeat at Cannae. How much less would any firmness and constancy be experienced in Africa by the Carthaginians, who are, themselves, faithless allies, oppressive and haughty masters. Besides, we, even when deserted by our allies, stood firm in our own strength, the Roman soldiery. The Carthaginians possess no native strength. The soldiers they have are obtained by hire: Africans and Numidians—people remarkable above all others for the inconstancy of their attachments. Provided no impediment arises here, you will hear at once that I have landed, and that Africa is blazing with war; that Hannibal is preparing for departure from this country, and that Carthage is besieged. Expect more frequent and more joyful dispatches than you received from Hispania. The considerations on which I ground my expectations are the good fortune of the Roman people, the gods, the witnesses of the treaty violated by the enemy, the kings Syphax and Masinissa, on whose fidelity

I will rely in such a manner as that I may be secure from danger should they prove perfidious.

"Many things that are not apparent at this distance, the war will develop, and it is part of a man, and a general, not to be wanting when fortune presents itself, and to bend its events to his designs. I shall, Quintus Fabius, have the opponent you assign me, Hannibal: but I shall rather draw him after me than be kept here by him. I will compel him to fight in his own country, and Carthage shall be the prize of victory, rather than the half-ruined forts of the Bruttians.

"Let Italy, which has so long been harassed, at length enjoy some repose. Let Africa in her turn be fired and devastated. Let the Roman camp overhang the gates of Carthage rather than we should once again behold rampart of the enemy from our walls. Let Africa be the seat of the remainder of the war. Let terror and flight, the devastation of lands, the defection of allies, and all the other calamities of war, which have fallen on us, through a period of fourteen years, be turned upon her.

"My discourse would be tedious and uninteresting to you if, as Fabius has depreciated my services in Hispania, I should in like manner endeavor, on the other hand to turn his glory into ridicule, and make the most of my own. I will do neither, conscript fathers, and in nothing else, though a young man, I shall certainly have shown my superiority over this old man in modesty and the government of my tongue. Such has been my life and such the services I have performed, that I can gladly rest content in silence with that opinion which you have spontaneously formed of me."*14

Listening to Publius Scipio's speech, I strongly suspected that Quintus Fabius had met more than his match in oratory as much as in generalship. It also seemed to me that Quintus Fabius Maximus was, indeed, jealous of Publius Cornelius Scipio, and would stoop to any depth to undermine him.

The senators had heard rumors that if Publius Scipio did not prevail upon the co-operation of the senate, he would take his case to the people. Jealously guarding their privileges, they demanded that he openly declare in the senate whether he submitted to the conscript fathers to decide respecting the provinces, and whether he would agree to abide by their determination or put it to the people. At first, Scipio resisted their demand, but upon consultation with his co-consul, he agreed to abide by the determination of the senate. A compromise of a sort was reached. The consul to whose lot Sicily fell would receive thirty ships of war which Caius Servilius had commanded the previous year. This consul would be permitted to cross over into Africa if he conceived it to be for the advantage of the state. The other consul would be assigned to Bruttium and the war with Hannibal. As it happened, the province of Sicily fell to Scipio.

Even so, the support of the senate was grudging. Scipio was not permitted to levy troops but only allowed to enlist volunteers. He rapidly built a fleet of thirty ships, twenty quinqueremes and ten Quadriremes in the space of 45 days. During this time he enlisted seven thousand volunteers, including myself. We were transported in ships to Sicily where my assignment was to train the cavalry, mostly raw recruits who had no experience whatever in warfare or horsemanship! Scipio told me that the key to victory in this war would be cavalry and that, within a year, we must build a formidable force from virtually nothing. It was a very tall order, and I spent nearly every day out on the field training and drilling my men.

A military tribune has the power of life and death over his men, but I preferred to use persuasion rather than brute force in training and disciplining my soldiers. If I saw that any of my men were not up to my standards of strength and accuracy with his weapons, or if any were overindulging in drinking or the pleasures of the flesh, I would assign them extra hours of training while allowing leisure to the others. I constantly reminded my men that, in battle, their lives were on the line. "Atilius! If your aim is that far off when you throw your spear at a Carthaginian, you'll be dead before you get another chance!" Slowly, gradually, my three hundred volunteers, mostly rustic Latin villagers, became a well-trained and effective cavalry unit, and, much to Publius Scipio's satisfaction, we showed off our skill to good effect when a delegation from Rome arrived to inspect Scipio's preparations for the invasion of Africa.

After fourteen years, the two legions of survivors of Cannae were still in Sicily. After Cannae, a spiteful senate had decreed that these survivors would be stationed in Sicily and not allowed to retire from service until the war ended. The conditions of service were also arduous as they were not allowed to lodge in towns. They had repeatedly petitioned the senate to modify this decree, averring that it wasn't through fault of their own that the battle of Cannae had been lost but through the fault of their generals, and that they were treated unequally with noblemen survivors of the battle who were allowed to keep their privileges. All of these entreaties over the years had come to naught and were treated with cold indifference by the Roman senate. Scipio was sympathetic to their cause because he, himself had survived the defeats both at Ticinus and at Cannae and escaped the ensuing carnage in both cases. He took the two legions under his command, personally interviewing each of the veterans and weeding out those who were disabled or infirm. He then augmented the legions to full strength with his volunteers. I was gratified to see him treat the survivors of Cannae with respect. I had always believed that they had been unfairly treated and, I myself had fled the battlefield after the battle of the Upper Baetis.

CHAPTER 15

As Scipio was about to embark to Africa a setback came in the form of an embassy from King Syphax. Syphax had married Sophonisba, the beautiful daughter of Hasdrubal Gisco and was passionately infatuated with her. He felt that the demands of the marital bond superseded the obligations of the treaty he had signed with Scipio, and informed Scipio that he could no longer rely on him for support. He urged Scipio to carry on the war elsewhere besides Africa, and that he wished to remain neutral, but if Scipio could not keep away from Africa, and should advance his army to Carthage, it would be incumbent upon him to fight for the land of Africa, which gave him birth and for the country of his spouse, for her parent and household gods.

Scipio sent reply through the ambassadors warning him, in no uncertain terms "not to violate the laws of hospitality which bound us together, the obligation of the alliance entered into with the Roman people, nor make light of justice, honor, their right hands pledged and the gods, the witnesses and arbitrators of compacts."*15 Not wanting to demoralize the troops, he did not reveal Syphax' defection to them, but told them that the ambassadors were urging his forces to invade Africa as soon as possible.

Scipio sent Gaius Laelius into Africa where he encountered Masinissa. Masinissa had been on the losing end of a power struggle in his own country and had very few troops, but his knowledge of the land would prove valuable even so. He had become staunchly pro-Roman, and would remain so the rest of his life.

We sailed to Africa from Lilybaeum on Sicily, 16,000 foot soldiers and 1600 horse. There were fifty men of war and 400 transports. The entire population of the city turned out to see us off. Scipio spoke to the troops from the ship of the commander-in-chief:

"Ye gods and goddesses who preside over the seas and lands, I pray and entreat you, that whatever things have been, are now, or shall be performed during my command, may turn out prosperously to myself, the state and the commons of Rome, to the allies and the Latin confederacy, and to all who follow my party and that of the Roman people, my command and auspices, by land, by sea and on rivers. That you would lend your favorable aid to all those measures and promote them happily. That you would bring these and me again to our homes, safe and unhurt, victorious over our vanquished enemies, decorated with spoils, loaded with booty and triumphant. That you would grant us the opportunity of taking revenge upon our adversaries and foes, and put it in the power of myself and the Roman people to make the Carthaginian state feel those signal severities which they endeavored to inflict upon our state."*16 After these prayers, he threw the raw entrails of a sacrificial victim into the sea, according to custom, and with the sound of a trumpet, gave the signal for sailing.

Our landing caused panic in the local population and consternation in Carthage. The day after landing, the Carthaginians sent five hundred horsemen against our forces under their young general Hanno (yet another Hanno!) But we routed them and pursued them, killing most of them, including Hanno. Scipio sent his light-armed troops to plunder the country all around.

Masinissa arrived very promptly with 200 horsemen, and he helped us defeat a body of nearly 4000 horsemen led by Hanno son of Hamilcar. We slew or captured more than half of them and made Hanno prisoner.

Scipio endeavored, without success, to lay siege to the city of Utica, which lay about 25 miles distance from Carthage, hoping to use it for a base, the way he had used New Carthage in Hispania. During this time, Hasdrubal, son of Gisco, now the most influential man in Carthage, and the leader of the Barcine faction, raised an army of 30,000 infantrymen and 3,000 horse, but he dared not move against Scipio until Syphax arrived. Syphax came with 50,000 foot and 10,000 horse, and took up a position not far from Utica and the Roman works.

During the Winter, Syphax attempted to make peace between Scipio and the Carthaginians. Scipio had no intention of entering into an agreement mediated by Syphax, but he used the negotiation as a pretext of sending emissaries into the camp of the enemy to reconnoiter, sending centurions into the camp in the guise of servants to the emissaries. They found that the huts of the Carthaginians, and especially those of the Numidians would be highly flammable once the dry season was underway. Scipio told Syphax that he would take up the question of peace with his council. The next day he sent word to Syphax that the council had rejected any terms of peace and that Syphax might hope for peace only if he abandoned the cause of the Carthaginians.

This Syphax declined to do, and Scipio marched his forces out of his camp toward evening. We marched in darkness to the camp of Syphax, where he directed Masinissa and Laelius to set fire to the huts of the Numidians. Then Scipio took the rest of the troops to the camp of Hasdrubal Gisco. A great conflagration arose in the camp of Syphax and most of his soldiers either died in the flames or were cut down in flight by the our troops who had surrounded the camp. Once Scipio saw the fires of Syphax' camp he set fire to the camp of Hasdrubal Gisco, and a similar slaughter ensued. Out of over eighty thousand soldiers in the two camps combined, only thirty-five thousand foot and five hundred horsemen escaped, many of them wounded and scorched. Forty thousand men were either slain or destroyed by the flames and more than 5000 captured. Among the captured were many Carthaginian nobles, eleven senators, with a hundred and seventy-four military standards. More than two thousand seven hundred horses were taken and six elephants. A great quantity of arms was also seized.

Hasdrubal Gisco escaped and made his way back to Carthage. Syphax took up a position in a fortified place about eight miles distant.

There was debate in Carthage about what course to pursue next. Some wanted to sue for peace, others suggested that Hannibal be returned from Italy to defend the city. The third opinion, which prevailed, was that the army be repaired and that Syphax be exhorted not to abandon the war.

Sophonisba implored him not to betray her father and her country, nor suffer Carthage to be consumed by the same flames which had reduced the camps to ashes, and news that the Carthaginians had been joined by a fine body of 4000 Celtiberians that had been recruited in Spain gave Syphax courage. Syphax set about to build an army of Numidian rustics, furnishing them with arms and horses. After a few days Hasdrubal and Syphax united their forces. This army consisted of about thirty-five thousand fighting men.

Scipio, during this time had renewed the siege of Utica and was bringing up his siege engines when he got a report of the mobilization of the Carthaginian armies under Hasdrubal Gisco and Syphax. Leaving a small force at Utica, he took the main body of his forces to a place called the Great Plains. Skirmishing took place over the next two days. On the fourth day both sides came down in battle array. Scipio placed the light armed spear men in front of the van with the more experienced principes behind and kept the triarii in reserve behind them. I commanded the Italian cavalry on the right wing. I had trained these men almost from scratch, and now would be the test of how good a leader I was. The Numidian cavalry under Masinissa formed the left wing.

Hasdrubal placed his Numidians opposite my cavalry and the Carthaginians were placed opposite to Masinissa. The Celtiberians were placed in the van.

The Carthaginians, mostly raw, inexperience soldiers, quickly gave way to the forces of Masinissa, and my cavalrymen easily routed Syphax' Numidians. We then set upon the Celtiberians who fought bravely, knowing that they would find no refuge in Africa if they escaped, and would receive no pardon from Scipio if they were captured. During the ensuing carnage I recognized one of the Celtiberians. He was a nephew of Armon, and he had been an adolescent in Carrach when I lived there. A skinny boy with sandy red hair and intense blue eyes, he had grown into a comely young man. "Andor!" I shouted in Celtiberian. "Yield to me, I'll spare your life!"

"You speak Celtic!" he replied "Who are you?"

"Lucius. I was a friend of Armon. Yield to me."

"No! Fight me!" he said "I won't be a slave!"

"Andor, trust me. I'll buy you and free you. Armon was my friend. Yield to me!"

Andor could see the slaughter going on all around him and, after a moment of hesitation, dropped his weapon. I ordered two of my men to take him to our camp. The carnage continued until nightfall. When I returned to our camp I went to the stockade where the prisoners were kept. Important prisoners would be taken to Rome to be displayed in Scipio's triumph, once the conquest of Carthage was complete. The others would be sold as slaves. Andor was the only Celtiberian prisoner taken and he had been placed in chains. He clearly appeared to be regretting his decision to surrender. I told the centurion in charge of the prisoners that I wanted Andor released from chains and paroled to me. "I don't have the authority to do that" He said.

"I will take complete responsibility." I said "I've known Scipio since we were boys."

"I don't care how long you've known Scipio!" He said. "I can't release a prisoner to you. If you wish, I'll summon the quaestor."

The quaestor was Marcus Porcius Cato. He was the same age as me and had also been in the army from the age of seventeen. He was an intimate friend of Quintus Fabius Maximus, and an continual thorn in the side of Scipio. He was renown for strictness and parsimony and was continually complaining to Rome of Scipio's extravagance and decadent Greek influenced habits. I seriously doubted that I would get any co-operation in this matter, but I repeated my demand.

"Certainly not" said Cato. "Why do you want him? For Greek vices?"

I tried to control my temper. "Porcius, I do not indulge in Greek vices. He's a kinsman to my woman."

"You have a Celtiberian woman?!" He shouted, genuinely shocked "What is Rome coming to when Roman men take up with barbarian women?!" I don't think he would have been more shocked had I professed an appetite for Greek vices!

"Porcius, do I have to bother Publius Scipio about this matter at a time like this?"

"Do you think I take orders from Publius Scipio?" he asked. "What you're asking for is completely irregular and unlawful! This man must be sold and the funds go to the state. And that's exactly what he deserves for coming here and fighting for Carthage against Rome."

"Porcius, if anything happens to my wife's cousin, one of us is going to die, and if my past history is any indication, that person will be you!"

"Are you threatening me?" He shouted. "I'm not afraid of you!"

"Well, If you're not, you should be!" I replied.

I stalked off and went to find Publius Scipio. I was loathe to bother him at a time like this, but I knew that the next morning I would have to lead my men in pursuit of Hasdrubal and Syphax and I was afraid that something bad would happen to Andor at Cato's hands. It violated my sense of honor to think I had lured this poor man into slavery when he could have had an honorable death on the battlefield!

"Where have you been, Lucius?" Publius Scipio seemed annoyed with me that I had not been there when he was discussing his plans for the next day with his staff. I sat quietly through the meeting and when it was over and most of the officers had left, I continued to sit there and pout.

"Lucius, is something the matter?" I told him about Andor.

"It's our policy to execute Celtiberian mercenaries who hire themselves to the Carthaginians" he said.

"Fine." I said. "I'd rather see him executed than sold into slavery. He, himself, would rather be executed than enslaved. He only agreed to surrender when I promised to buy his freedom. Now my word is dishonored and I'm made to be a liar! Kindly do him the favor of executing him. Me too while you're at it!"

"Calm down, Lucius. I'll talk to him." He sent his lictors with written orders to summon Andor. Even Marcus Porcius Cato would not defy lictors.

Scipio asked Andor questions as I translated. "Were you among the Celtiberians who abandoned my uncle Cneius Scipio before the battle of Upper Baetis?" he asked.

Perhaps hoping to be executed, Andor replied "Yes, I think so. We were told to stay out of the battle."

"Do you Celtiberians have no sense of honor or loyalty?" asked Scipio.

Andor did not flinch at the question. "We have honor and loyalty to our own kind." he said. "We know no loyalty to Rome or Carthage. None of us ever asked Rome or Carthage to come to our land. We sell our services to the highest bidder. If your uncle was stupid enough to trust us when he knew there was a party who could pay more, than he merited his fate! And if you want to execute me in revenge for your uncle's death, I won't beg you for mercy! I will show your men how a Celtiberian man dies." I translated the man's words properly, regretting that his honesty would cost him his life.

Scipio made a gesture toward the battle field. "We've already seen how a Celtiberian man dies. Some 4000 of your Celtiberian countrymen lay dead out there from today's battle. Do you think that I'm not so glutted with revenge upon your countrymen that I care whether there's one more or one less?

"Out of respect for Lucius, and for your uncle who worked for Cneius Scipio and took poison rather than betray us, and for your kinswoman who saved Lucius' life, I'm going to release you without ransom. We have no means at this time to return you to your native country, so I recommend that you enter the service of Lucius. He will see to it that you go home when the time is opportune."

I whispered "Thank you, Publius, for preserving the honor of my word." Andor would sleep in my hut. I told him that there was no point in running away because there was no refuge for him here in Africa, and I was the only person around that spoke a word of Celtiberian. He would have to be patient and I would see to it that he returned to Celtiberia when it became possible.

When we turned to leave, Scipio asked me "Do you really think you can trust this man?"

I said "Certainly. As long as there is no one around who can pay more!"

Chapter 16

Knowing that I would have to rise at dawn to join in the pursuit of Syphax and Hasdrubal, I asked one of my soldiers, a young man named Metellus, who had been slightly wounded and would not be able to accompany us, to companion Andor and see that he behaved himself and that his needs were met. I told Andor that he should try to make himself useful in the camp, reminding him of how, when I lived in his village, we had gone out together to chop wood, fetch water, and clear land for farming.

While we were slaughtering the Celtiberians, Syphax and Hasdrubal had made their escape. The following day Scipio sent Laelius and Masinissa along with both the Roman and Numidian cavalry and light infantry to pursue them. He himself, with the main strength of the army, set about to reduce the neighboring towns.

Carthage braced for an attack. Walls were repaired and protected by outworks, and provisions were collected to withstand a long siege. It was decided to send a fleet out to Utica to attempt to raise the siege there, and to send an embassy to Hannibal to recall him home to Carthage. They also sent an embassy to Mago who had established a base in Liguria and Cisalpine Gaul. Scipio seized the city of Tunis, and while raising a rampart there, caught sight of the Carthaginian fleet on their way to Utica. Scipio hastily returned to Utica and blocked the harbor with transports to prevent the Carthaginians from capturing or destroying the Roman ships in the harbor.

Failing to capture either Syphax or Hasdrubal, Laelius and Masinissa made a journey to Masinissa's kingdom, where the people joyfully flocked to their long-absent king. They expelled the garrisons of Syphax from the kingdom. Syphax himself set about to raise yet another army of Numidians, collecting all who were fit for service and outfitting them with horses, armor, and weapons. He organized them according to Roman fashion, dividing his horsemen into troops and his infantry into cohorts. But this new army was entirely raw and undisciplined. He pitched his forces not far from ours. Skirmishing gave way to all-out battle, but Syphax' troops were no match for experienced Roman cavalry and infantry, nor for Masinissa's horsemen. Syphax did all he could to rally his men, and riding up to the enemy to try to shame them into stopping their flight, he was thrown from his horse, overpowered and made prisoner. He was dragged alive into the presence of Laelius, a spectacle which gave Masinissa great satisfaction.

After this battle Masinissa took his horsemen to Syphax' capital at Cirta. Laelius planned to follow with the infantry. Once the people saw their king in chains, they agreed to open the city to Masinissa. Syphax' beautiful wife, Sophonisba, the daughter of Hasdrubal Gisco, met him at the very threshold of the palace and, falling down on her knees, she begged him not to deliver her to the Romans.

"The gods" she said "Together with your own valor and good fortune, have given you the power of disposing of us as you please. But if a captive may be allowed to give utterance to the voice of supplication before him who is sovereign arbiter of her life or death; if she may be permitted to touch his knee and his victorious right hand, I entreat and beseech you, by the majesty of royalty, which we also a short time ago possessed; by the name of the Numidian race, which was common to Syphax and yourself; by the guardian deities of this palace, that you indulge a suppliant by determining yourself whatever your inclination may suggest respecting your captive and not suffer me to be placed at the haughty and merciless disposal of any Roman. Were I nothing more than the wife of Syphax, yet I would make trial of the honor of a Numidian, one born in Africa, the same country which gave me birth, than of a foreigner and an alien. You know what a Carthaginian, what the daughter of Hasdrubal, has to fear from a Roman. If you can not effect it by any other means, I beg and beseech you, that you will, by my death rescue me from the Romans!"*17

Her supplications moved Masinissa and he promised to do anything in his power to keep her from falling into the hands of the Romans. Then he conceived a plan which he believed would both effect her safety and satisfy his own carnal desires. He would marry her!

Laelius arrived shortly after the nuptials were completed and expressed strong disapproval, even threatening to drag her from the marriage bed and send her with Syphax and the rest of the captives to Scipio. Masinissa prevailed upon him to leave the matter up to Scipio. The two commanders then proceeded to reduce Syphax' province to submission. Masinissa would become sovereign of both his own kingdom and that of Syphax.

When Scipio asked Syphax what had been his reason for not only renouncing his alliance with the Romans, but in making war with them without provocation, he blamed it on his passion for Sophonisba.

"Then it was that I was mad, then it was that I banished from my mind all regard for private friendship and public treaties, when I receive a Carthaginian wife into my house. It was by flames kindled by those nuptial torches that my palace has been consumed. That fury and pest had, by every kind of fascination, engrossed my affections and obscured my reason, nor did she rest until she had, with her own hands, clad me with impious arms against my guest and friend. Yet ruined and fallen as I am, I derive some consolation in my misfortune when I see the same pest and fury transferred to the dwelling and the household gods of the man who above all others is my greatest enemy. That Masinissa is neither more prudent nor more firm than myself, but even more incautious by reason of his youth. Doubtless he has shown greater folly and want of self control in marrying her than I did."*18

In public, Scipio took care to bestow the highest praises and honors upon Masinissa, but in private he let him know that he was not at all pleased with his conduct.

"I suppose, Masinissa" He said "that it was because you saw in me some good qualities that you first came to me in Hispania, for the purpose of forming a friendship with me, and that afterward in Africa you committed yourself and all your hopes to my protection. But of all those virtues, on account of which I seemed worthy of your regard, there is not one in which I gloried so much as temperance and control of my passions. I wish that you also, Masinissa, had added this to your other distinguished qualities. There is not so much danger to be apprehended by persons at our time of life from armed foes, as from the pleasures which surround us on all sides. The man who by temperance has curbed and subdued his appetite for them, has acquired for himself much greater honor and a much more important victory than we now enjoy in the conquest of Syphax. Beware of how you deform many good qualities by one vice, and mar the credit of so many meritorious deeds by a degree of guilt more than proportioned to its object."*19

Masinissa was reduced to tears by this speech and retired in confusion to his own tent. He felt himself under obligation to keep his promise to Sophonisba not to allow her to fall into the hands of the Romans. Consequently, he sent one of his servants to her with a cup of poison, informing her that he would gladly have fulfilled the first obligation which as a husband he owed to her, his wife, but those in power had deprived him of the exercise of that right, so he now performed his second promise, which was to give her the means to avoid coming into the power of the Romans. That, mindful of her father, the general, of her country, and the two kings to whom she had been married, she would take such measures as she, herself, thought proper.

When the servant brought this message and the poison, she said "I accept the nuptial present, nor is it an unwelcome one, if my husband can render me no better service. Tell him, however, that I should have died with greater satisfaction had I not married so near upon my death."*20 Then she took the poison without qualm or hesitation.

Scipio, fearing that Masinissa might, in his distempered state of mind, adopt some desperate resolution, lavished him with honors and gifts, after gently rebuking him for expiating one act of temerity with another and rendering the affair more tragic than it needed to be. He ordered an assembly summoned, and saluted Masinissa with the title of king and distinguished him with the highest encomiums, presenting him with a golden goblet, a curule chair, and ivory scepter, an embroidered gown and a triumphal vest. Masinissa's mind was thus soothed and he continued a faithful ally of Rome for the rest of his days.

Scipio then sent Gaius Laelius to Rome with Syphax and the other prisoners and led us back to Tunis.

When I got back to our camp I found young Metellus and Andor living in my tent, as I had left them. They had become friends and Metellus would take Andor along on forageing parties. Andor, in turn was teaching Metellus to hunt. He was also starting to pick up some Latin.

One evening, a day or two after we returned, Marcus Porcius Cato came to my tent. "I'm leaving for Rome, Varro," he said, "Scipio has arranged for Gaius Laelius to become Quaestor. I know I'll never get any satisfaction from either Gaius Laelus or Scipio so I plan to file a complaint against you with the military authorities in Rome. I will accuse you of insubordination, threatening a superior, and trying to persuade a centurion to disobey orders."

"Will an apology be of any benefit, Porcius" I asked.

He looked surprised, not having expected a soft answer, but I had gotten my way concerning Andor and I wasn't keen on cultivating powerful enemies. He almost smiled. "It depends on how abject it is."

"Abject enough" I said. "I was carried away by my anger, it impaired my judgment."

Always one to encourage self-improvement he said "You would do well to study the philosophy of the Stoics, Varro. It will help you learn to control your passions."

"Well, I may have time to do that now." I said. "I will be retiring from the army as soon as we conquer Carthage, or arrange a peace."

"There can be no peace between Rome and Carthage!" he declared "Carthage must be destroyed! If Scipio is so foolish as to allow the walls and the city of Carthage to stand, he will have a life-long enemy in me.

I will not cease, until the end of my days, to call for the destruction of Carthage! I'm sure that Quintius Fabius would agree with me.

"I have investigated you and you have the reputation of being a mild mannered man, so I may be persuaded to overlook this lapse." He said. "You might even be a decent person were you not so strongly influenced by Scipio in his profligacy and decadence! And your conduct so un-Roman. You have a perfectly fine Roman wife and children, yet you consort with a barbarian woman! You have no dignitas at all!"

"Porcius, it doesn't require any dignitas to run a stable in Subura, which is all I want to do right now. Have a good trip back to Rome, and give my salutations to Quintus Fabius."

"I suppose you're one of those who would criticize Quintus Fabius for the way he conducted the war" said Marcus Porcius Cato.

"No, not at all," I replied. "I think he did exactly the right thing."

"You do?" said Cato, looking surprised.

"Well, of course." I said, then quoting what Scipio had said, years ago: "When you're facing a military genius like Hannibal, and you know you're not one, than the intelligent and sensible thing to do is to avoid engaging him!"

"You're hopeless, Varro, absolutely hopeless!" he said. "I suppose you think Publius Scipio is a military genius."

"I do indeed, Marcus Porcius Cato." I replied "And you would too, if you had been at Ilipa!"

To my knowledge, Cato never filed charges against me. He was too busy running a campaign against government fraud and waste after he returned to Rome. He was, without question, the most insufferably self-important and self righteous man I have ever met.

Chapter 17

After the battle of the Great Plains, Carthage sent an embassy to Scipio to sue for peace. Considering all that had transpired over the past 16 years, the terms of the proposed peace could be considered mild. The Carthaginians must restore the prisoners, deserters and fugitives, withdraw their armies from Italy and Gaul, give up all claims to Hispania, retire from all the islands between Italy and Africa, deliver up all their ships of war except twenty, and furnish five hundred thousand pecks of wheat and three hundred thousand pecks of barley. A fine of five thousand talents would be levied. Scipio gave the Carthaginians three days to accept these terms of peace. When they returned, saying that they had accepted the terms, Scipio declared a truce and a Carthaginian embassy was sent to Rome to solicit peace. In the mean time the Carthaginians sent embassies to both Hannibal in Bruttium and Mago in Liguria to summon them home to defend their city.

Laelius arrived in Rome before the Carthaginian ambassadors and his arrival and the news he carried occasioned great joy in the city. King Syphax was sent to Alba to be kept in custody.

During this time, Publius Quinctilius Varus, the praetor, and Marcus Cornelius, the proconsul, marched against Mago in the territories of the Insubrian Gauls. The battle went back and forth, the contest undecided until Mago was wounded in the thigh and carried off the field. His men immediately betook themselves to flight. There had been heavy losses on both sides. Mago managed to reach the sea coast in the territory of the

Inguanian Ligurians, where the ambassadors from Carthage were waiting with ships to carry him and the remains of his forces back to Carthage, but Mago died of his wound during the passage.

Hannibal, in Bruttium, was also visited by an embassy from Carthage and ordered to depart Italy and return home. It is said that when Hannibal heard the message of the ambassadors he gnashed his teeth and scarcely refrained from shedding tears. He said "Those who have for a long time been endeavoring to drag me home, by forbidding the sending of supplies and money to me, now recall me, not indirectly, but openly. Hannibal, therefore, hath been conquered, not by the Roman people, who have been so often slain and routed, but by the Carthaginian senate, through envy and detraction, nor will Publius Scipio exult and glory in this unseemly return so much as Hanno, who has crushed our family, since he could not effect it by any other means, by the ruin of Carthage."*21

It is said that rarely has any person leaving his own country to go into exile exhibited deeper sorrow than Hannibal did on departing from the land of his enemies, that he frequently looked back upon the shores of Italy, and arraigning both gods and men, cursed himself and his own head that he did not lead his troops, while reeking with blood from the victory at Cannae, to Rome.

After sixteen years, Italy was quit of Carthaginian forces.

The senate in Rome was not impressed with the Carthaginian ambassadors, who asked for a renewal of the treaty of Lutatius without even knowing its terms! Quintus Fulvius Gillo had conducted the Carthaginians to Rome and he and Laelius told the senate that Scipio had grounded his hopes of effecting a peace on Hannibal and Mago not being recalled from Italy, and since they had both been recalled to Carthage, it was clear that the proposal for a treaty was merely a ruse to buy time until their generals arrived. The Carthaginian ambassadors were dismissed and sent home.

The Carthaginians wasted little time before violating the truce that Scipio had declared. A convoy commanded by Cneius Octavius, while crossing over from Sicily with two hundred transports and thirty men-of-war ran into bad weather within sight of Africa. His ships were scattered and many of the transports were driven to Aegimurus, an island filling the mouth of the bay on which Carthage stands, the rest driven on shore directly opposite the city, near the warm baths. The Carthaginians had all the ships, which had been abandoned by their crews, towed to Carthage and their contents plundered.

Scipio sent three ambassadors, Lucius Baebius, Lucius Sergius and Lucius Fabius to remonstrate with the Carthaginians about this theft. The three narrowly escaped violence from the assembled multitude. On the way back they were set upon by three quadriremes dispatched by Hasdrubal and barely escaped with their lives.

Scipio declared and end to the truce and prepared for war.

Hannibal arrived at Adrudentum and, after allowing his men a few days to rest and recover from the voyage, he proceeded by forced marches to Zama, five days distant from Carthage.

Hannibal dispatched some spies to our camp, and these were intercepted by the guard and brought before Scipio. Everyone, including the terrified spies, expected that he would call upon the services of Appius Virginius, the executioner, but instead, he turned to me, and said, with a grin: "Lucius, give these men a tour of our camp. Let them inspect everything they wish to their complete satisfaction." When they were done, I brought them back and he asked them if they had found out everything they were sent here to discover. He then released them and sent them back to Hannibal. Hannibal could only surmise that Scipio was supremely confident about the outcome of the coming battle.

At this time we were also joined by Masinissa with 6000 infantry and 4000 horse.

Hannibal sent a message to Scipio requesting permission to confer with him. Upon Scipio's assent, both generals brought their camps forward in order to shorten the distance between them and facilitate the meeting. Scipio asked me to accompany him and record the proceedings. Each of the generals had with him an interpreter. I kept a copy of what was said at this meeting and years later I gave it to Gaius Laelius, with whom

I have maintained a friendly acquaintance for all these years. He was being interviewed by a Greek named Polybius, who had come to Rome as a hostage and was now writing a history of Rome. I have long since committed to memory everything that was said at this meeting between the two most brilliant generals or our time. The two sat for a time regarding each other in silence, then Hannibal spoke:

"Since fate has so ordained it, that I, who was the first to wage war upon the Romans, and who have so often had victory almost within my reach, should voluntarily come to sue for peace, I rejoice that it is you, above all others, from whom it is my lot to solicit it. To you, also, amid the many distinguished events of your life, it will not be esteemed one of the least glorious, that Hannibal, to whom the gods had so often granted victory over Roman generals, should have yielded to you: and that you should have put an end to this war, which has been remarkable by your calamities before it was by ours. In this, also, fortune would seem to have exhibited a disposition to sport with events, for it was when your father was consul that I first took up arms; he was the first Roman general with whom I engaged in a pitched battle, and it is with his son that I now come to solicit peace.

"It was indeed most to have been desired, that the gods should have put such dispositions in the minds of our fathers, that you should have been content with the empire of Italy and we with that of Africa: nor, indeed, even to you, are Sicily and Sardinia of sufficient value to compensate you for the loss of so many fleets, so many armies, so many and such distinguished generals. But what is past may be more easily censured than retrieved. In our attempts to acquire the possessions of others, we have been compelled to fight for our own; and not only have you had a war in Italy, and we in Africa, but you have beheld the standards and arms of your enemies almost at your gates and on your walls, and we now, from the walls of Carthage, distinctly hear the din of a Roman camp. Peace is proposed at a time when you have the advantage. We who negotiated it are persons whom it most concerns to obtain it, and we are the persons whose arrangements, be they what they will, our states will ratify. All we want is a disposition not adverse from peaceful counsels.

"As far as relates to myself, time, (for I am returning to that country an old man which I left as a boy) and prosperity, and adversity, have so schooled me, that I am more inclined to follow reason than fortune. But I fear your youth and uninterrupted good fortune, both of which are apt to inspire a degree of confidence ill comporting with pacific counsels. Rarely does a man consider the uncertainty of events whom fortune hath never deceived. What I was at Trasimenus and at Cannae, that you are this day.

"Invested with command when you had scarcely attained the military age, though all your enterprises were of the boldest description, in no instance has fortune deserted you. Avenging the death of your father and uncle, you have derived from the calamity of your house the high honor of distinguished valour and filial duty. You have recovered Spain, which had been lost, after driving thence three Carthaginian armies. When elected consul, though all others wanted courage to defend Italy, you crossed into Africa: where having cut to pieces two armies, having at once captured and burned two camps in the same hour, having made prisoner of Syphax, a most powerful king, and seized so many towns of his dominions and so many of ours, you have dragged me from Italy, the possession of which I had firmly held now for sixteen years.

"Your mind, I say, may possibly be more disposed to conquest than to peace. I know the spirits of your country aim rather at great than at useful objects. On me a similar fortune once shone. But if with prosperity the gods would also bestow sound judgment, we should not only consider those thing that have happened, but those also which might occur. Even if you forget all others, I am sufficient instance of every vicissitude of fortune. For me, whom a little while ago you saw advancing my standards to the walls of Rome, after pitching my camp between the Anio and your city, you now behold here, bereft of two brothers, men of consummate bravery, and most renowned generals, standing before the walls of my native city, which is all but besieged, and deprecating, in behalf of my own city, those severities with which I terrified yours.

"In all cases, the most prosperous fortune is not to be depended upon. While your affairs are in a favorable and ours in a dubious state, you would derive honor and splendor from granting peace, while to those who solicit it, it would be considered necessary rather than honorable. A certain peace is better than a victory in prospect; The former is at your disposal, the latter depends upon the gods. Do not place at the hazard of a single hour the successes of so many years. When you consider your own strength, than also place before your view the power of fortune, and the fluctuating nature of war. On both sides there will be arms, on both sides human bodies. In nothing less than war do events correspond to men's calculations. Should you be victorious in a battle, you will not add so much to that renown which you now have it in your power to acquire by granting peace, as you will detract from it if any adverse event should befall you. The chance of a single hour may at once overturn the honors you have acquired and those you anticipate. Everything is at your disposal in adjusting a peace, but in the other case you must be content with that fortune which the gods shall impose upon you.

"Formerly, in this same country, Marcus Atilius Regulus would have formed among the few instances of good fortune and valor, if, when victorious, he had granted a peace to our own fathers when they requested it, but by not setting any bounds to his success, and by not checking good fortune, which was elating him, he fell with a degree of ignominy proportioned to his elevation.

"It is indeed the right of him who grants, and not of him who solicits it, to dictate the terms of peace, but perhaps we may not be unworthy to impose upon ourselves the fine. We do not refuse that all those possessions on account of which the war was begun should be yours; Sicily, Sardinia, Spain, with all the Islands lying in any part of the sea between Africa and Italy. Let us Carthaginians, confined within their shores of Africa, behold you, since such is the pleasure of the gods, extending your empire over foreign nations, both by sea and land.

"I can not deny that you have reason to suspect the Carthaginian faith, in consequence of their insincerity lately in soliciting a peace while awaiting the decision. The sincerity of which a peace will be observed, depends much, Scipio, on the person by whom it is sought. Your senate, as I hear, refused to grant a peace in some measure because the deputies were deficient in respectability. It is I, Hannibal, who now solicit peace;, who would neither ask for it unless I believed it to be expedient, nor will I fail to observe it for the same reason of expedience on account of which I have solicited it. And the same manner as I, because the war was commenced by me, brought it to pass that no one regretted it until the gods began to regard me with displeasure, so will I also exert myself so that no one may regret the peace procured by my means."

I had to admit that Hannibal showed more respect and admiration for Publius Cornelius Scipio Africanus than ever his countryman Quintus Fabius Maximus had.

But Scipio replied as follows:

"I was aware that it was in consequence of the expectation of your arrival, that the Carthaginians violated the existing faith of the truce and broke off all hopes of a peace. Nor, indeed do you conceal the fact, inasmuch as you artfully withdraw from the former conditions of peace every concession except what relates to those things which have for a long time been in our power. It is incumbent upon me to endeavor that they may not receive, as a reward for their perfidy, the concessions which they formerly stipulated, by expunging them now from the conditions of peace. Though you do not deserve to be allowed the same conditions of peace as before, you now request even to be benefited by your treachery. Neither did our fathers make war respecting Sicily, nor we respecting Spain. In the former case the danger which threatened our allies, the Mamertines, and in the present, the destruction of Saguntum, girded us with just and pious arms. That you were the aggressors, both you yourselves confess, and the gods are witnesses, who determined the issue of the former war, and who are now determining and will determine the issue of the present according to right and justice.

"As to myself, I am not forgetful of the instability of human affairs, but consider the influence of fortune, and am well aware that all our measures are liable to a thousand casualties. But as I should acknowledge that my conduct would savor of insolence and oppression, if I rejected you on coming in person to solicit peace, before I crossed over to Africa, you voluntarily retiring from Italy, and after you had embarked your troops: so now, when I have dragged you into Africa by manual force, notwithstanding your resistance and evasion, I am not bound to treat you with any respect.

"Wherefore, in addition to those stipulations on which it was considered that a peace would at that time have been agreed upon, (and what they are you are informed), we must also propose a compensation for having seized our ships, together with their stores, during a truce, and for the violence offered our ambassadors. If you agree to such terms I shall than have matter to lay before my counsel. But if these things also appear oppressive, prepare for war, since you could not brook the conditions of peace."*22

No agreement could be reached and both generals returned to their armies to prepare for the coming battle. This would be the final battle in a war that had lasted for sixteen years, and would determine whether Rome or Carthage would give laws to the world.

Scipio called us to assembly and said "Bear in mind your past battles and fight like brave men worthy of yourselves and of your country. Keep it before your eyes that if you overcome your enemies, not only will you be unquestioned masters of Africa, but you will gain for yourselves and give your country undisputed command and sovereignty of the rest of the world. But if the result of the battle be otherwise, those who have fallen bravely will be forever shrouded in the glory of dying thus for their country, while those who save themselves by flight will spend the remainder of their lives in misery and disgrace. For no place in Africa will afford you safety, and if you fall into the hands of the Carthaginians it is plain enough to those who reflect what fate awaits you. May none of you, I pray, live to experience that fate.

"Now that fortune offers us the most glorious of prizes; how utterly craven, nay how foolish shall we be, if we reject the greatest of goods and choose the greatest of evils from mere love of life. Go, therefore to meet the foe with two objects before you, either victory or death. For men animated by such a spirit must always overcome their adversaries since they go into battle ready to throw their lives away."*23

Andor had volunteered his services to Scipio and I vouched for his fidelity. He was placed among the hastati (light armed, inexperienced troops) and I hoped that he would survive the battle.

Our forces consisted of 34,000 Roman infantry, 3000 Roman cavalry, and 6000 Numidian cavalry. Hannibal's consisted of 45,000 infantry of various nationalities, 6000 cavalry, Numidian and Carthaginian, and 80 elephants.

Scipio placed his troops in the usual formation with velites and hastati in the van, principes behind them and triarii in reserve. I was with Laelius and the Italian cavalry in the left wing, and Masinissa and the Numidian cavalry were in the right.

Of significant concern were Hannibal's elephants, which could seriously disrupt our ranks. Gaps were left between the maniples, allowing enough room for the elephants to pass through. To make this less obvious to Hannibal, velites were stationed in those gaps. The velites were instructed that upon the charge of the elephants, they should run into the ranks and get out of the way, affording passage to the elephants between the maniples.

Hannibal placed his elephants, eighty in number, in front, and behind these, his Ligurian and Gallic auxiliaries, intermixed with Balearians and Moors. In his second line he place the Carthaginians, Africans and a legion of Macedonians. Leaving a moderate interval he formed a reserve of Italian troops, consisting mostly of Bruttians. He placed his cavalry in the wings, with the Carthaginian occupying the right and the Numidian on the left.

The first thing Hannibal did was to unleash his elephants and send them charging toward our lines. We in the cavalry blew loud horns to frighten off the beasts and several of them charged back toward the Carthaginian lines. This so disordered the Carthaginian left wing that Masinissa charged it and was thereby lured off the field. The velites did as instructed and cleared a path for the elephants and they passed harmlessly through the Roman ranks to the rear, where they were destroyed. Our Roman cavalry, lead by Laelius and myself, charged the Carthaginian cavalry and were also lured away from the battle.

Our two centers then confronted each other and the Roman hastati pushed back Hannibal's first line. Hannibal now charged with his second line and the hastati were pushed back with serious losses. Scipio then reinforced the hastati with the second line of principes. These renewed the attack and defeated Hannibal's second line. Hannibal had kept his third line, his battle hardened veterans, in reserve, but once his first two lines had been eliminated, they were now pressed into service. Scipio reorganized his troops and sent them to meet with Hannibal's veterans, and heavy fighting ensued in which neither side had the advantage. In the mean time, the Carthaginian cavalry, which had lured our cavalry away from the battlefield, turned and attacked us, but in the end, we routed them and rode back to the battlefield to join the battle. Our arrival, and the return of Masinissa turned the tide of the battle as we attacked the Carthaginian infantry in the rear, and a great slaughter ensued. By this time we had long used up our projectile weapons and carried on the slaughter with our swords. Early on, I lost count of the number of enemy soldiers I slew, but this was the last day I ever had to kill anyone.

Victory was ours in the battle and in the war. On the Carthaginian side there were 20,000 killed and 20,000 made prisoner. 11,000 escaped, including Hannibal. Our own losses amounted to 2500 Romans and 3000 Numidians.

At the behest of Hannibal, the Carthaginians sent thirty ambassadors to Tunis, where Scipio had his camp, to sue for peace. Their pleas received little sympathy from Scipio and the other Roman notables who had come to take charge of affairs. But although there was a great desire to demolish Carthage, when they reflected upon the magnitude of the undertaking, and the length of time which would be consumed in a siege of so well fortified and strong a city, and Scipio himself being worried that his successor would have the glory of terminating the war, rather than himself, it was decided that the Carthaginians would be offered peace terms. The Carthaginian ambassadors were rebuked again and again for their perfidy, and warned that, instructed by so many disasters, they would at length believe in the existence of the gods, and the obligations of an oath. Then the Romans dictated the terms of peace, which the Carthaginians had no choice but to accept.

No more would the Carthaginians be enabled to make war outside of their own territory. At the behest of Scipio, the Carthaginians sent a delegation to Rome to plead that the treaty of peace be ratified. The senate decreed that Publius Scipio should make peace with the Carthaginian people on what terms he pleased. They sent two hundred Carthaginian prisoners back to Carthage from Rome, with instructions that, if peace were concluded, they should be released without ransom.

Upon conclusion of the peace, the Carthaginians delivered up their man of wars, their elephants, deserters, fugitives and four thousand Roman prisoners, including a senator, Quintus Tarentius Culleo. The ships were taken out into the harbor and burned. As for the deserters, those who were of the Latin Confederation were decapitated, while the Romans were crucified, as Scipio had long ago said he was inclined to do.

After the battle had ended I returned to our camp. I found Andor, wounded in two places by spears, but alive and in good spirits. I made sure that his wounds were attended to.

Several weeks after the battle, Andor and I sailed back to Italy with a convoy of Scipio's veterans. I had been away for nearly three years, and Silvia introduced me to our little daughter Aelia whose existence came as a complete surprise since I had not received word from home in all that time. I told her that I was now home to stay.

I went with Andor to visit Ala, and, to my surprise, she also presented me with a little daughter, of like age to Aelia, whom she called Erda. She had Ala's fair hair and green eyes. "Mine?" I asked. She nodded. She and Andor embraced and spent hours chattering away in Celtiberian. It was decided that he would stay with her until such time as I could arrange passage for him to Emporion.

I went to see Silvius with the notion in mind of getting employment with him as a trainer of horses, or as a manager of the stables, as he was getting on in years. He said "I was blessed with four wonderful daughters and no sons, Lucius, but I've always thought of you as my son and I would like to adopt you as my son and heir." I was astounded! "I would be honored and grateful, Silvius, because I've always thought of you almost as a father, and you were kinder to me than my actual father ever was!" So documents were drawn up and I became the heir and eventual paterfamilias of the Silvian family. I added the cognomen Silvius to my name. When Silvius got too old to manage the stables, I took charge of the business. Publius Cornelius Scipio Africanus arranged that each of his veteran soldiers receive two iugera of land from the ager publica for each year of service, which gave me thirty-two iugera in Apulia. On these I installed Brunius to homestead and raise and train horses. Brunius purchased the freedom of one of Silvius' slaves and married her. They have five children.

With the tacit consent of both Silvia and Ala, I remained a bigamist until such time as Silvia passed away after more than fifty years of marriage. My life has been tranquil since the end of the war and I have a large family with many grandchildren.

I wish I could say that Publius Cornelius Scipio Africanus passed the rest of his days in happiness and tranquility, but I can not. He had incurred the enmity of Marcus Porcius Cato, who yearly became more powerful and influential in Rome, and became consul and later censor. He brought charges of corruption against both Publius and Lucius Scipio, and although they were absolved by public acclaim, Publius was soured on public life and went into a bitter retirement at his estate at Litinum on the Campanian coast. He died in his early fifties. His sons, Publius and Lucius were men of no great accomplishment and both died without issue, but his daughters, especially the younger, Cornelia, the wife of Tiberius Gracchus, are greatly esteemed by the Roman people.

It was some six or seven years after the war ended that the most amazing thing occurred. One evening after I'd come home from the stable the servant announced that there was a man who wanted to see me. The man was about my age, tall, thin and ragged with a scraggly growth of beard, and was accompanied by a small, dark woman and two half grown children, a boy and a girl, all undernourished and poorly clad. The man looked vaguely familiar.

"I went to see Aunt Tullia" he said. "your half brother is paterfamilias, but he's not related to me and I didn't want to ask him for help. She said that perhaps you could help me. She says you have a kind heart."

"Enneas?" I said "Papa said you died at Trasimene!"

"I was in the cavalry. We escaped the battle but were surrounded the next day by Maharbal and his Numidians. He told us we'd be freed if we surrendered but instead he put us in chains and we were transported to Greece to be sold as slaves. I was a slave for twenty-one years, until Titus Flamininus came to negotiate an alliance with the Achaeans against Phillip of Macedon, and my master, who was one of the negotiating committee, volunteered to Flamininus that he had a Roman slave and offered to free us as a good-will gesture."

I brought them into the house and Silvia ordered the servants to bring them food and wine. It was such a shock that I began to weep. Tears I had been holding back for years suddenly poured from my eyes. Enneas looked alarmed. "Please don't . . ." he said "I came to you for your help, not for your pity."

"I'm sorry." I said. "I never got the chance to weep for you or Gaius. There was just too much happening at the time."

"Perhaps Marcus Porcius Cato was right" I thought to myself. "I might benefit by studying the Stoics." Enneas needed no such instruction. Even Cato would have admired his stoicism.

"Aunt Tullia said that Gaius died at Cannae. I never knew." said Enneas. "The Greeks said I must be a Trojan, on account of my name. Just to defy them I gave my children Trojan names: Hector and Andromache."

"Of course I'll help you." I said. "What would you like me to do?"

"I only want employment." He said "If I could have work at your stable, a room and whatever you can pay me. My wife Efigenia is a good seamstress. Together we might make enough to feed ourselves."

"Of course." I said. "And I know someone who will help Efigenia sell her clothing."

I installed them in Brunius' old cottage, and hired Manlius, Ala's lame bookkeeper, to tutor Efigenia and the children in Latin. Hector, whom we called Ectorius, in the Roman fashion, had an ambition to become a military tribune so I trained him in horsemanship and had him go with my son Titus to the Campus Martius to train with weapons. Enneas still bore the stigmata of slavery-scarred wrists and ankles from the chafing of irons, and stripes on his back from floggings, but his manner was sober and dignified and one could tell that he came from a good family of Romans of the first class. Eventually, when Brunius got too old to run the horse farm by himself, I sent Enneas there to assist him. With my permission he raised a herd of sheep on the land and became reasonably prosperous.

Enneas never wore the cap of liberty that is customarily worn by freed slaves. He was, unquestionably, a free born Roman citizen and enslavement in Greece didn't change that. It was the senator, Quintus Tarentius Culleo, freed from long captivity in Carthage, who insisted upon wearing the cap of liberty the rest of his days. It was his way of paying homage to the man to whom he owed his liberty: Publius Cornelius Scipio Africanus.

I have maintained a friendship with Gaius Laelius, and whenever he arranges a gathering of old Punic war veterans, he invites me. We eat and drink and tell stories all through the evening. Recently these gatherings have been attended by a Greek hostage named Polybius, a well educated man, who tutors the sons of Aemilius Paullus. Polybius seems to have an insatiable curiosity about all things Roman and has the intention of writing a history of Rome. Laelius has asked me to sit with him when he talks to Polybius so that I can remind him of things he might leave out in his accounts of the war. We still laugh about what happened to me at the Sucro mutiny (although it didn't seem funny at the time) but I've asked Polybius to please not put that in his book!

My sons, influenced by their mother, and with my tacit consent, declined to become soldiers and have now taken over from me the management of the stables. My three daughters by Silvia all married men of our own class, and my daughter by Ala helps her mother in the jewelry business, which she will inherit. She is married to a Celtiberian immigrant and has four children.

A man of means and leisure now, I often go to the forum and listen to the political discourse. Frequently Marcus Porcius Cato addresses the senate and people, discoursing on the decline of Roman morality, the corruption of the youth, and the need for strong laws to prevent waste and fraud, on the perils of adopting the decadent ways of the Greeks, or on the means by which Rome might improve its agriculture. But whatever the subject of his oration, he always ends it with the proclamation "Delenda est Carthago!" (Carthage must be destroyed!)

CAPTIVUS

What would I say is the worst thing about being a slave? Some would say it's the experience of being flogged. Others would say it's the deprivation of food and other comforts. Others would say it's the experience of being chained when transported from one place of servitude to another. Many would say it's the low status of your condition, and the disdain with which free men regard you, and if you were born a free man, as I was, this loss of status is particularly painful. Then there is the threat of sexual assault by those who have power over you, an experience that I avoided only by credible threats of suicide. No, slavery is not a happy condition, and I really don't blame those of us who took their own lives to avoid it. Unfortunately, nature makes suicide difficult, and at the tender age of seventeen, I, Enneus Tullius, was not up to the task.

But getting back to the question, for me, the worst thing about my situation was being completely deprived of learning and knowledge. I was born with an insatiable curiosity, an unquenchable thirst for knowledge that impelled me to become a voracious reader. I grew up in a prosperous Roman family of equestrian status, the class of plebeians just below the patricians. My father was a client of one of the important men of the gens Livius. This man, Tiberius Servilius Livius had a client who was a freed Greek slave, and who tutored Livius' sons and nephews. My father somehow obtained permission for me and my brother Gaius to study under this tutor. The man had taken the name Livius as his cognomen, as is the custom among freed slaves and his Greek name was Andronicus. Livius Andronicus was the first person to translate the Iliad and the Odyssey from Greek into

Latin. Under his tutelage I memorized pretty much the entire texts of both books. Livius Andronicus also had a modest library which contained works of history by Herodotus and Thucydides, and works of philosophy by Plato, Aristotle and others and he encouraged my bent for learning and allowed me to borrow any books I wanted. I'm sure, that by the time I took on the toga virilis, I had devoured every book in his library.

My father would not permit me to neglect my military training, however. Once Gaius and I reached puberty, we were sent to the Campus Martius nearly every day to be trained as soldiers. I never questioned the necessity of training for war, as I knew that the normal state of affairs in Rome was war on one or more fronts. Often when we would go to the Campus Martius, Gaius and I would run into our cousin Lucius. Lucius was a year older than I and was far more diligent in his pursuit of martial excellence than either Gaius or myself. While Gaius and I trained with the younger boys, Lucius had the privilege of training under the guidance of Publius Cornelius Scipio, the sixteen year old nephew of the Consul Cneius Cornelius Scipio. Lucius also had the advantage of having been married at a very young age to the daughter of a stable owner, and he had access to the best horses and the best training in horsemanship available in Rome.

One day as we were leaving the Campus Martius, we ran into cousin Lucius and he greeted us with a grin. "Why don't you two come to my father-in-law's stable in Subura tomorrow and we'll teach you to ride. It's a lot more fun than drilling here on the Campus Martius and no one could possibly object to your learning a new skill. I'm learning to hurl pila and javelins from horseback!" Gratified by his generosity, we eagerly accepted his offer and showed up at the stables the next day. He was right, riding horses was a lot more fun than drilling. He arranged with his father-in-law to allow us to train with him twice a week and we looked forward eagerly to those sessions. But we never came close to matching Lucius in his skill with horses or at throwing weapons.

I envied cousin Lucius, not only for his martial abilities but also for his easy-going personality and his happy marriage. He seemed to consistently have the favor of the goddess Fortuna. I, on the other hand, was definitely no favorite of that goddess. Father had arranged marriages for both Gaius and I with two sisters who were daughters of Marcus Aurelius, another client of the Livius family. I had never met the girls, who would not be of marriageable age for several more years. Of course, as events transpired, there would be no such marriages for either Gaius or myself.

The first of a series of misfortunes took place when I was fifteen: the death of my father. It started with an intense pain on his right side. He took to his bed, vomiting frequently and unable to eat. After a few days the pain eased, but he had developed a high fever and was clearly dying. He called Gaius and myself to his sickbed. "Enneus" he said "Livius' Greek physician came to see me but he says he can't help me. A piece of the gut has burst and released its poison. I will die soon. You, my son, are now the man of the house. I give to you all of my worldly goods and the responsibility for the welfare of your mother and brother. I am sorry to leave you with these burdens." His breathing was labored and he could say no more. I took his hand and sat with him until I could no longer stay awake. He died the next day.

Mother seemed to age twenty years in an instant. She was paralyzed with grief. I had no experience with funerals and scarcely knew what to do. Fortunately, Papa's sister Tullia came to our aid. She was the mother of Lucius, and she got her husband, Titus Licinius Varro to make the funeral arrangements. He knew all about funerals since he was in the business of providing funerary monuments. Traditionally it is the duty of the eldest son to give the eulogy for the father, but at my age and in my present emotional state I was not capable of a good performance so I deferred to Uncle Titus and to Tiberius Livius, both of whom gave creditable eulogies. We buried Papa in the Tullius family plot, and uncle Titus provided a suitable monument for the grave site.

War began the following year. The Carthaginian general Hannibal attacked and destroyed the city of Saguntum, a Roman ally, in Hispania, and the Roman senate declared war on Carthage. The centuries elected Publius Cornelius Scipio, brother of the above-mentioned Cneius Cornelius Scipio and father of young Publius Cornelius Scipio to be consul, along with Tiberius Sempronius. Cousin Lucius was recruited to the cavalry of consul Scipio and soon boarded a transport to Massilia. Massilia is a seaport in southern Gaul. It was founded by Greeks. The Gauls, of course, are not civilized and thus, they have no cities. I was still too young to enlist in a legion, but, at Lucius' request, his father-in-law, Silvius, allowed Gaius and myself to continue training at his stable.

After a few months we got word that the Carthaginian general Hannibal had crossed the Alps and had invaded Italy with a force of some 40,000 foot soldiers and 8000 cavalry. He had, in addition, recruited soldiers from some of the tribes in the north, the Cis-Alpine Gauls and the Ligurians. The Consul Publius Cornelius Scipio had returned by ship from Southern Gaul to hastily recruit an army of Romans and allies to meet him. Most of Scipio's own forces, including, apparently, my Cousin Lucius, had gone on to Hispania with Publius Scipio's brother Cneius. Unfortunately, Scipio's new recruits were relatively inexperienced, and, when the two armies met at the Ticinus River, Hannibal got the better of them and they were routed. Consul Scipio himself was badly wounded and escaped with his life only because his son, young Publius Cornelius Scipio led a charge through Carthaginian lines to rescue his father. Consul Scipio managed to retreat with his forces to Placentia, but the next night the Roman camp was attacked by a force of 2200 allied Gauls who had decided to join forces with Hannibal and they invaded the camp at night and took heads of sleeping soldiers and brought them to Hannibal who received both the Gauls and the severed heads joyfully. Learning of these events, Scipio did not wait until dawn but retreated with his forces southward along the Trebia river.

The Roman senate summoned the other consul, Tiberius Sempronius Longus from Sicily to join forces with Scipio. The battle of Ticinus had taken place in November, and by the time that Sempronius arrived in the vicinity of Placentia it was already December, and the weather had turned intensely cold. Scipio opposed an immediate engagement with Hannibal, telling Sempronius that his troops should take the winter to train and drill. Sempronius was having none of it. He was eager to engage Hannibal and gain credit for saving Rome. Unfortunately, he was not aware that, as a general, he was completely outclassed by his opponent! The Roman and Carthaginian camps were on opposite sides of the Trebia River. Hannibal sent his Numidian cavalry early in the morning to attack and harass the Romans in their camp. Sempronius ordered his unfed troops to pursue the Numidians across the frigid river. They waded into the river and the chill penetrated to their bones. Barely able to hurl their weapons, they were easy prey for the Carthaginians. What is more, Hannibal had sent his brother Mago with 1000 cavalry and 1000 infantry to set an ambush for Sempronius' troops in the territory between the river and the Carthaginian camp. By day's end there were close to 30,000 Roman and allied losses.

In the elections held at the beginning of the following year, Gneius Servilius Geminus and Gaius Flaminius were elected consuls. Flaminius was a plebeian like myself, and considered a "new man"-that is, an upstart. In his political career he had proposed and supported various measures which were unpopular with the patricians and popular with the common people. He declined to follow the usual practice of taking auspices at his inauguration as Consul. Now, I can not truthfully say whether this impiety actually affected the events that followed, but it did have the effect of making many Romans, including many of the common soldiers, anxious, and thus adversely affected our morale.

I turned seventeen in the winter of that year, and was now eligible to be inducted into the Roman army. In normal times, as head of the household, I might have been able to decline the honor, but these were not normal times. Rome was under serious military threat, and every able-bodied free male between the ages of seventeen and forty-five was liable for service. Facing the inevitable, I continued to go to the Campus Martius to train. Young Publius Cornelius Scipio had returned to Rome and was busily recruiting. He approached me one day in March. "You're Lucius Tullius Varro's cousin, aren't you?" he asked. When I told him I was, he said "I have Lucius sending me reports from Hispania. I just received one recently, so if you see his family you can tell them that he is alive and well."

"Thank you" I said "I will."

"I understand that Lucius' father-in-law has permitted you and your brother to train to ride horses at his stables." he continued "How is that going?"

"I'll never be a good as Lucius." I said. I felt that my modesty was fully justified.

"Few men are." he said "But at this point we need every reasonably competent horseman we can get. I think you would be fine for Consul Flaminius' cavalry."

There was no way that I could say no to young Scipio, and two weeks later I found myself on my way to Arretium, where Flaminius had his camp. The worst part was saying farewell to my Mother and my brother Gaius. Mama, who had so lately lost her husband, was inconsolable. In all honesty, I could not even promise her that I would be back. I felt that my chances of dying in the coming battle with Hannibal were greater than my chances of surviving it. "I'm sorry, Mama" I said "but I have no choice. Hannibal must be stopped or he will destroy Rome." I embraced her and kissed her cheeks. "Gaius," I said "Take care of Mother. If we defeat Hannibal, perhaps you won't have to go." Gaius and I had been inseparable all of our lives and we needed no further words. I turned to go. I would never see either of them again.

Silvius, Cousin Lucius' father-in-law provided me with a horse, which was paid for by the public treasury, as is customary for equites who are recruited to the Roman cavalry. I joined about a dozen other young recruits and we rode off to Arretium.

I was housed with in a tent with seven other young equites in the cavalry section of Flaminius' camp.

It seemed that Hannibal had marched his forces through marshland from Cis-Alpine Gaul to Etruria and was camped at the edge of the marsh not too far distant from our camp at Arretium. Hannibal's troops were ravaging and plundering the land all around. Even from the camp you could see fires in the distance where farms and settlements were being burned. Etruria is a rich land and Hannibal was able to feed his troops quite well from the plunder. Flaminius, of course, was enraged, and he feared censure for allowing Hannibal to ravage the territory he had been sent to protect. He was eager to bring the invader to battle. Some of his officers tried to restrain him, reminding him that the Carthaginians were superior in cavalry and that he should at least wait until the other consul, Gaius Servilius Geminus, could arrive and join forces with us. Gaius Flaminius would not be deterred.

It was the day of the Summer solstice that Flaminius led us right into Hannibal's trap. Hannibal was marching his forces toward Rome, keeping the city of Cortuna and its hills on his left and Lake Trasimene on his right, devastating the countryside as he moved. We followed in pursuit. The road passed through a narrow and level valley enclosed on both sides by an unbroken line of lofty hills. At the eastern end of this defile rose a steep eminence with sheer slopes which were difficult to climb, and at the western end lay lake Trasimene, from which the only access to the valley was a narrow passage which ran along the foot of the hillside. During the night, Hannibal made his troop dispositions in preparation for an ambush. Hannibal himself occupied the hill at the eastern end of the valley with his African and Spanish troops, he posted his Balearian slingers and his pike men at the right end of the valley, and his Celts and cavalry at the left end of the valley.

I was in the vanguard with a detachment of horse. Suddenly we were attacked on all sides! The fog was so heavy we could hardly see ahead of us but we charged forward and after heavy fighting we managed to break through the Carthaginian lines. I quickly used up my pila and javelins. I believe I killed or wounded at least two of the enemy. After that, I had only my sword and I used it to fight my way through the enemy lines. After several hours some 6000 of us managed to reach the hills at the east end of the valley. The fog had lifted and we could see the devastation below. The valley below was littered with dead and dying Roman soldiers. It was clear that the Carthaginians had destroyed most of our forces. Returning back to the valley would be futile and suicidal. We rode eastward and took refuge in nearby Etruscan village.

The next day Hannibal's Numidian cavalry, under his general Maharbal, surrounded the village. Our highest ranked officer was Marcus Trebonius Mancinus and Maharbal sent a delegation including an interpreter to confer with him. Maharbal offered that if we surrendered and disarmed, he would allow us to depart with a single garment. We knew that we were in a hopeless situation and we didn't want to endanger the lives of the villagers, so we accepted what we could only consider to be a generous offer. We filed out of the village and we each laid our weapons on one pile and our armor on another. Maharbal's men would no doubt make good use of the spolia. We were dressed only in our military tunics. We were marched under guard to the Carthaginian camp. As we passed back through the valley we saw thousands of Roman corpses which were already beginning to stink. It was fortunate that my stomach was empty or I would have heaved up its contents.

The next day, Hannibal assembled all of the prisoners. There were some fifteen thousand of us. He announced that Maharbal had not been authorized to make an agreement with us to let us go with a single garment and that he would not abide by any such agreement. He said that any soldiers among us who belonged to the Latin confederacy or other such alliance would be freed without ransom. He said he was not here to oppress the Italians, his only quarrel was with Rome itself, and that allied troops should return to their homes and tell their countrymen of the generosity of Hannibal and persuade them to make alliance with him. If they did that, then they might spare themselves the devastation that they had lately witnessed in Etruria. Those of us who were Roman citizens would be sold into slavery. The interpreter added that since Carthage had no wish to import a large number of Roman soldiers to their own territory because even as slaves such a population could cause problems, Hannibal had arranged with Greek slave traders to transport us to Greece and sell us there. That was at least some small consolation to me since I at least could speak some Greek but didn't know a word of the Carthaginian tongue.

It didn't come as a great surprise to any of us that the Carthaginians went back on their word after promising to release us with a single garment if we surrendered. Among Romans the failure to keep one's word is considered a distinctly Carthaginian trait and is known as "Punic faith."

We Roman prisoners were put in chains and we were grudgingly fed one bowl of porridge a day. The highest ranked among us, Mancinus, was only a military tribune so there were no important prisoners. We learned that Flaminius had been slain in the battle. Hannibal had no wish to spare us more food than he absolutely had to, and no wish to slow his movements by transporting thousands of prisoners, so it was only a few days before he turned us over to his Greek buyers and we were marched in a column to the Adriatic sea. Try marching for a week with your wrists and ankles in chains. I bear the scars from the chafing of iron to this day. Those of us who fell faint due to hunger and illness were quickly dispatched with an ax blow to the scull. Our captors would not leave a live person behind even if he were obviously sick, for fear that that would encourage malingerers to fain illness to avoid their fate. The Greeks were at least a little more generous with the food than Hannibal. We were fed twice a day.

We were taken to a small seaport at the mouth of the Metaurus river. Over the course of the next few weeks we were loaded, a few hundred at a time, onto transport barges. We were kept below deck in the hold, chained to benches. The smell was indescribable. The journey to Megalopolis took about a week. I had never been at sea before and was seasick for the first few days, unable to keep food down. I thought I might die, but somehow I did not. Everyday some of the weaker prisoners did die and their bodies were removed from the hold and unceremoniously tossed overboard.

As the name may imply, Megalopolis is a big city, and it belongs to the Achaean League, a group of Greek city-states to the north and west of the Peloponnese. We were housed in sheds in the vicinity of the slave market which was situated near the harbor. We were kept in chains and guarded by spear men.

After our ordeal we were gaunt and ill. The slave traders evidently wanted to improve our appearance so they fed us decently and gave us clean robes of the Greek style. At intervals we were taken to a bath house and allowed to bathe. It was only after a few weeks of such treatment that we were taken out to the public area of the slave market and put on display.

When a prospective buyer wanted to examine us we were forced to disrobe. I found this appalling and refused to look at anyone on these occasions. I probably looked sullen. In any case, I was not immediately purchased. One day a man came by and examined me. I just stared off into space. At seventeen I had still not grown a beard and the man said "The Romans must be in a bad way indeed if they're recruiting children for their cavalry!" Then he asked the dealer "How much do you want for this one?"

The slave dealer knew that the man was a brothel owner in a nearby town and he said "I don't recommend him for you. The Romans, even the young ones, are not suitable for your type of work. I sold one of them to a brothel in town and he strangled his first customer and then hanged himself.

When nobody emerged from the room after a few hours the owner opened the door and saw for himself the whole horrible scene! After that, none of the brothel owners will purchase a Roman."

The story cheered me and I smiled. Seeing this, the slave dealer said "You speak Greek, young man? Why do you smile at such a tragedy?"

"What tragedy?" I asked "The customer got exactly what was coming to him and the Roman boy did the only honorable thing!"

"Insolent pup!" said the slave dealer, and he boxed my ears.

"So this is what you advertise as a placid man?" said the brothel owner. "I don't think I want to meet any of your fierce ones!"

After being thus punished for my insolence I was not inclined to ask the slave dealer how it was that he thought that a soldier who had recently slain half a dozen foe men in battle might be described as placid. I suppose that, disarmed and shackled, I did not appear to be a threat to anyone.

I think that the brothel owner must have spread the story around because weeks went by and I was not purchased. I had acquired the reputation of being sullen and anti-social. But one day the slave dealer said to me "Well, young Roman, we have found a place for you on a large estate to the south of here. The owner is an influential politician in the league. He'll be sending his man with a wagon tomorrow to transport you to the estate."

The next day, early in the morning, the overseer Nicander and his son Menander came to get me. I was loaded, still fettered, onto a wagon drawn by two horses. The trip to the estate took all day. When we got there it was getting dark so they gave me a meal of bread and porridge and allowed me to relieve myself and put me in a hut with a few other slaves. I was the only one among them who was fettered. I wondered when they would remove the chains.

The next day I was summoned to see the overseer. "Do you understand my speech, Roman?" he asked.

"Yes, Kyrios" I replied.

"I am not Kyrios" he said "I am only the overseer. You may call me Nicander. You will meet Kyrios in a few days. Right now I just want to be sure that you understand a few things. Firstly, you must do whatever you are told. If you disobey you will be flogged. Do you understand?"

"Yes, Nicander." I said.

"Secondly, If you try to escape you will be flogged." he said "Do you understand that?"

"Yes, Nicander." I replied.

"Our shepherd has died and you have been purchased to replace him." Nicander said "Do you know anything about sheep?"

"No, Nicander," I said "I was raised in a city."

"Then Chiron and his sons will teach you." he said "and you had best learn quickly because we count the sheep every evening and if any are missing it's ten lashes."

I stared at him in horror. As little as I knew about sheep, I did know that they had a tendency to wander off. Seeing my expression he said "You're a slave now, Roman. You'll just have to learn to endure the whip like all slaves do from time to time. If we didn't flog the shepherd for losing sheep the sheep would soon all be stolen and eaten. What shall we call you?"

I was so shaken I could barely reply "My. . . my . . . my name is Enneus."

He laughed "Aeneus! Why that's a Trojan name! You must be a Trojan!"

"Yes," I said "It is said that we Romans are descended of the Trojans."

"Very well, Trojan." said Nicander "We will remove your chains now. Tomorrow Chiron will introduce you to the sheep." He took off my chains. "Menander" he said to his son. "Escort Trojan here to his hut." The shepherd's hut was located out by the sheep enclosure, some distance from where the overseer and most of the other slaves were housed. It was a very small hut but I had it to myself. I was at last unchained after some three months but my wrists and ankles now bore the scars which would easily identify me for the rest of my life as either a slave, or at best, a freedman.

The next day I met Chiron and his oldest son, Myron. He appeared to be about fifty and the boy appeared to be about fifteen. He explained the daily routine for the sheep. "The sheep are taken up to the pasture to feed everyday. Your job is simply to bring them up there, watch them so that they don't wander off and then bring them back to the pen before nightfall. When sheep graze, they pretty much denude the pasture so we can't bring them to the same pasture for more than a few weeks. Once a pasture is used up you will have to take them to a different pasture until the vegetation in the first one grows back. Every year, around late Spring we shear the sheep to harvest the wool. You will also have to learn to do that. The rutting season is over for this year, but next year you will learn how to deal with the ewes and lambs."

Chiron seemed not to experience the slighted distress over his enslaved condition, which led me to believe that he had been born a slave. "How do they treat people on this estate?" I asked him.

"They treat me well enough." he said "But I'm in a different situation from you. I'm a voluntary."

"A voluntary?" I asked "What do you mean."

"I was born a Helot in Lacedaemonia." he replied. "You may not know anything about how Sparta treats its Helots, but all Greeks are aware that we are treated with great cruelty. I had a dispute with the Spartans and ran off years ago. I came here and volunteered my services on condition that they do not send me back. Kyrios has no great love for the Spartans so he agreed to the deal. But I can leave whenever I wish. I've made myself so useful here that no one ever gives me any trouble. I mend fences, keep up the pens, build huts and do anything else that needs to be done on this estate.

"You, on the other hand, are an involuntary." he continued "You are subject to flogging if you disobey or try to escape, and I suggest that you pay careful attention to me when I tell you how to keep the sheep safe, because you will be flogged if you lose one."

Kyrios was mostly an absentee landlord who preferred living in Megalopolis. He was involved in the politics of the Achaean League and this absorbed much of his time. It was several weeks before he came to visit his estate, but when he did, he requested to meet the new shepherd so I was summoned to his villa to meet him.

"Philophides the slave dealer tells me you speak Greek, young man. Is that so?" He asked me.

"I read it better than I speak it, I'm afraid." I replied.

"Why would a Roman boy want to learn to read Greek?" he asked, clearly surprised by my answer.

"Well, Rome has almost no literature of its own, so if we want to learn anything or have anything to read, we have to borrow from the Greeks." I replied.

"So you're a scholar?" He asked.

"If not for this war." I replied.

"A pity" he said "I need a shepherd, not a scholar, and if I did need a scholar I would certainly employ a Greek scholar in preference to a Roman."

"Yes, Kyrios" I replied.

"Philophides also says that Roman soldiers make good slaves because they are taught strict obedience and discipline from a very early age." he said.

I was not about to rise to the bait. I just said "If you say so, Kyrios."

"Philophides also says that you're insolent and that is why he had such difficulty placing you." He said.

"Yes Kyrios."

"And do you think a slave ought to be insolent, young man?" he asked.

"I don't think your sheep will much care." I replied.

He laughed heartily. "You really are an insolent fellow!" he said. "But you're right, the sheep won't care. That's why the best situation for you is to be a shepherd on an estate like this one. Very well, you'll do. You may go now."

Kyrios seemed like a reasonable person. Kyrios actually was a reasonable person. I had no reason to resent or hate him. He was just what he was in the scheme of things. A soldier captured in war can expect one of three things, to be ransomed (rare), to be slain, or to be sold into slavery. That's just the way it is. I could blame Hannibal or I could blame Flaminius for my plight, but I had no way to take revenge on either of them.

The only way out of this situation that I could see was suicide. And I did give the idea quite a bit of thought. But I only came close to doing it one night when Nicander got a little drunk and invited me to dine with him. I did not dare disobey him and I went to his hut. He started asking me questions that made me uncomfortable. Was I married? Had I ever been intimate with a girl? With a boy? He plied me with wine. Not the watered down swill which slaves usually drank, but strong wine. Finally, when he expressed a desire to see my private parts I said "Nicander, I am not a catamite, and I know how to write Greek well enough to write a suicide note." Inebriated as he was he got my gist and left me alone after that. Like Kyrios, Nicander was just part of the scheme of things and I bore him no resentment.

For the first month or two that I was on the estate Chiron taught me all he could about herding sheep. He was usually accompanied by one of his sons. After a time he became too busy doing other chores to accompany me to the pastures, but even then one of his sons would usually come along to help me. Myron was friendly enough. He was full of questions about Rome and its customs and was impressed that I had been a soldier and had been in a war. He said that someday he would like to join the Achaean military forces under Philopoeman and perhaps fight the Spartans who had so oppressed his family. But I told him that he was lucky to have a choice as to whether to join the military or not. I hadn't had any choice and that if I were him I would stay out of the military. "Battle," I told him "is not a pleasant experience in the least, and you're very likely to get seriously wounded or killed."

It was only after several months that they thought I could handle the flock on my own. Life settled into a routine. I would rise early and breakfast on a porridge made of barley or wheat. I would pack a lunch of flat bread and cheese to eat later in the day when I got hungry. I would go to the pen and persuade the sheep to come out and then lead them up to one of the pastures. It was usually a walk of an hour or two before we reached a suitable site. In late afternoon, as indicated by the position of the sun, I would herd the sheep back to their pen. My needs in terms of food and clothing were seen to by the female slaves on the estate, primarily by Chiron's wife in those days. When Winter came she gave me a sheepskin cloak that she had made for me. She was skilled at sewing, weaving, spinning and knitting and she taught these skills to her daughters.

For a couple of years I had no great difficulties. Life was boring but tolerable. I would keep my mind active by reciting poetry to myself. Sometimes I would wonder what was happening in Rome, how my Mother and brother were faring, and whether Rome would be victorious in the war, but there was no way for me to find out any of these things and I concerned myself with them less and less as time went on.

One day, however, a most unwelcome excitement came into my life. A wolf came out of nowhere and attacked one of the sheep. I picked up a rock and threw it at the beast, than another and another, but I did not land a decisive blow and the wolf dragged off the still bleating young lamb. I took the flock back to the pen and reported the loss to Nicander.

He frowned and said "That will be ten lashes, Trojan"

"But Nicander." I said "It wasn't my fault! The wolf . . . ."

"You know the penalty for losing a sheep, Trojan." he said "Next time you'll keep on top of it."

Nicander's son, Menander, led me toward the hut where the flogging would take place. "Don't resist me, Trojan, or it will be much worse for you. I'm sorry but I can't go easy on you. I will have to leave welts to prove my handy work." he said. He ordered me to strip down to my loin cloth, then he bound my wrists to a post and proceeded to scourge my back with a rawhide thong. I had resolved not to cry out, but after the first few lashes I just couldn't help myself.

My back now confirmed what my ankles and wrists had already proclaimed: that I was a slave. It was only now that I fully understood all the implications of my situation. Only slaves are flogged, so I definitely must be a slave!

Menander released me and I picked up my tunic. I couldn't put it back on because my back was oozing blood and I didn't want to get it bloody, so I had to walk back to my hut dressed in only my loincloth. I had to endure the pitying glances of the other slaves. I probably looked sullen and resentful, which may in part account for the events that followed. When I got back to my hut I lay down on my stomach. I knew I ought to be hungry, but I wasn't. I wondered if I would be fit to work the next day, and if the wolf would be back, and what I would do if he were. I reasoned that if a wolf were successful at dragging off a sheep, it would come back every day and I would have to endure daily floggings! I wondered if that was what had caused the previous shepherd to die.

I resolved that I would take the sheep in the opposite direction the next day and at least put some distance between the flock and the wolf. I also resolved that I would kill the wolf. How would I kill the wolf? Obviously my attempt with rocks was not effective. I just did not have good enough aim. I had never learned how to use a sling like the soldiers of the Belearis Islands, so I would have to make a spear. I had been taught in my military training how to make spears. Roman weapons are generally tipped with iron, but even if iron were not available, certain hard stones such as flint, obsidian, and chert could be used. I suppose I could have asked Aristides the blacksmith to make me some iron points, but he was a mean drunkard and I didn't really like him. I borrowed a knife and an ax from Myron and when I had gotten the sheep up to suitable pasture I looked around for branches which would be good material for a spear shaft. I also looked for stones that might be used for the points, and I found some good flint. I spent much of my time the next few days carving my shafts and knapping my flint and I fashioned myself several good spears. I made no secret of what I was doing and, naively, I carried my spears around with me as I went about my work of herding the sheep. I practiced throwing the spears at a target just as I had years ago on the Campus Martius. I was pretty confident that the next time the wolf made its appearance it would fall prey to my spear.

It came as a complete shock to me when three rather burly spear men approached me while I was up in the pasture with the sheep. They had Myron in tow. "Roman," they said. "Put those spears down and come with us. Myron will attend to the sheep." They escorted me back down to the estate and brought me before Nicander.

"Trojan" he said "It is a capital crime for a slave to have weapons."

"But . . . . but . . . ." I was at a complete loss for words.

"I understand that you are angry about your punishment the other day, but you've gone to extremes. Now you will have to be executed." He said.

"Very well then." I said "please make it quick!" I started to remove my tunic so it wouldn't be bloodied. I assumed that they would spear me through the heart.

"Not so quick" said Nicander. "We can't destroy Kyrios' property without his permission and he won't be back from Megalopolis for a few weeks, so you will have to be kept in chains until he gets back."

The took me to the same hut where I had been flogged a few days before, and chained me to the post. Chiron's wife or one of their children would bring me food twice a day and empty the container with my bodily wastes. "I'm sorry" said Myron, who brought me food one evening after he had returned from the pasture with the sheep. "I should have asked you why you wanted the knife and ax and advised you against it. Nicander would jump to the wrong conclusion."

"Not your fault, Myron," I said "and if I'm going to be flogged every time a wolf eats one of the sheep, and am not even permitted to kill the wolf with a spear, don't you think I'll be better off dead?"

"It isn't right, Enneas" he said "It isn't right!"

"Well, we can't do anything about it, can we?" I said.

One morning it was Ephigenia, Chiron's daughter, who brought me food. She was a solemn-looking child of about nine or ten and had olive skin and large brown eyes. "Mama isn't feeling well and the boys are all working now so she sent me with the food."

"Thank you, Ephigenia" I said.

"Mama and Papa feel sorry for you" she said, with a child's frankness.

"That's kind of them Ephigenia, but there's not much that can be done." I said "The goddess Fortuna is not on my side."

"Is that a Roman goddess?" she asked.

"Yes" I replied.

"Well, maybe you need a Greek goddess." She suggested. "I will make an offering to the goddess Artemis for you and maybe she can persuade your Roman goddess to kindness."

"Thank you" I said, "But what do you have to offer Artemis?"

"Oh, I'll find something." she replied.

Somehow the child's good-heartedness cheered me and after I ate I lay down to sleep and had good dreams.

I had been in this confinement for more than three weeks when Menander and his henchmen came in dragging a miserable whining creature who was begging for mercy. Menander unfastened me from the post and said "Move out of the way, Trojan." I crawled to the edge of the hut, as far from the post as I could get. Then Menander bound the wretch to the post and scored the man's back with more enthusiasm than he had mine. Loud screams filled the hut. I gritted my teeth and shut my eyes, but there was no way to shut out the screams and in my present distempered state they made me shudder. I don't know why, but sometimes being in the presence of such extreme brutality feels almost as unpleasant as being the recipient of it. I was appalled that Menander would have the satisfaction of seeing my distress, but I could not control my reaction. I was trembling and gasping for breath.

Finally it was all over and Menander admonished the man "That will teach you to steal! Now get back to work!" One of Menander's assistants lead the wretch from the hut.

"Alright, Trojan, come back here." I move back toward the post and he refastened the chains. Then he said "Kyrios will be back tomorrow or the next day and your execution will end your misery. My father thinks you intended to kill both him and me with those spears. Is that so?"

"No, Menander" I said "I intended to kill the wolf that was eating the sheep."

"Well," said Menander "maybe Kyrios will believe that, and maybe he won't."

A few days later Nicander and his son took me from the hut and brought me, still in chains, to see Kyrios. As they marched me up to Kyrios' villa they conversed as though I was not there to hear them.

"How shall we slay this man, Father?" asked Menander.

"The usual execution of a slave is by hanging or strangulation." Nicander replied.

"I've never slain anyone before." said Menander. He seemed a little doubtful that this was something he really wanted to do.

"You won't have to do it." replied his father. "Well get Aristides to do it. We'll offer him a wineskin, and a second wineskin if he agrees to dig a grave for him and bury him."

"Edepol!" I thought to myself. "Slain and buried for two wineskins!" Then I said out loud "Aristides won't even have to strangle me. I'll die from inhaling his foul breath!"

Both Nicander and Menander appeared shocked, and then they both broke into laughter.

"Trojan, we're going to miss you!" proclaimed Nicander.

"This Trojan is a strange bird" Said Menander. "He frets when he sees another wretch flogged, then he makes jokes about his own impending death!"

When we got up to the villa Kyrios' man servant admonished Nicander. "You can't bring this filthy slave in here. He probably has lice. Kyra will have a fit!"

"Can you not ask Kyrios to come outside then?" asked Nicander.

We waited in silence for about twenty minutes and finally Kyrios emerged from the villa. He addressed himself to me:

"Enneas" he said "Why were you making spears?"

"To protect your sheep, Kyrios." I said. "A wolf was attacking them and I wanted to kill it."

"Nicander believes that you intended to kill him and Menander in revenge for a flogging they had given you." Said Kyrios.

"A reasonable assumption" I said "but wrong. My intended victim was a wolf."

"You have been trained to kill, Enneas, and you have killed people in battle, is that not so?" Asked Kyrios.

"Kyrios" I said "you yourself said that the Roman soldier is obedient and disciplined. The Roman soldier kills only in obedience to orders from his military superior. Any other sort of homicide is a capital crime. I'm a war captive, not a criminal."

"Would you kill a man if I ordered you to?" he asked.

"No," I said "I will only kill under orders of my Roman military superior. Anything else you may command me. Well . . . . almost anything."

Kyrios laughed. Then he said to Nicander: "Give this young man some spears, real spears with iron points. I want him to kill the wolf that's been eating my sheep. And for every wolf he kills, henceforth, I will give him a sheep. And get this man to the barber. He's beginning to look like a Spartan!"

Nicander was more than a little shocked. "But Kyrios," he said "How do you know Trojan doesn't want to slay me and Menander?"

Kyrios replied "If Enneas does anything to harm you or Menander he won't experience a quick death by strangulation. We will do with him what the barbarian Romans do to their slaves. I will personally nail his hands and feet to a cross. It's a prolonged and very painful death. Is that agreeable to you Enneas?"

"Well," I replied "If a slave man may be said to agree to anything . . . ."

"Insolent as always" laughed Kyrios. He dismissed us and returned to his house.

After they removed my chains Menander accompanied me to the bathhouse for much needed ablutions. He said "I suppose you're pleased with yourself, Trojan."

"Yes I am." I replied "Depriving Aristides of two wine skins may have spared his wife from a beating!"

Menander threw back his head and laughed. Then he said "One of these days, Trojan, your insolence will get you into serous trouble!"

I resumed my work of shepherding and, indeed, the wolf came back. I killed it with one of my spears and was given a sheep for my pains. I had it sheared and butchered and gave the meat and the wool to Chiron and his family. They invited me to take part in a good feast of mutton.

I became quite good at protecting the flock and thus avoiding floggings. Time passed and I learned to tolerate poverty and loneliness. Occasionally the slaves on the estate would be allowed to take part in religious ceremonies to some god or another. There would be a cessation of work and a feast. Sometimes Kyrios would even come to lead the ceremonies. One time I happened to be close by and he began to recite a passage from the Iliad. He seemed to get stuck and I finished it for him. He stared at me in amazement, and then he joked "The Trojan remembers the battle of Ilium better than the Greek does! No doubt with good reason!" Everyone laughed.

After a few years of my stewardship the size of the flock increased so much as to become unwieldy.

It became clear that either a second shepherd must be assigned to the flock or some of the flock should be sold off. One day Kyrios summoned me to see him and said "I have arranged to sell some of our flock to Lycortis on a neighboring estate. I want you to bring forty animals to him. Chiron has been there and knows the way. He will come with you and help you drive the sheep. Myron will watch the rest of the flock in your absence."

I had not been off of the estate in the five or so years I had been there, so at least it would be a change in routine. The drove took most of the day but we got there about an hour or two before sunset. Since it was too late to return the same day, we were invited to stay the night and eat with the slaves on Lycortis' estate. Chiron knew some of the men and introduced me. "This is the Roman, Enneas Tullius whom we call 'Trojan.'"

"Ave Conterraneus!" (Greetings, countryman!) said one of the men. It turned out that Lycortis also had a Roman slave. I grinned at the man. "A long time since I've heard Latin. What's your name?"

"Marsius Iulus" He replied. It is not difficult to ascertain the class status of a Roman and I could tell from this man's speech and mannerisms that he was neither a patrician nor an equite but was most likely a member of the head count. It was also likely that he wasn't a true member of the gens Iulii but more likely a descendant of one of their slaves. The first name indicated to me that he might have been descended from a Marsi captured in a long-ago war. I myself am a true member of the gens Tullii and am descended from one of the founding families of Rome. All of this hardly mattered now. We were both Roman citizens, and both slaves.

"Were you also captured at the battle of Trasimene?" I asked him.

"Nay." he said. "There was another battle the following year which was far worse even than Trasimene. The battle was fought at Cannae in Apulia. We must have lost some 50,000 dead. After all of the disasters with Hannibal the Roman government was getting desperate and started levying from the head count. But we low-lifes don't train on the Campus Martius that much and don't make such effective soldiers so when the battle started they assigned my unit to guard the camp. The day after the disaster the Carthaginians surrounded the camp and we surrendered. Hannibal was willing to ransom us but the senate in Rome said 'nothing doing.' so here I am.

"But you're no head count type, are you?" he added.

"No," I said "I had a public horse. But is doesn't matter now. You and I are equals here."

"Right you are!" He laughed "Both slaves!"

It was good to hear the Latin tongue after all this time and Iulus and I drank watered-down wine and chatted by lamp light until it was time to go to bed. He himself spoke almost no Greek and he was just assigned to menial work on Lycortis' estate. As I lay waiting for sleep I pondered about the profound class divisions in Rome and it occurred to me that that might be one of the reasons that Rome seems to prefer being at war to being at peace. Every time Rome is at peace the conflicts between the classes come to the fore and there is civil unrest. The state of war tends to put a lid on such conflicts.

I had been on the estate some seven or eight years when one day I came back to my hut after the day's work to find a young woman there. She was sitting there weeping. I did not recognize her at first because the Greek women seldom leave the house and I had not seen Ephigenia in a long time.

"Miss," I said "What are you doing here? Who are you? Why are you crying?"

She just continued to sob. I took her hands and said "Please stop crying. You can't stay here. We'll both be flogged!"

She sniffed and calmed herself. "I'm Ephigenia, Chiron's daughter. They say I must marry old Aristides, the blacksmith. He lives in the hut next to ours. I used to hear him beating his wife when she was alive. I heard her screams. I won't marry him, I won't!"

I tried to reason with her. "Ephigenia, I can't help you. We're both slaves. We have no rights whatever. And if you stay here we will both be flogged."

"I won't do it, I won't!" she cried. I could see that she was hysterical and there was no reasoning with her so finally I said "Very well, Ephigenia. We'll go to Menander and I'll ask for your hand in marriage." This at least got her to get up and come out of the hut.

Much as I expected, Menander said "Trojan, a slave can't just marry anyone he wants. This girl has been promised to Aristides and as a blacksmith he is more valuable than a shepherd." I squeezed her hand. "Well, we tried." I said.

"I will not marry Aristides!" she shrieked "I will not! I'll jump in the well first!" She continued to cry and carry on and they took her to the punishment hut and beat her. For days she persisted in her stubbornness, refusing to eat and threatening to kill herself, and finally Menander gave up.

"Trojan," He said "If you want a very stubborn and disobedient wife, she's yours. Good luck!"

My trepidations about marrying Ephigenia were soon resolved because she was a most loving and devoted wife. I now looked forward to coming home from my chores to a good hot meal and kisses and affection. I experienced for the first time in my life the pleasures of making love to a woman. She was also very industrious and spent her time making and repairing garments, skills that her mother had taught her from a very early age.

Within the year she became pregnant. I said to her "They call me 'Trojan', well I'll show them a Trojan! If it's a boy we'll name him after the Trojan hero Hector, and if it's a girl we'll name her after Hector's wife!" She laughed "You're so funny, Enneas!" The first child was a girl and we named her Andromache. Little Hector came along the following year.

I threw myself into the tasks of being a loving husband and father and pretty much forgot that I was supposed to be a poor and miserable wretch! Was I happy? I would say I was as happy as my unfortunate circumstances would permit.

Andromache was a strong healthy baby but Hector was colicky and fretful and always a bit frail and small for his age. He was, however, very bright and easily learned to talk. I wanted both of the children to learn Latin so I spoke to them in Latin while their mother spoke to them in Greek. Somehow they were able to sort out the languages and rarely mixed them. It was my intention that when Hector reached manhood, I would somehow arrange for him to escape and go to Rome, although I had no idea what conditions would be like in Rome by then, or even if there would still be a Rome. When he was about five or six years old I started bringing him with me to the pastures. I started teaching him to read, both Greek and Latin. I used my memories of Homer's poetry, which I knew both in Greek and Latin to teach him. I would carve letters on logs or write them in the dirt. I tried to teach him new things every day. I think he could sense that I thought that education and literacy were very important, and he seem to easily absorb most of what I tried to teach him.

One morning, sometime before I started bringing Hector with me, I was up in the pasture with the sheep when I saw two men approach the flock. One of them had a knife in his hand and appeared intent upon killing and stealing one of the sheep. I grabbed my spears and ran toward them. "Stop!" I yelled in Greek. I brandished my spear at them. The two men were bearded and ragged and bore the markings of chains on their wrists. I could see that they were Romans or allied nationals, captivi like myself.

"Ave, Tullius, our countryman" Said one of them "Surely you could let us have one of your sheep!"

"They're not my sheep. They count them every evening and if there's one missing I'll be flogged." I answered in Latin. "How do you know my name?"

"Word is that there is a Cannensis named Tullius who guards the sheep on this estate." the man said. "Surely you would help fellow countrymen who are trying to escape from slavery. Why don't you come with us? Are you not weary of this servitude?"

It seemed that "Cannensis" was a name prisoners taken at the battle of Cannae referred to themselves by. I did not bother to explain that I had not been at Cannae. "I can not go, I have a wife and small children. But where do you intend to go? Where is there a safe place for you?"

"We have heard that there is a Roman legion in Illyria." He said "We will go there and join them"

I took out the sheepskin pouch that contained my lunch. "I can not let you have a sheep, but I have some bread and cheese you can have. Please leave the estate quickly. I won't tell anyone I saw you."

I tossed the pouch to the nearest man, not wanting to approach within knife range. "Good luck to you."

"Thank you, countryman." said the one who had been speaking. "But could you not lend us one of your spears?"

"Nay" I said. "If you were caught Kyrios would recognize his blacksmith's handiwork and would know you got it from me. And if you're caught with a spear you will be slain, but if you are unarmed you might get by with just a flogging."

"Very well then." said the man. "If we make it to Rome, is there anyone you would want us to inform as to your whereabouts?"

"No" I said "I don't think so. It would only cause them suffering."

Sadly, the incident tended to prove Nicander's contention that it is necessary to flog a shepherd who loses a sheep in order to prevent the shepherd from selling, giving away or stealing the sheep. Had I not feared a flogging I might well have spared the Roman fugitives a sheep. Slavery has a twisted logic all of its own.

The men finally left and I was grateful that I had had my spears close at hand. This had surely saved me from a flogging! That evening I told Ephigenia what had occurred and asked her to make me another sheepskin pouch. "It must have been difficult to choose between your loyalty to your countrymen and your loyalty to Kyrios." She said.

"I have loyalty to neither." I replied "My loyalty is to my back, which doesn't want to be flogged!"

I had been on the estate some fifteen years when Kyrios summoned me to his villa. "Enneas" he said "You've always been a straight—forward fellow and I will be straight—forward with you. I think that it will please you very much to learn that Rome has been victorious in it's war with Carthage. Rome has defeated Carthage and has made peace with the Carthaginians on Roman terms." I grinned, delighted with this news.

"Unfortunately, this will not affect your present situation, at least not anytime soon." said Kyrios. "We Achaeans believe that, now that Rome has been victorious over Carthage, the Romans will turn their attentions eastward toward Greece and Macedon. Even as the Romans were fighting against Carthage they maintained a conflict with Phillip III of Macedon, and we believe that there will soon be another such conflict. We Achaeans will be caught in the middle. We think that Rome is now very much a power to be reckoned with and we would wish to come to some sort of accommodation with her. We wish to maintain our own laws and our independence as far as possible. There are still thousands of Roman prisoners like yourself enslaved in Achaea and you are a bargaining chip, so eventually some sort of repatriation may take place, but, as I said, not in the immediate future.

"I misspoke years ago when I said I had no need of a Roman scholar, Enneus. I want you to teach me and my sons to speak Latin. I'm afraid that I can't relieve you of your shepherding duties, but perhaps you could bring the sheep back to the pen an hour early and come up here in the evening. You will dine with us on those nights when we are here and converse with us in Latin, and we will give you a container of foodstuffs to take back to your family."

I began to dine with Kyrios and his sons every few days. When I would come to the villa his servant would bid me to wash my body and provide me with a clean robe and sandals. I asked Kyrios if he had a copy of Homer's works, explaining that I had learned Greek from them and that I had actually helped my tutor, Andronicus to translate the works from Greek into Latin. Andronicus would translate a section and then show it to me and I would tell him whether his Latin made sense, and, if not, I would suggest wording that did. At that young age I was capable of memorizing whole texts and I learned both the Iliad and the Odyssey in both languages. Kyrios had a board made of slate and a stylus of chalk and I used this to teach him and his sons the Latin alphabet. It's not easy to learn a foreign language, but I was able to teach them the common words and phrases and after a time they were able to carry on a limited conversation in Latin. I enjoyed these evenings, partly because I was well fed on these occasions and partly because they provided me with my first opportunity in many years to converse with educated people, something I had sorely missed since leaving Rome.

These sessions continued for the next few years but became less and less frequent with time because Kyrios and his sons were involved in the affairs of the Achaean League and the league was involved in a war with Nabis, the tyrant of Sparta. Megalopolis was under siege by Nabis and Kyrios and his sons could not readily travel back and forth.

It was during one of Kyrios' long absences that an occurrence took place that was a jolting reminder of my enslavement. I regularly brought Hector with me when I went up to the pastures with the sheep, and lately, to encourage him in skill and independence, I sent him to a different pasture with part of the flock, usually between ten and twenty animals so he would be able to keep count of them. That day when he brought them back, he told me that there was one missing. I left him with the flock and went to look for it. I found its mangled carcass. The wolf, having already eaten its fill, and having gotten scent of me had run off and I could only catch sight of it in the distance. When we returned I reported the loss to Menander, who had some time ago replaced his deceased father as overseer, and he ordered me to be flogged. He did, however decrease the usual number of lashes to five, saying that I had come forth about it on my own. I sent Hector to his mother and allowed myself to be led to the punishment hut.

Hector was absolutely beside himself when I returned. I had never seen him throw such a fit! I finally had to order him to stop. I put my arms around him "It's alright Hector. I'm not dead. I'll be fine"

"But it's not fair, it's not fair, it's not fair!" exclaimed Hector.

"Hector, life is not fair. That's the way it is. If you expect it to be fair you will be sorely disappointed!" I said.

"Papa, it should have been me that they flogged and not you." He said. I was impressed with his loyalty and such a noble sentiment in one so young, but I said. "Nay lad, you're too little for that. I'm sure you'll have plenty of opportunity for a flogging when you're older."

"Papa" he asked "Why are we slaves?"

"Well son," I said "there are several ways to become a slave. Some people are born as slaves, some people become slaves because they have committed some crime or have gotten too far into debt. I became a slave because I was captured in war. I was a citizen of Rome and Rome was at war with Carthage. The Carthaginian general Hannibal invaded our country and I was in the Roman cavalry under consul Flaminius. Hannibal defeated Flaminius in battle and I was captured and sent here to Achaea to be sold as a slave. I've been here ever since. I think you could say that I was abandoned by the goddess Fortuna.

"Will we always be slaves, Papa?" he asked.

"I don't know, Hector." I said "Fortuna is a very fickle goddess and sometimes she returns to the one she has abandoned."

Indeed, the goddess Fortuna did seem to return to my side in the years that followed. Perhaps Ephigenia's Artemis had put in a good word for me! Some two years later Kyrios summoned me to his villa. He had not been mistaken six years earlier when he had predicted that Rome would soon become heavily involved with Greek affairs. "Enneas" he said "I don't know how much you know about the war that has been going on between Rome and Phillip III of Macedonia. The Achaean league initially sided with Macedonia but we have been so occupied with our conflict with Nabis of Sparta that we have not taken any active part in this war. Phillip, for his own part has given Achaea no help, and some months ago, the Romans, under Titus Quinctius Flamininus defeated Phillip decisively at the battle of Cyanocephalae in Thessaly. Now the Achaean League has decided to enter into negotiations with Flamininus in hopes that he will aid our cause against Nabis. I'm sure Chiron has informed you of how cruel and barbaric the Spartans are."

"Yes, Kyrios" I said "More than once."

"Well" he continued "I am on the negotiation committee and I have informed Flamininus of your presence on this estate and have offered to give you and your family up to him for repatriation to Rome."

My jaw dropped open! "I can go home? Kyrios!"

Kyrios smiled. "I hate to lose you, Enneus, you've been very helpful to me. But I really think it's time that you went back to Rome. I think that in exchange for Rome's assistance in the matter of Nabis, we Achaeans may be persuaded to repatriate all of the Roman war captives we acquired from Hannibal. But you and your family will be the first."

I knelt and clasped his hand. "I will be forever grateful to you, Kyrios!"

"One of Flamininus' tribunes will be coming in a few days with a wagon to take you and your family to Flamininus' camp in Thessaly. It will be up to them to arrange your transportation back to Rome."

I returned to our hut and told the good news to Ephigenia and the children. Hector was overjoyed. He had chafed at the prospect of a life of slavery. Part of this was my doing since I had attempted to educate him far beyond his station in life. Ephigenia and Andromache were far more subdued. They were apprehensive about leaving their family and friends and the only existence they had ever known. Women, whether slave or free, are so restricted in their activities that the whole concept of freedom means little to them. But both Ephigenia and Andromache knew only too well what liberty meant to Hector and myself and neither of them ventured to discourage us from seeking it.

"Papa" said Hector "Does this mean that I will never have to be flogged and that I'll never have to wear chains?"

"Hector" I replied "There are no certainties in life. The last thing I ever considered when I was your age was that I might someday be enslaved. What it does mean is that you will now have a chance to live your life as a free man. Just don't get into debt or get captured in war."

A few days later one of Flamininus' military tribunes, a man named Fulvius, came to the estate with a wagon to transport us to Flamininus' camp in Thessaly. We had few possessions, although the women on the estate got together and each contributed a supply of wool or yarn to Ephegenia so that she and Andromache could occupy themselves with knitting on our journey. Hector was in awe of Fulvius and promptly made up his mind that he wanted to be a military tribune when he grew up.

After about a week's journey we got to proconsul Flamininus' camp in Thessaly. The next day we were summoned to his presence. I knelt before him and clasped his hand. "How can I repay you?" I asked.

He smiled. "I intend to triumph when I come back to Rome and you may repay me by marching in the procession. I am hoping to secure the release of every surviving Roman captive in Achaea. Even mounds of gold and silver do not impress the Roman people as much as hundreds of liberated captives."

"I will be there with my son whenever your triumph takes place" I said.

"Were you captured at Cannae?" He asked me.

"No, Proconsul," I said "at Trasimene."

"Ah" he said. "A sorry business that was. I was just a boy at the time, but I heard stories . . . . And how have they treated you here?"

"Like slaves are treated anywhere." I said "It could have been worse."

"Next week I am discharging a legion of veterans to go back to Rome." He said. "You and your family will follow in their train. They will travel to the port of Epidamnus in Epirus, and from there they will board transports to Brundisium. I'm sure some of them will be willing to bring you to Rome. How long were you in the Roman army before you were captured?"

"About three months, Sir." I said.

"Infantry or Cavalry?" He asked.

"Cavalry." I replied.

"Good." he said. "I'll see that you get your back pay, three denarii per day."

Thus I had some two hundred and seventy denarii when we left Greece, but I knew I would have to be frugal with it since I had no idea how we might survive when we got there. I assumed that after twenty one years absence, any wealth or property I had had would have been long since appropriated by someone else.

We traveled with the discharged soldiers to Epidamnus and thence to Brundisium. The soldiers had just been paid for their tours of duty and were generous in sharing their provisions with us. Hector would eat his fill, a new experience for him, and then fall asleep. He became sort of a mascot for the soldiers and it was difficult to restrain him from pestering them with questions. He reminded me of myself as a child in that way, because I was always pestering the grown-ups with questions. When we got to Brundisium I was able to arrange transportation for us to Rome in a wagon. It was a slow journey which took over a week.

When we got to Rome we went to the property my family had owned in Quirinal. There were head count types living there and after twenty-one years none of those who lived there remembered me or my family. The squatters were not inclined to admit that the property, which was quite dilapidated, belonged to me. "We would have to see proof." said their leader. I was not in any position to press any claim on it, and since no one could give me any information about the whereabouts of my mother or my brother Gaius, I decided to try to find my Aunt Tullia, the mother of Cousin Lucius.

Aunt Tullia still lived in the household of her husband, Titus Licinius Varro, who was by then deceased. The paterfamilius of the family was now her step son, the eldest son of Titus, also named Titus. Aunt Tullia shrieked with joy when she saw me and smothered me with kisses. "We thought you were dead, Enneus! We thought you had died at Trasimene! And you have children!" She kissed and hugged Ephigenia and the children and invited us to dinner. We ate what was, for us, a sumptuous meal with pork shoulder and vegetables and bread and mulsum to drink, and even a dessert of fruit filled tarts. But for me the occasion was bitter sweet because she informed me that Gaius had been killed at Cannae and that my Mother had just wasted away and died not long after that. She asked me what my life had been like since Trasimene and I told her my story but spared her some of the more disturbing details.

"What are you going to do now that you're back?" She asked.

"I don't know" I replied. "I have very little money and it seems futile to try to reclaim property after twenty-one years. I guess I will just have to find some paid employment. It's not as though I'm unused to manual labor." I laughed, somewhat bitterly.

"You remember my son Lucius? He's been adopted by his father-in-law and now runs the stables. He uses only free labor and he might be able to use you."

"Why does he use only free labor?" I asked.

"Oh, it's just his preference." She said "He says he'd rather have the gratitude of those who work for him rather then their resentment."

"I will go to see him." I said "I still remember where Silvius' stable was. Gaius and I were there many times learning to ride horses."

"I wish I could have given you better tidings of Gaius and your mother. But I am so thrilled to see you and to know that you've survived! I never thought it possible!" Then she looked sad "So many have died. So many."

We had no lodgings for the night so I decided that we should go straight to the stable and visit Cousin Lucius. He and his family were now living in the compound that had housed the Silvius family when Gaius and I had frequented the stables. Silvius was still alive but he was quite old and frail. His widowed daughter Aelia looked after him. Cousin Lucius didn't recognize me at first but when I told him who I was he bade us to enter. "Enneus . . . Enneus . . . . by Hercules! It's good to see you!" Then he started to weep!

I was a little embarrassed. "Lucius," I said "I'd be grateful for your help, more than for your pity!"

This startled him out of his lacrimose state and he said "Of course! Whatever I can do . . ."

"I'm not asking for charity. I want employment." I said "Employment and a roof over our heads. Ephigenia is a good seamstress and Andromache is learning to be one as well. If you hire me and pay me what you can spare, we can probably scrape together enough to feed ourselves. I was a shepherd for twenty-one years. It shouldn't be too much of a shock to deal with horses."

"Certainly" said Lucius. "I'll have you start tomorrow. I've been wanting to sent my son Lucius out to Apulia anyway to see how Brunius is doing with the horse farm out there. You can take over his duties. And as for your wife and daughter, my Ala has a shop in Quirinal and she can sell their clothes for you."

"Who is your Ala?" I asked.

"Oh, well . . ." said Lucius "I'll explain about her later. But your boy . . . your boy will need to be educated. Does he speak Latin?"

"He speaks Latin pretty well, I taught both of the children." I said "But I don't think that his vocabulary is up to what a Roman child of his age would have. We had no access to books."

"I think for now I will hire Manlius, Ala's bookkeeper, to tutor your wife and children in Latin." Said Lucius "When he's ready, you son can share tutors with my son Titus. What's the boy's name?"

"Hector" I replied.

"Edepol! You really went Greek over there!" Lucius exclaimed.

"Well no" I said "They took 'Enneus' for a Trojan name and nick-named me Trojan. Just to defy them I gave the children Trojan names: Hector and Andromache."

Cousin Lucius laughed "I see." he said "But I think that Hector would be better off here in Rome if we Romanized his name. We can call him 'Ectorius.'

"Brunius' hut is empty now since he and his family have gone to Apulia." He said. "Would you and your family mind living there for the time being? It's not a very fancy domicile, I'm afraid."

"I haven't exactly been living in a palace these last twenty-one years." I said "I'm sure it will do fine for us."

Lucius invited us to dine with him and his family and introduced us to his wife Silvia, whom I did remember vaguely because I had attended their wedding, and his two sons and three daughters. His elder son was twenty-one, and his younger son was thirteen. His daughters were seventeen, fifteen and nine.

Silvia fussed over us and collected a pile of clothes for us as she could see that we were poorly clad. Hector was delighted with the togae praetextae she gave him and Ephigenia and Andromache were thrilled with their new robes. I told her I only wanted work clothes. Silvia was an accomplished seamstress in her own right so she and Ephigenia exchanged knowledge as far as their linguistic abilities would allow, and Silvia instructed Ephigenia and Andromache on how to make clothing in the Roman style. Greek style clothing would be much more difficult to sell.

Lucius was our salvation and I will be forever grateful to him and Silvia. I don't know what we would have done if he had not taken us under his wing.

I found that horses were quite a bit more intelligent than sheep and could be far more ornery. Lucius had an old stallion he had named Indibilis which had been with him in Hispania when he was stationed there. This animal was prone to kicking people as both Hector and I found out the hard way. Lucius was very fond of the beast and I did not think I could persuade him that Indibilis would be worth more as horse meat. He said he had named the horse after a chieftain of one of the Hispanian tribes.

Aside from Indibilis I got along well with the horses and the other stable workers. All in all it seemed an easier job than shepherding.

Lucius often invited me to dine with him. He told me a lot about his experiences in Hispania and in Africa. He was very devoted to his commander Publius Cornelius Scipio Africanus. That same Publius Cornelius Scipio who had recruited me to Flaminius' cavalry. One could almost say he worshiped him. And I also found out who Ala was. He practically worshiped her too! She had been his servant girl in Hispania— not a slave, but a free employed servant. After the Romans had been defeated at the battle of the Upper Baetis, he had been captured by Celtiberians who were going to sell him to Hasdrubal, the brother of Hannibal. He had been part of Cneius Scipio's intelligence operation and thus he was facing not merely death, but torture at the hands of Hasdrubal. She had followed his captors and she suddenly burst in on his captors and slew them all with a sword! Lucius considers her much like a second wife, although that's not lawful in Rome. At her request, he set her up with a jewelry shop in Quirinal and has remained at her beck and call. They even have a daughter. Silvia seems to take it all with surprisingly good humor.

I was reluctant at first to talk about my experiences in captivity, but Lucius was easy to talk to and I soon found myself unburdening myself to him. It was good to have someone to whom I could talk freely. I was not the least interested at this point in Roman politics, but Lucius wanted me to see what was going on and insisted on taking me to the forum to listen to the discourses. There was an election going on and we heard the candidates for consul and other offices speak. One of them was a man named Marcus Porcius Cato. Lucius detested him. He was an avowed enemy of Scipio and had been a thorn in his side during Scipio's African campaign. Lucius himself had had a couple of unpleasant run-ins with the man. Lucius was appalled when this Cato was elected consul.

On our expedition to the forum, I noticed that one of the senators was wearing a cap of liberty such as is customarily worn by a freed slave. I asked Lucius who he was and why a senator would be wearing such a head covering. Lucius replied that this was Senator Quintus Tarentius Culleo who had been taken prisoner during the war with Carthage and had been held there for years. He had been freed only when the treaty of peace was signed. He wore the cap of liberty to symbolize his gratitude for regaining his freedom. Personally I had no inclination to wear the cap of liberty. Not that I wasn't grateful for my freedom, but I had ample evidence on my own body to remind me that I had been a slave.

Well, I soon got to meet this Cato because he came to the stable in person to shop for horses. He was wearing the Toga Praetexta that Consuls wear, with the purple stripe, and he had two flunkies with him. He looked at me with disdain, it being obvious to him that I was a slave. I let him examine the horses, but when he got to Indibilis I said "Don't get too close to that horse, he'll kick you." the consul glared at me as if to say "How dare you tell me what to do?"

"Do you know who I am?" He asked.

"I do, consul Cato" I said "But the horse doesn't, and he'll kick you." I could see that Hector was making a great effort to suppress his laughter.

The consul asked to see Silvius and I sent Hector to escort him to Lucius. I found out later from Hector that Cato did, indeed, think I was a slave, and he complained to Lucius about my insolence! One thing is certain: I wouldn't want to be Cato's slave!

Hector and Lucius seemed to get along famously and the boy followed my cousin around peppering him with questions, which Lucius did not seem to mind answering. One evening when I was dining with Lucius he said "Hector has mentioned that he has ambitions of becoming a military tribune. I think that we might want to discourage that ambition. For one thing he's small for his age and he may not ever reach the height and weight requirements to even be allowed to enlist in the Roman military. He's been going with Titus to the Campus Martius, but Titus says that it's a struggle for the boy to keep up with the others in their skills. This could change, but, let us say that at this time he's not promising military material."

"I'm not sure I'd want him to be a soldier anyway." I said. "Obviously, with the invasion by Hannibal we had no choice, but there's no Hannibal these days and Rome is in no danger. Quite the contrary, I think Rome is the danger for the rest of the world." I laughed.

"I think that Hector should take advantage of a unique ability he has." said Lucius. "He speaks Greek as a native, and he speaks Latin at a level that could quickly become as good as native. He could be a translator and work either in the military or in business. I think we should educate him to that end and steer him in that direction."

"Yes," I said "I think you're right. Poor little fellow, he never had any of the advantages you and I had. I tried my best to teach him to read and write in Greek and Latin, but it's been a struggle without books, styli or parchment."

"You did a great job with him considering." Said Lucius. "Now he'll have a chance to catch up. And let's hope he'll also never have to undergo the trials you and I have had to undergo, especially you!"

We had been back in Rome for two years when Titus Quinctius Flamininus returned to Rome and the senate voted him a triumph. It is customary that the general honored with a triumph not enter the city until the day itself so we assembled at the Temple of Bellona outside the city. I brought Hector, but not Ephigenia or Andromache as they were both uncomfortable in public. Flamininus had, indeed, procured the release of 1200 Roman Punic war captives who had been enslaved in Achaea. He had not forced the issue but the Achaeans, grateful for his help against Nabis, the tyrant of Sparta, had acted on their own and purchased each man's freedom for five mina each. Each of the newly freed men had shaved his head and was wearing the felt cap of liberty. As I mentioned before, I had always declined to wear the cap of liberty and I had no desire to shave my head. The only thing I had promised Flamininus was that I would march in his triumph, so Hector and I were somewhat conspicuous.

As Flamininus had predicted, his spolia of twelve hundred war captives impressed the Roman people far more than his booty did and the cheers of approbation as we freed men passed by were deafening.
Hector was small for his age and looked closer to eleven than to thirteen so he, in particular, excited the sympathy of the matrons and he had to endure their embraces and their clucking and cooing over him all day. There were

very few other children. Most of the captives had been low in the hierarchy of slaves and had not been given the opportunity to marry.

After the triumphal procession there was a feast and there were tables especially designated for Flamininus' freed captives. Flamininus himself went among us and greeted as many of us as he could. Conspicuous as I was, he recognized me and said "Ah, Enneus, You've kept your promise. How is it going with you and your family?"

"We are doing very well" I said "I found work with my cousin, and as you can see, we're well fed." He smiled and went on to greet someone else.

I recognized only one man whom I knew had been at Trasimene, but as I barely knew him I did not go out of my way to talk to him. But then I heard a voice behind me "Ave, Trojan!" I turned and recognized Marsius Iulus. We grinned at each other "It's been a long time, Marsius! Good to see you! How do you like being a freeman?"

"Better than being a slave, certainly." he said "And you, have you gone back to being an equite?"

"No such luck." I said "I work in a stable full of horses but I have no public horse. I vote with the head count, like yourself."

"At least you have work." he said "I don't know what I'm going to do with myself."

"Come with me after the feast" I said "and we'll ask my cousin Lucius if he can use you, either here or at his horse farm in Apulia."

Lucius said that if I would train Marsius in horse husbandry he would offer him a job at the farm in Apulia. Marsius, having few other options, took up the offer gratefully.

Hector was persuaded by Lucius to perfect his Latin and his Greek and become a translator. At fifteen he took on the toga virilis, and Lucius took him to meet Publius Cornelius Scipio Africanus with an eye to securing him a position as a Greek translator for the army. Rome had gotten into a war with Antiochus III of the Seleucid empire in Asia, and Publius Scipio's brother Lucius had been elected consul and was preparing to go to Asia to deal with Antiochus. Publius Scipio had a son, also named Publius, who, due to some infirmity was not able to become a soldier and was training for the priesthood of Jupiter with the goal in mind of eventually becoming the Flamen Dialis. As part of his training, his father wanted him to learn how to perform the taking of the auspices before battle, and decided to send him to Asia to participate in the rite, if a battle with Antiochus were to occur. Young Publius, it seemed, was not adept at speaking Greek, and his father decided to hire Hector to accompany him and translate for him on occasions where his Greek might not be adequate. Once in Asia, Hector could then join Lucius Scipio's army as a translator.

Nothing went as planned. The transport that Hector and young Publius were on was blown off course in a storm and was captured by the Seleucids. Upon learning Publius' identity the Seleucids sent the boys to Antiochus' palace in Antioch. They were very well treated there but detained for a few months until Antiochus made a visit back to the palace from his camp and sent them back to Publius Cornelius Scipio Africanus without ransom. It was shortly after that the Lucius Scipio defeated Antiochus at the battle of Magnesia and forced him into a treaty on Roman terms. Hector later told me that the worst problem he had was to persuade young Publius to admit to being the son of Publius Cornelius Scipio Africanus. He had the fear that if the Seleucids knew who he was, they would cut his head off and throw it into the camp of his father, just as Nero threw the head of Hasdrubal Barca into the camp of his brother Hannibal!

I can only be thankful that Ephigenia and I knew nothing of these events as they were transpiring. We would have been beside ourselves with anxiety!

While Hector was away in Asia, Lucius received word that Brunius, his freed slave, had become infirm and was no longer able to direct operations at the horse farm in Apulia. Lucius invited me to dine with him one evening and proposed to me that if I would move to the farm in Apulia and take over operations there, he would give me a half interest in the venture. "I wonder if I might also raise a flock of sheep there" I asked. "That might make the place more profitable, with the mutton and wool."

"I think that's a great idea," said Lucius "and if you have any iugera to spare, that land is also good for growing olives. It's only 32 iugera, but I think that it could be used to much greater advantage than it is now. It just needs a knowledgeable and competent person to develop it."

I asked Ephigenia and Andromache what they thought of the idea, and neither of them were particularly attached to Rome, so they said that would be fine if that's what I wanted to do.

Lucius supplied us with a wagon and two horses and we loaded our worldly possessions into it and journeyed to the horse farm in Apulia. The farm was not far south of the Aufidus river. To get there we passed by the battlefield of Cannae, where my brother had been killed. By this time, twenty-six years later, there were no obvious signs that a battle had been fought there, but farmers who worked that land often found human bones not far below the surface. Gaius . . . . Gaius and I had been the closest of brothers. How could we have been torn asunder so violently?

I had only been to the horse farm once, five years before, when we had brought fifty horses from there to Rome to sell to the consul Marcus Porcius Cato for his cavalry. Brunius was now in his early sixties and had developed some arthritis and his movements were slow.

Brunius had been Lucius' groom for the whole time Lucius had been in Spain but had not gone with him to Africa. About the time of Publius Cornelius Scipio's consulship, he had bought the freedom of one of Silvius' slave women and married her. They had three boys and two girls, all under fifteen years old.

Marsius Iulus was still living at the farm and had married a local girl and had a baby. We stayed in his hut in the early days because Brunius' hut would have been too crowded with ten people living in it. Given Brunius' physical condition, most of the work had to be done by myself, Marsius and Brunius' eldest two sons Gaius and Atilius. The three of them helped me build our own hut. I promised Ephigenia that when we started to prosper, I would build an actual house for ourselves with multiple rooms and a bathing pool. I told her that it would probably take several years before he could afford to do that, but it would be the first thing on my agenda when our income increased.

While Marsius, Gaius and Atilius saw to the needs of the horses, I busied myself with procuring and herding sheep. With money that Lucius had given me, I was able to get some good stock from one of the neighboring farms. There was good pasture land along the Aufidus river and I would usually take the sheep there. I also planted several iugura of land with olive trees. It would take some years for them to grow to maturity and produce a crop, but when they did, it would be a good source of income. Ephigenia and Andromache planted a large garden and it produced enough vegetables to feed the thirteen people who lived here with some surplus to sell to the neighbors. Ephigenia and Andromache also made clothing of both cotton and wool to sell to the local farmers and villagers.

I began to teach Brunius' children how to read and do sums. It seemed to me that Lucius's sons, Lucius and Titus would not be interested in coming out here to live, and I doubted that Hector would either. They were all city boys and would probably find rural life boring. The management of affairs here would probably fall to Brunius' sons and they would do a much better job if they could read and do sums. In the years that followed, I taught every child growing up on this farm basic literacy and arithmetic, and if a child was interested, I would teach him or her history and philosophy as well. Eventually I gained the reputation as a scholar and a good teacher and prosperous villagers started sending their sons to me to tutor as well. There are few educated men in these parts and I filled a void.

A frightening incident did occur soon after we moved to Apulia. In my five years in Rome, after coming home from captivity in Greece, there had never been any such incidents, probably because Lucius had taken care to protect me from the consequences of looking like a slave. I was shy by nature and two decades of servitude hadn't helped matters. Lucius had to remind me to look men in the eye when I talked to them. He also persuaded me to make a habit of shaving. He himself had taken up that habit while serving under Scipio Africanus, who encouraged his men to be clean shaven. At first he tried to get me to go to the public bathhouse but he stopped once he realized the reason for my adamant refusal. Any man who had grown up in Rome would realize the moment he heard me speak, that I was a Roman equite. It was only provincials like Cato who would mistake me for a slave, but while I lived in Rome, Lucius was always there to set such people straight.

In Apulia I was on my own. As soon as I got there I started shopping around for sheep and for olive seedlings. I had to interact with the local population, townsfolk from Canusium and local landowners. As in Rome I avoided going to public bathhouses and made do with a basin for my ablutions. But Apulia is hot in summer and I wore a simple tunic which did not cover my scarred wrists. I began to perceive odd looks from the neighbors I dealt with. Rumors began to circulate that I was an escaped slave who was squatting on Lucius' land.

There was a Roman army garrison in Canusium and one day I received a summons. When I got there I was taken to see the military tribune and be began to interrogate me. He appeared to be about half my age and, from his speech I could tell he was not from Rome. He introduced himself as Gabinus.

"What is your name?" he asked.

"Ennius Tullius" I replied.

"Who owns the land you are living on?" He asked.

"It was assigned to my cousin Lucius Tullius Varro Silvius as recompense for seventeen years of service during the second Punic war." I replied "He has deeded half of it to me in return for making it productive. He and his sons prefer to live in Rome."

"Are you his slave, or his freedman?" He asked.

"Neither" I said. "As I said, I'm Silvius' cousin. I'm a Roman citizen from an equite family."

"Show me your wrists." he demanded. When I complied he said "Now tell me the truth. Where do you come from and who is your master?"

With difficulty I restrained my fury. I looked the man straight in the eye. Lucius would have been proud of me. "I wore these chains for nearly four months. They were removed only after I was sold to a Greek landowner. But they were placed there at the command of Hannibal when I was captured by his general Maharbal after the battle of Trasimene. Now if you will excuse me, I have work to do and would like to return to my farm."

Young Gabinus looked completely flummoxed. The expression on his face made the whole unpleasant episode worth while!

"Uh . . . . let me talk to the praetor." he said.

I sat there for some time cooling my heels. Through the open door I could see a light armed sentry, so I did not dare to leave. Finally the praetor entered with Gabinus at his heels. He was a handsome man and he wore a fine toga. He introduced himself as Tarentius Servilius and I could see that he was a patrician.

"It seems that there has been some misunderstanding here." he said. "Aren't you one of Flamininus' returnees? I remember seeing you in the triumph. You stood out from the rest with no cap of liberty and your hair not shorn. And your boy in a toga praetexta."

"Yes." I said "My son wears the toga virilis now and has gone to Syria to serve the Scipioni as a translator.

"I wish I could have gone to Syria with them" Said Servilius. "Apulia is so boring these days that we have to invent problems!" The tribune Gabinus grimaced with embarrassment.

"Welcome back to Italia, and welcome to Apulia." he said. "Veteran, please accept our apologies for this inconvenience and take with you this amphora of Apulia's best vintage." He handed me an amphora of wine.

Brunius would have said that Apulia's best vintage does not equal Campania's worst, but I was mollified by his apology. I mumbled my thanks and asked if I might leave. "Of course." he said. "And we look forward to seeing you do good things with that farm."

As I was leaving I heard Gabinus say "But are you sure he's telling the truth?"

Servilius heaved the sigh of a man who is weary of dealing with fools and incompetents and replied "If you had been raised in Rome, Gabinus, instead of in Placentia, you would recognize the man's speech as that of an equite raised in Quirinal."

Henceforth there were no more such incidents and the locals treated me with respect.

We had been at the horse farm for about eight months when Hector came out for a visit. I'm sure he was shocked to see me herding sheep once again! But, as I explained to him, these sheep are for my own profit and I don't get flogged if I lose one. "A much better arrangement!" he had to admit. By this time I had about twenty five head of sheep. Hector, as I mentioned had had some harrowing adventures in the land of the Seleucids, and regaled us with his stories that evening. I asked Hector what he planned to do now that the war was over, and he said that he would be going back to Rome and would see if he could make a living as a translator. Hector's skills soon landed him a position as a translator in a Greek translating company and he was able to support himself, although not in any lavish fashion. One advantage to me was that whenever he had anything interesting to translate, he would make a copy for me because he knew that I enjoyed reading. I knew that this occupied many extra hours of his time so I really appreciated his efforts. He seemed to get great satisfaction from my obvious joy at receiving these writings. Hector would generally come out here for a visit about twice a year. He was always talking about getting married, but it seemed that he never felt affluent enough to start a family.

After three or four years the farm was starting to become prosperous and I decided to build a house for myself and Ephigenia and Andromache. I hired some workmen from the village of Canusium and one of them, a young man named Albinus took a fancy to Andromache and asked her to marry him. I had no dowry for her, but he didn't seem to care. She was twenty-one already and we were worried that she might never get married. He seemed like a nice young man so we were happy with the arrangement and about two years later we had our first grandchild, a healthy little boy. Babies followed regularly thereafter, until she had four sons and two daughters. They lived in Canusium but she came to the farm often to visit. Whenever Hector came to visit we would send for her and the children.

Somehow, Rome can never seem to refrain from war for very long, and some twenty years after the war against Antiochus, Rome went to war with Perseus of Macedon. The war went badly for Rome for a couple of years and then the centuries elected Lucius Aemilius Paullus, the son of that consul Lucius Aemilius Paullus who died at Cannae, to be consul, with a mind to bringing the war to a successful close. Aemilius Paullus was the uncle of Publius Cornelius Scipio, the son of Africanus, whom Hector had assisted in the war with Antiochus. This Publius Cornelius Scipio was now the flamen dialis, and he summoned Hector to see him and offered him a position as translator in Aemilius Paullus' legion. Hector, somewhat bored with life as a translator in Rome took up the offer eagerly. He would be well paid and given a share of any booty that might be obtained. Aemilius Paullus did, indeed, make short work of the war and at length took Perseus prisoner. Unlike my benefactor, Titus Quinctius Flamininus, Paullus' treatment of the Greeks was not entirely benign. He laid waste to the entire land of Epirus and took one hundred and fifty thousand Epiriots captive to be sold as slaves.

Hector was appalled at this action. He had conceived the notion that the whole idea of slavery was wrong. I, of course, share that notion, but I generally keep my mouth shut about it because I know what the response would be among my fellow Romans if I ever broached the subject! Ironically, Hector was expected to take part of his share of the booty in slaves! Well, Hector did a most amazing thing. I'm sure his friends and acquaintances all thought he was crazy, or at best eccentric, but I was very proud of him. He took as his booty an Epiriot peasant family, husband, wife and three small children, whose hut and farm had been destroyed by the Romans, and he brought them here to me. He manumitted them and told them that they were free to leave but could stay here and work if they wanted to. They chose to stay here and they have been a great help to us. Ephigenia, in particular, thought it was wonderful to have another Greek speaking woman on the farm and she and the wife, Althaea have become inseparable friends. I taught the man, Nikias, how to tend the sheep and the olive groves and since then I've been able to spend much of my time teaching. I have taught their children to read and write and do sums, as well as the children of Andromache and the children and grandchildren of both Marsius and Brunius.

Despite having sacrificed the profit that might have come from selling his slaves, Hector prospered enough from this stint in Aemilius Paullus' army to marry. He married a Greek girl, the daughter of his employer at the translating company, and now they have three small children. Ephigenia is thrilled to have a Greek speaking daughter-in-law, and equally thrilled to have these long-awaited grandchildren. Hector still comes out to see us about twice a year, and still brings me materials that he has copied for me to read. I find them very useful when I teach.

I am seventy now and I look back upon my life with amazement. I suffered the most appalling misfortunes and yet in the long run my life has been prosperous and satisfying. I have taken these thirty-two iugera of land and created a peaceful and prosperous community within it. This farm supports more than thirty people between Brunius' children and grand children, Marsius and his wife, children and grandchildren and Nikias and his wife, children and grandchildren. All of us who live here are either freed slaves or the descendants of freed slaves! And I have seen to it that all of the children who have grown up here are literate. Ephigenia and I now have nine grandchildren and several great grandchildren. I am satisfied with my life and its accomplishments. I'd rather have been who I have been than to have suffered the fate of Publius Cornelius Scipio Africanus who achieved unsurpassed fame and glory but who died in self-imposed exile, a bitter and dishonored man.

My biggest regret is that I never again saw my brother Gaius, who died at Cannae, not far from here, but perhaps we will meet again soon in the fields of Elysium.

The Death of Carthage

Hector's Odyssey

Marcus Porcius Cato the Elder

Chapter 1

"The Achaeans voted Titus many honours, none of which seemed commensurate with his benefactions except one gift, and this caused him as much satisfaction as all the rest put together. And this was the gift: The Romans who were unhappily taken prisoners in the war with Hannibal had been sold about hither and thither, and were serving as slaves. In Greece there were as many as twelve hundred of them. The change in their lot made them pitiful objects always, but then even more than ever, naturally, when they fell in with sons, or brothers, or familiar friends, as the case might be, slaves with freemen and captives with victors. These men Titus would not take away from their owners, although he was distressed at their condition, but the Achaeans ransomed them all at five minas the man, collected them together, and made a present of them to Titus just as he was about to embark, so that he sailed for home with a glad heart; his noble deeds had brought him a noble recompense, and one befitting a great man who loved his fellow citizens. This appears to have furnished his triumph with its most glorious feature. For these men shaved their heads and wore felt caps, as it is customary for slaves to do when they are set free, and in this habit followed the triumphal car of Titus."

Plutarch's Life of Titus Quinctius Flamininus

I started life in some of the most inauspicious circumstances imaginable. I was born in a slave's hut in Achaean Greece. My parents were both as loving and attentive to me and my sister as it was possible for slaves to be, but we were poorly clothed and poorly fed and we were completely at the mercy of our master and his overseers.

My childhood did have one advantage that children in more prosperous circumstances often lack: I was very close to my father. We were always together. From the time I was about five or six I accompanied him every day to the pastures where we herded sheep. For a foreigner, Papa really knew his Greek and had memorized much of Homer and he was constantly reciting stories from the Iliad and the Odyssey to me. He was literate and did his best to teach me to read and write in both Greek and Latin. We had no books, no parchment and no styli so he had to find ways to write on rocks or draw letters in the dirt, but he was determined to educate me, against all odds.

I was about nine years old when the harsh reality of being a slave became clear to me. For some time Papa had allowed me to take some of the sheep off by myself into a different pasture. One day I failed to pay sufficient attention to the sheep and discovered that one of them was missing. When I brought the rest back to join my father's herd and told him that there was one missing he said "We have to find it, there will be punishment if we don't." Papa went off to look for the missing animal while I watched the rest of the sheep. When he came back he looked grim. He had found the sheep but it was in the process of being consumed by a wolf.

We brought the sheep back to their pen and my father reported the loss to Menander, the overseer. "You know the punishment for this, Trojan." he said. "It's ten lashes, but since you came forth about it on your own, you'll get five." (Menander used the whip sparingly, not so much from kindness as that he preferred to have his slaves back at work the following day, and this was far more likely after five lashes than after ten.) He turned to his assistant, Alexias. "Five lashes. You don't have to bind Trojan, he can hold onto the post."

"Go to your mother, Hector." Father told me.

"Hector is it?" said Menander "Trojan takes our teasing much too seriously!"

"And he calls his daughter Andromache!" said Alexias Both men laughed. I had no idea what was so funny about our names.

I completely lost control of myself when I saw my father led away to be flogged. I ran home to my mother's arms and wept inconsolably. I was still weeping when Father came in. His back was oozing blood from five angry red stripes. I was horrified and started to bawl all the louder. "Hector, why are you screaming? What's gotten into you?" he asked quietly. "Stop these hysterics, you're a big boy."

His words shocked me into silence. When I was finally able to talk I said "It was my fault. It should have been me they whipped and not you, Papa." "Nay, lad" he replied "you're too little for that. And I'm sure you'll have plenty of opportunities for a flogging when you're older!" He grinned.

"Enneas!" Exclaimed Mama. She didn't always appreciate Papa's sense of humor.

"Papa," I said "Why are we slaves?"

"Well, son." he said "Some people are born into slavery, and others become slaves because they've gone too far into debt, or have committed some crime, but I became a slave because I was abandoned by the goddess Fortuna. Fortuna is a very fickle goddess. She may be with a man one day and then abandon him the next. And some day she may even return to the one she abandoned. I was born a free man in Rome, but one day my country was invaded by an army from Carthage, under a general named Hannibal. I joined the army under the consul Gaius Flaminius, and went to fight against Hannibal but we were defeated in battle and I was captured and sold as a slave to the Greeks. It may be that Fortuna abandoned the Romans that day, because Gaius Flaminius was impious, or perhaps, Hannibal was just the better general."

"Papa," I asked "why does Menander call you Trojan, and why does he laugh at our names?"

"You've listened to me recite the Iliad to you many times, Hector." said Papa. "The Iliad is about the war, hundreds of years ago, between Greece and Troy, where the Greeks defeated Troy and destroyed the city. It's no disgrace to be called a Trojan, they fought bravely for ten years and were only conquered through a ruse. One of the Trojans was a man named Aeneas and he escaped the burning city and traveled to Italy where his descendants founded Rome. My name probably derives from his, so Menander jokes that I'm a Trojan. Hector was the king's son and a hero among the Trojans. I named you after him because I'm proud to be considered a Trojan. Andromache was Hector's wife, and a very virtuous woman, so I named your sister after her."

Our deliverance came two years later. Rome was at war with Phillip of Macedon and the proconsul, Titus Quinctius Flamininus sought to make a treaty with the Achaeans in alliance against Phillip. Our master, the owner of the estate on which we herded sheep, was among the influential Achaeans involved in negotiating the treaty. As a gesture of good will toward Rome, he told Flamininus that he owned a Roman slave and that he would be willing to give him and his family up to be repatriated to Rome. Flamininus inquired as to whether where were other Roman citizens enslaved in Achaea, and he was told that thousands of Roman captives had been sold to Achaean buyers during the war with Hannibal and perhaps one or two thousand were still alive. Flamininus decided that he would try to prevail upon the Achaeans to accept payment for all of their Roman slaves so that they could be repatriated. Eventually some 1200 were returned to Rome. He eagerly accepted our master's offer and sent a military tribune to fetch us to Thessaly where he had his camp. I was awestruck by the military tribune. His name was Marcus Fulvius Sextus and he was very tall, dressed in a red cloak, plumed helmet, chain mail, shield and greaves. I suddenly knew exactly what I wanted to be when I grew up!

When we got to the Roman Camp in Thessaly, we were taken to see Flamininus. Father knelt before him and grasped his hand in gratitude. "How can we repay you?" he asked.

Flamininus smiled. "If I'm successful here against King Phillip I will return to Rome in triumph. You may repay me by marching in my triumph. I intend to secure the liberty of every Roman citizen enslaved in Greece. The Roman public is not more impressed by mounds of gold and silver than by hundreds or thousands of freed Roman prisoners. Were you captured at Cannae?"

"No." said Papa. "I was captured at the battle of Trasimene."

"And how did they treat you?" asked Flamininus.

"Like slaves are treated anywhere." said Papa. "What can I say? It could have been worse. I'm glad to be going back to Rome a free man."

We were then taken to Epidamnus, a port city in Epirus. I had never been away from the estate before, and certainly had never seen a city. Everything was new to me and very exciting. The Roman soldiers treated us kindly and, for the first time in my life I found out what it was like to have a full stomach! They said I could eat all I wanted! But I also noticed that everyone else was dressed much better than we were and had all kinds of material things that I had never dreamed of. We had no possessions and no money and we were dressed in rags.

Chapter 2

As for his outward appearance, he had reddish hair, and keen grey eyes, as the author of the well-known epigram ill-naturedly gives us to understand:—

Red-haired, snapper and biter, his grey eyes flashing defiance,

Porcius, come to the shades, back will be thrust by their queen

Plutarch's Life of Cato the Elder

The trip to Rome, first by sea and than over land, was long and arduous. I thought we'd never get there. Papa went to his childhood home. None of his family remained. He was told that his mother had died years ago due to grief over the loss of her sons. He learned for the first time that his brother Gaius had been killed at Cannae. He still had an aunt who had married an old widower so he went to visit her. Her husband had died and she was now the responsibility of her stepson who was the *paterfamilias* of the household. Aunt Tullia made a great fuss over us and gave us a good meal, but as her stepson was not related to us in any way, Papa did not want to impose on the household. "I have a son who is your cousin." She said. "He was adopted by his father-in-law and now runs a stable in Subura. He is a kind person and I'm sure he would help you. Perhaps he could give you a job." She gave him directions to where he lived.

Papa had been away for twenty-two years and his cousin Lucius was so shocked to see him that he began to cry! But when he got over his shock he did everything for us. His wife, Silvia gathered up clothing to give to us. I was given some nice togae praetextae that had belonged to his son Titus. Mama, Papa and Andromache ware also given decent clothes.

Lucius asked me what I wanted to be when I grew up and I said "a military tribune."

"I was a military tribune myself!" he said. "I served in Spain and Africa under Scipio Africanus."

To me he really didn't seem quite dignified enough to be a military tribune. In my concept of a military tribune such a person wouldn't weep under any circumstances! But then I decided there must be some explanation that I didn't understand. "If you want to be a military tribune, Ectorius, you should start training now." he said. "Have you ever ridden a horse?"

"No" I said.

"Well, as soon as you and your family are settled, we're going to teach you how to ride a horse. And when my son Titus goes to the Campus Martius to do military training, you'll go with him. In the meantime we need to get someone to teach you and your mother and sister Latin, and when you're good enough at speaking and understanding it you can be tutored in mathematics, history and Greek along with my son."

I asked Papa "Why did cousin Lucius cry when he saw you?"

"I don't know." said Papa. "I guess it must have been too much of a shock to see someone that you thought was dead for so many years."

"Did you ever cry Papa? I mean after you were grown up?" I asked him.

"Well, when was first taken to Greece I was very lonely and unhappy and I did cry sometimes, but I was too embarrassed to do it in front of anyone." He replied.

187

I quickly came to love cousin Lucius. It was like having a second father. I followed him around like a puppy, and he didn't seem to mind at all! Still puzzled that a military tribune could be so kind and gentle, I asked him "Cousin Lucius, when you were in the war, did you kill people?"

"Well, of course." he answered "When the enemy is trying to kill you, you have to kill him to stay alive. I didn't much like doing it, but I didn't have much choice. And if you're a military tribune you may even have to execute your own men if they desert or mutiny. I never had to do that because Scipio Africanus was a very understanding man and sensed my aversion to doing that, but your general may not be so understanding. Are you sure you want to be a military tribune?"

I was beginning to have second thoughts. "Well, I guess I should find out more about it. I really admired Fulvius, the man who came to free us from slavery. He looked so splendid in his Roman military uniform, but I don't know that I'd want to execute anyone."

"I know how you might serve Rome in a way that few others could." said Lucius "Very few Romans speak Greek as well as you, and your Latin is getting better all the time. Rome, these days has gotten very much involved in conflicts in Greece, and I don't think these will end anytime soon. You could volunteer your services as a translator."

"Well, that's an idea, cousin Lucius. It would be interesting to go back to Greece as a free man."

One day I was helping my father at the stables when three important looking men came by and started walking around and inspecting the horses as if they owned the place. They were dressed in fancy togas and one of them had the purple stripe of a consul on his toga.

Papa said "Please don't get too close to that horse. He'll kick you." The man in the purple striped toga looked annoyed. "Do you know who I am?" He asked. "I do, Consul Cato," said my father. "but the horse doesn't. He'll kick you."

"Very well." said the man, sourly. "Where do I find Silvius. I'm going to my province in Spain and need to buy some good horses."

"Hector" said my father "Please take these men to see Silvius."

As we walked to Lucius's compound, Consul Cato said "How did you get the name of Hector, boy?"

"You may call me Ectorius, sir" I said. "My father admires the Trojans, so he calls me Hector."

"Is your father Greek?" He asked.

"No, my mother is Greek, my father is Roman. His name is Enneas and he is descended from the Trojan Aeneas, who came to Italia centuries ago and whose descendants founded Rome."

"Really!" smirked Consul Cato, evidently quite amused.

When we reached the house of Cousin Lucius and he opened the door and saw Consul Cato, he stiffened noticeably.

"I've come to see Silvius." said Cato. "I'm going to my province in Spain and I want to obtain some good horses."

"Fine," said cousin Lucius "How many do you need?"

"I'll talk to Silvius about that, thank you." said the Consul

"I am Silvius." said Lucius

"I recognize you." said Cato. "You're Varro. I would prefer to speak with Silvius himself."

"My father-in-law, Silvius, adopted me as his heir, and I have taken his cognomen.

189

'Varro' got to be a bit of an embarrassment after Cannae. (Cato smirked at this.) My father-in-law is old and infirm and I run the business."

"Old Silvius must have great respect for you if he adopted you as his son and heir!" said Cato. "Is he aware that you're a bigamist?"

"I don't know what he knows about that." replied Lucius, mildly

"I understand most men." said Consul Cato. "but I completely fail to understand you! You seem to have absolutely no shame about such a manifestly shameful situation!"

"Since you seem to have such an abiding curiosity about my affairs, which are none of you business, Porcius, I'll enlighten you." Said Lucius. "I served Cneius Scipio in his intelligence operations in Spain. After the battle of the Upper Baetis I was captured by three Celtiberian ruffians who planned to sell me to Hasdrubal Barca, who would have tortured me for the information I could give him. This woman, my Celtiberian servant girl, single-handedly killed all three with a falcata. I serve this woman in any way she wants, and if that includes conjugal relations, so be it."

The consul reddened noticeably. He was a fair skinned man with reddish hair and gray eyes, and when he was embarrassed the change in color was rapid and striking. "Very well, then, about the horses . . . ."

"How many do you need" said Lucius "Is this to be a donation?"

"Are you implying that Marcus Porcius Cato takes bribes?" said the Consul "You'll be paid what they're worth, I assure you. I'll take all that you have that are suitable for cavalry use."

"I have about thirty here in Subura, and about fifty at my farm in Apulia." said Lucius. "I can get them for you in about ten days."

"Very good. Eighty then." said Cato. "By the way, your slave man is rather insolent."

"I don't have any slave men here, Porcius." said Lucius "I use only free labor."

"Well, he must have been a slave once, I could see the scars on his wrists." said Cato. "Why doesn't he wear his cap of liberty?"

"If you're talking about my cousin Enneas," said Lucius, "He's a free born Roman of the first class, like you and me. He had the misfortune of being captured by Maharbal at Trasimene and enslaved in Greece. He need not wear the cap of liberty. Don't you have anything better to do than to meddle in the affairs of my family, Porcius?"

The consul reddened once again. "I'll trouble your family no more, Silvius. Bring all the horses in ten days to the Campus Martius. Cneius Aemilius here will give you a voucher to be paid by the treasury."

The government officials departed and cousin Lucius looked immensely relieved. I was incensed. "Imagine that man. Taking Papa for a slave and trying to get him flogged!" I said. "He only warned him to stay away from Indibilis because the horse would kick him. But you shamed him."

"You shame a man like that at your peril, Ectorius" said Lucius, "But I couldn't resist!"

"Why does Consul Cato hate you?" I asked

"Oh, It's nothing personal. Ectorius." he said "He knows I'm Scipio's man to the core, and he and Scipio are bitter political rivals."

"I'd love to meet Scipio some time!" I said.

"Well, if you study hard and get really good at speaking and writing both Greek and Latin, after you take on the toga virilis I will introduce you to Scipio and see if he can use his influence to get you a position as a translator for the army." Said Lucius "I really think that would be much better for you than to become a foot soldier or even a cavalryman. That I ever survived the war with Carthage was due to miracle upon miracle. Few men have had Fortuna's favor as consistently as I have. Believe me, of the Roman man children who were born the year that I was, I doubt one in ten is alive today."

"Papa once told me that he was enslaved because he had lost Fortuna's favor." I said. "But maybe that was how Fortuna protected him, if what you say is true."

"He was not as fortunate as I was." said Lucius. "I certainly wouldn't have wanted to spend 21 years as a slave in Greece."

The next day Lucius, his sons Lucius and Titus, Papa and I and two of Lucius' other employees rode out to Apulia to round up the fifty horses that would be brought back to Rome and sold to Marcus Porcius Cato's legion. It was a three day ride and we camped out in the open for two nights. We each carried spears in case we might be set upon by robbers, and just as in a military camp, men were assigned to four hour watches during the night. I had started training on the Campus Martius, but it seemed that I wasn't very good with weaponry and I wasn't too confident about being able to use my spear effectively. I hoped that we would not encounter bandits. Cousin Lucius was reputed to have been one of the best spear men in the Roman cavalry, and I knew that my father had killed enemy soldiers at Trasimene, but the rest of us had had no experience in combat.

The horse farm was just south of the Aufidus river and just north of that river was the battlefield of Cannae, where my father's brother had been slain. My uncle's bones were probably still buried somewhere in the field. Cousin Lucius pointed this out to my father and my father bade us to stop there for a few moments. He got down from his horse and knelt upon the ground. He recited a poem he had memorized in Greek, a lament by a father who had lost a son in war. Perhaps Priam. I didn't know but didn't have the heart to ask. In it he substituted the name Gaius for the name of the dead son. He ended with the words "Gaius, I have not forgotten thee." Tears sprang from my father's eyes as he remounted his horse, and we rode in silence to Lucius's farm. I understood for the first time the depths of my father's pain.

Time was of the essence so we did not stay long at the farm, but rounded up the fifty horses and headed back to Rome with the herd the next day.

We left only a couple of stallions and about a dozen brood mares. Brunius would have light work for a while.

A few days after we got back to Rome there was great excitement among the women in Silvius' household. It seemed that the tribune Lucius Valerius was proposing to repeal the Oppian Laws. The Oppian Laws had been passed some nineteen years before after the disastrous battle of Cannae. The deaths of many prominent Romans in the battles of Ticinus, Trebia, Trasimene and Cannae had created an abundance of wealthy Roman widows and the government wanted to tap into this wealth. The funds of all single women, wards and widows were deposited with the state. Women were allowed to possess only a small amount of gold, were not allowed to dress in purple (the color of mourning), and were not allowed to ride in carriages. After nineteen years the law, which had been passed in a time of extremity, was still in effect and the women of Rome were chafing under it.

Silvius' Celtiberian mistress, Ala, who owned a jewelry shop in Quirinal, particularly hated the law because it severely limited the amount of gold jewelry she could sell.

All over Rome women were pouring out into the streets to proclaim their desire for the Oppian law to be repealed. Silvia gathered her three daughters, Tullia, Lidia and Aelia together and went to Quirinal to recruit Ala and her daughter Erda. I tagged along out of curiosity. Mama, who followed the stricter Greek custom where women are concerned, would not let Andromache come along. When we got to Ala's shop she and Silvia kissed and embraced like old friends. I was astounded by the warmth and friendliness between two women whom one might have expected to hate each other: Cousin Lucius' wife and his mistress!

I met Ala's daughter Erda for the first time and was immediately smitten by her. She was only about nine, the same age as Aelia, but she was the most beautiful girl I'd ever seen. She had Ala's honey colored hair and green eyes and she was very fair with pink cheeks. She had inherited from Cousin Lucius a high forehead and strong chin. She would probably be tall, like her father, because she was already as tall as I was.

We joined a procession of women who were heading toward the Palatine. When we got there Silvia suggested that I go into the forum and listen to the speeches and report to them what was said. Women have no place in the political life of either Greece or Rome, although they seem to have more personal freedom in Rome. I had never been to the forum before but I slipped in unnoticed and got as close as I could to the rostrum. Consul Cato spoke first, and as I strongly disliked the man, I decided that I would be in favor of whatever he opposed, and vice-versa.

As might be expected of the man, Consul Cato vehemently proclaimed his opposition to repealing the Oppian law. He made the following speech:

"If each of us, fellow citizens, had established that the rights and authority of the husband should be held over the mother of his own family, we should have less difficulty with women in general; now, at home our freedom is conquered by female fury, here in the Forum it is bruised and trampled upon, and because we have not contained the individuals, we fear the lot.

"Indeed, I blushed when, a short while ago, I walked through the midst of a band of women. I should have said, 'What kind of behavior is this? Running around in public, blocking streets, and speaking to other women's husbands! Could you not have asked your own husbands the same thing at home? Are you more charming in public with other's husbands than at home with your own? And yet, it is not fitting even at home for you to concern yourselves with what laws are passed or repealed here.'

"Our ancestors did not want women to conduct any-not even private-business without a guardian; they wanted them to be under the authority of parents, brothers or husbands; we (the gods help us!) do not let them snatch at the government and meddle in the Forum and our assemblies. What are they doing now on the streets and crossroads, if they are not persuading the tribunes to vote for repeal? Give the reins to their unbridled nature and this unmastered creature, and hope that they will put limits on their own freedom. They want freedom, nay license, in all things.

"If they are victorious now, what will they not attempt? As soon as they begin to be your equals, they will have become your superiors! What honest excuse is offered, pray, for this womanish rebellion? 'That we might shine with gold and purple,' says one of them, 'That we might ride through the city in coaches on holidays as though triumphant over the conquered law and the votes which we captured by tearing them from you.'

"Pity that husband-the one who gives in and the one who stands firm! What he refuses, he will see given by another man. Now they publicly solicit other women's husbands, and what is worse, they ask for a law and votes, and certain men may give them what they want.

"I vote that the Oppian law should not, in the smallest measure, be repealed; whatever course you take, may all the gods make you happy with it."

The tribune Lucius Valerius got up to defend his motion for repeal and spake thus:

"I shall defend the motion, not ourselves, against whom the consul has hurled this charge. He has called this assemblage 'succession' and sometimes 'womanish rebellion,' because the matrons have publicly asked you, in peacetime when the state is happy and prosperous, to repeal a law passed against them during the straits of war. Not too far back in history, in the most recent war, when we needed funds, did not the widow's money assist the treasury?

"What, after all have they done? We have proud ears, indeed, if, while masters do not scorn the appeals of slaves, we are angry when honorable women ask something of us.

"Since our matrons lived for so long by the highest standards of behavior without any law, what risk is there that, once it is repealed, they will yield to luxury? Should we forbid only women to wear purple? When you, a man, may use purple on your clothes, will you not allow the mother of your family to have a purple cloak, and will your horse be more beautifully saddled than your wife is garbed?

"By Hercules! All are unhappy and indignant when they see finery denied them and permitted to the wives of the Latin allies, when they see them adorned with gold and purple, when those other women ride through the city and they follow on foot, as though the power belonged to the other women's cities, not to their own. This could wound the spirits of men; what do you think it could do to the spirits of women, whom even little things disturb?

"They can not partake of magistracies, priesthoods, triumphs, badges of office, gifts, or spoils of war; elegance, finery, and beautiful clothes are women's badges, in these they find joy and take pride. This our forebears called the women's world.

"Of course, if you repeal the Oppian Law, you will not have the power to prohibit that which the law now forbids; daughters, wives and even some men's sisters will be less under your authority—but, never, while her men are well, is a woman's slavery cast off. It is for the weaker sex to submit to whatever you advise. The more power you possess, all the more moderately you should exercise your authority." *1

In the end, the tribunes who had threatened to veto the repeal were persuaded not to, and the vote was put to the centuries. All of them voted for the repeal. I was quite happy to see that Consul Cato did not always get his own way. Ala, in particular, benefited from the repeal of the Oppian law, as she was now able to do a brisk business in selling gold jewelry.

Chapter 3

In return for his promise about his son, he (Scipio) would give him (Antiochus III) a piece of advice equal in value to the favour he offered, and that was to consent to everything and avoid at all cost a battle with the Romans. Heracleides, after listening to this, returned, and on joining the king, gave him a detailed report. But Antiochus, thinking that no more severe demands than the present could be imposed on him even if he were worsted in a battle, ceased to occupy himself with peace, and began to make every preparation and avail himself of every resource for the struggle.

Polybius, History of Rome. Book 21

Two years after we were repatriated to Rome, Titus Quinctius Flamininus came back to Rome and was granted a triumph by the senate. He had succeeded in repatriating 1200 Roman citizens who had been enslaved in Achaea. Father and I marched along with the others behind Flamininus' chariot. All of Rome seemed to go mad with joy at seeing us! There were few children among us, but the matrons insisted on hugging and fussing over us.

During the five years after coming to Rome, Lucius saw to it that I had all the advantages of a Roman boy of the first class. He paid Titus's tutors to tutor me as well. I learned to speak my native language in its proper form, rather than the rustic dialect we'd spoken in Achaea. I learned both the Ionian and Dorian dialects. I also studied classical literature, mathematics, and history. I became adept at translating from Greek to Latin. At fifteen, I took on the toga virilis, and was considered a man by Roman custom.

True to his word, Lucius took me to meet Publius Cornelius Scipio Africanus. It was clear that Lucius and Scipio were old and dear friends. Where Lucius had been tense and wary with Cato, he was his usual warm and effusive self with Scipio.

"It looks as though we will be going to war with Antiochus in Asia." Said Scipio. "He seems to think that now that we Romans have subdued Phillip of Macedon, he has free rein to encroach upon the Greek cities in Europe. And now he has retained Hannibal as his adviser. Hannibal, of course, will advise him to invade Italy. That could have been avoided had they taken my advice and stayed out of the internal affairs of Carthage. We merely spooked Hannibal into going into exile. He was harmless while he was in Carthage, now he's a menace. We'll have to nip Antiochus in the bud."

"Are you going to go?" asked Lucius

"Probably," said Scipio. "My brother Lucius is going to stand for consul along with Gaius Laelius. Whichever gets Greece as his province, he'll will probably want my help dealing with Antiochus." He smiled at me "And we will definitely be able to use translators who are fluent in both Greek and Latin. I still remember your father, Ectorius, from when he was a boy on the Campus Martius. He came of age for military duty the year after the battle of Ticinus and we recruited him for the cavalry of Gaius Flaminius. He was reputed to be brilliant at his studies. I wish we could have left him to them, but times were desperate then."

"Desperate indeed." said cousin Lucius. "Enneas hadn't even grown a beard back then and he told me that when he was exhibited for sale at the slave market in Megalopolis a prospective buyer looked at him and said 'The Romans must be in a very bad way these days if they're recruiting children for their cavalry!'"

"I'm surprised they didn't try to make him a catamite." said Scipio.

"Well, according to Enneas, the Greeks learned very quickly the hard way." said cousin Lucius. "That same prospective buyer expressed an interest in doing just that with Enneas but the slave dealer told him that the Roman prisoners, even the young ones, are unsuited to that work. One of them when forced into that situation strangled the first client and then hanged himself. When the client failed to emerge from the room the brothel owner opened the door and saw the whole shocking scene. Enneas said that he smiled when he heard the slave dealer tell that tale and the man noticed and said. 'You understand Greek? Why do you smile at such a tragedy?' Enneas replied 'What tragedy? The man got exactly what he deserved and the Roman boy did the only honorable thing.' The slave dealer growled 'Insolent pup!' and boxed Enneas' ears. The buyer departed saying 'if this is what you advertise as a placid man, I don't think I want to meet any of your fierce ones!'"

Scipio was married to Aemilia Paulla, the daughter of Aemilius Paullus, the consul who was killed at the battle of Cannae. Paullus had been hit in the head, early in the battle, by a rock slung by one of Hannibal's Balearian slingers, and had refused all offers of succor, preferring to die in the battle. Publius and Aemilia had four children, two boys and two girls. The oldest boy, also named Publius Cornelius Scipio was my own age. Young Publius was not endowed with any of the manifest gifts of his father. He was shy and awkward and of not much more than average intelligence. His father encouraged our friendship. He was hoping I'd help him improve his Greek. I tried, but with little success. Publius, in fact, refused to speak it. I couldn't figure out whether he lacked the ability or just stubbornly refused.

He complained bitterly about having to live up to his father's reputation. "It's really tough being the son of the most illustrious and popular man in the Roman Republic. People expect me to be extraordinary and I'm just not!" "Right" I said, not very sympathetically. "You'd rather have been born the son of a slave, like I was!"

That year Lucius Scipio and Gaius Laelius were both elected consuls, and both of them wanted Greece as their province, as they both wanted the opportunity to deal with the threat from Antiochus. Publius Scipio and Laelius had been friends from childhood, but Scipio favored his brother, announcing that if Lucius Scipio were selected to go to confront Antiochus, he, Publius, would go along as his lieutenant.

Young Scipio was in training for a priesthood in the temple of Jupiter, and it was arranged that he would sail to Piraeus after this training was completed and that his father would meet him in Athens. Scipio Africanus thought it would be a good idea for his son to have experience in assisting with the auspices that are always taken before a battle. The plan was that after meeting with his father in Athens they would travel by ship to Pergamum and join Scipio's brother, the consul, in his camp. Scipio asked cousin Lucius if I could come along and accompany his son in case he might need a translator. He was afraid that his son's Greek might not be adequate for him to travel in Greece by himself. I could then join the army in the capacity of a translator.

The goddess Fortuna decided to play one of her little tricks. Or perhaps I should actually put the blame on the god Neptune. Shortly before we were to dock at Piraeus a storm arose and our ship was blown right past the port and eastward. When the sea finally calmed, we were surrounded by triremes belonging to Antiochus!

The captain announced that it would be futile to resist and urged us all to remain calm and not give the Seleucids any provocation. Young Publius looked absolutely terrified. "Don't tell them I'm the son of Publius Scipio Africanus!" he said

"Don't be stupid, Publius!" I said "If your name is Publius Cornelius Scipio Scipionides, you'll be ransomed. If your name is Marcus Nemo Nemonides (Marcus Nobody, son of Nobody) you'll be sold as a slave! Just ask this former slave which is better!"

We were duly surrendered and put in chains. The crew and passengers of our vessel were divided up among several triremes. We were put in the hold, which was dark, damp and foul smelling. One of the sailors yanked the gold ring off of Scipio's finger, telling him he wouldn't need it anymore. Two sixteen year old boys were not a high priority to the minions of Antiochus so it was a couple of days before we were interrogated. We were fed on porridge made with barley, and goat cheese and flat bread, both of which were a little moldy. I was very much afraid that Publius would deny his parentage out of pride or fear and I set out to put the fear of the gods, or at least the fear of slavery, into him.

"Publius," I said "these chains are only the beginning. This is the food you will eat the rest of your life. I'm puny so I may be assigned to farm work or domestic work, but you will be seen as fit for the quarries or the galleys and you will labor from dawn to dusk. And there are floggings for any disobedience. My father was flogged when I lost a sheep! And, very likely, you will be violated."

"Violated?" He said. I thought: "Surely this fellow couldn't be so completely innocent that he doesn't know what I'm talking about!" I said, "That's customarily the lot of slaves. My father protected Andromache and me while we were under his roof, but he couldn't have protected us forever." I may have been a Greek and Roman hybrid, but in matters of the bedroom I was strictly Roman.

"When old Nicander, the father of the overseer Menander tried to take my father to bed, my father told him 'I write Greek well enough to write a suicide note.' That made him reconsider because he didn't want to get blamed for losing his master's investment. I will do the same thing when the time comes, but you don't even know enough Greek to do that! Publius, we must convince them that you are who you are: the son of Publius Cornelius Scipio Africanus! It's our only hope! You won't survive slavery. Patricians never do. Papa and I walked in Flamininus' triumph with the other Romans liberated from slavery in Greece, and he did not see even one patrician and only a very few knights, and his cavalry unit, 6000 strong was all patricians and knights. Only men from the lower classes, inured to hardship, can survive slavery."

"Well, if it's Fortuna's will that I die, I will die," said Publius "but I'd rather die alone and unknown than have my head cut off and thrown into the camp of my father, like Claudius Nero did with the head of Hasdrubal, the brother of Hannibal!"

So that was his great fear! "They won't do that, Publius, that was a very different circumstance! Trust me, these are Greeks. They would never pass up a chance for a big ransom!" Publius didn't seem to be listening to me. He appeared to go into a trance. It seemed I was on my own.

The officer who came to interrogate us didn't bother to introduce himself but just started asking questions. In his consternation, poor Publius seemed to have totally forgotten all the Greek he'd ever learned. I told the officer I would have to translate for him as his Greek was not that good and Greek was my mother tongue. I told them that he came from a very illustrious Roman family and would fetch a fine ransom.

"So what are your names?" asked the officer

"My name is Ectorius Tullius, and this is Publius Cornelius Scipio the son of Publius Cornelius Scipio Africanus."

"And I'm Hannibal!" replied the officer, sarcastically. "Are you Greek or Roman?"

"My mother is Greek and my father is Roman. I'm a Roman citizen. Scipio is a Roman of noble parentage. His uncle is Consul." I said. "His grandfather was Aemilius Paullus, the general who was killed at Cannae."

"Do you think I'm stupid?" said the officer "Why are you telling obvious lies? Where did you learn Greek?"

"I was born in Achaea." I said.

"If your father is Roman, what was he doing in Achaea?"

"He was captured in battle by the Carthaginians and transported there."

"A slave then."

"Yes," I said "I was born in a slave hut"

"And now you'll die in one too!" he said. I was starting to get flustered.

"I think not!" said Publius in Latin. He had followed the conversation better than I thought.

"What did he say?" said the officer.

Publius continued. "Ectorius's family are clients of the Scipioni, and we will not allow him to be sold into slavery. If you find the man who stole my signet ring, you will see that it bears the seal of Scipio. And if you want to die in your bed rather than nailed to a cross, I suggest that you not incur the mortal enmity of the conqueror of Carthage!" Finally young Publius was acting like a Scipio! I translated.

"Are you threatening me?" Asked the officer. I translated.

Young Scipio smiled and held up his manacled hands. "Do I look like I'm in a position to threaten anyone? I'm merely letting you know what will happen to anyone who harms the son of Scipio Africanus. My father crucified Roman soldiers who deserted. What do you think he will do to the man who harms his son?" I translated.

The officer gathered the ship's crew together. "Which one took your signet ring?" he asked. Publius pointed him out. "Demetrios! Give this boy back his ring!" The man took the ring from a leather pouch that was tied about his waist. The officer took it and showed it to several other men. They murmured and nodded. He put the ring back on Publius' finger.

"We will be taking you to Antiochus." he said. "He'll decide what to do with you both."

Publius spoke again and I translated: "You have the word of a Scipio that we will not try to escape or make trouble if you take these chains off." The officer took out his key and released us.

When we were alone Publius asked "How did I do?"

"Splendid!" I said "That was perfect! But how come you won't even try to talk to them in Greek?"

"I really can't" said Publius. "They would laugh at me if I tried, and I don't like to be laughed at."

"I wonder who these people are" I said "They speak a sort of Greek, closer to Ionian than to Dorian, but a lot of them look more like eastern barbarians."

"My Greek tutor said that when Alexander the Great died, his three generals each took a part of his empire for himself." said Publius. "Ptolemy took Egypt, Antigonus took Macedonia, and Seleucus took all of Asia. Antiochus is a descendant of Seleucus and he has ambitions to restore the empire to it's former greatness and to bring all of Greece under his influence. Father thinks that he has designs on Italy as well, and we have to stop him in Asia before he invades Italy. The fact that he has Hannibal in his employ makes him more of a threat because we know that Hannibal would jump at a second chance to destroy Rome."

We were transferred to a large transport ship and after about eight days we arrived in Antioch, the capital of the Seleucid kingdom. We were taken to the palace of the king, Antiochus III. I overheard one of our guards from the transport ship tell the sentry at the palace "The little one is a chatterbox but the big one is as silent as a post."

The opulence of the palace amazed even Publius, whose standards of luxury were much higher than mine. We shared a large room with colorful carpets, comfortable beds and beautiful murals on the walls, and we were wined and dined splendidly. I had never eaten dates before, and they used them to make all kinds of delicious desserts! Antiochus had a library full of books in Greek and I was allowed to take them to our room and read them. I read to Publius some of my favorite passages from the Iliad and the Odyssey, translating them directly into Latin for Publius' benefit. I was also able to read Thucydides account of the Peloponnesian War. Accompanied by one of the palace guards, we were allowed to wander around in the garden during the day. Antiochus himself was not there. He and his sons were away with his army preparing for battle against Publius' father and uncle. His young wife, Euboea, whom he had recently married after the death of Laodice, his first wife, was there, and, despite the fact that we were enemies of her country, she treated us with the utmost courtesy and kindness. She was strikingly beautiful and I could understand why King Antiochus was smitten with her. We also met Antiochus's daughter Laodice, who had a four year old girl child named Nysa. Publius was shocked to learn that Laodice's husband had been her own brother, Antiochus, now deceased. The royal family practiced incest and seemed to think that there was nothing strange about it! In fact, Laodice planned to marry her next older brother Seleucus if he survived the war.

The only person, other than servants, who was near our age was Lysander, Euboea's younger brother who was visiting from Chalcis. Euboea encouraged him to befriend us. He and I got along well enough but he began to get miffed at Publius who was aloof and wouldn't speak Greek.

"It's a little difficult to become friends with someone who won't speak to you" he complained to me. When I translated Publius replied in Latin "We're not friends, we're enemies. Our two countries are at war, and Ectorius and I are hostages here. These are fine accommodations for prisoners, but detention is detention. And as for speaking Greek, when I can laugh at your Latin, I'll let you laugh at my Greek." I translated.

"What will the Romans do to us if they conquer Antioch?" asked Lysander. I translated.

Publius thought for a few moments, then said, in Latin "If you surrender, like Carthage did, you won't be harmed. If you persist in fighting and we have to take Antioch by siege, all men over the age of puberty will be put to the sword and the women and children enslaved. I fear that you are old enough to be killed. It's possible, though, that my uncle Lucius will take both you and your sister to Rome to march in chains behind his chariot in his triumph. You might do well to return to Chalcis before Rome besieges Antioch." I translated.

Lysander looked alarmed. "Your friend scares me." he said. When I translated this, Publius smiled and said "If you're afraid of a Roman priest, wait until you meet a Roman soldier!" I translated.

"You're a priest?" asked Lysander. I translated.

"I'm in training to be one." said Publius. "I can't be a soldier, I have the bleeding disease. Both me and my brother Lucius have it. It comes from mother's family. Any injury will cause my death. I wasn't even allowed to train on the Campus Martius. Some of mother's cousins died after receiving minor injuries there." I translated.

I was completely shocked. What if the Seleucid officer had beaten Publius for his insolence? We had so narrowly escaped catastrophe! And we certainly weren't safe yet. I could not bear the thought of facing Publius Cornelius Scipio Africanus if anything should happen to his son!

Lysander must have mentioned the disorder to his sister because the household became even more solicitous toward us after that.

After a few weeks Antiochus arrived and we were taken to see him. He was tall and lean and a rather handsome man. He looked Greek rather than Asian. Publius still refused to speak Greek, so I translated.

"When will you ransom us?" Publius asked.

"I will be sending you back to your father without ransom." replied the king. "Your father is one of the two most renown generals of our age, and it seems to me that I might lose this war. I think I might be better off if he owes me a personal favor. I'm sorry to tell you this but your father has been taken ill and is recovering at Elaea near Pergamum. My ambassadors will escort you to him. You leave tomorrow."

Publius was overjoyed at this news. I translated his response "Many thanks, King Antiochus. I will be so happy to see my father again. And I will do my best to persuade him not to crucify you when he conquers your country."

"Oh, I'm not too worried about that." said King Antiochus. "If he didn't crucify Hannibal . . . ."

"He may now, if he catches him" replied Publius.

We traveled on horseback to Elaea in the company of Antiochus' ambassadors, a journey of three days. We spent the nights in comfortable inns along the way. I asked Publius "What would you have done if I hadn't been there to translate for you?"

Publius considered this for a minute or two and then said "I think I'd be living in a slave hut by now, or, quite possibly, dead."

When we reached Elaea we were taken to the house where Scipio Africanus was recovering from his illness. I hung back because I did not want to distract from a reunion which was so intimate and emotional. The elder Scipio rose from his sick bed to embrace his son. "I was so worried about you, Publius!" "Sit down Father, you're not well!" Said Publius. "It's ok, they treated us very well, after the first couple days anyway."

"Were you afraid?" the father asked "A little," replied the son. "It's better not to show them your fear. I was not going to tell them I was your son, but Ectorius convinced me that I must."

"Ectorius was right." said Scipio Africanus. "Where is he? Come on in, Ectorius!" I entered the room and the general gave me a bear hug. "Such a fine young man you are, Ectorius, I'm so glad you were with my son during this time, but it must have been hard on you!"

"Oh, I don't know," I said "I could get used to living in Antiochus' palace!"

The Seleucid ambassadors who had accompanied us to Elaea met with Scipio Africanus. He told them that, while he was personally grateful to Antiochus for sending him back his son, it could not, in any way, affect his public conduct toward the king or his kingdom. He would, however, advise the king not to do battle with Roman forces until he, Scipio, was well enough to join the Roman forces. This implied that Scipio might advise his brother to spare the life of the king if he defeated him.

Lucius Scipio, however, pressed Antiochus to battle before Publius Scipio Africanus could join him and he defeated the Seleucids at the battle of Magnesia. Publius Scipio, now sufficiently recovered, was summoned to

Sardis to deliver the terms of the peace. Young Publius and I accompanied him. Antiochus was to retire to the other side of the Taurus mountain range, to pay fifteen thousand Euboic talents toward the expenses of the war, and hand over 20 selected hostages as pledge of his good faith. In addition, he was to give up Hannibal to the Romans. Of course, this last condition was never fulfilled. Hannibal, nobody's fool, fled to Crete as soon as he got wind of it.

I never got much chance to use my translating skills in this campaign. Lucius Scipio was eager to return to Rome and have a triumph, and he took on the agnomen Asiaticus. Now that the war was over, I had no great desire to remain in Greece and I accompanied young Publius and his father back to Rome. Scipio Africanus paid me well for the time I served as translator for his son, and I had enough money to live on for several months. When I got back to Subura, cousin Lucius greeted me warmly, but said that my parents and sister were no longer there. They had gone to settle in Apulia at Lucius' horse farm because his man Brunius was getting too old and infirm to manage the place. My father's plan was to not only manage to horse farm but to raise a large flock of sheep and reap the profits from the wool and the meat. Lucius thought that was an excellent idea.

I wanted to see my family after being away for so many months so I borrowed a horse from Lucius and rode out to Apulia. I had only been there once, when we had brought fifty horses to Subura for the use of the Consul Cato. Seeing Papa there herding the sheep gave me the most intense sense of déjà vu! Papa and I hugged and he said "I think you've grown since I last saw you!" "It must be the good food I had in Antioch" I said. Papa was shocked "You were in Antioch?" "Yes." I said, "I had a big adventure. I'll tell you all about it at supper when Mama and Andromache can hear about it. It's just so strange to see you herding sheep again, just like when we were in Greece!"

"There's a difference though" my father grinned. "These are my sheep. I keep the profits from the wool and the meat. And if I lose one to a wolf, I lose money, but I don't get flogged!"

"Yes, you're right, Papa," I said, "A much better arrangement!"

I asked Papa a question that I had been wanting to ask him for years. "How did you and Mama come to be married, Papa?"

"Well," he replied "I must have been in Greece about eight years. One day I came back to my hut after the sheep were penned and there was this girl sitting in the hut weeping. She must have been about fifteen or sixteen year old. 'What are you doing here, miss' I asked her. She just kept on weeping. I took her hand 'it's all right, miss, please stop crying. You can't stay here. We'll both be whipped. Please calm yourself. What's your name?' She finally stopped crying and said "I'm Chiron's daughter, Efigenia. They want me to marry old Aristides, the blacksmith. We live in the hut next to his. He gets drunk and he used to beat his wife all the time when she was alive. I won't marry him! I'll die first!"

"I'd really like to help you, Efigenia, but you know I can't. We're both slaves. We have no rights whatever." But nothing I could say would persuade her to accept her fate. 'I won't do it, I won't! I'll die first!' Finally, just to get her out of the hut I agreed to go with her to Menander and ask for her hand in marriage. He said 'Trojan, you know slaves can't just decide for themselves whom they want to marry. She's been promised to Aristides, and as a blacksmith he has more value than you.' I squeezed her hand. 'Well, we tried,' I said.

"She was having none if it. 'I won't marry him! You can't make me! I'll jump in the well!' They took her away and I heard screams from the punishment hut as they beat her. But she was very stubborn. She refused to eat and swore to kill herself.

"After a few days Menander threw up his hands and came to me saying. 'Trojan, if you want a very stubborn and disobedient wife, she's yours. Good luck!' And so we were married and she has been a very good wife to me and she and you children have been my comfort in my lonely exile. I would say I was a very lucky man. You may wonder why I would even consider bringing children into the world who would be born into slavery, but I always expected that you would find a way to better yourself, which is why I taught you how to read and write, and how to speak Latin."

I still remembered Chiron, my grandfather. Sometimes I was sent to help him with his work, which was repairing fences and otherwise maintaining facilities on the estate. He had been a helot in Lacedaemonia and had run away from there in his youth. The Spartans were notoriously cruel to their helots. Knowing no other existence than slavery, he volunteered his services on my master's estate on condition that they did not send him back to Lacedaemonia. He worked hard, was well treated and was never flogged. He had married a slave girl and had several children besides my mother. His wife had died in childbirth.

CHAPTER 4

"Shame on the unjust citizens who will deprive of home and country a hero who has done such things!"
The Sibyl, prophesying the fate of Publius Cornelius Scipio Africanus. From Punica by Silius Italicus, book xiii, 513

When I returned to Rome I was somewhat at loose ends. With my family away I felt like an orphan. I had three marketable skills, shepherd, stableman and translator. None of these were very remunerative, but of the three, translator seemed the least arduous. I joined a company of Greek translators and was put to work. Commerce between the Roman Republic and Greece was expanding by leaps and bounds, so we were kept very busy. A lot of my work dealt with business contracts and negotiations. Occasionally we were called upon to translate books, usually from Greek to Latin. Whenever I got something interesting to translate I would make an extra copy to give to Papa, who loved to read.

One day, Anaximander, the leader of our group called me into his office and said "Hector, I have an important assignment for you. A well known senator wants a book translated from Greek to Latin. He's a man reputed to be difficult to deal with and I would just as soon not deal with him because he is reputed to dislike Greeks. He's also reputed to be a tightwad. But this assignment may benefit you because you will be able to say that you worked for such a prominent man and that will enhance your reputation and your ability to obtain plum assignments in the future, and he may find you less objectionable since you are a Roman citizen and speak Latin perfectly."

I found my self on the way to visit Senator Marcus Porcius Cato, a man whom I loathed. He recognized me and was actually rather affable. "Well, if it isn't Ectorius, the young fellow from Silvius' stable! How is Silvius these days? And your father, what was it? Enneas?" I was amazed at his memory!

"They're both well. Papa's gone to Apulia to raise sheep." I said.

"You seem perplexed about something." said Cato.

"I . . . I thought you didn't much like my cousin Lucius." I said.

"Nonsense" said Cato. "Your cousin Lucius is the salt of the Earth. Rome could use more like him. I am even willing to believe that his bigamy is the misguided result of profound gratitude. After all, when a man is governed by lust, he will seek to consort with as many women as he can. Your cousin appears to limit himself to just two. Imagine that! A profound virtue leading to a significant vice. Most curious."

"How do you know so much about my cousin, If I might ask."

"Ectorius, a man like myself has many enemies, and when a man threatens my life I find it prudent to keep an eye on that person thenceforth." Said Cato

"Cousin Lucius threatened your life? Cousin Lucius? You have got to be joking!" I said.

"Your cousin may seem completely harmless to you, Ectorius, but I can assure you that after sixteen years in the Roman cavalry, serving during the entire second Punic war, he is supremely adept at homicide! Oh, I have long since decided that where I was concerned he's quite harmless. He got carried away by a desire to rescue a kinsman of his barbarian woman, whom he had persuaded to surrender during the battle of the Great Plains. I wouldn't release him and your cousin threatened to kill me. I could have caused him a great deal of trouble by reporting the offense to the military authorities in Rome, since, clearly, he was out of line, but he ventured to apologize and I decided to let it go. The only thing I really have against

Lucius is that he's Scipio's man. Now Publius Cornelius Scipio Africanus is a man I truly detest, and I plan to ruin him!"

At once horrified and intrigued, I asked "Why do you hate Scipio Africanus? Has he not done great service to Rome?"

"He has." said Cato "But then he did a profound disservice to Rome, which negates all of that! He left Carthage intact with it's walls still standing. He should have destroyed that city! And do you think that if he had destroyed the city, and sold it's inhabitants into slavery that we would have had the least bit of trouble with Phillip of Macedon after that? Or with Antiochus? No, we would not!"

I fear that I found that argument a little difficult to refute.

"Furthermore." he went on, "Scipio and his ilk bring decadent and degenerate influences to Rome. Oh, I know you're part Greek, and I mean no offense, but Greek ways may be fine for the Greeks but they're poisonous to Rome! We Romans need to stay strong and the Greek influence brings effeminacy, profligacy and corruption. I have fought against these influences all my adult life, and plan to continue doing so while I have breath in my body!"

Still curious, I asked: "And just how do you propose to ruin Scipio Africanus?"

He smiled. "In the usual Roman fashion. There appears to be a slight discrepancy in the amount of payment Antiochus made to Lucius Scipio, versus the amount that actually went into the Roman treasury. A simple matter of fiscal malfeasance, such as caused the ruin of the likes of Marcus Livius. I will get the plebeian tribunes to bring the matter up and urge charges to be filed. Even if the charges can't be made to stick, their reputations will be ruined.

"But getting to the subject at hand, I am planning to write a definitive handbook on agriculture, a subject with which I am intimately acquainted having grown up on a farm and having taken over the management of that farm at a very early age. I have acquired a book by a Carthaginian named

Mago, called 'On Agronomy.' It's been translated into Greek, but not into Latin. I would like you to translate it into Latin for me. It's not that long a book. You'll get one denarius per page."

Appalled as I was by the character of my prospective employer, I couldn't see the harm in translating a book on agronomy, so I accepted the commission.

I kept my self very busy those days to avoid dwelling too much on my situation and my loneliness. I was very frugal with my income, and tried to put money away for the day that I might marry. The girl of my dreams was the beautiful Erda, the daughter of cousin Lucius by his Celtiberian mistress, Ala. But I knew that Erda, while always kind and pleasant to me, had no interest in any sort of serious relationship with me. For one thing, she was three inches taller than I was! I wasn't ugly but I wasn't remarkably comely either, and she was strikingly beautiful. Actually I would have settled for a girl closer to my own size, status and degree of attractiveness, but the sad fact was that I couldn't afford to marry and it would be many years, if ever, before such a thing might become possible.

In addition to my usual translation work, I worked on Mago's book for a couple of months. I periodically brought sections of it to Cato for his inspection. "Very good work, my boy," he said "Now I understand what he's trying to say much better than I did when I tried to read it in Greek! When you're finished with this book I will have you translate Zeno's work *On Ethics* into Latin. I intend to publish it. I think that Romans should have more exposure to the philosophy of the Stoics." As I turned to leave he said "If you've got some time, go to the forum and see what's going on. The tribunes are soon going to be denouncing Publius and Lucius Scipio!"

"Why are you telling me this?" I asked "Aren't you afraid that I might warn them?"

"Please do!" replied Cato. "Marcus Porcius Cato doesn't stab his enemies in the back. They should be able to see him coming after them from two furlongs away! Do you think I prefer that they sleep soundly at night?"

I only learned of the event afterward, but it became the talk of Rome. When the tribunes brought charges against Lucius Cornelius Scipio that he had misappropriated funds that King Antiochus had paid as an indemnity to Rome, he brought out his account books. Publius Cornelius Scipio Africanus grabbed the books from his brother and tore them to pieces on the Senate floor! "Why are you so concerned about a missing four million sesterces" he said "when Lucius Cornelius Scipio Asiaticus has enriched the Roman treasury by two hundred million?" The charges were dropped. Cato had lost a battle, but he would persist, and he would be victorious in his aims eventually.

My own dealings with Cato came to an abrupt end a year or so later. Cato had finished his book on agriculture (*De Agri Cultura*) and he wanted me to translate it into Greek. Everything went along well until I got to the part concerning the treatment of slaves. I found his recommendations so odious that I could not in good conscience have any part in promoting them. They included the notion that you should wring every ounce of effort out of your slaves, cut the rations of ill or infirm slaves and sell them off when they became too old or infirm to do the requisite amount of work. Didn't the Greeks treat their slaves badly enough without these recommendations? I sent a boy to Cato's house with the book and a note that said I could no longer participate in translating this book and that he need not pay me for the work I had done on it hitherto.

A few days later the Senator appeared at my door. "Don't you think you owe me an explanation, Ectorius?" He said.

"I suggest that you find someone to translate this book, Senator Cato, who has never been a slave!" I replied.

For once in his life, Cato was at a complete loss for words. And he didn't turn red, he turned white! Then he turned his back toward me and stalked off! Cousin Lucius had said that you shamed a man like Cato at your peril, but I didn't care. I felt more exulted just then than I ever had in my life!

Two years after he had tried to bring charges of financial malfeasance against Lucius Cornelius Scipio Asiaticus, Cato had his tribunes, the brothers Petilii, accuse Publius Cornelio Scipio Africanus of taking a bribe from Antiochus in exchange for moderation in the peace terms. On the day of the hearing Scipio was accompanied to the forum by a vast throng of Romans. The tribunes held forth all day repeating Cato's old canards about Scipio's Greek influenced decadence and profligacy, his mishandling of Locri and the fact that his son had been returned without ransom by Antiochus and that Scipio himself, and not Lucius, the actual victor at Magnesia, had delivered the peace terms. Cato had upped the ante. Fiscal malfeasance is a fineable offense. Bribery is a capital offense.

The proceedings adjourned for the day and Scipio was called upon to return the next day to answer the charges. A proud man, Scipio had no intention of dignifying these insults with an answer. Instead he proclaimed to the multitudes "Tribunes of the people, and you Romans, on the anniversary of this day I fought a pitched battle in Africa against Hannibal and the Carthaginians, with good fortune and success. As, therefore, it is but decent that a stop be put for this day to litigation and wrangling, I am going straightway to the Capitol, there to return my acknowledgments to Jupiter, the supremely great and good, to Juno, Minerva and the other deities presiding over the Capitol and citadel, and will give them thanks for having on this day and many other times, endowed me with the will and ability to perform extraordinary services to the commonwealth. Such of you also, Romans, who choose, come with me and beseech the gods that you may have commanders like myself. Since from my seventeenth year until old age, you have always anticipated my years with honour, and I your honours with services." *2 And as he proceeded to the Capitol, the whole of the multitude followed him, so that only his accusers were left in the deserted forum.

But Scipio Africanus was disgusted with the politics of Rome, as practiced by bigoted and narrow-minded souls such as Cato, and he retired to his estate in Liternum and remained there until he died, two years later. An attempt was made to force him to return to Rome to face trial, but this was thwarted by Tiberius Gracchus, who said "Shall Scipio, the famous conqueror of Africa stand at your feet-tribunes? Was it for this that he defeated and routed in Spain four of the most distinguished generals of Carthage and their four armies? Was it for this that he took Syphax prisoner, conquered Hannibal, made Carthage tributary to you and removed Antiochus beyond the Taurus mountains-that he should crouch under two Petilii? That you should gain the palm of victory over Publius Africanus?"*3

There were rumors that Scipio Africanus met his end by suicide, but I don't believe that. He had long suffered from serious illness. It is also said that when asked if he wanted to be entombed in Rome, he gave the bitter reply. *"Ingrata patria, ne ossa quidem habebis."*
"Ungrateful fatherland, not even my bones shalt thou have!" He was about fifty three years old when he died.

Shortly after Scipio Africanus died, Cato contrived once again to have Lucius Scipio and several of his lieutenants and staff arraigned for financial malfeasance concerning a missing portion of the tribute from Antiochus. I accompanied cousin Lucius to watch the proceedings. Lucius Scipio no longer had his record books, as his brother had dramatically torn them up four years before, and he was unable to prove his innocence. When the verdict *"Condemno."* was announced I briefly observed the exact same expression of shock and horror on Lucius Scipio's face as I had seen on young Publius Scipio's face the day we were taken prisoner by the Seleucids. But the expression vanished almost immediately and was replace by another, equally familiar, expression: the trance-like visage that Publius had maintained during the following two days. When asked to put up money for the fine, Lucius Scipio asserted that all of the money from Antiochus' tribute had gone into the Roman treasury and that he did not have even enough money to pay the fine. At a word from the praetor the lictors put Lucius Scipio in chains and took him off to prison.

I had never seen cousin Lucius so incensed. "I should have killed that scoundrel, I should have!" he said, referring to Cato.

Then, to my utter astonishment, Cousin Lucius took the rostrum!

"Fellow Romans!" he proclaimed in a loud voice. "My name is Lucius Tullius Varro Silvius. I have never spoken here in public. I have never held office other than military tribune. I am an ordinary plebeian Roman who served Rome for the sixteen years of the war against Carthago. I have known Lucius Cornelius Scipio Asiaticus since we were both boys training on the Campus Martius. We boys who trained on the Campus Martius in those days, we all went to war and fought for Rome. Nearly all are dead now. They died at Trebia and Trasimene and Cannae and at the Upper Baetis. I am the only one left to speak for them now! I served in Hispania under the command of Publius and Cneius Scipio, they who perished in the battle of the Upper Baetis. Better that they should have perished than that they should be here today and witness their kinsman thus treated! Later I served under the command of Scipio Africanus in Hispania and in Africa. I have heard that in the old days in Carthago they crucified their generals who lost a battle. Cruel but understandable. Rome punishes generals who are victorious! Incomprehensible!

I say it's a sad day for Rome when Lucius Cornelius Scipio Asiaticus, who served Rome all through the war with Hannibal and, on his own, conquered King Antiochus at Magnesia, should be condemned on a trumped up charge of malfeasance and taken to prison in chains. Is this his reward for a life of noble service to Rome? A sad day for Rome! That's all I have to say."

Cousin Lucius may not have had the oratorical abilities of Cato, but his speech was from the heart and was received with approbation. Many in the crowd were in tears. Worried about the possibility of civil unrest, Tiberius Gracchus took the rostrum.

"Fellow Romans" he said "Citizen Silvius speaks well. Please remain calm. I will do everything in my power to see that no harm comes to Lucius Cornelius Scipio Asiaticus. You have all seen that I am a fair man and dealt justly with Scipio Africanus when he faced prosecution two years ago. Just have patience and allow me to do what is within my legal power to do."

Tiberius Gracchus was not reputed to be a friend to the Scipios, If fact he was said to have quarreled with Scipio Africanus and was his political adversary. Nevertheless he showed outstanding character by once again intervening in their favor. He ordered Lucius' released from prison on account of his services to Rome and decreed that the praetor should levy the sum of the fine from Lucius' property. No trace of the money allegedly received from Antiochus appeared, and, in fact, the money raised from the sale of Lucius' property was not even enough to cover the fine! It should have been clear to anyone who thought about it that whatever money was missing from Antiochus' indemnities, it did not end up in Lucius Scipio's coffers! Lucius Scipio's friends collected enough donations for him to more than make up the amount he had been fined, but Lucius refused all such donations and, sesterceless, lived off of the charity of close relatives the rest of his life.

Marcus Porcius Cato was censor at this time and removed Lucius Cornelius Scipio from the rolls of the senate and from the ranks of the equites. As censor Cato was very severe in his judgments concerning whom to expel from the senate and the equestrian order. Among many others he expelled the dissolute Lucius Quinctius Flamininus, the brother of my family's benefactor Titus Quinctius Flamininus. This Lucius had beheaded a condemned Gallic deserter at a banquet solely for the entertainment of his catamite. Cato also expelled the popular senator Manilius from the senate for embracing his wife in public in the presence of their daughter. I wondered if Cato might find a pretext for expelling cousin Lucius from the equestrian rolls, but he never did.

And so, Marcus Porcius Cato had achieved the first of his two great goals: The ruin of the Scipios. The second goal would take much longer to realize and only be achieved after his death, but it would be achieved: the destruction of Carthage. The remainder of my story concerns this second goal.

CHAPTER 5

"This Paulus had a daughter, Aemilia, who was the wife of Scipio the Great, and a son, Aemilius Paulus, whose Life I now write. He came of age at a time which abounded in men of the greatest reputation and most illustrious virtue, and yet he was a conspicuous figure, although he did not pursue the same studies as the young nobles of the time, nor set out on his career by the same path. For he did not practise pleading private cases in the courts, and refrained altogether from the salutations and greetings and friendly attentions to which most men cunningly resorted when they tried to win the favour of the people by becoming their zealous servants; not that he was naturally incapable of either, but he sought to acquire for himself what was better than both, namely, a reputation arising from valour, justice, and trustworthiness. In these virtues he at once surpassed his contemporaries."

Plutarch's Life of Aemilius Paulus

I continued to earn an adequate but modest living as a translator. Most of my work involved business correspondence but occasionally I would be given a book to translate. I was considered one of the best translators of Greek in the city and there was no lack of work for me. About twice a year I would travel to Apulia to visit Papa and Mama. Andromache had married a local boy and had three children. She lived in a nearby village. Cousin Lucius had generously deeded half of his property in Apulia to Papa, and Papa's sheep gave him and Mama a comfortable subsistence. I stood to inherit about 15 iugera of land and a fair amount of livestock, but at this point I was still not in a position to marry. I wanted to marry an educated girl, but this too would probably not be an obtainable goal. Papa had been born into an equestrian family, but having been considered dead, his name had been deleted from the list of Roman plebeians of the first class. Since this class maintained property qualifications and Papa had had no property when he came back to Rome, he never bothered to apply for his former status. Therefore, we were both considered members of the head count, the lowest class of free Romans. My chances of marrying a girl of any higher class than the head count were negligible, unless I acquired a substantial amount of property. Fifteen iugera of grazing land in Apulia would impress nobody.

I was already well into my thirties and still unmarried when I unexpectedly got the opportunity to travel, once again, to Greece. One day I received a summons to come to the temple of Jupiter to meet with the Flamen Dialis. I was completely mystified. I had very little knowledge of Roman religious practices, and equally little interest in them. The only thing I could think of was that he might want me to translate something for him. When I got there I was warned not to touch his person, especially if I was wearing any metal, as he was not allowed to touch metal. I was ushered into his chamber. The Flamen Dialis was dressed in elaborate priestly garments and it took me a moment or two to recognize him. Publius Cornelius Scipio the younger! My companion in our misadventure in the Seleucid empire!

"Ectorius!" he proclaimed "It's so nice to see you again after all this time! You are reputed to be the best Greek translator in Rome!"

"You flatter me, Publius." I said, "but it is very nice to see you. The priesthood becomes you."

"Better than being a soldier, I guess," he said. "Especially when the best of soldiers is treated so shabbily by this country!"

"Indeed they are." I said. "Both your father and your uncle."

"I heard about the speech your cousin made after my Uncle's condemnation. Thank him for me when you see him. I can't believe it's been fifteen years!

"You may wonder why I summoned you here today." said Publius "My uncle Lucius Aemilius Paullus is preparing to go to Macedon to deal with King Perseus. He's been throwing his weight around in the region, much to the distress of his neighbors. It is said that he convinced his father, king Phillip, to have his brother Demetrius, a friend of Rome, executed. I would like to recommend you to my uncle as his translator. You will be paid a good salary and receive a share of the booty if he is victorious."

"I think I may take you up on that." I said. "I'm still not married, and I'd like to be. But It's difficult to make an adequate living as a translator here in Rome. And I'm getting bored of my hum-drum existence. You've never married either?"

"No, I seem to be heir to a multitude of the family infirmities and I don't want to pass them to progeny." said Publius. "But I have adopted my cousin, Aemilius Paullus' second son to be my heir. He's sixteen years old now. He's one of two sons by Paullus' first wife, whom he divorced. The other boy has been adopted by Quintus Fabius Maximus. (Grandson of Quintus Fabius Maximus Cunctator of Punic war fame.)

"I will talk to my uncle and you will hear from him soon. I believe he plans to sail to Greece next month." I thanked Publius and took my leave.

You may wonder why Aemilius Paullus would adopt out his two sons by his first wife. Romans have the custom of primogeniture, by which only the oldest son may inherit the family property. If he adopted out his sons by his first wife, than the oldest son of the second wife would be able to inherit his property, and two wealthy, but childless Romans would have heirs. Everyone would benefit. In the case of Aemilius Paullus, he had two sons by his second wife, both of whom still wore the toga praetexta.

I was soon summoned to the quarters of Aemilius Paullus who had been elected consul for that year and would assume office on the ides of March. He would immediately be going to Macedon. I met his sons Quintus Fabius and Publius Cornelius Scipio Aemilianus, and their friend Publius Cornelius Scipio Nasica, the son of a cousin of Scipio Africanus who bore the same name. Cousin Silvius had offered to lend me a horse and I asked Aemilius Paullus if I could bring the horse and ride with the cavalry. "Do you think you could keep up with the cavalry?" he asked. "I grew up at my cousin's stables and I handle and ride horses pretty well." I said. "Don't expect me to be much good in combat, though, if it comes to that."

"You won't be in combat." he said. "If the cavalry is attacked ride away as fast as you can and save yourself. There are always risks on military maneuvers, but as a non-combatant you are permitted to leave the battle."

Shortly after that I went to pay my respects to cousin Lucius, whose wife, Silvia had just died. They had been married over fifty years and he was utterly heartbroken. No matter what anyone said about his infidelity, he had been a fond and devoted husband to her. For her part, she had been a paragon of a wife and mother, and I will always be grateful for her kindness to my family and myself when we were destitute.

Despite his grief, cousin Lucius was attentive to me and congratulated me on my new position with Consul Paullus. He gave me several of his old military tunics and asked his daughter Aelia to alter them to my own size, as he was about eight inches taller than me. We went to the stable and he introduced me to the horse he would lend me for use in Macedonia.

Before leaving for Macedonia I rode out to Apulia to visit Papa and Mama and give them the sad news of Silvia's death. I brought Papa several books that I had copied for him and told him I was afraid that it might be some time before I would be able to copy any more for him. He was always grateful for whatever literature I could provide for him. Brunius had died several years before but his sons still lived in his hut and Papa paid them to help him tend the horses and sheep and grow crops. Papa had planted a grove of olive trees on some of the land and had a large vegetable garden. The whole operation was prosperous and self-sufficient. Andromache came to visit from a nearby village. She and her husband now had five children, and the two eldest boys already wore the toga virilis.

From Apulia I went straight to Brundisium, from which the Consul's fleet would be leaving. On the Nones of April we embarked and landed in Illyria, from which we proceeded to Macedonia. I was grateful that I had a horse and didn't have to walk. After two weeks journey we set up camp on the river Elpeus. The forces of Perseus were camped on the other side of the river. Roman military camps are always on the same plan, and everyone knows exactly where their tent will be set up. I was housed with the scribes in one of the tents not far from the consul's quarters.

Not long after we arrived I was summoned to the Consul's tent. Polybius, the hipparch of Megalopolis in Achaea had arrived with 1500 horsemen, offering assistance in the coming battle. Consul Paullus was fairly fluent in Greek and, Polybius, for his part, spoke quite a bit of Latin, but I was asked to attend their meetings and meals just in case there might be a problem in communication. Consul Paullus told Polybius that he did not need the Achaean cavalry at this time but he was grateful for the offer. He invited the hipparch to dinner. Polybius was highly educated and a brilliant and charismatic man, and he had a wealth of knowledge about Greek culture, literature and history. He held forth on a great variety of subjects and we were all spellbound, especially consul Paullus' sons Quintus Fabuis and Publius Scipio Aemilianus. He was also well versed in military tactics and he and the consul must have spent over an hour discussing strategy and tactics for the battle. The next day Polybius sent his troops home but asked the consul if he could stay and observe the preparations for battle, and hopefully, the battle itself. He was planning to write a book on military strategy and tactics and wanted to compare Roman practices with Greek. Quintus Fabius prevailed upon his father to let him do this.

He and I had a few conversations and he said "Your Greek is so perfect I have a hard time believing you weren't born in Achaea!"

"I was born in Achaea." I replied. He looked as though he expected some elaboration, but I said nothing more. In my experience Romans were sympathetic to my father's situation but I suspected that Greeks would not be, and I was hesitant to reveal my lowly origins to any Greek.

.

It may be said that Rome had not always been sympathetic to its soldiers who were taken captive after a defeat in battle. To my knowledge there was never any attempt to ransom the prisoners captured by Maharbal after the battle of Trasimene, but after the battle of Cannae, some 10,000 prisoners were taken who had been left to guard the Roman camp. Ten of them were sent to Rome to plead with the senate to ransom themselves and their fellow soldiers. The senate adamantly refused on the theory that if they ransomed the captives it would give the message to soldiers in future battles that there might be salvation after losing a battle. Rome wanted its soldiers to go into battle knowing that they must either be victorious, or die. When Quintus Fabius Maximus arranged a prisoner exchange with Hannibal, and needed money to ransom those that were in excess of the number of the Carthaginian prisoners, he had to sell his estate in Etruria to raise the money, as the senate refused to provide it. By this time the estate had become a political liability for Fabius in any case because Hannibal, when laying waste to all the surrounding area, completely spared Fabius' estate just to damage his credibility in Rome. And Fabius' kind—hearted ransoming of the excess Roman prisoners was not looked upon favorably by the elite of Rome.

By the time of the second Macedonian war, however, over 20 years after the battle of Cannae, the Romans were quite sympathetic to the enslaved Trasimenenses and Cannenses and we were warmly welcomed home.

The battle of Pydna, in which the forces of Consul Aemilius Paullus were victorious over those of Perseus of Macedon took place about ten weeks after we left Italy. As a non-combatant I stayed in our camp while it was taking place. The fighting started in the mid-afternoon and lasted only a short time.

The Greeks had a very effective fighting formation called the phalanx, in which the soldiers in close formation form a wedge, with their long pikes sticking out in front of the formation. Polybius mentioned to Consul Paullus that this formation is invincible as long as the soldiers can maintain its integrity, but if the terrain becomes uneven, there will be gaps and the formation can be attacked at the flanks and broken apart. Once this happens it is possible to destroy it. So the consul's strategy was to retreat slowly and lure the phalanx to rough and unstable terrain. The line lost its cohesion and the Roman swordsmen attacked the Macedonian infantry on their flanks. Our soldiers were better equipped then the Macedonians and had longer and more effective swords and the Macedonian infantry were soon cut to pieces. The Macedonian cavalry fled, along with their king. The Macedonians lost about 25,000 killed or wounded out of some 44,000 troops, while our forces suffered only one to two thousand casualties out of some 38,000 troops.

With this victory, Roman hegemony over Greece was now an accomplished fact. After a few weeks on the run, Perseus and his family surrendered and were sent to Rome as prisoners. The one hundred fifty year old Antigonid dynasty was at its end. Macedonia was divided into four Roman client states, and would eventually become a Roman province.

Rome now had to decide what to do with the various states of Greece. The senate appointed fifteen commissioners to advise consul Paullus on the affairs of the Greek states. The Roman victory over Perseus precipitated the rise of pro-Roman governments in many of these states and the leaders of these governments ingratiated themselves with the commissioners by providing lists of influential citizens who were accused of being on the side of Perseus, or even neutral during the war. These citizens were ordered to go to Rome to defend themselves against charges of sedition. The commissioners Gaius Claudius and Cnaeus Domitius were to go to Achaea to investigate anti-Roman activity there and Consul Paullus offered my services to them as a translator. Thus I found myself back in the land of my birth after an absence of some twenty-six years.

The leader of the Achaean league was a man named Callicrates. He gave the Romans the names of about 1000 influential Achaeans who, he claimed, were part of a conspiracy against Rome. These were rounded up and interned in a camp, with the expectation that they would be sent to Rome to face trial. One by one, they were interrogated by the commissioners' staff, and it was my job to act as interpreter between the Roman interrogator and the Achaean prisoner. My tent mate, Arennius the scribe, recorded everything that was said. The prisoners were understandably perplexed, angry and unhappy about what had befallen them. Some of them admitted to having been in favor of Perseus, others professed to have always been loyal to Rome. Many, perhaps a majority, averred that they had never cared a wooden drachma for either side. Not one admitted to ever having been a part of any conspiracy against Rome.

There are ways that angry but powerless men express their contempt for those that they feel are oppressing them, and I found myself on the receiving end of such expressions. They would curse me and call me foul names and spit when I happened to walk by. I dressed as a civilian in the toga virilis and went about unarmed so perhaps they perceived that I was a safe target. I thought of dressing in a soldier's tunic and carrying a spear, but given my small size I would have looked ridiculous. I preferred to be abused by the Greeks rather than laughed at by the Romans. I felt that reporting this behavior would only make my situation worse. I also felt that I was participating in something that was unjust and unwholesome and I became more depressed every day.

Then one day they brought in Polybius!

"Polybius! What are you doing here?!" I exclaimed

"You know this man?" asked the Roman officer.

"Why yes!" I said. "Polybius is the hipparch of Megalopolis. He brought a whole company of cavalry to help Consul Paullus in the war, and he even advised consul Paullus on Greek military matters. He's not the least bit anti Roman!"

But the officer told me to sit down and do my job. I translated the usual questions for Polybius and when I asked questions regarding the alleged conspiracy, Polybius replied "the only conspiracy here is the conspiracy between Callicrates and the Romans to eliminate all of Callicrates' possible political rivals!"

When the interrogation was over I whispered to Polybius that I would send word to Consul Paullus that he had been arrested, and surely Paullus would intervene to set him at liberty. Polybius thanked me and then the guards escorted him back to his tent.

I did write to Aemilius Paullus concerning Polybius and entrusted the letter to a courier, but I never found out if my letter ever reached him.

After this, Polybius would occasionally seek me out and ask for small favors for himself and his friends. He was always congenial and friendly, in contrast to the others, and gradually the frequency of incidents of abuse diminished. There were still sneers and icy stares, but, at least, when Polybius was around the more obvious signs of contempt were suppressed.

One evening after my work was done, I was passing by the tent where Polybius and other men from Megalopolis were lodged. They were having supper and Polybius called out to me "Ectorius, my friend! Come have some bread and wine with us." I hesitated, but there was something in Polybius manner that compelled me. As I sat down, two of Polybius companions got up to leave. "Eumenides!" said Polybius "where are you going.?"

"To find better company!" replied Eumenides

"You won't find any better company in this place than us!" said Polybius "sit down!"

To my surprise, both men sat back down. Polybius had a way about him that compelled men to do his bidding. Callicrates was correct in perceiving him a credible rival for power.

"So, Ectorius," said Polybius "What do you Romans plan to do with us?"

"I think they plan to send you to Italy." I said "Originally they planned to charge you with sedition, and compel you to defend yourselves in court, but there doesn't seem to be much evidence against any of you. Nothing was found in the royal archives of Macedonia to implicate any Achaeans. I think you are right that they really just want to make things safe for Callicrates. You will be hostages to ensure the good behavior of the Achaeans."

"Thank you for your candor, Ectorius." Said Polybius "But do you think that these proceedings are in any way just or fair?"

"Polybius" I replied "I intend no flattery, but you are, by far, the most intelligent person I have ever met. So how is it that the first thing that I ever learned in my infancy has thus far escaped your notice?"

"And what might that be?" asked Polybius

"That there is no such thing as justice or fairness in human affairs!" I replied

Polybius laughed. But then he said "Does that mean that you think that human beings are incapable of being just and fair?"

"No" I replied. "Human beings are just and fair when it suits them to be just and fair, and unjust and unfair when it suits them to be unjust and unfair. Human beings are capable of both great kindness and great cruelty. Sometimes the same person is capable of both. You take Scipio Africanus. He was magnanimous in releasing the Spanish prisoners without ransom after the battle of Baecula, but when he took the town of Iliturgis, where they had put to death Roman soldiers fleeing the defeat at the Upper Baetis, he killed every man, woman and child in the city."

"But I must say" said Polybius "that we Achaeans expected better of the Romans than to be treated this way."

"And so you should." I replied. "Unfortunately, I can not do anything about this. I can not even refuse to do this work. Years ago I was hired by the powerful senator Marcus Porcius Cato to translate one of his works into Greek. I found some of his ideas abhorrent and refused to finish the work. As powerful as he was, Cato had no way to punish me. But when you join the Roman army, even as a translator, you take an oath of obedience and they hold you to it. If I refused to follow orders I would be scourged with rods and then decapitated. That's how Rome maintains military discipline. And as for myself, I expected better of the Achaeans than to be cursed and spat upon!"

Polybius looked embarrassed. "I think that does you credit in a way because your Greek is so flawless that they think you are a traitor. There is nothing Greeks despise more than a traitor."

"A traitor?" I asked. I was shocked. Finally all of this uncalled-for abuse was starting to be comprehensible.

"But perhaps you could provide us with a different explanation." suggested Polybius.

I felt that I had been backed into a corner. I switched to Latin, which I knew Polybius would understand but the others probably would not. "What have I ever done to you, Polybius, that you would seek to humiliate me?"

He looked shocked. "Ectorius" he replied, also in Latin "that's the last thing I would seek to do!"

"Then which do you suggest would be better for me to do, Polybius?" I asked, still speaking Latin "Admit to being a traitor, or reveal that I was slave born?"

Polybius was momentarily taken aback, but then be replied, again in Latin "If a man is a traitor it's something he has a choice to be, and it's an ignoble and ignominious choice, the sign of a vile character. If, as you say, you were slave born, you had no choice in the matter, and it reflects well on your character that you have become an educated and refined man. Agathocles of Syracuse rose from humble beginnings to become king, and once he was ruler of all he surveyed, no one cared that he started out as a potter! And as far as being humiliated, you must remember the story of how Diogenes, when told that men had derided him replied 'but I am not derided!' No one can humiliate you unless you, yourself, consent to be humiliated."

Only Polybius could have given me an answer so complete and so flawless.

"Are we to sit here listening all night to the Roman tongue?" asked Eumenides "Won't we hear enough of that when we are sent to Italy?"

"Tell them, Ectorius." said Polybius softly, in Greek.

I turned to Polybius' companions. "I understand that some of you call me a traitor" I said. "I am a Roman soldier and the son of a Roman soldier. When the Carthaginian, Hannibal, invaded Italy the Roman soldiers fought bravely, but our generals were no match for Hannibal so we lost all of our battles in the early days. My father was captured and transported here to Achaea in chains to be sold as a slave. He was here for twenty-one years and during that time he married a slave girl and fathered my sister and me. His name was Enneus and they jokingly called him Trojan. He liked being a Trojan so he named me Hector, and my sister Andromache." This brought about some laughter, the first smiles I'd seen this evening, but the memory of Menander and Alexias laughing at our names made me wince.

"We were freed by Titus Quinctius Flamininus when I was about eleven years old and sent back to Rome." The mention of Flamininus brought murmurs of approbation. He had been very well thought of by the Achaeans. "I learned Achaean Greek on my mother's knee, but in Rome, as in Greece, nationality and citizenship follow that of the father. Therefore I am a Roman citizen and you are mistaken to think that I am a traitor.

"I am sorry about what is happening here, I think it's wrong, but I can do nothing about it. I wish that Rome were still run by people like Flamininus. If it were, then this would not be happening. I think, perhaps, that too much success has made Romans arrogant and we have become too accustomed to domination and privilege, but perhaps it is only because I was slave born that I see this."

An elderly man who had been listening spoke up. "The man is correct." he said "Whichever way you look at it. If you consider him a slave born in Achaea, he's not a citizen of the Achaean League and can not be considered a traitor. If you consider him a free-born Roman, then he's a Roman citizen and can not be considered a traitor to the Achaean league no matter how well he speaks our language."

When I got back to my tent, Arennius, the scribe, said "Where were you? We were so worried about you. We were just about to send the guards looking for you! We thought they might have killed you, they seem to hate you so much! We've seen how they treat you. Why do you think they hate you?"

"Well, I just found out why, Arennius." I said. "My Greek is so good that they thought I must be a traitor!"

But after that evening, all harassment ceased and my relations with the Achaeans became cordial. I had Polybius to thank for that.

If I felt that Rome's treatment of the Achaeans had been shabby, Rome's treatment of the Epiriots was far worse. Wanting to provided his soldiers with more booty, Paullus permitted his men to pillage the whole country. But they didn't stop there. The Romans razed seventy cities and sold 150,000 Epiriots into slavery. Epirus would be a wasteland for generations to come. I could not fathom the reason for this harsh treatment as Rome had had some assistance from Epirus during the war, and Rome did not deal nearly as harshly with the Macedonians, nor the Illyrians, both of whom had been their enemies! Could it be that this was revenge on Epirus for the damage that their King Pyrrhus had done in Italy nearly one hundred and fifty years before? It all seemed so senseless to me!

Since there were so many Epiriot captives, Consul Paullus' soldiers were expected to take part of their booty in slaves, which they could either transport back to Italy or sell to local slave dealers. Generally, only those who owned estates transported their slaves, the vast majority were sold to local dealers. I was allotted five slaves as part of my booty. The whole notion of slavery appalled me and at first I just thought to decline the booty, but as I wandered through the slave market in Epidamnus, where the captives were being held, it occurred to me that I now had the power to redeem five people from slavery. Most of the captives were not in chains but were guarded by spear men. I ran a across a ragged and forlorn family, a man, women and three small children huddled together. Both parents appeared to be in a state of shock and the children had dirty faces and runny noses and were whimpering. I told the quaestor that I would take them as my share of the booty. "I presume you will be selling them to one of the dealers" he said "you'd do much better to take five adult men and not bother with women and children."

"No, I'll take these." I said. "Let me talk to the man privately." The quaestor shrugged and I approached the family. I felt awkward. How do you tell a free born man that you are his new owner? I decided not to put it in those terms. "Are you hungry?" I asked him. He nodded. "I'll be right back, I want to talk to you." Then I went to the market and purchased a large pot of fish stew and bread and some cheap wine, and water for the mother and children and returned with it to the family. They thanked me and ate as though they had not eaten in days. "What's your name?" I asked the man.

"Nikias." he replied. "This is my wife Althaea, and my children Nikias, Chloe and Melina. Who are you?"

"My name is Ectorius Tullius, and I will be the person responsible for you and your family." I said.

"You're not Greek?" he asked "You sound like you come from Achaea or Lacedaemonia, but you dress like a Roman!"

"I am a Roman, but my mother was Greek." I replied

"Why are you Romans doing this to us?" he asked "What have we done? You've taken all our crops and burned all our houses and now you take us away to be sold as slaves! What have we done?"

"Nikias" I said. "I really don't understand any of this. I wish it weren't happening. I don't have it in my power to help Epirus, but I do have it in my power to help you and your family. Please do everything I tell you to do and you and your family will stay together and have your freedom as soon as I can arrange it."

"Why would you do that for us?" he asked.

"I have my reasons, which you will know some day. Please trust me and co-operate with me."

"You won't touch my wife?" He said

"Nikias" I said "I'm not the kind of man who would violate a married woman. You are under my protection. No man will touch her."

"What are you going to do with us?" he asked

"You and your family will have to come with me to Italy. My father has a farm in Apulia where you will be safe. I will manumit you as soon as I can and then you will be free to stay or leave, or even return to Epirus if you choose. Please co-operate with me. If I have to sell you, your fate will be much worse."

Nikias nodded. I was soon approached by slave dealers who asked me how much I wanted for this family. "They're not for sale." I said "I'm taking them to my father's farm in Apulia. He needs people to herd sheep and tend his olive grove."

"You're making a big mistake!" said the slave dealer. "It's very dangerous to handle a free born man who has just been enslaved. Such a person must be professionally trained. He will give you all kinds of problems."

"My father is well acquainted with the methods used to transform a free born man into a slave." I said "He'll know what to do with them." The slave dealer shook his head and left.

Nikias looked alarmed. "What methods does your father use to transform a free born man into a slave?"

"Nikias," I said "I was just telling the slave dealer that to get rid of him. My father is indeed well acquainted with the methods used to transform a free born man into a slave, but that's because he was a free born man who was forced into slavery. And the methods used are not anything you want to know about."

As much as I was anxious to go back to Rome, I decided it would be better to stay in Epidamnus for a week before sailing, as Nikias and his family needed time to recover from their ordeal. I was afraid that the children, in particular, might not survive the passage, as they all seemed to be suffering from respiratory illnesses. I sent my horse ahead of time with instructions to board him in a stable in Brundisium. I inquired around the city and found a small house that was vacant and could be rented for a week. I took them to the market and allowed Althaea to buy whatever food she needed to feed the family. There was a clay oven in the house and Althaea was able to cook their accustomed fare, including a heavy barley bread, dipped in wine, goat cheese, and stews made with various types of peas and beans. Her cooking reminded me of what I had grown up eating in Achaea.

I had brought a few books with me and spent my time reading them and copying sections that I thought my father might be interested in. The little boy, Nikias, appeared to be about seven years old. He had lost his front teeth and the permanent ones were beginning to grow in. He was interested in what I was doing; he had known nothing of reading or writing. I read him some stories from the Odyssey and gave him his first reading lessons. Both the parents and the children seemed to be recovering their health and their spirits after several days and I booked passage for them as well as myself on a transport to Brundisium.

The day before we were to leave, the little boy said to me "Kyrios, I'm scared! I don't want to go to Italia! Mama says we'll drown! I want to go home!"

"Nikias, my child" I said "I know you miss your home, but you can't go back there. Your hut has been burned, and there is no food. You'll all starve. As for drowning, If you drown, I'll drown too because I will be on the same boat as you. I'm not asking you to do anything I wouldn't do. Where we're going there's plenty of food, and there are horses. You'll get to learn to ride horses. And there will be other children for you and your sisters to play with. It's really a very nice place. Come with me to the market and we'll get you and your family a treat." We went to the market and came back with little cakes sweetened with raisins and spiced with anise. I also purchased a supply of foods that are easily preserved, bread, olives, dried meat, dried fruits and the like, and I bought blankets for each of us because I knew it might get cold and windy aboard our vessel.

When we were waiting to board the ship we ran into Arennius. I was carrying the youngest child because Althaea was feeling a little weak. Arennius laughed and said in Latin "Ectorius, are you transporting slaves or have you adopted a family?"

"Neither one, actually," I said. "I'm taking these people to my father's farm in Apulia where I plan to settle them and have my father hire them to work for him. Father uses only free labor, so I will manumit them."

"Ectorius," said Arennius "You have got to be the oddest man I've ever met!"

"Well," I replied "Marcus Porcius Cato would probably say that I'm what you get when you have miscegenation between a Roman equite and a Greek slave woman!" Arennius practically doubled over with laughter.

"Were you allotted some slaves, Arennius?" I asked "Yes," he replied "But I sold them, all except one, a man who can read and write and can assist me when I have too much work for one scribe. I will be transporting him on this ship."

We boarded the vessel and found a relatively sheltered area on the deck. Last to board the ship were the slaves that were to be transported to Italy. They were mostly men but there were a few women and adolescent boys. There were no small children. They were all in chains and most of the women were weeping. They were taken down into the hold. It was only while watching this dreary procession, that Nikias suddenly seemed to awaken to the gravity of his situation and he dropped to his knees and clutched my hand, much as I had seen my father do with Titus Flamininus years before. But where my father's gesture of obeisance had been an expected formality, Nikias' was spontaneous and heartfelt. He had tears in his eyes. "Kyrios!" he cried.

"What is it, Nikias?" I said "What ails you?"

The tears continued to flow and for a while he seemed unable to reply. Finally he said "Kyrios, you might have put us in chains, but you didn't. You might have sold the children, but you didn't. What can I do to repay you?"

"We are going to a place where you and your family will be safe" I said "And you may stay there as long as you like. If you take it upon yourself to help my father, who is getting too old for physical labor, he will pay you a laborer's wage and I would be gratified. If you think you can find a better place for yourselves, you will be free to do so."

The sea voyage lasted three days and Nikia's family huddled together for warmth. When we arrived at Brundisium I rented a wagon to transport them to Papa's farm in Apulia, while I rode along on horseback. When we got there I introduced them to Papa and Mama and said "Papa, see if you can put Nikias to work and pay him a freed man's wage. When I get back to Rome I will arrange for them to be manumitted." Anyone else would have thought that I was insane, but Papa just grinned and said "Whatever you say, son." He and Brunius' sons helped them build a hut on Papa's property.

CHAPTER 6

Polybius' note to Demetrius contained the following Maxims:

"The early bird catches the worm"

"Night favors all alike, but most the brave."

"Be bold, meet danger, act now: lose or win"

"Do anything rather than give yourself away"

"Keep a cool head-piece and take leave to doubt"

"These are the sinews of the mind . . ."

From Polybius' History of Rome

At the end of Aemilius Paullus' term as consul, he returned to Rome where he would have his triumph for his victory over Perseus. At that time, the thousand or so Achaean prisoners were also transported to Italy as hostages. Most of them were quartered in various towns in the Italian countryside, but Polybius was allowed to live in Rome and, in fact, became tutor to Quintus Fabius and Publius Cornelius Scipio Aemilianus, the elder two sons of Aemilius Paullus. Paullus evidently did not have enough clout to secure Polybius release in defiance of Rome's policy toward Callicrates.

Sadly, the younger of Paullus' two sons by his second wife died three days before his triumph, and then the elder died ten days after it. He was left without a male heir.

I went back to work as a translator in my old company, now run by Anaximander's son Antenor. I had accumulated my wages during my year abroad, and I did receive a share of the booty taken from Macedonia, Illyria and Epirus, although it didn't amount to a fortune and I had sacrificed some of it by freeing my slaves rather then selling them. I felt that it was time I married and I decided to marry Antenor's daughter Sophia, who was seventeen. She was plain, but not ugly, and at least she was literate and intelligent. We rented a small apartment and I hired an elderly widow from the head count class to help Sophia with domestic work. It was nice to be able to come home to a meal of lamb stew and freshly baked bread and to have someone to talk to about the day's events. Greek girls are far more shy and conservative than Roman girls and I knew that she would not run around on her own or spend money extravagantly. We got along well and within a year, we had a baby boy. I named him Enneas, after my father and when he was old enough to travel we took him with us to Apulia to visit his grandparents. They had waited a long time for this grandchild and were absolutely thrilled with him. My mother was very pleased that I had married a Greek girl and she and Sophia got along famously.

Nikias and his family were still living at the farm. He and Papa had gotten along well and he was hard working and useful. A fourth child had been born to them. The family seemed to have recovered their equilibrium and expressed their gratitude toward me for helping them when they were in dire straits. Papa was teaching the oldest boy, little Nikias, to read, along with some of Brunius' grandchildren. Papa loved to teach and some of the more prosperous locals sent their children to him for tutoring. Mama gave Althaea instructions in sewing, spinning yarn and knitting, and the two of them frequently sat together chatting and making clothing and woolen blankets to sell to the locals. One would have thought that they were mother and daughter, they seemed so intimate.

Having married into the Greek community in Rome, and having complete command of the language, I now became active in its social life. Greeks, with the exception of the Lacedaemonians, are great talkers and love to gather together over food and wine and discuss history, philosophy and current events. Naturally these activities brought me into frequent contact with Polybius, who rapidly became a leader in the Greek expatriate community in Rome. Polybius, through his friendship with Aemelius Paullus and his sons was the best connected of any Greek expatriate in Rome. To say that he had made the best of a bad situation would be a profound understatement!

When we met at social gatherings Polybius would greet me warmly and tell me all the things he had been up to. "What you said about Rome having become too accustomed to domination and privilege, Ectorius, has given me an idea. Rome has, within two or three generations, gone from practically a backwater to become the ruler of the civilized world, and I want to find out how and why! I plan to write a complete history of Rome which will include not only the events that happened but also its political system and its military practices. And I think that one of the keys to the whole thing is the second Punic war, in which your father was captured and enslaved. You seem to know a lot about Scipio Africanus. Do you know anyone who actually served under him?"

"Well, yes." I said "My cousin Lucius, who was like a second father to me after we returned to Rome, served under him in Hispania and Africa. He trained the Roman and Italian cavalry in Sicily in preparation for the invasion of Africa. And I, myself met Scipio years later when I volunteered as a translator during the war against Antiochus. I was barely in the toga virilis at that time." I told him the story of young Publius and my adventures in that war. He listened intently and said "So you actually met Antiochus' daughter Laodice?"

"Yes, she and the others were all very kind to us." I said

"Demetrius! Come here!" he called to a young man who was across the room. A youth of perhaps nineteen years of age came over and Polybius introduced us. "This is Demetrius, Laodice's son born after she married Seleucus. He must have been born about five years after the war." then he said "Demetrius, this is Ectorius who was in Antioch during the war between Rome and your grandfather Antiochus III. He says he met your mother and your half sister Nysa." We exchanged greetings and Polybius continued. "Demetrius was brought to Rome as a hostage. We would like to have him go back to his kingdom and take his rightful place as its ruler. His uncle Antiochus Epiphanes is entirely unsuitable as ruler. His behavior is so erratic and bizarre that the Greeks have renamed him Antiochus Epimanes (Antiochus the insane). The Judeans have some of their own names for him, but those are better left untranslated in polite company."

"How did you like Antioch?" asked Demetrius

"I have rather fond memories of the palace." I said "despite being a prisoner there. Everything was so luxurious and the library . . . The library was splendid! I passed my time there pleasurably, eating and drinking, reading books and walking in the garden."

"But how did you happen to be a prisoner there?" He asked.

"Well, briefly, Scipio Africanus sent me to accompany his son on a voyage to Athens and we got blown off course and seized by your grandfather's navy. Young Publius Scipio was too valuable a hostage to take any chances with so they sent us to Antioch."

Demetrius grinned "Well, if I ever get back there and assume the kingship, come and visit me and you can have your pick of the books in the library." Then he went off to find companionship closer to his own age.

"I have taken the poor fellow under my wing and have been teaching him how to hunt." said Polybius "As I said, Antiochus Epiphanes is quite mad and Demetrius would be a better king, but I think that all of these royal Seleucids are a little bit unstable. It must be all the inbreeding. The place might actually be better off under direct Roman rule. I understand that cousin marriage can happen here, but nothing any closer."

"But getting back to my proposed book," he continued "You said that your cousin served under Scipio Africanus. Would I be able to meet this man?"

"I don't see why not." I said "He's very friendly and he loves to tell war stories. Sometimes he goes to Gaius Laelius' gatherings of veterans and they stay up half the night reminiscing."

"Gaius Laelius?" said Polybius "He must be the father of Scipio Amelianus' friend by that same name."

"Well," I said "If you want to know everything about the second Punic war, Laelius is the one to talk to. He and Scipio Africanus were boyhood friends and he was with him the whole time. Ticinus, Trebia, Cannae, New Carthage, Ilipa, Zama, everything!"

"Well," said Polybius, "I would love to talk to your cousin and Gaius Laelius and anyone else who participated in the war."

"You'd better do that quickly, then, because these men are getting into their seventies." I said. "I can arrange for you to meet cousin Lucius. I think I owe you, after what you did for me in Achaea. Everything was much better for me after your intervention."

"I didn't do that entirely out of kindness, I'm afraid." said Polybius "This was a situation with tremendous potential for tragedy. All that was necessary was for you to retaliate and get some of those fools punished. Achaeans are high spirited. That would have led to a riot and then we would have all been put to the sword. We were very lucky that didn't happen. Most men wouldn't have put up with what you did."

"I told you, Polybius," I said "That the first thing I ever learned in infancy was that there was no such thing as justice or fairness in human affairs. The second thing I learned as a slave born child was never to retaliate against or resist my tormentors."

"Those concepts are not appropriate for free men, Ectorius." said Polybius "As free men it is our duty to resist oppression and injustice."

"But Polybius." I said "As long as slavery exists, there really isn't any such thing as a free man. Anyone of us can be enslaved at any time. My father was condemned to slavery for the crime of defending his country. You may feel that you have been unfortunate in being forced to come to Rome as a hostage, but if you had been Polybius the Epiriot rather than Polybius the Achaean, you would more than likely be a slave right now. The Romans devastated the land of Epirus and enslaved 150,000 unresisting Epiriots, and Rome wasn't even at war with the country! As far as I could tell, they just did it to increase the booty for the troops. I myself got slaves as part of my share of booty, but I freed them."

"That's amazing!" said Polybius "You are a very generous man. So you think that slavery should not exist? What would we do with prisoners taken in war? Slay them all?"

"I don't know." I said "My cousin Lucius says that after the conquest of New Carthage in Hispania, Scipio Africanus put all the artisans to work making weapons and other products for the war, and put young and healthy men to work as rowers in the fleet, but gave all of them their freedom when they were no longer needed for the war effort. They worked hard knowing that they would be manumitted. Maybe that would be a better practice."

"An end to slavery would be a wonderful thing, and so would an end to war." said Polybius "but neither of those things are ever going to happen, or if they do happen it will be in hundreds or thousands of years from now. At this point such things are not even worth thinking about."

Clearly Polybius thought that my views on the subject of slavery were little short of insanity, but we've remained friends over many years. Whenever I hold forth on the subject I'm met with incredulous looks and glassy-eyed stares, so I generally only do that when I've had more wine than I should.

Polybius was quite serious about his plan to write a history of Rome and he spent hours in the archives researching the ancient history and the events of the first Punic war. From time to time he was puzzled by materials he read in Latin and would come to me for an interpretation. I was usually able to clarify things for him. "I'm beginning to figure out where Rome derives its great strength" he said. "It's largely a function of the political system itself!"

"What do you mean?" I asked

"Well, Plato and others describe three political systems that have at various times been developed in Greek city-states" he said. "There is monarchy, aristocracy, and democracy.

"Each of these can be sound and effective governments, but each will eventually deteriorate into their bad forms which are tyranny, oligarchy and mob rule, respectively, so that under any of these forms, sound government is temporary and unstable. What the Romans have done is to combine all three forms of government into one very stable system. The consuls, two of whom are elected each year, is the monarchic component, the senate is the aristocratic component and the assemblies of the plebs are the democratic component and they each put a check upon each other. The system of having tribunes of the plebs prevents the government from becoming too oppressive to the people because the tribunes have veto power over whatever the senate proposes. The system is particularly strong from a military point of view because the consuls are chosen from men with strong military and leadership experience, and they spend their terms actually leading their legions in warfare. Part of my book will be an analysis of this system."

"Do you think that Rome will continue to grow stronger?" I asked "and that this system will last?"

"I don't think anything lasts forever." said Polybius, "But it has already lasted longer as a stable and effective government than many other governments we've seen and I think, that in the short term at least, Rome is irresistible. The Romans will give laws to the rest of the civilized world, and will civilize much of the uncivilized world while it's at it. But, I do think that in the long run, perhaps hundreds of years, Rome will be undone by its own success. Already we are beginning to see signs of decadence, particularly among the youth. I fear that the youth have acquired the luxurious habits of the Greeks. So far has the taste for dissipation and debauchery spread among them they they think nothing of paying a talent for a male prostitute and 300 drachmae for a jar of Pontic pickled fish! Cato commented upon this the other day, declaring that anybody could see that the Republic was going downhill when a pretty boy cost more than a plot of land and jars of fish more than a plough man!"

"Oh, Polybius," I said "Don't mention Cato to me. I detest him."

"Sorry, Ectorius, I had forgotten!" replied Polybius "But you know, Cato worries me a bit too. Every time he makes a speech, no matter what the subject, he ends it with 'and furthermore, I think that Carthage should be destroyed!' I think that one of these days he will persuade enough people to that notion and some event will precipitate another war."

"Exactly what Rome needs, a third Punic war!" I said. "Fortunately, Cato and I don't run in the same circles. I spend much of my time with Greeks and he dislikes Greeks." I said. "Incidentally, speaking of the Punic war, Cousin Lucius says there will be a get-together of Punic war veterans at the house of Gaius Laelius next week. He says it's fine if I bring you. There will be a number of veterans you can interview for your book." Polybius thanked me and left.

Polybius came to the gathering and met my cousin Lucius, Gaius Laelius, the scary looking Appius Virginius, and a number of other veterans, and he arranged with a number of them to record their experiences. His biggest prize was Laelius, who could furnish him with innumerable anecdotes about the incomparable Scipio Africanus. My cousin Lucius was able to furnish him with information about events in Hispania from the battle of Cissa to the aftermath of the battle of the Upper Baetis, when Hispania was the province of the elder Publius Cornelius Scipio and his brother Cneius Scipio. This period of the war came to an abrupt end with the Battle of the Upper Baetis in which both of the elder Scipios were killed. About a year after that, Scipio Africanus took command of Hispania, and marched on New Carthage. Within four years he had driven the Carthaginians completely out of Hispania. Between cousin Lucius and Gaius Laelius, Polybius received complete accounts of the Spanish campaigns.

Two years after little Enneas was born, Sophia gave birth to another boy, whom we named Lucius after my cousin, and a year after that a little girl arrived whom we named Silvia. Antenor was a doting grandfather, and he made me a full partner in the company. It was now my job to distribute assignments and supervise the work. My income rose accordingly, but I was very busy. Still, I made periodic visits to Apulia to see my parents. I had to go alone since the babies were too young to travel. It was always a pleasure to go to the farm in Apulia and see what my father had done with it. It was a beehive of activity with all of the Brunius clan, consisting of three sons and fourteen grandchildren pitching in and Nikias' family, which now had five children, and the widow and children of Marsius Iulus whom my father had met in Greece. Iulus had been a slave on a neighboring estate and had also been freed through the efforts of Titus Flamininus. They still bred horses, which they either sold locally or sent to Silvius for his stables, and they raised sheep, sold the wool and the meat, and the olives had started producing so they sold olives and also produced olive oil. None of the workers were wealthy but they all seemed happy and healthy. Aside from having my own children, I don't think anything has ever given me as much satisfaction as seeing Nikias and his family flourishing and happy. I shudder to think of what may have happened to them if I had not intervened. My only regret is that I wasn't able to do more.

Soon after I returned from this last trip to Apulia, a messenger came from Polybius asking me to visit him. He was sick and confined to bed. "Ectorius, I have a big favor to ask of you" He said. "We have arranged for Demetrius to escape from Rome and return to Syria, now that Antiochus Epimanes is dead. Demetrius has twice petitioned the senate to allow him to return and make his rightful claim to the throne, but both times they refused him. I suppose they think it in the interest of Rome to have the Seleucid Kingdom governed by a boy. I wanted to take charge of the action, but as you can see, I've been ill. There is a Carthaginian ship moored on the Tiber that is chartered to go to Tyre. Demetrius will have an entourage of eight companions and five servants. The plan is that he will send some of his servants to Cerceii with instructions to wait for him to arrive with a hunting party, and tell those who remain at home that he has gone to Cerceii, that way neither party will miss him right away. In order for him not to be missed at his lodgings, we have arranged for him to attend a banquet at the house of Apraxias tomorrow. What I'd like you to do is bring this note to him there before he gets too drunk, and make sure he leaves when he should. Then accompany him and make sure he gets to the ship. His friends who are going with him will meet him there."

I laughed. "I'll be happy to do this, Polybius, but why me?"

"Because of all the Greeks I know," Polybius said "You're the one who can best pass for a Roman, and therefore you're the least likely to attract attention. I just want to make sure Demetrius gets to where he needs to go. We've arranged it so that it will be days before he is missed."

Demetrius was only slightly inebriated when I got to the banquet the next day and when he read Polybius' note, he was eager to leave. I had borrowed two horses from Silvius and he and a servant rode one and I rode the other and we headed to the Tiber where the Carthaginian vessel was moored. When we said farewell, he reiterated his promise to supply me with books if I should ever again visit his palace in Antioch. I wished him the best.

It was four days before anyone in Rome was aware that Demetrius had escaped and by this time the ship had already passed the straits of Messana. The matter was taken up by the Senate and they decided that it would be useless to pursue him. When he arrived in his kingdom the soldiers there supported his claim to the throne and they killed his half brother, the boy king Antiochus Eupator and his regent Lysias and Demetrius assumed the throne. To this day, Polybius is quite proud of his role in helping Demetruis to escape, but for my part I have serious doubts that it was one of the better things I've done in my life. I hesitate to say that any good came of it. Nevertheless, I continued to let Polybius involve me in his various schemes, as I found that his company always livened up an otherwise uninteresting existence.

CHAPTER 7

"For who is so worthless or indolent as not to wish to know by what means and under what system of polity the Romans in less than fifty-three years have succeeded in subjecting nearly the whole inhabited world to their sole government, a thing unique in history? Or who again is there so passionately devoted to other spectacles or studies as to regard anything as of greater moment than the acquisition of this knowledge?"
Polybius, The History of Rome

Shortly after this, Rome witnessed the funeral of Aemelia Paulla, the widow of Publius Cornelius Scipio Africanus and sister of Aemilius Paullus. She had been greatly admired and huge throngs flocked the streets of the city to watch the procession. I accompanied cousin Lucius as he paid his respects. Scipio Africanus had provided well for her and she was known for her lavish life style and luxurious tastes. Both of her sons, my friend Publius, the Flamen Dialis, and the dissolute Lucius, had predeceased her, and her fortune went to Publius' adopted son, Publius Cornelius Scipio Aemilianus, the second son of Aemilius Paullus, with provision for each of her daughters to receive fifty talents of silver for their doweries. Much to everyone's surprise, Scipio Aemilianus gave all of this fortune to his mother, Papiria Masonis, who had been divorced from Aemilius Paullus for over twenty years. After Papiria Masonis died, Scipio Aemilianus bestowed the money on his two sisters. Both of Aemelia Paulla's daughters had made distinguished marriages, the elder, Cornelia Africana Major to Publius Cornelius Scipio Nasica Corculum, the grandson of Cneius Scipio, and Cornelia Minor to Tiberius Gracchus. At the time of her mother's funeral,

Cornelia Minor had recently given birth to the couple's first son, named Tiberius after his father.

It was not long after this occasion that cousin Lucius appeared at my door along with Gaius, one of Brunius's sons. They told me that my father was gravely ill and that they were about to travel to Apulia. They had brought along a third horse and bade me to come with them. I hastily packed foodstuffs and clothes and we set out on our journey, which would take two or three days. Cousin Lucius was in remarkably good condition for seventy two and, being a very adept horseman, had no trouble keeping up with Gaius and myself. We rode during the day and camped at night.

"What was my father like as a boy?" I asked cousin Lucius when we were sitting around a fire eating supper.

"What I remember is that he was full of curiosity, always asking questions." said Cousin Lucius. "He wanted to know how everything worked, why people behaved the way they did, how everything came to be the way it was. He would pester the grown-ups with questions, until, at some point, he realized that none of the grown-ups knew the things he wanted to know. He strongly suspected that the Greeks knew more than the Romans about all sorts of things so he threw himself into the study of Greek. It's ironic that captivity in Greece put an end to his intellectual pursuits for so many years. In personality he was mild mannered. He never bullied anyone but also, he bore himself with sufficient dignity that no one ever bullied him. Everyone liked and admired your father."

"My friend Polybuis is like that in a way, always brimming with curiosity," I said. "You met him at Gaius Laelius' house. What did you think of him?"

"I thought he was very talented at gathering information from us." said cousin Lucius. "He even learned things from Appius Virginius. He pumped him about Roman military discipline. I think that your Polybius has a deeper understanding of Rome than anyone I've ever met, with the possible exception of Scipio." Then my cousin began to laugh. "I'll never forget the time I vomited while watching an execution. Appius Virginius was the centurion in charge of the executions. I was the gentle soul that Scipio had put in charge of the female hostages found at New Carthage. I thought Scipio would be furious with me, but he just said 'What would have happened if I had put Appius Virginius in charge of the female hostages and you in charge of executions?' No one was better than Scipio at using men according to their talents."

"Did you tell that story to Polybius?" I asked

"Yes," said cousin Lucius "but I told him not to use it in his book."

When we got to the farm in Apulia it was too late. Papa had passed away the night before. The feelings of grief hit me suddenly and were so intense that it was all I could do to keep my composure. It was only the thought that Papa would want me to be strong for everyone else that kept me from complete disintegration. Mama was inconsolable. Andromache and Althaea took turns trying to comfort her. Cousin Lucius took her hands and, told her in his awkward Greek of how difficult it had been to bear the loss of Silvia, to whom he had been married for over fifty years, and that he knew exactly how she was feeling. She seemed to take some comfort from this.

Many of the locals who had known Papa for years, and had respected and admired him, came by to pay their last respects. They praised Papa for having made a very productive farm out of nothing and for his skills as a tutor. It was clear that in the twenty-eight years he had lived among these people Papa had become a pillar of the community. We invited them to come to the funeral which would be the next day.

There must have been two or three hundred people at Papa's funeral. All of Brunius's clan, of course, Nikias and Althaea and their five children, Andromache and her husband Albinus and their children and grandchildren, and perhaps two hundred locals. I helped the men dig the grave in the plot my father had designated for this purpose. There were a few grave markers there already, one for Brunius and others for some of his grandchildren who had died in infancy and one for Marsius Iulus who had died several years before. It is the Roman custom that the eldest son gives the funeral oration when the *paterfamilias* dies, but I didn't think I could do it and asked cousin Lucius to speak in my stead. Cousin Lucius rose to the occasion just as he had after seeing Lucius Scipio taken to prison in chains and he gave a most eloquent and heart felt eulogy. I took heart from his performance and told a few anecdotes about Papa including how he had taken a flogging on my behalf and, my favorite, of how he had told Consul Cato to please stay away from Indibilis the horse because it would kick him, and when Cato asked him if he knew who he was, he had said that he did, but the horse didn't, and it would kick him. This drew some laughter from the crowd.

We had bought an ample supply of wine and the women had prepared a feast. We butchered several of the sheep, and there were vegetables from the garden and the women baked bread. Local women also brought food so there was plenty for everyone to eat and drink. I spent some time talking to Nikias. He told me that he had come to love Papa dearly and that he and I were the two finest people he had ever met. He said he was sure that he and his whole family would have perished if I hadn't helped them. Young Nikias was about thirteen now and had picked up the local dialect, a rather different speech from Latin, but Papa had taught him proper Latin and Greek as well. I suggested to them that it might benefit the boy if I took him to Rome and trained him as a translator. It wouldn't make him rich, but would make a more comfortable living for him than farm work. Both father and son were agreeable to the idea and it was decided that he would come to live with me and Sophia and the children in Rome.

"Who will be in charge of the farm now?" I asked cousin Lucius.

"Well, I don't think either of my sons want to come out here to live," he said "and I doubt that you do either. All of you are too spoiled by living in Rome. I guess it will have to be Brunius' son Gaius. Nikias seems to be a very good man but he doesn't read or write and his Italian is limited. You know that I deeded half of the property to your father in exchange for his taking charge here, so this now belongs to you. Your father was far-sighted enough to teach Gaius and his brothers to read and write and do sums so I think they can handle affairs with a minimum of supervision. I will be sending Lucius or Titus out here every few months and I hope you can also come out here from time to time to make sure everything is going smoothly. Will your mother be staying here now that your father has passed away?"

"She hasn't expressed any desire to leave, but I'll ask her." I said. I went to see her. "Mama, would you like to come to Rome and live with me and Sophia? I'm sure she and the children would love to have you." She sighed and said "I'd love to see more of Sophia and the children. Bring them here when the babies are old enough to travel. But I will stay here. Althaea is like a daughter to me and I want to stay close to Andromache and the children. I feel at home here which I never did in Rome." She sighed again. "I was so lucky to have your father for all these years, the best husband, the best father, the best person in the world. My one consolation for the misfortune of being born into slavery." I embraced Mama and said "Slave or free, I could not have asked for better parents than you and Papa."

The next day Silvius, young Nikias, and I departed for Rome. Nikias rode the horse that had brought Gaius to Rome and back. When we got back I arranged for Nikias to have a bed in the children's room. I soon began teaching the boy how to translate documents from Greek to Latin and vice—versa. He had a lot to learn but caught on quickly. I would give him an assignment then correct his mistakes and make him do it again and again until it was acceptable. Within a few weeks he was doing serviceable work.

Not long after my father died a man came to me and asked where he might find Enneas Tullius. "My father or my son?" I asked. He smiled. "Your father, I believe."

"My father died several months ago." I said "What would you want with him?"

"Well, in that case, I suppose it's you I need to talk to." He said "I'm Marcius Vitellus, a publican." He showed me his documents.

"My father only owned 16 iugera of land out in Apulia, which now belong to me, but my understanding is that these are not taxed." I said, somewhat annoyed.

"I'm not concerned with your 16 iugera out in Apulia." he said "In any case that would be the interest of a some other publican, I only handle tax matters in Rome itself. I have been researching your father's case and, what I've found will certainly be to my benefit, but, even more so, to yours."

"What have you found?" I said. This sounded like it might become interesting.

"Your grandmother was married to Marcus Entellus Tullius, and they had two sons, Gaius and Enneas. Your grandfather died shortly before the beginning of the second Punic war. Both your father Enneas and his brother Gaius were recruited into the Roman cavalry. Your father went missing at the battle of Trasimene but was found many years later by Titus Quinctius Flamininus in Greece. Your uncle died at Cannae. Shortly after the battle of Cannae, the Oppian laws were passed, and as a widow with no male relatives to look after her, your grandmother's money and property were put in trust of the Roman treasury. Your grandmother died well before the Oppian laws were repealed and this wealth has never been claimed."

"And how much money and property might there be?" I asked

"The property requirement for an equite at that time was 25,000 denarii, so there would be at least that much. There is a property in Quirinal that belonged to your grandfather which is presently rather run down and dilapidated and is inhabited by tenants who have not paid rent in generations."

"And what would be your share?" I asked
"The taxes involved are inheritance taxes, five percent for transfer to your father, and another five percent for transfer to you." he said

"That hardly seems fair, since my father never saw a sesterce and lived a hardscrabble existence out in Apulia for 28 years." I said

"Well, if it wasn't for my diligence you wouldn't have seen a sesterce either, so I think that ten percent is not unreasonable." He said "and I only get to keep a third of that. The rest goes to the Roman treasury."

"Very well." I said "How do I claim this inheritance?"

Marcius Vitellus guided me through the intricacies of the Roman financial bureaucracy and I found myself in possession of 42,000 denarii and a run down property in Quirinal. I gave notice to the tenants that they must leave and I hired workmen to tear down the building and built a nice house for my family. It cost me 20,000 denarii to build the house, but since we no longer had to pay rent, and could actually make some money by renting out a room or two, we could live very nicely on my salary and even accumulate a nest egg for our old age.

The house was only a few blocks from where Ala, cousin Lucius' Celtiberian mistress had her jewelry shop. Sometimes I would find an excuse to go by there just to look at the beautiful Erda, whom I had admired ever since we were children. But as she was married to a Celtiberian immigrant and had four children, I never revealed my feelings toward her. I would end up buying a nice piece of jewelry for Sophia who would squeal with delight and proceed to treat me like a king. It made me realize that it was better to appreciate what I had rather than pine for what I could not have.

Now that I had a presentable home and a nice dining hall I began to fulfill long delayed social obligations by inviting friends and relatives to dinner. After the period of mourning for my father was over I gave a party for Silvius and his children and grandchildren, and soon after that I gave a party for Antenor and all my in-laws and co-workers. To this party I invited Polybius and some of our mutual friends from the Greek community.

"I love your new house!" said Polybius. "Fortuna has certainly smiled on you lately."

"My only regret is that my father never got a chance to enjoy this inheritance" I said. "And I would give this all up if I could have my father back!"

"Unfortunately, I've never seen anyone return from Hades," said Polybius "So you may as well enjoy your new-found affluence."

Young Nikias wandered over. "Have you met my new assistant, Polybius? I said "This is Nikias, one of the Epiriots I brought over to Italy seven years ago. I'm training him to be a translator. His family still live in Apulia at my late father's farm."

"Well, Nikias," said Polybius "Ectorius is said to be the best translator in Rome, so you've come to the right place to learn the trade. How do you like Rome?"

"I'd love to see more of Rome." said Nikias, smiling "but Ectorius keeps me very busy."

"Well, that might be the best thing for you." said Polybius "Because Rome can sometimes change a young man like yourself for the worse.

"Speaking of translators, Ectorius" he continued "Scipio Aemelianus thinks that I should have my histories translated into Latin and I think I could probably get him to sponsor the work if you're interested."

"Well, of course I'd be interested." I said. "I've always been curious to read your histories and I think that they'd be of more interest to a Latin speaking readership than to a Greek."

So it was that I came to translate Polybius' works into Latin. His works were written in a Greek which was very plain and somewhat colloquial and lacked the style of earlier Greek historians like Herodotus and Thucydites, but I found his material fascinating. They were a lens through which I could see and understand Rome. As a hybrid I had always been torn between my Greek and Roman halves. I belonged at once to both cultures but wholly to neither. When I first came to Rome through the beneficence of Titus Quinctius Flamininus, I had embraced my Roman nationality and culture fiercely and completely, but with time, and my harrowing experiences in Achaea and Epirus, I had begun to develop a certain ambivalence and perhaps even a dislike for Rome and started to feel more comfortable in the company of Greeks. Reading Polybius I began to feel that the best days of the Romans were already passed. Rome of the last few generations had produced some of the most memorable and marvelous characters like Quintus Fabius Maximus, Marcus Claudius Marcellus, Marcus Livius and Gaius Claudius Nero, the victors over Hasdrubal Barca at the battle of Metaurus, my benefactor Titus Quinctius Flamininus, and, of course, the Scipios. These days the only people in public life that I could admire were Tiberius Sempronius Gracchus and Publius Cornelius Scipio Nasica Corculum. Certainly most Romans would consider Marcus Porcius Cato a great man but his cruelty during his consulship in Hispania, and his mistreatment of his own slaves, not to mention his treatment of Scipio Africanus and his brother Lucius lead me to despise him. As I've said before, I learned very early in my life not to expect justice or fairness in human affairs, never the less, I decline to call any man great unless he treats lesser souls with kindness.

CHAPTER 8

"Ceterum censeo Carthaginem esse delendam."
(*Moreover, I advise that Carthage must be destroyed*)

Marcus Porcius Cato

Polybius, through his connections with patrician Romans kept me abreast
of political developments in Rome. Cato, it seemed, was ceaselessly
advocating that Rome go to war once again with Carthage and destroy
the city once and for all. For nearly fifty years the Carthaginians had duly
paid their yearly indemnity to Rome and had adhered to the terms of the
treaty made with Scipio Africanus. The major irritant in relations between
Rome and Carthage was the Numidian state ruled by king Masinissa.
Masinissa had been an ally of Carthage during the second Punic war
but had gone over to the side of Rome after the Roman victory over the
Carthaginians at Ilipa in Hispania. His neighbor Syphax had treated
with Scipio but had subsequently married Sophonisba, the daughter
of the Carthaginian general Hasdrubal son of Gisco, and Syphax had
then returned to the Carthaginian fold. After Scipio defeated Syphax at
the battle of the great plains and subsequently took him prisoner, both
kingdoms of the Numidians were granted to Masinissa. Subsequent to
the treaty imposed upon Carthage by Scipio, Masinissa would invade the
Carthaginian territory approximately every ten years on the pretext that
he was reclaiming ancient lands. The treaty forbade Carthage to go to
war with any nation without approval from Rome, and on the occasions
of these invasions Carthage was reduced to sending embassies to Rome

to complain about the Numidians. Rome nearly always sided with the Numidians.

The Romans would send embassies to Carthage periodically to investigate affairs between the Carthaginians and the Numidians and on one of these Marcus Porcius Cato was present. He must have been about eighty at the time. He was incensed and alarmed when he saw how prosperous the city was and he redoubled his efforts to promote its destruction. One day he was orating in the senate and a large juicy fig dropped from the folds of his toga. The other senators admired it and he said "This fig come directly from the lands of Carthage, only three days from Italia by ship!"

Cato's opponent in the senate was Publius Cornelius Scipio Nasica Corculum, who made it clear that he did not favor another war with Carthage. He made his own embassy to Carthage three years after that of Cato, and, upon returning rendered a rare decision in favor of Carthage and against Masinissa. Whenever Cato would proclaim "Carthage must be destroyed!" Scipio Nasica would answer "Carthage must be saved. It is my view that Carthage should be maintained as a rival to Rome to ensure that we Romans maintain our vigilance and as a check upon our arrogance!"

Masinissa was not to be deterred by Scipio Nasica's adverse decision and continued to make incursions into Carthaginian territory. Fifty years had passed since the end of the second Punic war and the Carthaginians had finally paid off the heavy indemnity imposed upon them by Scipio Africanus. The Carthaginians themselves thought that that meant that the treaty with Rome had expired. The senate in Rome thought otherwise.

It was around this time that Polybius came to see me in a state of great excitement and ebullience. "Scipio Aemilianus brought a motion before the senate a few days ago to allow all the surviving Achaean hostages to go home" He said "We were expecting opposition from Cato but he just groaned and said 'Are we to sit here all day arguing whether a bunch of aged Greeks are to be buried in Italy or Greece? Let them be buried in Greece!' and now, after seventeen years, I'm free to go home!"

"That's wonderful news, Polybius!" I said

"But, of course, I won't have the same position I had there when I left." said Polybius. "We went back to the senate a few days later to ask that our honors be restored to us. Cato smirked and said 'Polybius, you seem like some Odyssius going back to the cyclop's cave to retrieve the belt and cape he left there!' I suppose I over-reached."

I laughed "The presence of Cato would certainly make the senate seem like a Cyclop's cave to me!"

"Scipio Aemilianus is going to Hispania to serve under Lucius Licinius Lucullus." said Polybius. "The Celtiberians are in revolt again."

"That country will never be pacified" I said "Cousin Lucius was there for ten years and he says the tribesmen there are fierce and unruly. Even the women are fierce! He witnessed his servant girl kill three men with a falcata! The provinces there have been consistently misgoverned for fifty years so I can't really blame the inhabitants for their rebellion."

"I think it won't be long before Rome is once again at war with Carthage." Said Polybius "The Romans have been doing everything they can to provoke and prepare for another war. This time the Carthaginians are sitting ducks. They no longer have fierce Numidian mercenaries to recruit and, having been at peace for fifty years, their citizens are not trained for war. I suspect Scipio will soon see service in Africa. If that happens I may just come and join him so I can witness first hand whatever happens. I may extend my history to cover these exciting times."

We embraced and said farewell and a few days later Polybius and a number of his fellow hostages boarded a ship to Megalopolis.

Polybius was correct in his prediction. Not long after he left for Achaea, the Carthaginians decided that it was high time that they put an end to Masinissa's incursions and they gathered up an army of fifty eight thousand soldiers to give battle. As it happened, Scipio Amelianus had been sent to Numidia from Hispania by Lucullus to procure elephants for the campaign against the Celtiberians and he witnessed the battle from a height. The battle between Masinissa, with 52,000 troops and the Carthaginian general Hasdrubal, with 58,000 lasted the whole day with many falling on each side but with Masinissa gaining the advantage. In the evening, when fighting had ceased, Scipio presented himself to Masinissa and Masinissa greeted him warmly. He had had a great liking for Scipio's adoptive grandfather, Scipio Africanus. Masinissa by this time was about ninety years old and had fathered forty-six children, the youngest only about four years old!

When the Carthaginians learned of Scipio's arrival they asked him to broker a truce between themselves and Masinissa. They offered to surrender to him the territory around the town of Emporium and pay him an indemnity of two hundred talents immediately and eight hundred talents later. But when Masinissa insisted that they give up any deserters, the Carthaginians refused and the two side failed to come to an agreement. Scipio returned to Hispania with his elephants.

Masinissa surrounded Hasdrubal's camp and laid siege to prevent any food from coming into the camp. Hasdrubal's first inclination was to give battle while his troops were still strong, but having learned that envoys were coming from Rome to settle this affair, he delayed. The envoys did, indeed, arrive from Rome, but they had been given orders from the Roman senate that if Masinissa were defeated, they should put an end to the strife, but that if he were victorious, they should spur him on. Finding that Masinissa had the advantage they told him to finish the work of destroying the Carthaginian army. The Carthaginians in this day and age did not seem to realize the degree of enmity that the Romans still bore toward them.

Hasdrubal's forces began to suffer from famine. They first ate their pack animals and then their horses, and then they boiled leather straps for food. They began to sicken for want of food and exercise and from exposure to the North African heat. When they ran out of fuel for cooking they burned their shields. They could not carry out the bodies of the dead because Masinissa kept strict guard and they could not burn them for want of fuel, so they suffered pestilence due to living in the stench of putrifying corpses. Finally realizing the hopelessness of his position, Hasdrubal agreed to give the deserters up to Masinissa and pay the Numidians five thousand talents of silver in fifty years. In exchange, they were to be allowed to pass out through their enemies, one by one, through a single gate and each wearing only a short tunic. But as they did this they were set upon by the cavalry of

Masinissa's son Galussa and many were killed. Only a few returned safely to Carthage, among them Hasdrubal and others of the nobility.

When the envoys returned to Rome they reported the battle between the Carthaginians and Masinissa to the senate. To the Senate the fact that the Carthaginians had given battle to the Numidians without the consent of Rome meant that they had deliberately broken the treaty imposed upon them fifty years before by Publius Cornelius Scipio Africanus. This gave Marcus Portius Cato the opportunity he needed to promote the case for war. When the Carthaginians sent envoys to Rome to complain about Masinissa they were asked why they hadn't done so before the battle, and they were told that they must satisfy the Roman people, but they were not told how they might accomplish this.

Fearing for their own city, the people of Utica, a well fortified city less than 20 miles from Carthage, decided to put themselves under the protection of Rome, thus providing an eventual base for the Romans to attack Carthage.

The Romans gathered up their forces and prepared for an invasion of Africa. About a year after the battle between the Carthaginians and the Numidians, Rome declared war. A delegation of envoys arrived from Carthage to find that war had already been declared and, still hoping to avoid the conflict they offered to surrender unconditionally. The Praetor informed the delegation that Rome would accept their surrender and grant them freedom and the enjoyment of their laws, and moreover all their territory and the possession of their other property, public and private, on condition of sending three hundred children as hostages to Lilybaeum within thirty days. The hostages were sent to Lilybaeum and were put in the charge of Quintus Fabius Maximus, the son of Aemilius Paullus, who took them to Rome and confined them in the dockyard of the six benched ships. The consuls themselves, Manius Manlius and Lucius Marcius Censorius then sailed to Utica with eighty thousand infantry and four thousand cavalry. They were given secret orders not to desist from the war until Carthage was razed to the ground.

The Carthaginians sent envoys to the consuls at Utica, asking them what they might yet do to avoid war. The consuls told them that they must hand over to the Romans all their arms and missiles. The Carthaginians complied with this demand, delivering more than two hundred thousand stands of arms and two thousand catapults to the Romans.

Then the Romans demanded that the Carthaginians abandon their city and remove themselves to a location at least ten miles from the sea where they would be free to build another city. Carthage would be razed to the ground except for its temples and cemeteries

This last demand proved to be intolerable to the Carthaginians and, at last, they determined to resist.

CHAPTER 9

"Even when an old man he was prone to indulge his sexual appetite, and at last married a wife when he was long past the marrying age. This was the way it came about. After the death of his wife, he married his son to the daughter of Aemilius Paulus, the sister of Scipio, but he himself, in his widowhood, took solace with a slave girl who secretly visited his bed. Of course, in a small house with a married woman in it, the matter was discovered, and once, when the girl seemed to flaunt her way rather too boldly to the chamber, the old man could not help noticing that his son, although he said nothing, looked very sour, and turned away. Perceiving that the thing displeased his children, Cato did not upbraid or blame them at all, but as he was going down in his usual way to the forum with his clients, called out with a loud voice to a certain Salonius, who had been one of his under-secretaries, and was now in his train, asking him if he had found a good husband for his young daughter. The man said he had not, and would not do so without first consulting his patron. "Well then," said Cato, "I have found a suitable son-in-law for you, unless indeed his age should be displeasing; in other ways no fault can be found with him, but he is a very old man." Salonius at once bade him take the matter in charge and give the maid to the man of his choice, since she was a dependent of his and in need of his kind services. Then Cato, without any more ado, said that he asked the damsel to wife for himself. At first, as was natural, the proposal amazed the man, who counted Cato far past marriage, and himself far beneath alliance with a house of consular dignity and triumphal honours; but when he saw that Cato was in earnest, he gladly accepted his proposal, and as soon as they reached the forum the banns were published."

Plutarch's Life of Cato the Elder

With Polybius gone back to Greece I had lost my source of inside information and was only vaguely aware of these events. I was now fifty six years old. Antenor had retired and I now ran the company with the able assistance of Nikias. I was also training Enneas and Lucius, ages sixteen and fourteen respectively to be translators. They had both learned good Attic Greek from their mother and both of them seemed to have a gift for the work.

One morning, before the boys and I left for work there was a knock on my door. It was Erda. At fifty four she was still strikingly handsome but now she looked disheveled and seemed quite upset. "Cousin," she said. "Mama's very ill and I think she may be dying. She wants to see Lucius. My husband, Carolo, is away in Emporion buying jewelry and I'm afraid to go to Subura by myself. Can you come with me?" In all these years neither of us had ever acknowledged our kinship before, although we both knew we had a set of great grandparents in common. "Yes, of course," I replied, "but it's a long walk."

"We have a carriage." she said "Please hurry!"

Cousin Lucius was now about eighty—two and looked frail. He had lost several inches in height and was slightly bent over. His mind, however, was a sharp as ever. He got into the carriage and we took him to see Ala. She was lying in bed and her breathing was rapid and shallow. "Lucius" she said "I think my heart is failing." Her hair was white now and, coated with sweat, it seemed plastered to her head. Her once beautiful face was now deeply lined and she appeared to be in pain. Cousin Lucius took a seat by her bed and held her hand. "Ala, my heroine, I won't leave your side." He kissed her on her forehead. Erda and I left them alone with each other and went to the kitchen. Erda offered me some cakes and wine. I did not feel up to going to work. I knew that Nikias could handle things and I thought that my services would soon be needed again, so I accepted her offer. We chatted for a while about the few things we had in common. "I still remember the first time I saw you, Ectorius," she said "The day the Oppian laws were repealed. Mama felt sorry for you because you looked so frail and small for your age, but you were very smart. You told us everything that was said in the forum. Mama said you had a very difficult life, just like she did when she was a child in Hispania."

"I think she had it much worse than me." I said "I was not an orphan. I had two very loving parents, even though we were extremely poor and lowly."

"Lucius was always very kind to me," She said "and Mama told me he was my father. He even provided me with a dowry. But I never really thought of him as my father, just the kindly lover of my mother. They could not be married under Roman law because he was married to Silvia. I really liked Lucius, but I could never understand why he and Mama were lovers all these years, and she never had any other lovers. And Silvia never seemed to have any problem with it!"

I told her how Cousin Lucius had once explained the situation regarding Ala to Marcus Porcius Cato in response to his prying. "Cousin Lucius was like a second father to me." I said "My family was destitute when we returned to Rome from Achaea, and if it hadn't been for Lucius giving Papa employment and seeing to my education I would have ended up a street urchin, perhaps become a beggar or, at best, a day laborer. I don't think that, given my small stature, I would even have been permitted to become a common soldier. What satisfaction and happiness I've had in my life, I owe to the magnanimity of cousin Lucius."

After about an hour we decided that we had better check on Ala and cousin Lucius. When we entered the room we saw that Lucius was still sitting there holding Ala's hand. But both of them had died! The old soldier, one of the last surviving veterans of the 16 year long second Punic war, and his heroic lover had entered Elysium together, hand in hand.

"Mama!" shrieked Erda. She was beside herself and began to wail. I wasn't much better off myself. I forgot all decorum and began to weep. For some time Erda and I sat there weeping, she for her mother and myself for Lucius. It had been forty-five years since I had seen Cousin Lucius weep over my father's misfortune, and at the time I could not understand how a grown man could weep, but now I understood and I wept for Lucius.

I don't know how long we wept, but after some time we were both spent and sat silently. Finally I said "If I might borrow the carriage, I'll fetch Cousin Lucius' sons, Lucius and Titus." She nodded and then got up and walked with me to the carriage house.

The death of a parent, no matter how old, always comes as a shock and both Lucius and Titus were stunned. Lucius got into the carriage with me and Titus brought along a dray to carry back their father's body.

"Papa said he wanted us to bury him between Mama and Ala." said Lucius. "I suppose we must comply with his wishes, no matter how strange it may seem. He will be in death as he was in life, the devoted lover of two women."

A few days later we had a double funeral in the Silvius' burial plot. I brought Sophia and the children. There were Erda and her children and grandchildren, and all of Cousin Lucius' children and grandchildren as well as the children and grand children of Silvia's sisters. He had outlived all of the veterans of the early part of the second Punic war with the exception of Marcus Porcius Cato, and we certainly weren't going to invite him! The only veterans who came to the funeral were Senator Aurelius Servilius, who had served under Cousin Lucius in Hispania, and some half dozen that he had trained for Scipio Africanus' cavalry for service in Africa toward the end of the war. These latter were all at least ten years younger than cousin Lucius.

But much to everyone's amazement and my personal chagrin, Marcus Porcius Cato showed up at the funeral! He was accompanied by a woman who appeared to be less than one quarter of his age, and who was carrying a small red haired child. "This is my wife Salonia." he said, "And my son Salonius." Then he explained "I always make it a point to pay my respects to Punic war veterans, although we are becoming so few that I fear there will be none left to come to my funeral!"

"I'll be glad to come to your funeral, Porcius Cato!"

Senator Cato turned around. It was Senator Aurelius Servilius, no great admirer of the Censor, who had spoken. "And the only reason I'm still around to do so is that Lucius Tullius Varro Silvius saved my life at the battle of Ilipa. I come to honor a parent, and one of the finest soldiers I ever served with!"

"Ah yes" said Cato. "Among all of my enemies, Lucius was my favorite. I always wished we could have been friends. And in every encounter we ever had, Lucius got the better of me. Few men can say that! Although it seems to run in the family!" He was looking directly at me, as though challenging me to say something.

It was my turn to smirk. I lifted my chalice and said "I drink to the memory of my Cousin Lucius Tullius Varro Silvius, by far the finest Roman I ever knew, and I drink to the memory of his commanding officer, Publius Cornelius Scipio Africanus, the conqueror of Carthago, and I drink to the memory of his brother Lucius Cornelius Scipio Asiaticus, my own commanding officer when I served in the Roman army in the war against Antiochus, and who conquered Antiochus in the battle of Magnesia!"

Everyone present, except Cato, seconded the toast, and I don't think anyone there was unaware of Cato's role in ruining the Scipios.

Conceding defeat Cato said "As I said, it runs in the family." But then he added "But I say, let us Romans finish the work Publius Cornelius Scipio Africanus started. Let us, once and for all, put an end to Carthage!" And, having had the last word, he left.

"The old coot!" said Aurelius Servilius. "He saw that his son disapproved of his liaisons with slave girls so he married the daughter of Salonius, his freedman scribe and fathered that little tyke. I heard that when his older son asked if he did that because he was dissatisfied with him he said 'Why no! I was so pleased with the way you turned out that I wanted to make more sons just like you!'"

CHAPTER 10

"He (Hasdrubal) was by nature corpulent, and he had now become pot-bellied and was unnaturally red in the face, so that it looked as if he were living like a fatted ox in the plenty of a festival, instead of being at the head of a people suffering from such extreme misery that it would be difficult to set it down in words. However, when he met the king and listened to Scipio's offer, slapping his thigh often and calling upon the gods and Fortune, he said that the day would never come on which Hasdrubal would look at the same time on the sun and on his city being consumed by fire; for the most noble funeral for right-minded men was to perish in their native city and amid her flames. So that when we look at his utterances we admire the man and his high-souled words, but when we turn to his actual behaviour we are amazed by his ignobility and cowardice. For, to begin with, when the rest of the citizens were utterly perishing from famine, he gave drinking-parties and offered his guests sumptuous second courses and by his own good cheer exposed the general distress. For the number of deaths was incredibly large and so was the number of daily desertions due to famine. And next by making mock of some and inflicting outrage and death on others he terrorized the populace and maintained his authority in his sorely stricken country by means to which a tyrant in a prosperous city would hardly resort."

Polybius, On the Third Punic War.

After cousin Lucius died I went through a period of profound melancholy and depression. There was a void in my life. Wanting to get away from

Rome for a while I went to Apulia and visited with Mama and Andromache. Nikias came with me and had a good time visiting with his family. The farm was still prospering under the care of Gaius Brunius, but without Papa it just wasn't the same. Andromache noticed my distraction and said "You seem sad, Hector."

"I feel empty." I said "Nothing entertains me or interests me these days. Papa's gone, Cousin Lucius is gone, my friend Polybius is in Greece. I'm getting tired of my work. Everything seems drab and colorless to me."

"Maybe you should go to Athens, or Corinth and see some of the marvelous places you've read about in Greece." she said "Maybe you just need a change of scene, have some adventures and new experiences. You should do this while you're still young enough and healthy enough to enjoy traveling. If you want company your nephew Dasius is eager to go to Athens. He wants to attend Plato's Academy there." Dasius was Andromache's youngest son and he took after his grandfather in his intellectual bent. Papa had taught him Greek, Latin, history, mathematics and a little philosophy before he died and Dasius chafed from the lack of intellectual stimulation in Apulia.

"You know, Andromache," I said "I think you're right! That may be just the thing for me! Let me get some affairs in order in Rome and I'll come back down here and get Dasius and we can sail from Brundesium to Athens! If we get blown off course, at least there aren't any Seleucid vessels these days to capture us. Rome controls the whole of the Mediterranean these days. They call it Mare Nostrum-our sea!" Andromache laughed. "Dasius will be thrilled when I tell him!"

I went home and told my plans to my family. I was engaged and happy for the first time in months. Sophia was used to my peculiar ways and made no dissent. It was my eldest son, Enneas who gave me grief. "Why are you taking cousin Dasius to be educated in Athens and not your own son?" he asked

"Since when have you ever been the least interested in history, philosophy, mathematics, medicine, biology or any of the subjects they teach at Plato's Academy, Enneas?" I asked him. "Your grandfather taught Dasius and he was a very willing and enthusiastic pupil. Your teachers remarked about your indifference to everything they tried to teach you. If that has changed, fine, but you will have to wait until you are older. Dasius is old enough and mature enough to live in Athens without succumbing to it's decadence."

"Well, Grandfather probably was a better teacher than any you hired for me!" he said. "and he died when I was very small."

"Enneas, let me know in five years if you still want to go to Athens to study and I will consider it." I said

I put Nikias in charge of the company and borrowed a horse from Lucius' stable and returned to Apulia. From there Dasius and I traveled to Brundisium and took sail for Athens. When we got there I rented a room where I would stay for a few weeks and where Dasius could continue to reside while he attended classes at the Academy. I decided to dress in Greek style because these days Romans were not well loved by the Greeks. I did not advertise my Roman citizenship, and as far as the Athenians could tell from my speech I could have been from Corinth or Megalopolis. Dasius told people he was from a Greek colony in Italy, which was, more or less, true, as Apulia had been settled, in part, by Greeks.

Applying to the Academy, Dasius was given both written and oral exams and impressed the admittance committee with his knowledge. He began to take classes there and I was invited to sit in on some of the discussions, which I found mildly interesting. The Scholarch at this time was named Arcesilaus, and he promoted a philosophy of academic skepticism, which holds that nothing is really knowable. The best you can do is weigh the probabilities. The skeptics were at odds with the Stoics, which inclined me to their favor as I associated Stoicism with Cato! But none of this was very relevant to my life as a worldly man.

I visited the Acropolis and various temples and other places of interest. I also visited a few of our company's clients who, over the years, had sent us documents to translate. I had known them only from their correspondence, but some of them were hospitable and invited me to dine with them, and they directed me to places that might be of interest to a visitor who had never been in Athens before.

After several weeks I grew restless and decided to travel to Corinth. I left Dasius with enough money for his rent, food and tuition for the year. I advised him that he might earn an income by offering his services as a translator, either of commercial documents, or for Latin speaking visitors. He thanked me effusively for my help.

Corinth was a splendid city and I enjoyed my time there, but the atmosphere was even more anti-Roman than it had been in Athens. The Roman backed puppet government was brutal and oppressive and rebellion was in the air. I suppose it's a blessing that, unlike Cassandra, the daughter of the Trojan king Priam, I could not see into the future while I was there, because, within the next year Rome would raze Corinth to the ground and the entire population would be slain or sold into slavery. I did meet with a few of our clients while I was there, and, as in Athens I was invited into their homes to dine. I am loathe to think of what may have happened to these kind people.

From Corinth I decided to travel to Megalopolis and determined to look up Polybius while I was there. I made inquiries as to where I might find him and it seemed that he was well known there dispite his seventeen year absence. He had inherited his father's estate and was living comfortably. He seemed delighted to see me. He asked me how I happened to be in Megalopolis and I told him everything that had gone on in my life since he had left Rome, and that I was just a tourist. He gave me his condolences on the death of cousin Lucius.

"I hear from Scipio Aemilianus that the Romans have really bungled things in Africa, and that Carthage is still holding out." He said. "Scipio has been elected Consul and is on his way to Africa to straighten out the mess. He's invited me to join him and perhaps advise him in siege tactics and I'm leaving in a couple of weeks. Why don't you come with me?"

"Wouldn't I be in the way?" I said. "Scipio doesn't need a Greek translator, the Carthaginians speak Phoenician."

"The fall of Carthage will be a major historical event and I plan to write about it for the final chapter of my History." He said "You can help me by taking notes and being an extra pair of eyes. I'll tell you what; when they sell the inhabitants into slavery I'll buy one for you so you can manumit him!" Polybius laughed heartily.

"You know me too well, Polybius" I laughed. "How could I resist an offer like that?"

Polybius invited me to stay with him until we were to leave for Africa and I earned my keep by translating more of his work into Latin.

After a few weeks we sailed to Utica and joined Consul Scipio Amelianus in this camp outside of Utica, where he was preparing to besiege Carthage. I shared a tent near the Consul's tent with Polybius, a Punic translator and a couple of scribes. The translator's name was Amandas and he was from Tyre. His native language was similar to that spoken in Carthage and he was also fluent in Latin, Greek, Aramaic and Hebrew. His father had been involved in commerce with both Rome and Carthage and he had traveled all over the Mediterranean world from an early age. I envied and admired his wide-ranging linguistic abilities which far outshone mine. I told him that if he ever wanted to take up residence in Rome, he could join our company and be our translator for Punic documents. I asked him to teach me a bit of the Carthaginian tongue. It was completely unrelated to Latin or Greek, although there are some borrowings from both languages. He told me that the Carthaginians had retained some ancient religious practices which had pretty much died out in his country. He said that in both languages the word "baal" meant god. That is the origin of the syllable "Bal" at the end of many Carthaginian names, such as Hannibal, Hasdrubal and Maharbal. The name "Hannibal" actually means "Grace of God." and the name "Hasdrubal" means "Help of God."

None of their gods would help the Carthaginians now. Scipio Aemilianus laid waste to the countryside around Carthage and blockaded the harbor. The winter was spent in preparing for an all out assault on the city.

Amandas heaped scorn on the consuls who had preceded Scipio and had only good things to say about the latter. Scipio had saved the Romans from complete disaster time after time. When the consul Manius Manlius took an expedition to Nepheris against the Carthaginian general Hasdrubal, counter to the advice of Scipio, the affair ended in a rout of the Romans due to the difficulties of the mountainous territory and the fact that the Carthaginians held the high ground. Four cohorts of Roman soldiers were cut off by the Carthaginians and took refuge on a hill. The Romans had given these men up for lost but Scipio took three hundred horsemen and found a way to secure a position above the enemy and drive them off, rescuing the men who had been trapped.

Scipio had also persuaded the Carthaginian general Himilco Phameas, a formidable foe, to abandon the fight and come over to the Roman side with 2200 of his horsemen.

"Now that Scipio is running things," said Amandas "We might finally see an end to this dreadful business. The consul Calpurnius Piso was even more incompetent than Manlius and he's let the soldiers fall completely out of discipline. The soldiers are given up to idleness, avarice and rapine. They go out to plunder for booty without permission and then they fight among themselves over the booty."

Indeed, the first thing that Scipio did was to re-establish discipline among his soldiers. Amandas, Polybius and I listened as he addressed them:

"Soldiers, when I served with you under the command of Manlius, I gave you an example of obedience, as you can testify. I ask the same of you, now that I am in command; for while I have ample powers to punish the disobedient, I think it best to give you warning beforehand. You know what you have been doing. Therefore why should I tell you what I am ashamed to speak of? You are more like robbers than soldiers. You are runaways instead of guardians of the camp. You are more like hucksters than conquerors. You are in quest of luxuries in the midst of war and before the victory is won.

"For this reason the enemy, from the hopeless weakness in which I left him, has risen to such strength, and your labor has been made harder by your laziness. If I considered you to be to blame for this I should punish you now, but since I ascribe it to another, I shall overlook the past. I have come here not to rob but to conquer, not to exact money before victory, but to overcome the enemy first.

"Now all of you who are not soldiers must leave the camp today, except those who have my permission to remain.

"For you soldiers, I have one order adapted to all occasions, and that is, that you follow the example of my habits and my industry. If you observe this rule you will not be wanting in your duty and you will not fail of your reward. We must toil while the danger lasts; spoils and luxury must be postponed until their proper time. This I command and this the law commands. Those who obey shall reap large rewards; those who do not will repent it."*4

After thus effectively restoring discipline, Scipio moved our camp from Utica to just outside the walls of Carthage. He set about to lay siege to Megara, a large suburb of the city. Unable to scale the walls, some of the soldiers gained entrance to the town by climbing a tower that lay just outside the walls and setting down planks to make a bridge to the walls. They descended into the town, broke open a gate and admitted Scipio with 4000 men. There was panic among the inhabitants and they rushed in mass to the citadel known as Byrsa. It was night time and Scipio, not knowing the layout of the city and fearful of a possible ambush decided to withdraw.

The following morning I awoke to the most horrible bloodcurdling screams. Polybius had already left to join Scipio and Amandas and I made our way to the city wall to see what was happening. The Carthaginians, under order of their beoetarch, Hasdrubal, were mutilating captured Roman soldiers on top of their walls in plain sight of the Roman camp. They tore out their eyes, tongues and tendons with iron hooks, they lacerated the feet of some and cut off fingers of others, and flayed some of them alive. When they were done they threw the victims from the walls. By Zeus, it was the most horrible thing I'd ever seen in my life! How in Hades had I let Polybius talk me into coming here? I was sick to my stomach and sick at heart. Amandas and I went back to our tent and I lay down and wept.

Even the normally exuberant Polybius was grim faced when he returned to our tent. "Why did they do this?" I asked him.

"I can only think that Hasdrubal did this to inform his people that there would be no hope of safety in surrendering to the Romans and to impress upon them the necessity of fighting to the end." said Polybius. "For how could they expect Scipio to spare any of them after this?"

I thought of going home but it would have been unsafe for me to travel alone through enemy territory. To make myself useful I volunteered my services as a scribe. Since one of the scribes had taken ill, I was welcomed. Scipio remembered me from the campaign against Perseus and put me on the military payroll. The work at least took my mind off of the horrors I had witnessed.

Scipio then took measures to starve the city. He built a camp on the isthmus and, in twenty days constructed a wall four and a half kilometers in length and three meters high so that the Carthaginian general Bithya, whose forces were stationed in Nepheris, could not bring in supplies by land. Bithya's ships, however, would wait until a strong wind blew from the sea and were sometimes successful in running the Roman blockade. When food did come, Hasdrubal distributed it only to his 30,000 soldiers, and the rest of the populace starved.

Scipio decided to build a strong embankment across the harbor to effectively close it, but the Carthaginians became alarmed and excavated another entrance at a different part of the harbor in mid sea, where an embankment was impossible due to the depth of the water and the fury of the wind. The work was done in secret and even the women and children helped to dig. When everything was finished the Carthaginians sent out fifty triremes and a variety of other craft in defiance of the Roman blockade. Had they made a surprise attack on the Roman fleet they might have done considerable damage, but it seems that their only purpose was to show the Romans what they were capable of, and they returned inside the harbor.

Three days later the Carthaginians sent their ships out to give battle. The naval battle lasted for two days but ended with Roman victory and Scipio decided to try to take the quay which was strategic for controlling the harbor. He assailed the parapet with rams and other siege engines and beat down a part of it. But the Carthaginians made a bold night time assault on the siege engines. Naked and carrying unlit torches they plunged into the sea and waded through water up to their breasts, and despite the arrows and spear points of the Romans they succeeded in lighting their torches and setting fire to the engines. They caused so much panic and confusion in the Roman camp that men began to flee and Scipio restored order only by killing some who would not desist from flight.

But the assault gave the Carthaginians only temporary relief. The Romans rebuilt their siege engines and soon succeeded in taking command of the quay. There Scipio built a brick wall of the same height as the walls of Carthage. He put 4000 men on the wall to discharge darts and javelins at the enemy.

Having effectively sealed off Carthage from any source of food, Scipio, in concert with Galussa, the son of Masinissa, proceeded to destroy the Carthaginian forces in the area of Nepheris, and lay siege to that city, taking it in twenty two days. Scipio now controlled all of Africa. All that remained was to take control of Carthage.

Hasdrubal, the beoetarch of Carthage was a vain and ostentatious man. He was corpulent at a time when his fellow citizens had been suffering from famine for many months. In his foolish desperation he sought to appeal to the Numidian King Galussa. Polybius, Amandas and I happened to be visiting the Numidian camp at this time and witnessed the meeting. Hasdrubal dressed in full armor for his interview with Galussa, with a purple dyed robe over his armor fastened by a brooch, and was attended by ten bodyguards armed with swords. Rather than going to King Galussa and making obeisance as would have been appropriate in his circumstances, he stood with his retinue twenty paces away and bade the Numidian king to come to him. Galussa, however, declined to take offense and approached him unattended. "Who are you afraid of that you come here in full armor?" Galussa asked him.

"The Romans" Hasdrubal replied.

"Then you should not have trusted yourself to Rome when there was no necessity for you to do so." said Gulussa. "But why are you here? What is it that you want me to do?"

"I want you to go to the Roman commander," said Hasdrubal "and tell him that we agree to obey every injunction: only I beg of you both to abstain from harming this wretched city."

Gulussa replied "Your demand appears to me to be quite childish! Why, my good sir, what you failed to get by your embassies from the Romans, who were then quietly encamped at Utica, and before a blow had been struck, how can you expect to have granted you now, when you have been completely invested by land and sea and have almost given up every hope of safety?"

"We do not despair for our own ultimate safety." replied Hasdrubal. "Above all, we trust in the support of the gods, for surely they would not disregard the flagrant violation of treaty from which we are suffering. We call upon the Roman commander in the name of the gods and Fortune to spare our city: with the distinct understanding that, if we fail to achieve this grace we will be cut to pieces to the last man sooner than evacuate it."

Gulussa conveyed these sentiments to Scipio who remarked "Oh, it was because he intended to make this demand that he displayed abominable cruelty to our prisoners! And he trusts in the gods after violating even the laws of men?" Scipio told Gulussa to tell Hasdrubal that he would offer safety for himself, his wife and children and ten families of his friends and relations. He would be allowed to take ten talents of his private property and bring out with him whichever of his slaves he chose.

King Galussa went to Hasdrubal with these concessions but when he heard them he slapped his thigh again and again, and appealing to the gods and Fortune declared that "The day will never come on which Hasdrubal will behold the sun and his native city in flames: for to the nobly minded one's country and its burning houses were a glorious funeral pyre."*5

Polybius thought that Hasdrubal, who ruled Carthage with an iron hand, cowing the common people by fiercely rebuking some, and by abusing and even executing others, was very similar to the tyrant presently directing the affairs of Greece.

Hasdrubal returned to Carthage and Scipio began his final assault on the city. He lay siege to the harbor of Cothon and then to the Byrsa. Most of the surviving inhabitants took refuge in the Byrsa. Fierce street fighting went on for six days and nights. I had no appetite to observe it and stayed in my tent, but I could hear shouting and screams from the city. There were fires burning everywhere in the city and the air was thick with smoke. On the seventh day Amandas was summoned to translate and I decided to go with him, bringing stylus and parchments in case the services of a scribe were needed. Some suppliants had come from the Temple of Eshmoun bearing sacred garlands and asking to speak to Scipio.

Our nostrils were assaulted by burning flesh as we ascended the Byrsa and we saw corpses everywhere. Polybius was already there when we arrived. Scipio asked Amandas to translate the words of the priests. They requested that he spare the lives of all who might wish to depart from the Byrsa. In reply, Scipio said that everyone might depart with the exception of Roman deserters. Immediately, 50,000 men and women came forth and were allowed to pass out through a narrow gate in the wall. These were all who had survived of a city that had once housed 700,000 souls. All of them would be sold as slaves.

About nine hundred deserters took refuge in the Temple of Eshmoun, along with Hasdrubal and his wife and two small sons. But after a time Hasdrubal came out and approached Scipio bearing an olive branch. Amandas translated as he pleaded for mercy for himself and his wife and sons. Scipio commanded him to sit at his feet, in plain sight of the deserters, who heaped scorn and imprecations on him. Then the deserters, preferring immolation to crucifixion, set fire to the Temple of Eshmoun. Caphonbal, the wife of Hasdrubal appeared on the roof of the burning temple with her two little boys and addressed Scipio:

"For you, Roman, the gods have no cause of indignation, since you exercise the right of war. Upon this Hasdrubal, betrayer of his country and her temples, of me and his children, may the gods of Carthage take vengeance, and you be their instrument."

Then she addressed Hasdrubal and shouted: "Wretch!, Traitor! Most effeminate of men! This fire will entomb me and my children. Will you, the leader of great Carthage, decorate a Roman triumph? Ah, what punishment will you not receive from him at whose feet you are now sitting?"*6

Amandas translated and I wrote everything down for Polybius, who stood as though frozen. I had not seen a woman with such a regal bearing since I had been a captive in the palace of Antiochus.

Then, as we watched in horror, Caphonbal slew her own children and threw them down into the fire and, finally, she flung herself into the flames.

It was over. Carthage, a city which had flourished for seven hundred years and which had ruled over so many lands, islands, and seas, rich with arms and fleets, elephants and money, equal to the mightiest of monarchies but far surpassing them in bravery and high spirits, was now utterly and completely destroyed

Much to our amazement, Scipio began to weep and publicly lamented the misfortune of the enemy. He compared the fate of Carthage to that of Troy, to that of the Assyrians, the Medes, the Persians, and, of late, the splendid Macedonian empire. Then he spoke the words of Homer:

"The day shall come in which our sacred Troy
And Priam and the people over whom
Spear-bearing Priam rules, shall perish all"

Polybius asked him what he meant by this and he said "When I consider the mutability of human affairs, I fear that someday this may also be the fate of Rome."*7

Scipio gave his soldiers leave to plunder the city and the surviving inhabitants were removed to Utica where they were put in the charge of the quaestor who would arrange for them to be sold. Polybius and Amandas and I went back to the camp outside of Utica, where, at least, the air was breathable. I had developed a bad cough from breathing all of the smoke. Polybius was anxious to return to Greece. He had heard that the Romans had destroyed Corinth and had done a great deal of damage in putting down a rebellion there. "Well," He said "If I were that eager to see a city destroyed, I might as well have stayed in Greece and not gone to all of this trouble!" He planned to see what he could do to ameliorate the situation there.

I had become good friends with Amandas and I invited him to come with me to Rome and be my guest for a while.

A few days before our ship was supposed to leave, Amandas and Polybius went off together and returned a few hours later with a twelve year old boy in tow. They both appeared to be struggling to keep a straight face.

"Well, here he is." said Polybius "The slave I promised you. Amandas helped me pick him out."

"What?" I said "I thought you were joking!"

"No joke." said Amandas "Here he is!"

"Well, what am I going to do with a slave?" I asked

"Manumit him, of course!" replied Polybius. Then, he and Amandas broke into gales of laughter. The poor boy looked like he wanted to run away, but he was weak and emaciated.

Well, what could I do? I couldn't in good conscience tell them to take him back to the slave market and get their money back. I couldn't just tell the child to go off and fend for himself. The only thing I could think of was to feed him. I made some porridge and gave it to the boy.

"Does he speak any Latin or Greek?" I asked Amandas

"He says he once studied Greek but the Greek tutor left years ago and he's forgotten all the Greek he once knew." Replied Amandas

"What's his name?" I asked

"Gillimas." answered Amandas

"I know you both find this very amusing." I said "But I really don't. Granted I took the Epiriot family and manumitted them, but it was a very different situation. I had a place for them and I could speak with them in Greek. This is a far more awkward situation!"

They looked at each other and both seemed a little embarrassed.

"Now, what you've done in jest can't be undone." I said. "I can't just throw away a child. I'm a person who does the right thing. But I hope you'll think twice about it next time before imposing a burden on a friend for your own amusement."

"Well," said Amandas "Since I'm going with you to Rome I can translate for you and start teaching the boy some Latin. Polybius and I will both contribute some of our booty to his upkeep and you can have him learn a trade and he will be able to support himself in a couple of years. It will all work out."

I thought of Marcus Porcius Cato and of all the years he had shouted out to the people of Rome "Carthago delenda est!" and now it had come to pass. This child was only one of hundreds of thousands of victims of his madness. I said to Amandas : "Tell Gillimas that I am sorry for what has been done to him and his family and his city in the name of Rome, and that, if he gives me permission, I will be his father."

Amandas and Gillimas had a long talk, back and forth, none of which I understood, but in the end the boy seemed reconciled.

"I told him he was very lucky." said Amandas "Because of all the people who might have bought him, you were the kindest and would treat him just like a son."

The night before he was to sail back to Greece, Polybius and I dined together and he said "I should apologize to you for persuading you to come here, Ectorius. This has been a very painful experience and I did you no favor by involving you."

"I don't understand it, Polybius. Why am I so different?" I said "Why am I the only person who thinks this was the wrong thing to do?"

"Well," said Polybius "Perhaps it's because you are really neither Roman nor Greek, but actually a Trojan, Hector Aeneides, and in seeing the destruction of Carthage you were reliving the destruction of Troy!"

"Polybius, be serious." I said

"Well, here's how I see it." he said "You were the child of a Greek slave woman and a foreigner, and you spent your childhood herding sheep. You did not absorb much of what makes a person Greek. When you went to Rome, it was too late for you to absorb much of what makes a person Roman. You learned both languages well enough, but you never really learned the rules of either Greece or Rome. You've invented your own rules. Now your rules are logical and humane. They're good rules. But they're not Greek rules and they're not Roman rules. The Roman rules permit, and even compel, the destruction of Carthage. Your rules do not. Do you understand now?"

I stared at Polybius in amazement. He had put in words what I had only vaguely sensed. "How do you know more about me, Polybius, than I know about myself?"

"It's easier to see things from the outside than from the inside." said Polybius. "I understand Rome better than the Romans do, and I intend to make Rome understandable to the Greeks, because Greece is now ruled by Rome, and may continue to be for centuries to come. If Greece does not want to end up like Carthage, we had better understand our new masters. I don't want to see any more Corinths."

"Will I ever see you again?" I asked

"Perhaps." he said. "When things are stabilized in Greece, I plan to do quite a bit of traveling. I want to try to chart the course Hannibal took over the Alps, and I want to visit various battle sites of the second Punic war. I think it's important for an historian to see historic locations first hand whenever possible. I'm sure my travels will take me to Rome from time to time and you and I can get together."

I booked passage for myself, Amandas and Gillimas to Brundisium. I wanted to visit Mother and Andromache in Apulia before going back to Rome. Two days before we were to leave, I saw Gillimas tugging on Amandas sleeve imploring him to do something for him. Amandas brought the boy over to me and said "Gillimas wants to talk to you and he wants me to translate." I nodded and motioned for them both to sit down. Amandas translated Gillimas' words.

"Amandas says that you are taking me to Rome." said the boy. "How can that possibly be a good thing for me? I hate Rome and Romans. You see what they've done. And even if I could bring myself not to hate Romans, they will hate me because I am Carthaginian. The Romans must truly hate Carthaginians to be so merciless to us. They will abuse me. How can I possibly go to Rome?"

I replied "I don't know what else to do, Gillimas. You are too young to fend for yourself. I know you probably did fend for yourself for a time, but you ended up in the slave market. You need someone to protect you or you will end up there again. My family and I live in Rome so we must go there. Do you have a better idea?"

The boy was silent for a while. "My father died in the battle with Masinissa. My mother and sisters starved to death. My grandfather Gillimas adopted me. He was a senator and an ambassador, but he was killed by Hasdrubal after he rebuked him for what he did to the Romans on the wall. I am the only one left. Why did the Romans come here to destroy Carthage? Why are they so cruel?"

"Gillimas" I said "Rome and Carthage fought two terrible wars in the past. The simplest answer I can give you is that Rome did this for revenge for injuries done by Carthage in earlier wars. It's more complicated than that, but perhaps you will understand these things better when you're older. What's done is done. We can not bring back Carthage. We can not bring back your grandfather or your mother and sisters. You need to consider what the best thing is for yourself. You don't want to be a slave. I was a slave once myself so I know."

"You were a slave?" asked Gillimas

"My father was captured and sold into slavery by the Carthaginians in the last war." I said "So I have as much reason to hate Carthaginians as you have to hate Romans. If Romans are cruel, we were well tutored in cruelty by the Carthaginians. But I, myself, don't hate Carthaginians. I was not in favor of destroying Carthage.

"I own part of a farm in Apulia" I continued "and we will be stopping there on our way to Rome. If you fear to go to Rome, perhaps you can stay in Apulia. You can decide for yourself when we get there."

Gillimas opted to stay in Apulia. Andromache owed me a favor after what I had done for Dasius and she took a liking to the boy and volunteered to house him and see to his education. I left with her the money that Polybius and Amandas had contributed for Gillimas and Amandas and I proceeded on to Rome.

Back in Rome I kept myself busy and tried to forget the horrors I had witnessed in Africa. I arranged marriages for my sons and daughter, all within the expatriate Greek community. The Rome I had once loved seemed to have died with Cousin Lucius.

One day Sophia remarked that she would like to live in Athens, where she had been born and spent her first ten years before Antenor had brought her and her sisters and brothers to Rome. She could use her dowry to buy a small house. The idea appealed to me and, leaving the company to Nikias, and the house to Enneas, we embarked for Athens to enjoy our old age. Our daughter Silvia and her husband decided to come with us. We passed through Apulia on our way and visited with Mama and Andromache. Gillimas was now fifteen and had done well at learning Latin and Greek. He was no longer the emaciated waif he had been but was now a handsome young man with black curly hair and a mischievous grin. Andromache had done a good job with him. He had asked Nikias for the hand of his youngest daughter and planned to be married next year. The irony of it was not lost on me. I had arranged for Nikias to come to Apulia twenty-five years before, and I had arranged for Gillimas to come three years before, and now Gillimas would marry into Nikias' family. I knew first hand what the Greek and Roman hybrid was like, and I wondered what the Greek and Carthaginian hybrid would be like. Perhaps some day I would find out.

After Word:
The Last Carthaginian

"The ruin of Carthage is indeed considered to have been the greatest of calamities, but when we come to think of it the fate of Greece was no less terrible and in some ways even more so. For the Carthaginians at least left to posterity some ground, however slight, for defending their cause, but the Greeks gave no plausible pretext to any one who wished to support them and acquit them of error. And again the Carthaginians, having been utterly exterminated by the calamity which overtook them, were for the future insensible of their sufferings, but the Greeks, continuing to witness their calamities, handed on from father to son the memory of their misfortune. So that inasmuch as we consider that those who remain alive and suffer punishment are more to be pitied than those who perished in the actual struggle, we should consider the calamities that then befell Greece more worthy of pity than the fate of Carthage, unless in pronouncing on the matter we discard all notion of what is decorous and noble, and keep our eyes only on material advantage. Every one will acknowledge the truth of what I say if he recalls what are thought to have been the greatest misfortunes that had befallen Greece and compares them with my present narrative."

Polybius comparing the fates of Carthage and Greece

My name is Gillimas Tullius and I am, to the best of my knowledge, the last Carthaginian. The last who remembers our splendid city with its two stunning harbors, its magnificent Byrsa with its awe-inspiring temples, the last who remembers Megara with its streams and ponds, gardens and fruit trees. Megara, the paradise of my childhood.

It is possible that some others survive, seventy years after the burning of Carthage, but I don't know of any. I don't know the fate of the three hundred young hostages, my elder brother among them, who were taken to Rome at the beginning of the third Punic war. Were they enslaved? Or where they adopted into Roman families? I just don't know. Whatever my brother's fate, he was at least spared from seeing his mother and brothers and sisters perish of starvation and disease, as I did. He was spared from hearing the screams of enemy soldiers being mutilated on the walls of Megara in plain sight of their comrades in the Roman camp, and knowing that we would all be made to suffer dire punishment for the crimes of a few. He was spared from witnessing the murder of our grandfather at the hands of Hasdrubal's thugs after he objected to the atrocity. He was spared from seeing his beloved city go up in flames.

I have no reason to complain. I was more fortunate than any other Carthaginian I know. Ironically, I owe my salvation to a joke. Tullius had been visiting Polybius in Greece when the consul Scipio sent word to Polybius asking him to come to Carthage and advise him on the siege. Polybius had been Scipio's tutor in his youth. Polybius in turn invited Tullius to come with him. He told him what when the war was over, he would buy him a Carthaginian slave. Polybius knew that Tullius, who had been born a slave, couldn't abide owning slaves, and whenever he happened to acquire any, he freed them immediately. Tullius thought that Polybius was joking and he said "How could I refuse an offer like that!"

When the Romans finally took the city and burned it, block by block, all of us who could took refuge in the temples of the byrsa, our citadel. We did not believe that Scipio would spare any of us after what Hasdrubal had done to the Roman soldiers on the walls of Megara, but when the priests came out to beg him for quarter, Scipio granted it. There were 50,000 survivors out of a population that had numbered 700,000. But quarter meant slavery, and I found myself tethered to a post in the slave market at Utica. I was twelve years old and the only survivor in my family, with the possible exception of my older brother who had been taken to Rome as a hostage. I had a great desire at that moment to have my mother's arms about me, but at the same time I was grateful that Abba and Uma were not around to see me in my present situation.

It was there that Polybius and Amandas found me. Amandas, the translator, was from Tyre, where they speak a language similar to ours. He recognized me from his dealings with my grandfather, who had been an ambassador. "Aren't you Gillimas' grandson?" He asked me.

"Yes." I said "But my grandfather is dead. Hasdrubal had him murdered after he rebuked him for what he did to the Roman Soldiers."

They conversed for a time in Greek, then Polybius went to fetch the Roman quaestor. Money exchanged hands and the quaestor freed my leg from the chain. Amandas took me by the arm and led me to the Roman camp where they had their tent. Then they presented me to Tullius, who looked unpleasantly surprised and Polybius and Amandas practically doubled up with laughter. A joke! I was a joke that Polybius and Amandas had played on poor Tullius. I wanted to run away but I was too weak. I prostrated myself before Tullius in the Carthaginian manner, not knowing at the time that such gestures were despised by the Romans.

The first thing Tullius did was heat up some porridge for me. Even without understanding his speech, I knew that Tullius didn't want me. It's difficult being a good man in this wicked world. Poor Tullius was stuck with me because he couldn't bring himself to take me back to the slave market and he didn't think I could fend for myself at my age. I had been fending for myself for some time, but with my city destroyed, it would have been difficult to survive. The best I might have done was to become a beggar in Utica. Amandas told me that I was really lucky to have a patron like Tullius, who would take me to Rome and treat me like a son.

There was the rub. I didn't want to go to Rome! I hated Rome and the Romans. They had destroyed everything I had loved. And it was not just that I hated them, I also feared them. "The Romans must hate Carthaginians passionately to have done this to us." I thought to myself "How could I possibly live among them?"

I persuaded Amandas to translate for me as I expressed my anxieties to Tullius. Tullius was blunt, almost to the point of being brutal. I asked him "Why did the Roman do this to us? Why did they come here to destroy Carthage?"

"There are complicated reasons that you won't understand until you're older" he said "but the simple explanation is revenge. Rome and Carthage fought two prolonged wars in the past, and if Romans are cruel, we were well tutored in cruelty by the Carthaginians." I thought of the treatment of the Roman prisoners on the walls of Megara. I did not see what they did to them but I heard their screams for hours. I hear them still, on my worst nights.

"In the last war my father was captured by the Carthaginians and sold as a slave." He said. "I have as much reason to hate Carthaginians as you have to hate Romans. But I don't hate Carthaginians. I was never in favor of this war. If you don't want to come to Rome, I own a part of a farm in Apulia and you may stay there if you wish. If you stay here and try to fend for yourself, you'll end up back in the slave market."

So I traveled with Ectorius Tullius to Apulia. His sister Andromache lived there with their aged mother. Andromache was about sixty and her six children were grown and were scattered about. She had grandchildren about my age who often came to stay with her. She seemed to have no problem with taking on another child. I felt comfortable there and decided to stay. She and her mother spoke Greek and I started to remembered the Greek I had been taught before the war. She agreed with me that, under the circumstances, I would be better off staying in Apulia than going to Rome with her brother.

The farm was an unusual place. Everyone who lived there was either a freed slave or a descendant of freed slaves. There was the Brunius clan, who were in charge of the horse breeding operations. They bred horses for Tullius' cousin who owned a stable in Rome and were descended from Brunius, a freed slave once owned by the cousin's grandfather. Brunius had been a Campanian and his descendents spoke the dialect of Campania. There were the children and grand children of Marsius Iulus who had met Tullius' father when both were enslaved in Greece. Then there was

Nikias and his family. They had been brought to Apulia by Tullius who had acquired them as booty in a war the Romans fought in Greece. They also spoke Greek although they had a different dialect than Andromache and her mother. Tullius had freed them but they had elected to stay here and work for wages for Tullius' father. They were in charge of the sheep and the olive groves, and his wife and daughters carried on a clothes making enterprise under the direction of Tullius' mother who had been a seamstress. Nikias worshiped the ground Tullius walked on. I felt that Nikias and I had a lot in common because we had both been completely dispossessed by the Romans. I came to think of him almost as a father, and I eventually married his youngest daughter. The only thing I had difficulty getting used to was the smell. Megara had smelled of jasmine. This place smelled of sheep and horse manure!

My nationality was never an issue with these simple and humble country folk. I never forgot Carthage or my true identity, but with time my memories of childhood began to fade. I was always aware, however, of the great animosity between Rome and Carthage, and I did not advertise my identity. I took on the cognomen of my patron, as is the custom among freed slaves.

Andromache saw to my education and had me tutored in Latin, Greek and mathematics. She noticed that I enjoyed carving and had a talent for it so she arranged for me to study sculpture with a local artisan. Eventually I started my own workshop where I specialized in funerary art. After a time, my work came to be in great demand. My artwork has a Carthaginian flavor to it, I can't help it. One day a grizzled old sea captain and his mate came into my workshop and they were looking over the stock. I heard him mutter "Carthago." as they were looking around. Then they came over to where I was working and he said "Poenus, are you?" I was so shocked I could not even reply. I just stared at the man. "Oh, don't worry" he said "We won't tell anyone."

It is a tragic and lonely thing, being the last of your kind, having no one to talk to who shared your childhood experiences. I've been lucky to have lived a long life, to have satisfying work, and a loving wife, children and grandchildren, but even to this day, seventy years after its death, I mourn for my beloved Carthage.

Footnotes from Carthage Must be destroyed

1. Ab Urbe Condita by Titus Livius Book XXI #X
2. Ab Urbe Condita by Titus Livius Book XXI #XIX
3. Ab Urbe Condita by Titus Livius Book XXI #XX
4. Ab Urbe Condita by Titus Livius Book XXII #LI
5. Ab Urbe Condita by Titus Livius Book XXV #XXXVIII
6. Ab Urbe Condita by Titus Livius Book XXVI #XLI
7. Ab Urbe Condita by Titus Livius Book XXVI #XLIII
8. Ab Urbe Condita by Titus Livius Book XXVI #L
9. Ab Urbe Condita by Titus Livius Book XXVII #XVII
10. Ab Urbe Condiat by Titus Livius Book XXVII #XXXIV
11. Ab Urbe Condita by Titus Livius Book XXVIII #XIX
12. Ab Urbe Condita by Titus Livius Book XXVIII #XXVII, XXVIII and XXIX
13. Ab Urbe Condita by Titus Livius Book XXVIII #XVIII
14. Ab Urbe Condita by Titus Livius Book XXVIII #XL,XLI,XLII, XLIII and XLIV
15. Ab Urbe Condita by Titus Livius Book XXIX #XXIII
16. Ab Urbe Condita by Titus Livius Book XXIX #XXVII
17. Ab Urbe Condita by Titus Livius Book XXX #XII
18. Ab Urbe Condita by Titus Livius Book XXX #XIII
19. Ab Urbe Condita by Titus Livius Book XXX #XIV
20. Ab Urbe Condita by Titus Livius Book XXX #XV
21. Ab Urbe Condita by Titus Livius Book XXX #XX
22. Ab Urbe Condita by Titus Livius Book XXX #XXX and XXXI
23. The Histories by Polybius, Book 15, Page 489

Footnotes to The Death of Carthage

1. Ab Urbe Condita by Titus Livius, Book xxxiv, #s ii, iii, iv and v.
2. Ab Urbe Condita by Titus Livius, Book xxxviii, #LI
3. Ab Urbe Condita by Titus Livius, Book xxxviii, #LIII
4. The History of Rome by Appian of Alexandria, The Punic Wars Book 17 #116
5. The Histories by Polybius. Book xxxviii.
6. The History of Rome by Appian of Alexandria. The Punic Wars, Book 19 #131.
7. The Histories by Polybius, Book xxxix.